THROUGH THICK
AND THIN

THROUGH THICK AND THIN

EARL SEWELL

sepia

★BET BOOKS™

BET Publications, LLC
http://www.bet.com

SEPIA BOOKS are published by

BET Publications, LLC
c/o BET BOOKS
One BET Plaza
1900 W Place NE
Washington, DC 20018-1211

All Kensington Titles, Imprints, and Distributed Lines are available at special quantity discounts for bulk purchases for sales promotions, premiums, fund-raising, and educational or institutional use. Special book excerpts or cus-tomized printings can also be created to fit specific needs. For details, write or phone the office of the Kensington special sales manager: Kensington Publishing Corp., 850 Third Avenue, New York, NY 10022, attn: Special Sales Department, Phone: 1-800-221-2647.

ISBN: 1-58314-358-0

First Printing: August 2004
10 9 8 7 6 5 4 3 2 1

Printed in the United States of America

For my uncles James Roy Sewell and Jesse Elijah Sewell.

For James Roy Sewell, who chose to serve in both the European Theater and the Pacific Theater during World War II because he refused to return to Mississippi in the early 1940s and live under the laws of Jim Crow. Thank you for not only surviving the war but for remaining compassionate, caring, and loving throughout the remainder of your life. Thank you for all the tickles, giggles, and memories.

For my Uncle Jesse Elijah Sewell, who to this very day can charm the whistle out of wind and the stars from the sky. Thank you for your humor, charisma, and most of all, for being there on the dark days as well as the bright ones. I love you more than the clouds love floating in the sky.

ACKNOWLEDGMENTS

To my father, Earl Sewell, Sr.: There are not enough words in the dictionary to express how I feel about you. Without you, none of my success would be possible.

To my Aunt Louise Studway: You're simply the best. Thank you for being a constant guide in my life. To Mary Griffin: Without you, I would have certainly gone crazy trying to write this book. Thank you for your invaluable wisdom, your willingness to listen, and your insight. To my cousin Quentin Robinson and his family, Shinobu (*She no boo*); Quentin, Jr., Emi; and Miki. Thank you so much for coming through for me at a time when I really needed the support of an extended family. You guys are a huge part of the jump start to my career.

To my agent, Sara Camilli: Thank you from the deepest chambers of my heart for all your hard work. You are one of the most wonderful human beings I've ever met.

To Linda Gill, Glenda Howard, Kay Driggins, and Guy Chapman: What can I say? You guys are an absolute joy to work with. Thank you for all the hard work you do.

To Zane (author of *Addicted, The Heat Seekers, Shame on It All, Sisters of APF,* and the *Sex Chronicles I* and *II*); Robert Fleming (editor of *After Hours: A Collection of Erotic Writing by Black Men*); Brian Egeston (author of *Whipping Switches and Peach Cobbler* and *Granddaddy's Dirt*); Vincent Alexandria (author of *If Walls Could Talk, Postal Blues,* and *Black Rain*); Timothy B. McCann (author of *Forever, Until, Always,* and

Emotions); Victoria C. Murray (author of *Temptation and Joy*); Nina Foxx (author of *Dippin' My Spoon* and *Get Some Love*); Eric Pete (author of *Real for Me* and *Someone's in the Kitchen*); Dr. Trevy McDonald (author of *Time Will Tell*); Nolan Douglas (of Full Circle Bookstore in Chicago, Illinois); Francis Utsey (of The Cultural Connection Book Store in Milwaukee, Wisconsin); and Lisa Williams (of Walden Books in Detroit, Michigan): Thanks to all of you for your willingness to help me spread the word about my work. All of you have most certainly helped me make my dream come true.

To the Urban Pages Book Club in Cleveland, Ohio; Black Women Who Read Book Club in Minneapolis, Minnesota; and R. A.W. Sistaz Online Book Club. I cannot say thank you enough for the support you've given me.

To Sherry Taylor, Regina Williams, Ladoris Hope, Leatha King, Tracey Miles, Katrena Dear, Stephanie Madgitt, Marie Walton, Martina Royal, Theresa Dawson, Tonya Howard, and Gerri Brown. Thank you for always insisting that I put my heart and soul into my work.

To Dr. Robert John and his dental team members: Rosita, Rose, Corina, Maureen, Lois, and Tamra. Thank you all for giving me a memorable smile, and for supporting my work.

To my teammates and friends in both my marathon training group and bicycling club: Shawn Stuckey, Mary Bethany, Kelly Gant, Symeria Smartt, Mr. Gino Weaver and Ms. Monica Weaver, Tony DeSadier, Tony Azu-Popow, Michael Simms, Tracy Boone, Larry Dawson, Craig Ashford, Jennifer Ellis, Andrea Sanchez, Tyronna Johnson, and Kristine Mrozek. Thank you, guys, for your friendship, your warmth, and for motivating me on all of the days that I wasn't performing at one hundred percent. All of you have taught me the meaning of de-termination, commitment, leadership, and team spirit. In all of my years of being involved with endurance sports, I've never been so proud to be associated with such a diverse and dedicated group of individuals. The fact that we all made it through subzero temperatures that made our eyelashes freeze, as well as scorching temperatures, is nothing short of awesome. You are all incredible athletes.

Love passionately all the time. Because tomorrow,
the person you love may not be there.
—Leo Buscaglia

1

RICHARD

Richard Vincent had been eagerly darting in and out of the kitchen from the living room all morning checking up on Nina, who was preparing New Year's Eve dinner. He was in a buoyant mood, and the delicious smells wafting through the house made him anxious. Nina, who was dressed in a comfortable pair of red sweatpants and Richard's old Clark Atlanta University T-shirt, was stirring a pot on the stove when Richard came sauntering yet again back into the kitchen.

"Can I taste anything yet?" he asked, attempting to nibble on her neck rather than food.

"Stop that." Nina spun around and smirked as she answered him. "If you keep on bothering me, the food may never get done. Now go on back in there with Nathan," she ordered and pointed her wooden spoon in the direction of the living room.

"All right, all right, I know when I'm not wanted." Richard lightly smacked her behind and rushed out of the kitchen before she could protest his naughtiness.

When Richard returned to the living room, Nathan, his five-year-old, greeted him with an impish smile, then he began punishing his Teken Two video game opponent on his Sony PlayStation.

"Hey, man, you're cheating," Richard said, then grinned at Nathan, who was sitting Indian-style in front of the black giant-screen television.

"No, I'm not," Nathan answered with a big voice and kept his eyes glued on the screen while he ferociously pressed the buttons on the video game's controller.

"You were supposed to wait for me to return before you began playing again."

"You were taking too long," Nathan answered.

"Then what are you doing if you're not cheating?" Richard asked, wondering how Nathan's five-year-old logic would justify what he was doing.

"Practicing," Nathan answered, still refusing to avert his eyes from the screen. Richard quickly moved closer to Nathan and attacked him from behind by tickling his belly to throw off his concentration. Nathan rolled over onto his side and then his back, laughing and snorting as he curled up in the fetal position pleading with his father to stop tickling him.

"Quit it!" he squealed at the top of his voice as he tried to catch his breath.

"What do you have for me?" Richard asked, lowering his voice to a deeper bass. "Looks like you've got a big belly for me to tickle."

"No, I don't!" Nathan disagreed as he kicked and laughed. Richard loved playing with Nathan like this because it reminded him of when he was a young boy and his father tickled him in the same fashion.

"Oh, yes you do." Richard pulled up Nathan's purple Barney the Dinosaur pajama shirt and exposed his brown tummy. Richard filled his cheeks with air, pressed his lips against Nathan's skin, then expelled the air from his mouth, making a loud flapping sound against Nathan's stomach. Nathan giggled even more while at the same time gasping to catch his breath.

"Yes, I just love a boy with a big full belly," Richard said as he allowed Nathan to catch his breath. At that very same moment, the voice of Donnie Hathaway singing his popular holiday song called "This Christmas" drifted into the room and captured Richard's attention. It made him reflect on the past year and all of the tragedy that had taken place. He thought back on his manipulating Mother-In-Law, Rubylee, whose constant interference ultimately caused the stress-related death of her daughter—his wife, Estelle. Rubylee's criminal activities then led to her and her other daughter, Justine, being tossed in the slammer. Despite the overwhelming tragedy, he was determined to make sure that the upcoming year would end on a positive note.

"The fireside is blazing bright . . ." Richard whispered a few lyrics from the song. Richard exhaled as he attempted to shove his upsetting thoughts about the past year aside. He had never been the kind of person who wished that the years would move by quickly, but this time, he couldn't wait for the old year to depart so that he could welcome in a fresh new one. Although he truly regretted the way his marriage ended, he was happy to have his new love, Nina Epps, in his life. She represented an entirely new beginning and a chance to build a strong family unit with his son, Nathan. He truly wanted their relationship to work out even though it had begun on the melody of infidelity. *That doesn't matter,* he thought to himself. *This relationship will work; I'll make it work.* The fact that Nina was an intelligent, drama-free woman who didn't have any dependents, who respected him, along with his son, was what mattered most to him. Now that Nina had consented to moving in with him, their courtship wouldn't have the black eye of betrayal surrounding it.

"Thankfully." He huffed the word under his breath. The treachery of his ex mother-in-law, who was hell-bent-for-leather on destroying his happiness, would no longer concern him. He would never allow anyone like Rubylee to manipulate his peace of mind and happiness again. He couldn't afford to have anyone like that alter his peaceful existence ever again.

"Do you think that Santa Claus has made it home yet, Daddy?" Nathan's voice breached Richard's train of thought.

Richard stood on his feet and then scooped up Nathan, who was still as light as a feather to him. Richard carried him over to the gas fireplace and flipped the wall switch, which caused the flame in the brick fireplace to shoot up. Nathan studied his father with childlike wonder and became fascinated by his dad's features so he began toying with his ear.

"You have hair in your ear," Nathan mentioned as he began pulling a strand of wiry hair.

"Hey, don't pull that!" Richard flinched when he felt a light-stinging tug, "and to answer your question, I would say yes. It's twelve noon on New Year's Eve. I'm positive that Santa is at home by now."

"Can we call him?" Nathan's innocence made Richard chuckle.

"Why do you want to call him?" asked Richard, smiling.

"Because I want to talk to him. I want to know if he can tell me what Mommy is doing." Nathan's remark caught Richard by surprise and reopened the wound of Estelle's death, threatening to cloud the holiday season. Richard thought that he had a better command over his emotions when it came to the loss of his wife. He thought that he could just switch them off but he was wrong. There was still a lingering sadness in his heart about how things had turned out. Nathan had also been struggling with the events surrounding Estelle's sudden death, along with Rubylee's bank-swindling conviction. Nathan's young mind just couldn't understand why he could no longer talk to his mother or see his grandmother, who was behind bars. Nathan was also experiencing difficulty with sleeping, especially alone in his room. He couldn't stand to sleep by himself and favored sleeping with Richard every night or he wouldn't sleep at all. He would stand in the middle of his bedroom and have a sobbing spell if he couldn't share the bed with his father. Richard felt guilty as hell about Nathan discovering that Estelle had passed away overnight in her sleep earlier that year, and as a result of that guilt, he couldn't bear the sound of his little man in pain. So he compromised by allowing Nathan to sleep with him for comfort and security. The only problem was that Nathan was a rough sleeper who would karate-kick him in the ribs at any given moment during the night. So most nights, Richard would leave the bedroom and go crash out in the La-Z-Boy chair in the family room.

"Remember how we talked about saying our prayers every night?" Richard captured his son's gaze.

"Yes, I remember," Nathan answered as he continued his finger examination of Richard's earlobe.

"Well, when you say your prayers every night, I know that Mommy is listening to every word that you say, and although you can't hear her, I know that she can hear you. So whenever you want her to listen to you, all you have to do is say your prayers, okay?"

"But what if she can't hear me?" Nathan asked, not fully buying what his father was telling him.

"Trust me, she can hear you," Richard responded.

"I want her to come back." Nathan began pouting. "Last Christmas we made cookies for Santa, and this year I didn't make anything for him. Mommy said that I made the best cookies in the whole world."

"Well, why don't you and I make some cookies together." Richard desperately wanted to fill the hole that was in Nathan's heart. "I know that it's a bit late for Santa to get them, but perhaps we can mail him some cookies with a little note. I know that an expert chef like yourself remembers how to make the best cookies in the world."

"Yeah, I remember, I think. Does that mean we can't call Santa at all?" Richard covered Nathan's face with the palm of his hand, like a basketball player cupping a basketball. "I think that Santa will have his phone disconnected until next Christmas." Nathan giggled while Richard swiveled his head from side to side. Nathan grabbed Richard's hand at the wrist and pulled it off his face.

"I think that Santa is probably sleeping. I think he's tired from delivering toys a few nights ago," said Nathan. Richard studied his son's features. Nathan had inherited his finer grade of black hair, which felt like goose feathers when his scalp was oiled, and Richard's ebony skin. He had his mother's eyes and nose, though. Nathan pressed his forehead against Richard's and the two of them gazed deeply into each other's eyes.

"I see you, Daddy."

"I see you too, Nathan. Let me see you smile." Nathan clenched his teeth together and showed all of his teeth.

"Would you look at those choppers you got in there."

"This one is sharp," Nathan said, sticking his finger in his mouth and pointing to his canine tooth.

"Oh, yeah," said Richard, "I see how sharp it is," Richard said. At that moment, Nina walked into the family room where Richard and Nathan were. She held her hand under a large wooden spoon, which had a scoop of turkey dressing on it.

"Richard, baby, I need you to taste this," Nina said, making sure that she didn't drop any of the dressing on the throw rug. Richard dropped his jaw open and Nina placed the scoop of food inside his mouth.

"Do you think that I have enough sage in it? I can't tell anymore because I've been in there tasting it."

"It tastes fine to me, baby," Richard answered.

"What about the turkey meat? Can you taste the turkey meat that I put in there?"

"Yeah, I can taste it," Richard said. "When do you think dinner will be ready? Nathan and I are starving."

"I'm not hungry," Nathan swiftly answered.

"Well, it's going to be a little while before all the food is ready, sweet pea." Nina reached out and rubbed Nathan's arm. "Maybe you'll be hungry later on." Nathan's eyes suddenly turned sad, like a lonely teddy bear. He broke his gaze and turned his head away from her and rested it on Richard's shoulder. Nina looked at Richard and he could tell that she was feeling a bit sensitive about Nathan having trouble adjusting not only to her but also to his new life. Richard put Nathan down and he quietly went back to the business of playing his fantasy video game. Nina turned and headed back into the kitchen, and Richard trailed behind her. Nina went to the center island, turned on the faucet, and cleaned the spoon.

"Give it more time, baby," Richard said, concerned about her feelings. Dealing with Nathan's emotional needs as well as hers was taxing his own emotions, but he didn't care about himself at this point; he cared only about making sure their relationship worked. There was no way he was going to allow the communication that they had to become extinct the way it had with him and Estelle.

"I'm okay," Nina answered. "He misses his mother, and that's understandable." But that wasn't the only thing on her mind. Although she'd agreed to move in with Richard, her thoughts about their future together had been getting the best of her. Cooking New Year's Eve dinner offered her some distraction from her thoughts but not much. She wanted to know what his plans were for the three of them. Richard had not even mentioned marriage, and shacking up with him wasn't exactly what she had in mind. Nina wanted a solid commitment, not just pretty words and promises. She was starting to question her decision about moving in with him. After all, she didn't want to make the mistake of tossing away her freedom twice.

Nina's thoughts were all over the map. No, she didn't want to make the same mistake, yet she wanted to be with Richard because he made her happy but she wasn't sure if that was enough. Nina tried to think more positively about their relationship, so she shoved her bad thoughts to the back of her mind and concentrated on the present.

She'd been doing that ever since Richard purchased this home a few months ago. She had been quietly planning out their life of happiness together. One of the first things she wanted to do, since she'd be living in the house with Richard, was to get rid of the furniture from the Chicago lakefront apartment he'd shared with Estelle. Nina took issue with having reminders from Richard's miserable life with Estelle crossing over into the life they were going to have. When she left her husband, Jay, the only things she took were her clothes; she left everything else behind. And in her mind, Richard should do the same thing. Another one of Nina's issues with Richard was the bed that he was sleeping in. Although he'd gotten rid of the mattress that Estelle had died on, she felt that he should have gotten rid of the entire bedroom set. Richard certainly had enough money to replace it, and she didn't understand why he was being so cheap about it, and that annoyed her.

Richard pulled out an orange slice from a bowl of fruit that she'd cut up as a snack until dinner was ready. Nina smacked the back of Richard's hand.

"Don't come in here plunking out of the bowl and you haven't even washed your hands."

"I'm sorry, baby, I didn't mean to upset you." Richard sensed Nina's irritableness.

"It's not you, Richard. I just suddenly have a lot of things on my mind."

"Well, do you want to talk about it?" Richard offered.

"No, it's not that serious. I mean, when I'm ready to talk, you'll be the first to know, okay? Besides . . ." Nina was about to shift Richard's attention off her. "If you keep plucking out of the fruit bowl, there will be none left for when Rose and John arrive." Nina moved over to the stainless steel blue and silver stove to check on the status of the boiling elbow macaroni to make sure she didn't overcook it. Richard moved over to the matching refrigerator, opened it up, and pulled out the one-gallon glass jug of apple cider that he'd picked up from the apple orchard over in Wauconda. He grabbed a drinking glass and set it down on the counter top of the center island. As he poured himself a glass, the phone rang. Nina swiftly moved over to the phone, which was mounted on the wall next to the white cabinet with glass windows.

"Hello?" Nina answered.

"Girl, I'm lost as hell." It was Nina's best friend, Rose, calling on her cellular phone. "I don't see anything out here except some damn horse ranches. Why in the hell did Richard want to move way out here in the damn boonies?" Nina chuckled, delighted to hear the sound of Rose's voice. "What street are you on?" Nina snapped her fingers to capture Richard's attention.

"The hell if I know. They don't have any street signs out here, you know that."

"Well, tell me what you see."

"A big-ass white fence with a bunch of horses standing around freezing their asses off. They're gawking at John and I like they've never seen black people before."

"Yeah, sister girl, you are lost. I'll let you speak to Richard. He knows this area better than I do. Hang on and I'll get him on the phone." Nina handed Richard the phone. "She's lost," Nina explained.

"Hey there, Miss Rose," Richard greeted as he took the phone from Nina and placed it to his ear. "Happy New Year to you."

"Happy New Year to you too," Rose returned the greeting.

"So, tell me where you are."

"Man, I don't know! You've moved way the hell out here in the boondocks with the horses, raccoons, and cows. Shit, I thought your ass was country, but I didn't know your ass was sho-nuff country with a capital K." Richard split open with laughter, and he also heard John laughing in the background. "Go on and tell the truth, Richard, you have a damn hog and chicken farm out here, don't you?" Richard laughed even harder. "Don't be ashamed to admit it. I'll bet you were out in the tool-shed in your overalls with your granddaddy's old pistol, loading it up to shoot a hog for dinner tonight." Richard was trying to catch his breath now. "Rose, you missed your calling, honey. You should be doing stand-up."

"Hey, I just keep things real, you understand what I'm saying? Now where in the hell am I?"

"I think I know where you are. Do you see a crossroad in front of you?"

"Yeah, there is a street right in front me but I can only go right or left. I can't go straight or I'll run into the damn woods."

"Okay, good, you're not that far. Make a right turn and

drive up to Sutton Road. Once you get there, make a left turn and drive down exactly one mile. You'll see my driveway on the left-hand side."

"Okay, now, if we get lost again, you're going to have to come out here and get us."

"I'll walk down the driveway to the road so you can see me. Okay?"

"All right."

"Rose, you and John are less than five minutes away," Richard said, reassuring her.

"Hell, we'd better be. It seems like we've been driving forever. I could have made it to Mexico and back by now with all of this driving that I've been doing."

"Lord have mercy," Richard said, laughing. "I'll see you in a few minutes."

2

CHARLENE

On New Year's Eve, Dr. Charlene Hayward stood at the foot of her walnut-stained sleigh bed. She studied the woven effect design on both the headboard and the footboard. She stared at the comforter and pillows she'd just purchased, which had a palm tree motif that blended in well with the palm trees painted in the various pieces of artwork hanging on the walls of her bedroom. Satisfied with the way the new comforter set blended in, she picked up the plastic wrappings off the brown sisal area rug, which had a palm tree pattern around its border. Everything in her bedroom had a Caribbean influence because she didn't want to be reminded of the fact that she was in Kankakee, Illinois, and had been there for almost two years, which was much longer than she'd anticipated on staying. Kankakee was a town located south of Chicago. It wasn't exactly the place she'd planned on settling down, but it was a good distance from the rocky romance and soiled friendship she'd escaped from.

She walked into the bathroom and tossed the trash in the wastebasket under the sink counter. She turned the knobs on the bathtub and listened to the light roar of the water as it spilled out and splashed into the tub. She opened up the medicine cabinet, grabbed her lavender-scented bath gel, and poured it into the water. She went back into her bedroom, kicked off her heels, removed her skirt and blouse, then tossed them into a basket so they could be taken to the dry cleaners later on. She removed her panties and bra and tossed them into the lime green dirty clothes hamper. She walked over to her walnut dresser, opened the top drawer, and pulled out her tiger print pajama pants and matching cami. She placed the items on the bed so that she could put them on once she got out of the tub. She walked back over to the dresser, grabbed a hair twist, and pulled her hair into a ponytail. She went over to the nightstand, clicked on the radio, and listened as the Stylistics sang, "People Make the World Go Round." Snapping her fingers to the smooth melody, she went and slipped into the comfort of her warm bath.

The night would be perfect once Raymond arrived, she thought to herself while extending her leg in the air and lathering it up with a soapy towel. Raymond was the reason that she'd stayed in Kankakee as long as she had. If it weren't for him, she would have left the moment she got back on her feet. She lowered her soapy leg back into the warm water, extended the other one, and began lathering it up. Her radio was now playing Erykah Badu's song called "On and On." Charlene mapped out a night of passion in her mind and her thoughts sent shivers of anticipation throughout her body. She'd met Raymond a year ago at a fund-raising banquet for a new cancer treatment center for a hospital that she had privileges at. She had just paid the hotel bartender for her drink and was stepping away so that she could hear Seth, her colleague, speak about the benefits of the state-of-the-art facility. Raymond, who was also there networking with business leaders for political contributions, walked right into her and almost spilled her glass of wine on her gray dress.

"I am so sorry," he said in a loud whisper. "It doesn't look like any of it got on your pretty dress." Raymond was a caramel-shaded man with short, wavy, and relaxed sandy brown hair, and brown freckles on his cheeks and nose.

"It's okay," Charlene said, grabbing a napkin from the bartender.

"I am really sorry. Let me replace your drink," he offered before she could refuse. "Bartender, please make her another one."

"You really didn't have to do that. I'm already past my limit," Charlene confessed. "I was only going to nurse this one last drink all night."

"It doesn't matter. I spilled your drink and it's my pleasure to replace it. When you get home, give your dress a close inspection. If you see any stains, give me a call, and I'll take care of the cleaning bill for you." Raymond handed her a card. Charlene looked at his card but didn't recognize his name.

"So, are you one of the investors for the new cancer center?" Charlene asked.

"I'm sorry, excuse me for being both clumsy and rude. Raymond Dolton is my name and I'm running for mayor of Hopkins Park, Illinois."

"Oh, really?" Charlene was suddenly interested in him. She lowered her eyes inconspicuously and examined his left hand in search of a wedding ring, but didn't see one. She'd been to the small town of Hopkins Park many times. It was only a short drive from where she lived.

"Yes," Raymond said, meeting her gaze fully for the first time.

"Are those really your eyes or do you have on contacts?" Charlene asked.

"No," he laughed, "they're mine. I got them from my grandmother. She has hazel eyes as well."

"They're pretty," Charlene said. In the back of her mind, she was adding up Raymond's credentials. A handsome single man with potential, she thought. Charlene had a rule never to date a man who had potential, but to date only the ones who had already reached their potential—that way they wouldn't blame her for their shortcomings. Although Charlene stuck to her rules, there were several problems with doing that. The biggest was that once a man had reached his potential, some woman, usually his wife, was already there reaping the benefits. That was the problem with Charlene's love life—she could never find a man on her level that was available, and so she was a repeat offender in the dating-a-married-man department.

"What would you like to see changed in my town?" Raymond asked.

"Why? Are you granting wishes?" Charlene responded sarcastically.

"No, but if I'm elected mayor, the first thing that I'm going to do is change whatever you want changed."

"Oh, really," Charlene chuckled with amusement. She had an undeniable weakness for men with social status, money, and power. Again, the problem was that when she met a man who fit those criteria, he was usually married. That was the biggest problem with her last rocky romance. The heart surgeon she was involved with was married to her girlfriend. Things got out of control when her friend decided to confront Charlene. One nasty word led to another and the next thing Charlene knew she was protecting herself by holding her girlfriend in a headlock while she pulled on a fistful of Charlene's long hair.

"Yes, anything you want. Just tell me and I'll fix it once I'm elected into office." Raymond smiled with confidence.

"Well, Main Street needs to be repaved. The potholes on that street are wrecking my car," she answered.

"You got it," he said with a large smile. "As soon as I'm elected, I will repave that street for you," he declared.

"Great," Charlene said, becoming irritated by his presence all of a sudden. He wasn't what she wanted at that point. But if he were the mayor, she would have made an exception and given him a bit more play.

A few weeks later Charlene was sitting in her apartment watching the local news and saw that Raymond actually had a real shot at becoming the mayor of the town. She located his card, phoned him, and that's when their courtship began. He told her that he was married, but separated from his wife. Charlene didn't care—as long as he wasn't with her, she had a shot at getting what she wanted. She devoted all of her spare time to working with him on his campaign and even loaned him money to buy advertising space on local radio stations. Not loaning money to a man was a rule she rarely broke, but she couldn't control the grand fantasies of how she'd become his wife and be one of the most powerful women in town. She would have him bestow the honor of having a street named after her, and a school. Everyone in town would treat her like a queen because she'd demand that they do so. Charlene was such a smooth operator with the way she stayed close to Raymond and gained his trust and confidence. Then during the November elections, Raymond defeated his opponent and was scheduled to take office in January.

Charlene got out of the bathtub, oiled her skin with Oil of Olay, and put on her pajamas. She went over to her window and took a peek outside to see if she saw his car. She was eager to make love to him. Tonight she wanted to get a bit rough and wild with their lovemaking. She wanted to break him off right so that she could get a few things that she wanted taken care of right way. She'd scheduled an appointment for him with a lawyer so that he could legally sever all ties with his wife. She wanted to be married before the ink dried on his divorce papers so that their life together as the town's number one couple could begin immediately. There was no way she was going to lose this time, she told herself. In her mind, her plan was simple, perfect, and reasonable. This time, things would work out in her favor. This time, she would not be made a fool of.

Charlene clicked off the radio and turned on the television. The local weatherman was talking about the massive snowstorm headed toward Chicago and its surrounding areas.

"This is going to be a major blizzard," he said. "Chicago and its outlining areas could see as much as two feet of snow.

Chicago hasn't experienced a storm of that magnitude in thirty years when the city was shut down by twenty-five inches of snow."

"Raymond, baby, where are you?" Charlene spoke out loud to no one. She went back over to the window and glared out of it again but still did not see his car.

"The current radar readings suggest that the storm will hit New Year's Day. So those of you who will be celebrating New Year's Eve outside of your home shouldn't have anything to worry about," the weatherman said. "Then after the storm passes, we're going to get hit with a blast of bitter cold arctic air from Canada, which will make temperatures dip down well below zero. So Kankakee can brace itself to see temperatures around minus five to ten degrees but with the wind chill, the air will feel more like twenty degrees below zero."

"Damn, it's going to be cold," Charlene hissed as she picked up the remote control and changed the channel to *Living Single,* the TV series. She sat on her bed and watched the show. Just as the program was going off the air, her phone rang. She looked at the caller ID on the nightstand, but before she picked it up, she wanted to make sure it wasn't her answering service calling her into the dental office for some emergency. She recognized Raymond's cellular phone number and picked it up.

"Hey, baby, where are you? Have you picked up the bottle of wine for us to celebrate with tonight?" she asked.

"Charlene." Raymond paused. "There's something I need to tell you." Charlene instantly picked up on the strange tone in his voice. Raymond sounded as if someone had just died.

"Raymond, what's going on? What happened?" Her tone and mood were suddenly going edgy because her instincts were telling her that something dreadful was about to happen.

"I hate to do this over the phone, but we think it's the best way to handle it."

"We? What do you mean 'we'?"

"She doesn't know who you are; she just knows that I've been dating someone." Charlene felt her temper flaring and it would not be long before it began to take control over her responses and actions. "You need to get your ass over here right now, Raymond, and stop screwing around with me," Charlene commanded, because no one blind-sided or manipulated her, especially not Raymond. She had plans to change and mold him into the perfect man for her.

"See there, that's one of the reasons why I'm doing this. Your temper, Charlene. You have a very bad temper. When things don't go your way, you can become a very evil person. You're mean and seem to enjoy confrontations."

"Raymond, just because you're not man enough to deal with a strong and opinionated black woman, don't take your shortcomings out on me, and I don't need a damn psychiatric evaluation from you!" Charlene growled as her face contorted itself into a hideous expression of rage.

"Look, I have to think about my public image now, okay."

"Public image!" Charlene felt insulted. Somehow Raymond made her feel as if she was not good enough to be by his side. She had a damn D.M.D. degree, which she worked her ass off to get so she would receive a certain amount of respect in society as a dentist.

"Yes, my public image. You and I can no longer continue our relationship. I'm spending my remaining years on this planet with my wife. We've been talking, and we're going to give our marriage another shot." His comment wound Charlene up like a cobra. Now, she was ready to strike back with a vicious amount of venom.

"You've been slipping around with her while you were still dating me, haven't you?"

"Charlene, that doesn't matter. What does matter is that it is over between you and me."

"Oh, this isn't over, Raymond," Charlene barked into the phone. "This is far from over. What, you think you can just charm your way into my life, play with my emotions, and leave just like that!"

"Hey, you knew I was still married. You knew I had a wife.

That's just the chance you take when dealing with a guy like me."

"Oh, no, you didn't just say that to me." Charlene was now clenching her teeth so hard that she felt as if she were going to crack them.

"Look, let's be adult about this. I'm going back to my wife and that's just the way it is. It's over between us. You take care of yourself and have a happy holiday season," he said and hung up the phone.

"Why, you bastard." Charlene dialed his number back. She didn't get an answer. She tried calling him two more times, in case she'd misdialed the number. She was in a fit of rage.

"Oh no, Raymond, you are not going to get away with this. No sir, nobody, and I mean nobody, screws with this sister and gets away with it." Charlene put on some clothes and hurried out of the house to confront Raymond at his apartment. She was about to spend New Year's Eve fighting, which was not what she had envisioned. When she arrived, she discovered that his name was no longer on the mailbox. She didn't want to think that he was savvy enough to move out without her realizing it. She was trying to comprehend what was going on but then it hit her.

"Why, you low-down son-of-a—" She caught herself as she got back into her car and slammed the door shut. Charlene sat in her car and began to think of all the evil shit that she could do to him to get revenge.

"You're going to get it, Raymond, one way or another," she snarled through her teeth. "I know that your ass is in that apartment just hiding out. Don't worry," she said to herself, "I'm going to catch you at home, and when I do, I'm going to get you for old and new."

3

NINA

When Rose finally made it to the house, the worries that were consuming Nina vanished. Rose's personality and presence had a way of infecting a room with laughter and merriment. So the moment she saw her friend's bright almond eyes and huge smile, there was no need for worry and uncertainty to consume her thoughts.

"Happy New Year, girl," Rose said as she greeted Nina with open arms awaiting her embrace. "I'm sorry that John and I couldn't make it for Christmas."

"Girl, don't even worry about that. Happy New Year to you too," Nina smiled, "Miss Thang." Nina teased Rose then cuddled her and gave her a kiss on the cheek. Nina then helped her out of her long gray winter coat.

"Where is John?" she asked Rose.

"Out there with Richard helping him with some grocery bags." Rose was protecting her hair from the cold weather with a matching gray silk scarf that was wrapped neatly around her head. Rose purposely took her time uncoiling the scarf, and once it was completely removed, Nina inhaled with a gasp of surprise.

"When did you get your hair braided like that?" Nina stepped closer and gave Rose's new hairstyle a full inspection.

"Do you like it?" Rose twirled around like a fashion model.

"Who braided it up for you?" Nina continued her inspection of the superb job that the hairstylist had done. Rose's braids were an Afrocentric interpretation of the Mohawk.

"Felicia, my new stylist, created this look for me by corn-rowing my hair toward the center and then she added braided extensions on the top with pins."

"What happened to the other lady who was doing the French rolls for you?"

"You know how heifers get when you've got more than a spit's worth of hair. They want to start cutting it off. I needed someone that knows how to deal with a black woman that has a head full of hair. Felicia was recommended to me by one of the volunteers at the hospital."

"Well, you look wonderful, Rose. Your eyes are bright, your skin is glowing, and you seem so happy. Mr. John must be doing something right."

"And you know this," Rose confirmed Nina's suspicion. "And look here, girl." Rose pulled down the collar of her green holiday turtleneck and exposed a beige square adhesive patch on her upper chest.

"What on earth is that?" Nina pinched her eyebrows with intense concern, trying to figure out the meaning of the object.

"It's a patch, silly," Rose explained. "I'm trying to stop smoking." Nina suddenly felt her heart warm. She'd been trying to get Rose to kick the habit for years.

"I am so proud of you." Nina hugged her friend once again. "If there is anything I can do to help you, just tell me, and I'll do it."

"Just be supportive okay? This shit isn't easy. I've been doing it for years, knowing what the risks were and well . . ." Rose paused for a moment and a strange expression came over her face that Nina had never seen before. Nina was about to ask if something was wrong, but Rose continued on before she could.

"I will admit, I feel better knowing that I'm trying to stop my bad habit."

"What made you decide to stop? You're not sick, are you?" Rose didn't answer for a brief moment and Nina's thoughts immediately got the best of her.

"Oh no, Rose, what is it? Cancer? Emphysema? What? Girl, I know that you're not about to tell me—never mind, I don't want to hear about you being sick. I just can't bear the thought."

"Would you slow down and stop being such a worrywart, my goodness." Rose was trying to figure out why Nina suddenly went off on a tangent. "I refused to stop before now because, well, shoot, I didn't have a reason to stop. Now that John is in my life, I think that I want to stick around for as long as I can. I want to make what we have last forever." Rose paused in thought once again. "I want to take one last shot at love, Nina. I'm tired of being by myself. I'm tired of being alone for the holidays. I'm tired of coming home to no one. I want to make my relationship with John last. My smoking is something that bothers him. And to be honest, it bothers me, too."

"I'm just glad that you're taking your health more seriously." Nina held Rose's hands in her own.

"I've always taken it seriously, Nina, even though I pretended like I wasn't. Smoking was the vice that relaxed me when nothing else would. A lot of my problem was loneliness." Rose laughed a little as she lost herself in her thoughts once more.

"John," Nina called out to him as he set some grocery bags on the grayish-blue countertop next to the white spice containers that Nina had purchased for the house.

"What are you doing to my girl?"

"What do you mean, what am I doing to her? You should be asking her what she's doing to me," John tittered as Richard took his coat and hat for him. John possessed a deep rich chocolate complexion and was a burly man. His arms and chest were thick, and his stomach was round but it fit his stout body type. His black hair, which was shaved close to his head, was turning the color of snow around the edges of his hairline. He was wearing a pair of tan Dockers, a navy blue dress shirt, and a silver Timex watch.

"Ever since I met Rose, my life hasn't been quite the same," John admitted as he crept up behind Rose, who had her back turned to him, and slid his arms around her full-figured waist, while at the same time placing his full lips on her earlobe.

"This exciting, courageous, and strong woman has me feeling like a teenager again. And as long as I have her with me, everything is going to be all right."

"Show-you-right," Rose said. "Watch yourself, baby. You know how I get when you start talking like that to me." John released a big laugh that filled the room. "Are you going to give me that special treatment plan that you like to prescribe later on?" He whispered in her ear.

"Man, please," Rose answered, behaving as if his words had very little effect on her, "you'd better get on out of here before I write you a prescription for total rest and relaxation."

"Lawd have mercy!" Nina bellowed out loud. She now had a much better perspective as to why Rose was trying to get her act together by dropping her smoking habit. She was trying to keep things hot between her and John.

"Hey there, tiger," John called out to Nathan, who had come into the kitchen to see what all the commotion was about. Nathan replied with a hello and then rushed to wrap his arms around Richard's thigh as he was coming in from another room, where he'd just hung up John's and Rose's wool coats.

"You must be that handsome man I've been hearing so much about." Rose looked at Nathan and smiled. "My name is Rose." She placed her hand flat against the top of her bosom. "But you can call me ladybug. All of my friends call me ladybug."

"Hi, ladybug," Nathan spoke softly.

"Come here, sweetie." Rose kneeled down to Nathan's height and extended her arms. To the surprise of both Nina and

Richard, Nathan walked directly over to Rose, which was un-usual because he never went to strangers, especially when he hadn't had a chance to warm up to them yet. Rose scooped him up in her arms and gave him a strong hug.

"So you like Barney, huh?" Rose asked, noticing his paja-mas.

"Yeah," Nathan answered, looking down and away from her.

"Well, I like Barney too. But do you want to know who I re-ally like?"

"Yes," Nathan answered, studying Rose's hair. She inhaled deeply, exaggerating her expression. "I really like Baby Bop. She's my favorite because she's always smiling like the sun and she loves to sing. Now, who is your favorite character?" Rose asked as she lightly poked him in his round chubby belly with her index finger. Her playfulness brought to Richard's mind the popular Pillsbury Dough Boy on the television commercials.

"BJ," Nathan answered with a slight giggle. "I like BJ be-cause he likes to sing and play. BJ also has a big imagination." Nathan stretched his arms all the way out.

"Oh, really?" Rose responded as if she were surprised. "I know a song that both BJ and Baby Bop like to sing. I think you know it too. Let me see if I can remember how it goes. She took a moment to think, then joyfully chanted the words. Nathan quickly joined in, and Rose scooped him tightly in her arms, bouncing him to the melody. When they'd finished the song, Nathan's mood was jovial.

"You're funny, ladybug," Nathan said now that he was a bit more comfortable.

"And you're cute," Rose said, rubbing her nose against his.

"That's called an Eskimo kiss," Nathan informed Rose.

"Well, you're very smart too," Rose remarked. "I'll bet that Santa Claus got you everything you wanted for Christmas, didn't he?"

"Yup, he did," Nathan answered as he began playing with his fingers.

"And I'll bet that a good little boy like yourself knows how to do all kinds of neat things."

"Yup, I know how to make cookies, I can tie my shoes, and I can count to one hundred by tens."

"Wow! You're not a little boy, you're a big boy if you know how to count that high." Nathan giggled at Rose's expression.

"Ladybug, I got my own room."

"You do?" Rose echoed with surprise.

"Yup, and I got lots of toys in there. I got action figures that you can play with."

"Oh, really."

"I'll go get them so that we can play." Rose sat Nathan down and he was about to take off running to his room to pull out all of his toys but Richard stopped him.

"Don't you bring all of those toys down here." Richard's tone was authoritative and stern.

"I tell you what, Nathan. I know that your dad is going to show my friend John and me around your house in a little while. When he does that, you can show me your room and action men then. Is that fair enough?"

"Okay, ladybug," Nathan said and hurried out of the kitchen to go back to the business of playing his video game.

"Now, that was real impressive," Nina, said sarcastically before she had a chance to take the sting out of her words. "You've gotten more conversation out of him in five minutes than I've been able to in days."

"Well, don't go wrinkling your face up over it. You know that being a nurse requires me to have a certain kind of magic with people, especially with children."

"Look," Richard interjected, "why don't I give you guys the grand tour of the place. A lot of the rooms are still empty but Nina and I are going to have this place put together really nice the next time you two come back over."

"Well, let me be the first to say that I love the fact that you have plenty of space around your house," said John. "I like the fact that it is far away from the noise and congestion of the city."

"That was one of the things that attracted me as well. I have two acres of land," Richard boasted.

"Richard, sweetie, before you do the tour, I need you to run to a 24-hour mini-mart. I just realized that I've run out of aluminum foil."

"Girl, why didn't you say something? I could have picked some up for you when I was in the store getting the ingredients for the pecan pies that I'm making for everyone."

"I didn't realize it until just now," Nina answered. "Hang on, let me get a piece of paper and pen so I can write down a few other things I need, now that I'm thinking about them." A few moments later, Nina returned with a list of items for Richard to pick up. Richard invited John to tag along on the errand with him. Richard also asked Nathan if he wanted to go and Nathan quickly answered yes. A short time after that, Richard, John, and Nathan said good-bye to the ladies and left the house.

"Where is the bathroom?" asked Rose. "I want to go in there and wash my hands so that I can come in here and help you clean the greens."

"Oh, there is one right over here." Nina walked Rose around a corner and opened up a small door that was the entrance to the half-bathroom. A few moments later Rose returned to the kitchen. She slipped off her shoes and slid them against the wall so that no one would trip over them. She walked over to the center island, sat down on one of the stools, and began washing the greens that Nina had dumped into the sink.

"So, what was that all about?" Rose asked.

"What was what about?" Nina responded, a bit puzzled.

"The remark about Nathan," Rose said.

"Oh, that. It's nothing. I'm just trying to at least get him to talk to me instead of tearing up every time I say something to him. He just seems so sensitive and I don't know how to deal with it. On top of that, I'm not sure if moving in with Richard is such a good idea. I mean it's a good idea, but... shit, Rose, I don't know what I'm trying to say. I have so many things on my mind."

"Well, just start talking. Perhaps we can figure some things out together. You tell me about your concerns and I'll tell you about mine."

"I'm just trying to figure things out in my mind, Rose. I want to be a good stepmother to Nathan, but I can't if every time I say something to him, his little eyes fill up with tears. Sometimes I feel as if he thinks that I'm some hideous monster from a bad dream he's having."

"Honey, you shouldn't feel that way. You are not the source of his pain. If anything, he is probably dealing with emotional issues from that wicked-ass grandmother of his. You did tell me that she was his primary babysitter, didn't you?"

"Yeah, she was."

"And from what we know, the woman wasn't the most stable individual walking the planet."

"No, she wasn't."

"Hell, she probably filled his little mind with all kinds of misinformation."

"I must admit, from what Richard has told me about the woman, she was nothing but a bad influence on everything and everyone. And the environment that Nathan was exposed to was filled with negativity."

"The little man has been through a lot, Nina. He is probably dealing with a lot of emotions. Don't add to his discomfort and uncertainty by rushing everything."

"Yeah, maybe you're right, Rose. Perhaps I am rushing things. Maybe I should reconsider my decision to move in with Richard."

"Hold on now, I didn't say that. The rules of the game are different today than they were when we were in our twenties. Keep your man, and keep him close to you. Some of the sisters out there these days just don't play. They're spiteful, disrespectful, aggressive, and just don't give a damn. I know, because I hear the conversations that these white-collar office jezebels have at the beauty shops. They talk about how they fly to a different city for a company convention and have a quick fling with the only brother wearing a suit in the company. This one sister was even so bold that she said she saw Charles Wilson, the owner of a new exclusive sports medicine complex for injured professional athletes. Mind you now, I had no idea of who this Charles Wilson dude was until she started flapping her jaws," Rose said.

"Oh, I've heard of him," Nina answered, "and from what I hear, his client list is a who's who in professional sports."

"Well, I got the impression that he was very wealthy. She said that she saw him sitting down eating dinner at a restaurant and bumped into him as he was leaving the rest room. They said their apologies and she watched him as he sat down at a table with a woman and a small baby. She said that she wanted to meet him but didn't want to put him in an odd situation. So this jezebel leaves the restaurant, gets in her car, calls the restaurant back on her cell phone, and has the hostess interrupt his dinner to have him come to the phone."

"What!" Nina shouted louder than she'd intended to.

"Honey, you heard me. She had the man paged."

"Well, what did she say when she got him on the phone?"

"She introduced herself, told him that she didn't want to put him in an odd position, and started talking to him." Nina was shocked into a still silence by what Rose was telling her.

"Wait a minute, girl. As her wanna-be sophisticated ass was talking loud and telling her story about how she crept off with him and got her freak on, a few of us ladies in the shop were looking at her like she'd lost her damn mind. Honey, let me tell you, that heifer was fearless and started snapping off with nasty words at everyone who was glaring at her."

"You're kidding me? She was saying all of this at the beauty salon?"

"Girl, you know how it is when you're hanging around

shops in the hood. Girlfriend got to loud talking and saying that if your relationship is tight, then you don't have to worry about a sneaky woman like her stealing your man."

"She must have been one of those young tack-headed tramps."

"Nope," Rose said, "she looked to me like she was in her early to mid-thirties." Nina was silent for a moment as she placed the greens in a pot of boiling water on the stove. "Why did you get so quiet all of a sudden?" asked Rose.

"Just thinking too hard, I suppose."

"About what?"

"The way my relationship began with Richard. We were cheating on our spouses."

"No, hold up. Stop right there," Rose interrupted Nina. "Don't go down that road, Nina. That is the past. You need to concentrate on the future, like I'm doing. You need to work on building up what you and Richard have. I'm not just talking out of the side of my head either, girl. You do like me and go with the flow. If your man is financially stable, doesn't do drugs, and isn't trying to sell drugs, I say keep him. If he doesn't beat on you, doesn't leach off of you, and enjoys spending time with you, I say keep him."

"I'm afraid, Rose," Nina admitted. "I worry about the future. I don't want to but I can't help it. I know that Richard loves me and I love him, but I'm not sure if that's enough."

"Nina, what are you really afraid of? Because you're not making any sense." Nina sighed and searched her feelings. "I guess the fact that things are going well between Richard and me is something new to me. I'm just so used to arguing about something. I was with Jay for twenty years, and I guess that some of my life with him is still in my system."

"You need to let that go and stop comparing your life with Jay to your new life with Richard."

"Yeah, you're right."

"Let me ask you something, and I want a straight answer from you."

"What?"

"Do you have absolute trust in Richard?"

"Trust is earned, Rose, and—"

"I didn't ask you for an analysis," Rose interrupted her. "Do you trust him?"

"He has not given me a reason to not trust him, so yes I do."

"Then if you two trust and love each other the way I feel you do, then baby girl, no one will ever come between you. Trust is everything, Nina."

"I know that, Rose."

"Let me tell you something that John told me about men. When a man loves you, he's passionate about you, and the only thing that matters to him is your well-being and the health of your relationship together. He told me that one of the things he has learned is that when other people who are miserable see your happiness, they'll throw stones at it. They'll test it, just to see if it is as strong as it appears to be. He told me that a man really loves you when he can turn his back on the temptation of being with another woman. John told me that's the way he feels about me. And I know that Richard feels the same way about you." Nina was moved to tears and hugged her girlfriend.

"Thank you, Rose, I really needed to hear that."

"Now come on, girl, stop that before you get me crying. Let's pull it together before our men get back."

4

RICHARD

"I thought that boy would never drift off to sleep," Richard murmured as he unbuttoned his gold silk pajama shirt. He'd just walked back into the living room, where Nina was relaxing comfortably in her blue silk pajama pants and matching top on the sofa in front of the glowing yellow light of the fireplace. She was nibbling on some fruit from a tray she'd prepared that had sliced oranges, red seedless grapes, and sliced Dole pineapples from the can. "He was determined to stay awake."

"I take it he finally drifted on off to sleep," Nina presumed as she adjusted the sofa pillow that she was lying on.

"Yeah, and he damn near took me with him," Richard admitted as he continued moving toward the kitchen for a bottle of wine and two wineglasses.

"Kids will do that to you," Nina stated. "You try to make them fall asleep and the next thing you know you are both knocked out and dead to the world, as my mother, Cora, use to say."

"Tell me more about your mother." Richard raised his voice so that she could hear him from the kitchen. "I like it when you tell me stories about her and your father. How long were they married for again?" Richard asked as he returned. He sat down on the floor in front of the sofa and leaned his back against it. He placed the wine glasses down near his left hip and began uncorking the wine bottle.

"Thirty-seven years," Nina answered. "My parents were good people and they loved each other deeply. It's still hard to believe that I lost both of my parents in the course of two weeks. Momma passed on a Monday and seven days later Poppa passed on. I truly believe that they honestly couldn't live without each other. Poppa was so hurt when she died. I could see the pain all in his eyes. I tried to get him to come and stay with me for a while after she passed but he refused to leave the house. Poppa lost the will to live when my mother died. The only thing that mattered to him was her, and he wanted to be with her no matter what."

"Wow," Richard said, "I believe in stuff like that, loving someone so much that you can't stand to be without them. I think that I understand how your father felt. My parents were in love similarly as well. I remember a conversation that my father and I had once when I was in high school. I thought that I was in love with this one girl named Ursula who dumped me and went off with the school's basketball star. He told me, 'Son, one day you're going to find a woman who loves you just as passionately as you love her. And when two people love and respect each other like that, they can't imagine living their life without that person. 'When a man loves a woman,' he said to me, 'life has no meaning to him without her'."

"I really wish that I could have met your parents," Nina said as she sat upright and took a sip of her wine.

"Yeah, I do too," Richard agreed. "Here." Richard patted the floor beside him with the palm of his hand. "I want you to sit right here next to me." Without complaining about being on the hard wooden floor, Nina sat down right next to him. Richard twisted his body and gazed deeply into Nina's eyes, noticing how the romantic glow from the fireplace was casting its shadows against her honey-shaded skin.

"I know that I'm moving rather fast and this may be a bit soon, but I don't care. The reason I asked you to tell me about your parents again is because I want our love to be that strong." Nina suddenly broke eye contact with him and she didn't know why. She just gazed at the flame in the fireplace trying to determine what the new feeling stirring her heart was. Richard used his index finger and swiveled her head back toward him so that he could step into her gaze.

"In every chamber of my heart, Nina, I feel the very same thing that you do. I also have that wave of emotion that I can't really name or explain. But I do know this . . ." Nina's eyes suddenly began blinking rapidly and uncontrollably. "I love you," Richard said, and dug into the pocket of his robe, "and I want you to have this." He pulled out a small ring box. When Nina saw it, something wonderful and magical began stirring deep within her. She was on the verge of cracking open with tears of shock, awe, and surprise, but she didn't want to ruin the moment so she held her emotions together as best she could.

"Open it," Richard spoke softly.

"I want to, but I'm nervous." Nina's voice was wound up and full of emotion. She couldn't get her words out. She bit down on her bottom lip, which was now twitching as rapidly as her eyes were blinking.

"Let me open it for you then." Richard turned the front of the box toward her and opened it up. The box made a small squeak when its lid locked in the open position. Inside, Nina saw what she was hoping and waiting for—an engagement ring.

"I want you to be a permanent part of my life. I want you to . . ." Richard paused and rephrased his words to get directly to the point. "Will you marry me?" That did it for Nina. She exhaled the breath that she was holding in and split open with tears of joy as she wound her arms around Richard's neck and entwined him in her embrace. She couldn't speak the word "yes."

"Is something wrong?" Richard asked nervously because she wouldn't say yes or even nod her head yes. "I took one of the rings from your jewelry box in order to make sure that I had the right ring size."

"No, it's not that," Nina said as she unwound herself and studied the engagement ring.

"It's polished platinum with side ornaments." Richard began telling her about the ring. "It has six tapered baguette diamonds on the band, and the mounting is solid eighteen-karat yellow gold. The center diamond is three karats."

"The ring is so beautiful." Nina smeared away a tear from her cheek, took the ring out of the box, and put it on. Looking at the ring on her finger, Nina wanted to take back everything that she'd thought about Richard being cheap. She exhaled and met his gaze once more.

"Sometimes I feel as if you're reading my mind, Richard." Nina spoke softly, and Richard could see the emotion in her eyes.

"I will admit that I really make an effort to study everything about you. In fact, I think that I have a Ph.D. in Ninaology." Nina laughed, which helped to relieve some of her intense emotions.

"No one has ever touched my heart like this before. It's kind of scary."

"Nina." Richard put Nina's face in his hands. "I'm only going to ask you this one more time. Will you marry me?" It was the question that made Nina's heart skip beats and lose her voice for a moment.

"Well, if you're not ready . . ."

"Yes." She finally got the word out through her trembling lips. "Baby, I am going to be such a good wife to you." Nina spoke straight from her heart. "I'm going to be the best mother that I can be to Nathan and I'll always be in your corner. Baby,

I'll never take you or your love for granted." Nina's thoughts were erupting in spurts.

"I know, Nina. That's why I'm making sure that I don't lose you."

"Richard, it means so much to me to hear you say that. I was having so many doubts about us. I was afraid that you only wanted to shack up with me. I was afraid that you thought that I wasn't trustworthy and never even considered a solid commitment like marriage. And—"

"Hey, hey, hey." Richard slowed her down. "Clear your mind of all of those doubts, okay?" Richard smeared away another line of her tears with his thumb and kissed her on her trembling bottom lip.

"Let's sit on the sofa," Nina said. Richard sat on the sofa and Nina straddled him and rested her behind on his knees. She reached over and plucked a few grapes from the fruit tray, which was sitting on the cocktail table.

"Open up," she told Richard. He complied and she hand-fed him the grapes. "I was talking to Rose about day care for Nathan, and shopping for some new clothes for him. Then there is the issue of the house. My goodness, Richard, there are so many things I want to do with the house. I want to get rid of this furniture, and replace it with some elegant furniture from Walter E. Smith. I want to get some drapes made, get some patio furniture for the pool, repaint this living room, get a new bedroom set, turn one of the bedrooms into a library where I can relax and read my books. I want to turn the coach house into a gym, so that we can keep on looking good to each other. Oh, and I can also put a desk and a computer in there so that we can help Nathan with his homework and—"

"Slow down, baby." Richard was delighted with Nina's eagerness but couldn't keep up with everything she was saying to him.

"I'm sorry." Nina attempted to contain her excitement by placing another grape in Richard's mouth.

"I thought you'd want to talk about our wedding plans."

"I do, but I'm looking beyond that. I'm just being sensible at this stage of my life. A big full-blown wedding would be nice but it is not necessary. I don't know tons of people to invite to the wedding. Well, I have quite a few former in-laws but I don't think we'd want them at our wedding. So for me something small, intimate, and romantic would be perfect."

"That's interesting, I thought that was what all women wanted," Richard commented.

"You shouldn't make broad generalizations like that, babes. Besides, I'm not just any woman."

"I know that's right. So now do you feel better about moving in with me?" Richard asked.

"Yes," Nina answered in a tone that made her sound like a schoolgirl with a crush. Nina then got up, walked over to the stereo, opened up the glass door, and pressed the power button. She quickly adjusted the sound because she didn't want to inadvertently wake Nathan.

"It's the eve of New Year's day," the smooth sultry voice of the female disc jockey announced. "I hope that you're all snuggled up with your lover, safe and warm, waiting for the blizzard to pass over. During this time of year, we often reflect on the past year and wonder what the New Year holds. Hopefully, the New Year will continue to bring you love, peace, and joy. The New Year is a popular time for lovers to get engaged, so if you've gotten engaged tonight, this song is just for you. 'This is for the Lover in You,' by Howard Hewett."

"Did you hear that, Richard?" Nina was excited by what she'd just heard. "It feels as if this night is turning into pure magic." Nina went and stood in front of the fireplace and extended her arms out for Richard to join her.

"Come here, baby, and dance with me." Richard got up from the sofa and stepped into Nina's embrace. He placed his hands on her hips and they grooved, slowly and sensuously, to the sound of Howard's voice.

"Promise me that you'll always love me like this," Richard said.

"I promise, baby. I'll never stop loving you," Nina said as she parted her lips, lowered her eyes, and kissed him.

"This feels so right," Richard uttered. "What is this thing that we have?" He drew her in and whispered in Nina's ear.

"Magic, baby," she answered. "Pure love and magic."

5

CHARLENE

It was 6:00 P.M. on January 1st 1999, and Charlene was lounging on her sofa with her legs propped up on the sofa pillows. She was glaring out the window at the falling snow, which was layering everything in its path in a blanket of white.

"'I have to think about my public image,'" Charlene hissed loudly as she wrestled with her rage about what Raymond had said to her. "What in the hell is that supposed to mean?" She'd been calling him all day leaving ugly messages on his voice mail.

"You know what, asshole," she barked as she picked up her cordless phone and pressed the redial button. When his voice mail picked up, she began shouting.

"You know what! I hope that you didn't call yourself being a damn playa or something. And I most certainly hope that you weren't around sleeping with your wife and me at the same damn time! And another damn thing!" The voice mail disconnected her. "I should have told his ass that I just found out I had chlamydia—that would have fixed his whorish ass. I can see his dumb ass now heading to the damn clinic to have someone jam a Q-tip down the tip of his puny dick!" Charlene was fuming and she couldn't contain her emotions or control her thoughts.

"What about all of the damn money I loaned you?" She sprung to her feet and began pacing the floor back and forth like a caged tiger. "And exactly when did you and your wife decide to get back together, Raymond?" At that moment she wished that she was Barbara Eden from the television show *I Dream of Jeannie,* so that she could blink his ass right in the room with her. "Why were you telling me, 'Oh, don't worry about that, we're getting divorced. I'm just waiting for a court hearing.'" Charlene mocked his words. She pressed the redial button on the cordless phone again and waited for his voice mail.

"You know what, Raymond, I want my damn money back. I want the three thousand dollars I loaned you back with interest, and if I don't get it, I'm going to make you regret it. I will destroy your precious public image! You don't know who I am! I'm not just some castaway woman you can use as you see fit. I will—" The machine cut her off again.

"Goddamn it!" She pressed the redial button again and waited for his voice mail.

"The voice mail box of the person you're calling is full. Please try again later," said a female voice on his service. Charlene was so aggravated that she snatched the plug from the wall and flung the phone across the room. It made a loud crashing sound as it hit the wall then tumbled to the floor.

"No, Raymond." Charlene bounced up and down on the balls of her feet as if she were a boxer getting ready to do battle. "You can't get rid of me that easily. I have invested my time, energy, and money into you. I broke my damn rule for you and this is how you treat me! Like some overworked and unappreciated secretary!" Charlene marched out of the living room and back to her bedroom. She yanked some blue jeans and a sweatshirt off hangers in the closet.

"I don't care if there is a blizzard outside, Raymond. I'm coming over to your place to see your ass!" She grabbed her boots and stuffed her feet into them. "You and I are going to have it out tonight!" Charlene flung on her coat, hat, and gloves and marched toward the front door and outside into the howling blizzard. The wind was as furious as Charlene was and was blowing the snow so hard that it was falling horizontally instead of vertically. The combination of the wind, snow, and bitterly cold air on her exposed skin angered her even more as she trudged across the parking lot to her car, which was buried in snow. She opened up her car door, got in out of the cold, and fired it up. The music jumped on and soul singer Aretha Franklin began screaming about getting a little R-E-S-P-E-C-T. She twisted her body, reached behind the passenger seat, and grabbed the snow scraper. She opened up the door, stepped back out into the howling wind of the blizzard, and scraped off only the driver's side of her windshield. She dusted off the driver's side mirror and got back in her car. She turned on the windshield wipers, and watched as the blades struggled to push the rest of the snow off to the side. Once the blades had done their job, she put the car in reverse and attempted to back up without being able to see out of the back window.

"Goddamn it!" she hissed because the rear tires of her Lexus were spinning in place. She snatched the gear shift back into drive, pulled forward a bit, yanked it back into the reverse gear, and pinned the gas peddle to the floor. The engine shrieked just as loud as her tires squealed against the snow. She finally got the car out of the parking space and drove off edgy and recklessly toward Raymond's apartment.

Normally it took twenty minutes to drive from her place to his, but tonight, in the madness of a blizzard, it took Charlene forty-five minutes to reach his apartment. When she pulled into the parking lot of his complex, she didn't bother with finding a legal parking space. She just double-parked in front of his building. She grabbed the window scraper from the passenger seat and locked her fingers around it tightly. She got out of the car and high-stepped it to the front door. She stepped inside and entered the small vestibule where the silver mailboxes and door buzzers were mounted on the wall. She instantly noticed that his nameplate was still no longer there.

"I know that this mother-fucker didn't move out and I didn't know about it!" Charlene cursed. She pressed the button where his nameplate should have been but got no answer. Charlene's heart began racing wildly as she pressed the button over and over again. "I know that I haven't been taken for a fool like that!" she snapped, not wanting to believe what she was discovering. She rang one of his neighbors doorbells.

"Who is it?" the female voice asked through the intercom.

"Yes, hi, I'm your new neighbor and I locked myself out. Can you buzz me in, please?" Charlene tried to sound as pleasant and nonconfrontational as possible. There was a short pause and then the door buzzed. Charlene raced up the staircase, marched over to his apartment door, and began banging on it with the side of her closed fist. When she got no answer, she began kicking the bottom of the door with her boot.

"I know that your ass is in there. You're not fooling a damn soul by taking your nameplate off the mailbox, Raymond. Bring your punk-ass on out here and face me like a real man." Charlene lost the last scrap of composure that she had and got ridiculously ghetto. "Come on out here! I've got something for your ass!" She still got no answer so she kicked the door harder, not caring who heard her loud talk.

"Come on, I'm waiting! I'll kick on this damn door all night if I have to!" she barked with venom in her voice. Charlene heard the lock on a door turn, but it was the neighbor's door behind her, on the other side of the hallway. A woman in a gray robe, with a butcher's knife in plain view, stood in her doorway, peering out at her.

"Dr. Hayward?" the woman called her name. Great, Charlene thought to herself as she rolled her eyes. "Dr. Hayward, why are you out here acting like that?" It was Miss Hernandez, a thirty-something Spanish-American patient that Charlene had once treated. *This town is too damn small,* she thought to herself.

"He can't be worth all of this aggravation, honey," she stated.

"I know that his ass is in there!" Charlene snapped at Miss

Hernandez, paying no attention to the presence of the knife or the tone of her voice.

"Dr. Hayward, that apartment is empty. The movers emptied that apartment out. It only took them a few hours to do it."

"What?" Charlene refused to believe what she was hearing because that would mean that Raymond had calculated his every move to exclude her from his life.

"Look, Dr. Hayward, there is a damn blizzard outside and you're over here kicking on a door like you've lost your damn mind. Do you realize that you woke up my six-month-old baby with all of your noise?" Miss Hernandez pinched her eyebrows into an expression showing her own aggravation.

"Look, I'm sorry about that," Charlene apologized. "Believe me when I say that I don't behave like this."

"I know that, you're just on the edge of madness tonight along with this blizzard." Charlene didn't appreciate being called crazy and so she rolled her eyes at Miss Hernandez. "Look, I've called the police on you, so if you don't want to catch a case for the New Year, I suggest that you leave, right now. This is a quiet working-class building and the police respond rather quickly, even on a night like this." Miss Hernandez said her piece and stepped back inside the safety of her apartment. Defeated, embarrassed, and humiliated, Charlene ran back down the stairs, rushed out of the building, got in her car, turned the radio off, and drove into the night.

She flipped on her bright beams as she drove down the dark highway at a snail's pace because she couldn't tell where the road was due to the fact that it was covered with snow. The stretch of narrow two-lane farm highway that she was on wasn't a priority for the salt trucks. As she made her way up to a main artery that would be passable enough to get her back home she saw the flashing squad car lights of a state trooper. As she approached the squad car, she slowed down. The state trooper was blocking the road. She blew her horn at him so that he could move out of her way. Instead of doing what she wanted him to do, the trooper got out of his car and approached her. Charlene let her window down.

"Miss, this road is closed. What are you doing on it?" asked the trooper.

"I'm just trying to get somewhere," Charlene replied with a nasty tone.

"Where do you live?" asked the trooper. The question ticked Charlene off because she didn't think it was any of his business where she lived.

"Miss, I'm only asking because most of the main roads as well as the side roads have been shut down. They're impassable because of the blowing and drifting snow." It was at that point Charlene realized that her emotionally guided decision to rush over to Raymond's apartment had been a bad one.

"The only roads that the salt trucks are concentrating on are the ones leading to the hospital," said the trooper. Charlene reached into her purse, pulled out her hospital identification card, and held it up for the trooper to see.

"I'm a doctor," she said, "I've been called in for an emergency."

"Why didn't you say so at first?" the trooper asked, noticeably annoyed. Charlene didn't answer his question; she just glared at him as if she really didn't have the time to have this conversation with him.

"Be careful and take your time. Do you have a cellular phone with you?" he asked.

"Yes," Charlene replied.

"If you get stuck or caught in a ditch, call for help, but stay in your vehicle until help arrives." The trooper had to raise his voice above the howling wind. "Don't try to walk in this weather."

"Okay," Charlene responded, feeling nervous for the first time. The trooper got back in his vehicle and moved it so that Charlene could pass. Her Lexus fishtailed and she had to handle the steering wheel quickly and aggressively in order to keep the car on the road. The dental office would be the ideal place for her to try to reach, so that she could wait out the storm. The dental office was one mile away from the hospital where she had privileges at. She would just sleep in one of the dental chairs since the office was closed. *How could I have let Raymond get under my skin like this?* she asked herself as she glanced in her rearview mirror, noticing that the squad car's lights had faded into the night. Driving along the dark road suddenly felt creepy as she followed the tire tracks of a vehicle that had been on the road recently. *"Just stay in the tire tracks,"* she said out loud as a way to comfort her twitching nerves. Suddenly the tire tracks disappeared, and Charlene thought that the car had perhaps run off the road, but disregarded that conclusion when she realized that she'd just passed an intersection. *The car had probably turned off onto the other street.* She continued on and listened to the sound of the deep snow scraping and knocking the undercarriage of her car. She turned the car radio back on in an effort to drown out the horrid scraping sound. She pressed the scan button on the face of the radio and listened as the radio scanned for about thirty seconds before it moved on. She pressed the frequency button and switched over to an AM radio station that was giving the weather report. As Charlene got closer to the dental clinic, the road became more passable. She could now also see the bright white parking lot lights of the dental office slashing through all of the darkness of the night.

Although it was only a brief walk from her parking space to the door of the dental office, once Charlene was inside she noticed that she was covered from head to toe with fluffy white snow. She flipped on the office lights, took off her coat, and tossed it in one of the waiting room chairs. She walked back to the office of Dr. Seth Wood, who was the owner of the practice, and took his portable color television off of the bookshelf behind his desk. Charlene then grabbed a fresh white lab coat from a closet to use as a blanket. She then went to an empty room, plugged up the television, set it on a countertop so that she could see it, and got comfortable in the dental chair. *It's a Wonderful Life* was on. The movie's main character, George

Bailey, was standing on a bridge in the middle of a snowstorm about to jump in the freezing water and kill himself when Clarence, his guardian angel, jumped in to prevent George from taking his own life.

"You should have jumped your ass in there, George," Charlene hissed at the television, still coping with the rage that was consuming her. "Life really sucks, George. One minute you think that everything is going great, and the next minute, your entire world can change." She glared at George Bailey mindlessly for a moment and chuckled when she came to the realization that George Bailey reminded her of her ex-fiancé.

"He certainly had trouble taking a hint." Charlene was drifting on a memory. "She only used him to get back on her feet after she finished her undergraduate degree. She used him until another man with deeper pockets and a generous cock came along." Charlene watched as George Bailey stumbled through his miserable life.

Charlene didn't remember when she had drifted off to sleep, but when she woke up, the entire town was in George Bailey's house dumping money in front of him.

"Lucky bastard!" Charlene got up and clicked off the television in a fit of agitation, because just like George Bailey, her ex-fiancé had been blessed with a large sum of money after she dumped him. His parents passed away and left him a large insurance policy, and then he sold his mother's dental practice. She'd made her move too soon with regard to that relationship. At that moment, Charlene's cellular phone rang.

"Hello?" Charlene answered her phone.

"Dr. Hayward, this is Kay from the emergency answering service." Kay had a light southern accent. "I've received a call this evening from a patient who has a dental emergency."

"What did the patient say?" Asked Charlene.

"The patient says that he is in extreme pain, and he believes he's split a molar tooth all the way down to the gum line."

"What's the patient's name?" Charlene asked.

"Mr. Raymond Dolton." Kay said. Charlene was silent for a moment as she processed the name that Kay had just given her.

"Tell him to come in, I'm already at the office." Charlene said.

"Do you think that it is safe for him to drive in the blizzard Dr. Hayward? I think that he was hoping that you'd call in a prescription for a pain killer."

"Kay." Charlene got irritated with her. "I'll give Mr. Dolton a call myself."

"There is no need to do that Dr. Hayward. I've got him on the other line. I'll just let him know that you're in the office waiting for him."

"Thank you," Charlene said and ended the call.

While waiting on Raymond, Charlene convinced herself that Raymond was coming to see her so they could be together. She figured that the dental emergency was just a trick to get away. She believed that Raymond had finally realized she was a much better catch than his wife. However, when Raymond arrived at the office, he wasn't alone. He was accompanied by a bony woman, who was about as interesting as a plank. Charlene knew right away, she was his wife.

"Are you the dentist on duty tonight?" she asked.

"Yes." Charlene's answer was sharp as a blade. She met Raymond's gaze, he was silent, and unspoken tension hung in the air.

"He was doing something crazy. He's been under a lot of pressure lately and I don't think he knows how to deal with it. You see, we just recently got back together and—" The woman was very frazzled, and the sound of her squeaky voice only added to Charlene's disdain for her.

"He had something on his mind so he decided to go outside and shovel the front porch to get his mind off of things. Well, he slipped and fell wrong, somehow hitting his jaw on the steps. One of his molars broke off all the way down to the gum line."

"Okay," Charlene met the woman's gaze. "I'll take care of

him. You wait right here in the waiting room," she instructed his wife. "This way, please." Charlene wanted to punch Raymond in his damn jaw, but she played it cool, for now. She escorted Raymond to a dental chair at the back of the office where she could work on him. He sat down in the chair, and she immediately closed the door, and stood in front of him with her arms crossed. Her heart raced, her eyes narrowed to slits, and the red wine of rage began to pump through her veins.

Raymond met her contemptuous glare and spoke as best as he could.

"I'm sorry, okay! I would have gone to another clinic, but—"

Charlene tossed up her hand and cut him off. "So that tiny twig of a woman out there is your wife?" she asked. Raymond answered her by nodding his head yes.

"Can you do something for the pain that I'm in?" he asked. Charlene could see his eye was twitching very badly. She didn't give a damn about his pain at that instant, because her twisted sense of vengeance demanded that he suffer a bit.

"You left me for fucking Twiggy!" She wanted to argue with him even though she knew that it would be difficult, if not impossible, for him to get a word in.

"Look, I don't have time to have this conversation." Raymond spoke through his clenched teeth and slightly swollen face. "Can you please do something about the pain!" Charlene felt something come over her that she'd never experienced before. A certain kind of maliciousness began attacking her logic, reason, and sense of compassion. She knew that she would be questioned if she began a procedure without explaining what she was about to do, and without the help of an assistant in the office, but she didn't care. She moved around the dental office methodically like a robot with a specific purpose. She broke the standard of care by not giving him a consultation, or taking an x-ray, or even giving him an oral exam. She sedated Raymond, and propped open his mouth so that she could work in it. Charlene didn't care about saving Raymond's tooth.

"Worried about your public image, are you," she said to Raymond, who was unconscious. "I understand," she said as she grabbed a tooth extractor. She inhaled deeply as her sense of being victimized gave way to the villain within her. She clamped the tooth extractor down on his upper incisor tooth and began viciously pulling and jerking on it.

"You-are-going-to-learn-that-you-shouldn't-toy-with-my-feelings!" She damned him as she continued to yank and pull on a perfectly healthy tooth. Her sudden act of passion clouded her professional sensibility and insisted that she ignore the cracked molar tooth that was causing him pain.

"You've got to pay the piper for crushing my heart like this!" She said and then finally ripped out his tooth, root and all, completely from his head. She took a few quick deep breaths but she still felt an unsatisfied fury rushing through her blood and Raymond was about to be a victim of her full unleashed treachery. Charlene clamped the tooth extractor down on the other incisor tooth and tore it out of his head, leaving part of the root in the gumline. She then clamped the jaws of the tooth extractor down on a canine tooth like a vicious mongrel and ripped it clean out of his head like an animal tears into flesh. Charlene locked down on the other canine tooth and extracted it as well. When she'd finally calmed down, she'd removed six healthy upper anterior teeth from Raymond's mouth. Charlene was now tired and her face was covered with light perspiration from all of the pulling and snatching she'd done. She gently placed several pieces of sterile cotton in his upper mouth and applied pressure so that several good blood clots would begin to form where she'd removed his teeth. Once all of the cotton molded itself to his mouth, she stepped back from him and began laughing wickedly at what she'd done.

"You're going to be speaking with a lisp like Mike Tyson now," she cackled like a phantom on Halloween. "You're going to say it's just ludicrous, plain old ludicrous." Charlene's haunting laugh trailed off and she immediately began to shed tears as regret crammed the chambers of her heart and mind. Several root tips where still embedded in Raymond's gum line, and would need to be surgically removed.

"What have I done?" she asked herself. "What on earth have I just done?" Charlene was more concerned about what she'd done to her career than she was about Raymond's oral health.

6

NINA

On the morning of Saturday, January 9ᵗʰ, Nina was sitting on the sofa in her apartment thumbing through a bridal magazine in search of the perfect wedding dress. She didn't want one with a long train that would trail behind her. No, she was looking for one that was a bit saucier. Something short that showed off her legs and her shape.

Nina's thoughts shifted from looking at wedding dresses to moving out of her apartment in Schaumburg and into the house with Richard and Nathan. There were so many decorating ideas that she had for the house. She wanted each room to have its own uniqueness. She wanted to start with their bedrooms. Nathan's room would be first, she thought to herself. She'd take him shopping with her so that she could get an idea of whether he preferred to have bunk beds or a bed in the shape of a car or some other toy. The outing would help build a stronger relationship between them. She would also do some shopping for him because she'd noticed that some of his clothes were getting a bit snug on him. Richard more than likely bought clothes that fit him, instead of thinking ahead and purchasing a size larger so that Nathan could grow into them. Then she'd work on their bedroom. Everything in that room had to go. She wanted a bed with posts and custom-designed drapes, bed linen, and dressy velvet throw pillows. She wanted their bedroom to have a romantic feel to it. She wanted to look forward to falling asleep every night wrapped in Richard's embrace. She wanted everything in her new house to say, "refined elegance." She would have gardeners come out and take care of the landscaping. She would purchase furniture for the pool deck, which she knew that she and Richard were going to enjoy tremendously once the weather broke. The in-ground lap pool was three feet deep at its shallow end and eight feet deep at its deepest end. A quick erotic fantasy formed in her mind. She would lure Richard down to the swimming pool late one night. She would have sensual music playing and undress in front of him, whetting his appetite of desire for her. She'd walk down the steps of the swimming pool completely naked and then invite him in. She imagined Richard removing his pajamas. His manhood would be thick with pressure, like a fire hose, and make her womanhood throb for him to be inside her. Once he got in the water, she'd lock her fingers behind his neck and lock her legs, at the ankles around his waist. She'd be as light as a feather to Richard in the water. They'd kiss each other and behave naughtily by fondling and exploring each other's erogenous zones. The thought of the fantasy was making Nina hot.

Nina entered her kitchen then took a green pear out of the wicker fruit basket that was on the counter beneath the wooden wall cabinet. She sat down at her small kitchen table and began going through the mail that she'd been neglecting. She separated the bills from the junk mail and pulled out her checkbook and calculator. It was difficult for her to believe that she'd actually been living on her own for almost a year. Breaking away from her marriage with Jay, was in her opinion, the best thing she could have done for herself. It was a bit dicey the first few months that she lived there, especially since she lost her job the same month that she got her place. If it wasn't for her good planning and solid savings account, her situation could have easily become a desperate one. Although Richard told her if she needed anything, just call him and he'd take care of her, no questions asked, she was her own woman. Her pride wouldn't allow her to ask for help. Lucky for her, two months after she lost her job, another opportunity at a small brokerage firm came along and she was able to maintain a comfortable living. Nina had to admit; she was going to miss her cozy apartment and the freedom that it represented.

Later that afternoon, Nina drove into the city and hooked up with Rose at Bloomingdale's Department Store on Chicago's Magnificent Mile. John's birthday was coming up later in that month, and Rose wanted to buy him something special, but she had no idea of what she was going to get him. Nina tagged along so that she could stop in Marshall Field's at the Water Tower Place to pick up a few things for Nathan, and possibly catch some good post holiday bargains. It was 6:00 P.M. when the two of them put their shopping bags in the trunks of their cars and then headed over to the Signature Room on the ninety-fifth floor of the John Hancock Building for dinner. The waiter seated them at a window table which had a spectacular view of Chicago's world famous Navy Pier. The Ferris wheel at Navy Pier was all aglow with bright lights, as was Chicago's Lake Shore Drive. The waiter brought them a basket of warm bread and some dipping oil for it. They ordered two iced teas and then excused the waiter.

"So finish telling me the exciting news about John," Nina said, unfolding her white napkin and placing it on her lap.

"Well, when he came up here over the holiday, he'd actually arrived a few days earlier to interview for a firefighter's position with the rescue team out at O'Hare Airport. He said the interview went well but he wasn't sure if he'd be called back since he was from out of state."

"Okay," Nina acknowledged that she was listening to Rose's every word. "Go on."

"Well, to his delight, they called him up and asked him if he could come back for a second interview."

"That must mean he is a very strong candidate," Nina concluded.

"Yes, it does, and I'm praying that he gets the position, because that would mean we wouldn't have to keep flying back and forth so much."

"Would they pay for him to relocate?" Nina asked.

"Yes, they would," Rose answered her, "plus his salary would increase considerably."

"Well, I certainly hope he gets it."

"I'm praying that he does, child. Lord knows I want my man here with me."

"Okay, here are your drinks," said the waiter, who had returned. "What will you be having this evening for dinner?"

"I'm going to have the salmon," said Rose.

"And I'll be having the shrimp and pasta," Nina followed up.

"Those are two very excellent choices. I'll put your orders in right way." The waiter bowed and excused himself.

"So how are things with you, Richard, and Nathan? Have you guys set a wedding date yet?"

"Girl, Richard is so frantic. Since we're having a small romantic wedding, he wants to get married on Saturday, May 22nd."

"Wow, that's only a few months away. Why didn't you tell me?"

"Wait a minute, child, there's more," Nina paused and took a sip of her iced tea. "He wants to purchase a dental practice as well."

"Damn, he is moving quickly," Rose agreed.

"That's what I said, but he explained to me that he's been wanting to purchase his own practice for a long time. When he talks about owning his own business, I can see the passion and fire in his eyes."

"Well, what about you, sweetie? What are you going to do?"

"I'm going to be right there by his side, honey. He told me

that I wouldn't be working for anyone else except myself, because I was going to be his office manager."

"Well, go on with your bad self, Miss Thang!" Rose smiled with pride.

"Let's toast, Rose." Nina held up her glass. "Here is a toast to friendship, love, and prosperity."

"Amen to that," Rose said as she clicked Nina's glass.

When Nina got back to her apartment later that evening, she took out the clothes that she'd purchased for Nathan and looked them over once more. She'd gotten him socks and underwear because in her opinion you could never have too much underwear. She'd purchased him some Oshkosh blue jeans and overalls. She just loved to see little boys in overalls. She'd also got him a few sweaters, some new snow boots, and some long johns for the cold days that were still ahead of them. Satisfied with what she'd purchased, Nina folded Nathan's belongings back up and placed them in their shopping bags. She went into her bathroom, opened a small linen closet, and removed a fresh washcloth. She adjusted the temperature of the water in the sink, moistened the washcloth, and began removing her makeup. Once she was done, she went back into her bedroom and pulled out a pair of her nylon walking shorts. She put the shorts on, turned on her boom box, walked into the living room, and got on her treadmill, which she'd purchased after she left her ex-husband. She placed her *Best of Sade* CD in her boom box, turned it up, and set the speed on the treadmill at six miles an hour. She loved the sound and melody of Sade's voice; to her, it was romantic, yet troubled, and uncertain about the future. Sade crooned "Ordinary Love" as Nina listened while getting into the rhythm of her run. The melody of Sade's voice made Nina's thoughts drift like a bottle in the ocean. Everything was going so well for her that she found it difficult to believe that she didn't have much to complain about. She had her health; she was deeply in love and about to marry a wealthy man who loved her with an equal amount of passion. This year she'd turn forty-one and life seemed to be only beginning. A second chance at this type of happiness was what she'd only fantasized about. Like Sade's voice, she questioned whether or not she could have it all—health, love, passion, wealth, and joy. In the deepest chamber of her heart she could feel the flame of her soul burning bright with hope and the discovery of true love.

Nina thought about the small, intimate, and romantic wedding that she was envisioning. Her wedding dress would be sexy, sassy, and have a bit of adventure to it. Nathan and Richard would have on matching tuxedos, while Rose, John, and Gracie, her daughter, would be in the background well-dressed for the occasion. Speaking of Gracie, she thought to herself as she wondered why she hadn't returned her phone calls. But then again, Gracie could be funny like that. The girl could go weeks at a time and not call or return a phone call. Perhaps everything wasn't perfect in Nina's world. Although Gracie was twenty-three and a grown woman, Nina still worried about her. She couldn't help it, Gracie was her baby; no matter how strange and selfish she could behave.

Nina began to think about Richard once again and what he'd told her after they'd made love on the night he proposed to her.

"I want you to quit your job," Richard had said to Nina as she lay nestled next to him in bed. "With your accounting background, I know that we would do well. You could run the office and manage the staff while I focused on the patients and their oral health."

"Richard, you just don't know how happy it makes me to hear you say that."

"What do you mean?" he asked, brushing her shoulder lightly with the palm of his hand.

"It just makes me feel good to know that you're not excluding me. I love it when you say what we are going to do. You don't say, 'I'm going to do this' or 'I'm going to do that.' You always say, 'We are going to do this or that.' I like hearing that because it lets me know that you're thinking about us as a unit, working together."

"Baby, I wouldn't have it any other way."

"That's what I like about you. I can tell that you want me to be around you."

Before Nina realized it, she'd run five miles on the treadmill and was saturated with sweat. She stopped the machine, got off, did a few stretches, and then went and took a shower. When she got out, she sat down on her bed and turned on the television to pass the time until she was ready to drift off to sleep. She flipped through the channels and started watching the cable television program *Sex and the City*. After the show ended, Nina got up and went into the kitchen for a glass of water before she turned in for the night. As she was pouring her glass, her phone rang. It was at that point that she noticed her answering machine was blinking a message saying FULL. Nina figured that all of the messages were probably from Richard trying to reach her. She picked up the phone.

"Hello, baby," Nina said.

"Hello, Mom?" Nina could hear trembling in Gracie's voice and was glad she didn't say more than she should have.

"Gracie?" Nina asked, surprised to hear her voice. "Are you okay?"

"No," Gracie answered. "Did you get any of my messages?"

"No, baby I haven't, I've been out with your Godmother Rose. Gracie, baby, what's wrong? You sound like you're crying." Nina's heart was suddenly jolted to life with adrenaline.

"Mom," Gracie sighed, "I'm so sorry to bother you." Nina could hear Gracie trying to hide her sniffling.

"Baby, what's wrong?" Nina asked as her concern increased by the second.

"Can you come and get me, please." Gracie's words were getting caught in her throat. Nina quickly scrambled for a pen and paper. "Where are you? I'll be on the next flight out there."

"I'm here, in Chicago, at the airport."

"Which one, baby? Midway or O'Hare?"

"O'Hare," Gracie said. "I'm in Terminal One, by United Airlines."

"Okay, I'll be right there," Nina said. "In about twenty minutes."

Nina tossed on a gray cotton sweatsuit and rushed out of her apartment. Her heart and mind were racing with strong emotions and unsettling thoughts. Something major had to have happened between Gracie and her husband, Mark.

"The slick son of a bitch probably left her all alone again," Nina hissed as she tossed her money into the toll basket, and waited for the green GO light. She never did care for Mark, primarily because he'd brainwashed her daughter into dropping out of school so she could sit at home and have his babies. His entire twisted concept of a woman's place rubbed her wrong.

"I knew that son of a gun was shifty. He probably just up and walked out on her." Nina's foregone conclusions were making her angrier by the minute. She finally arrived at the airport, which was bustling with activity. She pulled over in front of one of the United Airlines entrances and got out of the car to search for Gracie. She saw a woman sitting under an outside canopy with her head down. A brown tattered suitcase was at her side.

"Gracie?" She called out, but the woman was too far away to hear her so Nina got back in her car and pulled forward to the canopy. She honked her car horn at the woman, who glanced up. She was wearing a blue headscarf and dark sunglasses. Nina got back out of the car, and called out her name again.

"Gracie?"

"Yes, it's me," the woman answered as she stood up slowly, picked up her tattered suitcase, and walked over to the car. Nina pressed the trunk latch and walked around to the rear of the car so that she could help put Gracie's suitcase in the trunk. Once it was inside, Nina slammed the trunk door and hugged

Gracie, who felt tense and stiff to her. Gracie exhaled a large sigh of relief when Nina hugged her.

"Come on, get in the car," Nina said. After both women were safely situated in the car, Nina studied her daughter's slumping posture. It was as if she'd somehow been broken.

"Hey, it's okay," Nina said and placed her hand on Gracie's knee. "You're with me now, okay?" Gracie still refused to look at her mother; she just stared at the dashboard in front of her. Nina used her hand to turn Gracie's face toward her. She could see that Gracie's was bruised. She gasped as reality began to take shape.

"I've missed you, Mom," Gracie said as Nina noticed a tear fall from behind her dark sunglasses. Nina carefully removed Gracie's sunglasses from her face and got a glimpse of her swollen and battered right eye. Gracie grabbed Nina's arm and stopped her before she pulled the glasses completely off.

"I couldn't take it anymore." Gracie pushed the glasses back up. "I escaped," she said softly. "I finally escaped."

7

CHARLENE

On Friday, January 15th, city officials held a local press conference to disclose to the residents of Hopkins Park, Illinois, the
condition of its incoming mayor. When the local media received
the news of what had taken place the night of the blizzard, reporters and local cable access television and radio stations con-
verged on the city hall press room and swarmed around it like
flies hovering around a fresh pile of manure with a foul stench.
They were all trying to sniff out the details of why Dr. Hayward
would commit such a malicious act against the new mayor.
There were rumors and speculation that Raymond's defeated
opponent was at the core of what happened. Dr. Seth Wood, a
tall puny man, with an oversized Adam's apple, and the owner
of the dental practice, stood at the speaker's podium, which was
cluttered with microphones. A small gathering of city officials
stood in silence behind him. He appeared nervous to Charlene,
who was sitting Indian-style on her mattress with her eyebrows
pinched into an angry expression and her jaws clenched tightly.
She knew that she was about to be publicly bull-whipped, so
she set her VCR to the record mode because she wanted to be

able to defend herself against every lash that cut into her moral character.

"Let me start off by saying that the mayor is expected to make a full recovery," said Seth as Charlene watched his hands clutch and release both sides of the brown wooden speaker's podium. She could tell that he was nervous and under pressure.

"On the night of January first, Mayor Raymond Dolton was at home shoveling snow off his porch." Seth paused to place a clutched fist over his mouth and clear his throat. "The mayor lost his footing on the slick porch steps, fell, and hit his jaw against the banister. The impact caused the mayor to break the crown of a molar tooth all the way down to the gum line. The mayor was in a considerable amount of pain, and was driven, by his wife, to my dental office, which was less than ten minutes from his home."

"So, you're saying that his wife drove him to your office during the blizzard," a black female reporter interrupted him.

"Yes," answered Seth. Charlene watched as the reporter scribbled his answer down on her note pad.

"Stupid, heifer, that's what he just said." The female reporter annoyed Charlene.

"When the mayor arrived, one of my associates was waiting to treat him. At some point during the treatment process, a dispute between the mayor and the treating dentist took place." Seth paused, and looked down at his notes. Charlene could tell that he was looking to make sure that what he said was clear and accurate. "The treating dentist performed several unnecessary tooth extractions."

"How many extractions were there?" the same nosy female reporter asked.

"Who gives a damn!" Charlene howled at the television wishing the woman could hear her scolding words.

"A total of six upper anterior teeth, from cuspid to cuspid, or from one canine tooth to the other, were removed. The mayor has been seen by another dentist, who is treating him."

"Seth, at least tell them I got the man to the hospital and didn't let him suffer long? Those reporters want to make me out to be a gruesome woman," Charlene spoke to the television.

"What about the molar that was cracked?" asked the female reporter. It was at that point that Charlene realized that the reporter was Angela Rivers, a seasoned reporter with a solid reputation for getting exclusive interviews on high-profile news stories.

"The mayor is being treated for all of his needs," answered Seth.

"Is it true that the mayor was romantically involved with Dr. Hayward, the dentist on staff the night he came to the dental office?" asked Angela.

"Bitch, get out of my business!" Charlene snapped, again angered by Angela's persistence.

"I cannot comment on the mayor's private life," Seth responded.

"Where is Dr. Hayward now?" asked a male reporter.

"I acted swiftly and appropriately in this matter by terminating Dr. Hayward's employment without pay. There is also an ongoing investigation."

"How long has she been dating the mayor? Did she know that he was married?" Angela just wouldn't stay out of Charlene's business.

"Angela, let me be clear on this. I do not know and cannot comment on any of the mayor's romantic involvements. I can tell you that the mayor is getting the best care and will be fine."

"Has the mayor mentioned filing a formal complaint against Dr. Hayward?" asked some other female reporter.

"Bitch!" Charlene hissed at the woman. "It's none of your damn business whether or not he tries to file a lawsuit against me."

"Again," Seth answered, "I cannot comment on any legal action the mayor plans to take."

"What disciplinary action will be taken against Dr. Hayward?"

asked a third female reporter, and Charlene's stomach suddenly went sour as she waited to hear what her fate would be.

"As I said, I moved swiftly on this matter by terminating Dr. Hayward's employment."

"What about the Department of Professional Regulations? Have they been informed of what Dr. Hayward has done? And will they suspend her license?" inquired yet another reporter.

"Suspend my license?" Charlene gasped at the thought. "Why do you want to add fuel to the damn fire!"

"I cannot comment on that at this time," answered Seth, and Charlene clicked off the television because her heart was suddenly racing as the reality of what she'd done began to take its toll. After performing her vengeful act, she reasoned in her mind that the worst thing that could happen would be Raymond filing a malpractice claim against her. Her professional liability insurance would cover that for her. She never took into consideration the suspension of her license. Now she began thinking logically and realized that she was going to need an attorney.

The following morning she got up and watched the morning news. She soon discovered that once the reporters got the story, they'd rushed back to their computers and sensationalized every detail of what they'd been told. A newscaster was holding up to the camera some of the headlines from a local newspaper in the county. It seemed that every newspaper had its own unique spin on what happened to the mayor.

"Look at this one: 'The Tooth Fairy Gets Her Revenge,' said the male newscaster, who seemed to get a kick out of her newly inherited misery. "Here are two more interesting headlines, 'Pow! Right in the Kisser—Local Dentist Delivers a Knockout Blow,' and 'Toothless Mayor Doesn't Have Much to Smile About.' The newscaster then went to local footage of the reactions to the story from tax-paying citizens.

"I think the mayor needs to come forward and explain himself," said a waitress at a local diner. "I voted for him, and I want to know the truth. Was he having an affair with that woman?"

"What that woman did to the mayor is just horrible," said a male citizen who was exiting a local Quick Mart. "Doctors are not supposed to harm people, they're supposed to help them. She's crazy and she needs to have her license revoked. I know that I wouldn't want her to be my dentist."

"I think that the mayor got what he deserved," said another woman. "I bet he'll think twice before he decides to toy with a woman's emotions." Charlene's malicious act of sudden passion was the hot topic of conversation around the small town.

As unconfirmed rumors of her affair with the mayor took on a life of their own, her phone wouldn't stop ringing. Reporters had somehow obtained her phone number and began constantly calling to ask her to come forward with an exclusive interview to share her side of the story. However, none of them was as persistent as Angela Rivers, whom Charlene kept hanging up on. Angela just didn't get the hint. Every time she called, she just fired off questions like a machine gun and that annoyed the hell out of Charlene. A few days later Charlene was leaving her apartment to run an errand. She couldn't believe that Angela Rivers actually had the nerve to just show up at her building. She approached Charlene as she was walking to her car.

"Dr. Hayward," Angela called out as she got out of the news van and trotted across the parking lot to catch her.

"Do you have a minute? I'd like to talk to you about your romantic affair with the city's new mayor." Charlene was shocked by the woman's boldness. Charlene made it to her car and fumbled around with the key chain trying to find the door key to the car. Angela placed a tape recorder up to her mouth.

"Do you have any comment?" asked Angela. Charlene glared at her with damnation. *How dare she ask me questions about my personal life.* Charlene was fuming on the inside.

"I don't have anything to say," she answered Angela through clenched teeth while giving her an evil glare. However, Angela was truly fearless and paid no attention to the daggers in Charlene's eyes.

"Is it true that you and the mayor have a child together?" *Where in the hell did that rumor come from!* Charlene was trying to figure that one out.

"No! We don't have a damn child together!" Charlene exploded at Angela. Charlene then realized that Angela was drawing her out by making up the questions as she went along. She was attempting to get Charlene to slip up and provide her with something useful that would catapult her career to new heights.

"Perhaps that would be a good reason for you to come forward. It would help to clear your name and your reputation. The citizens of Hopkins Park have a right to know everything that transpired between you and your lover." Angela was stubborn and wouldn't give up. "In fact, if you give me an exclusive report, I can pull a few strings and make your story national news. By the time I'm done, I'll have you on *Good Morning America* telling your side of the story and a publisher waiting to print it."

"Listen, bitch! I am not going to get on fucking television and air all of my dirty laundry! Or print it in some damn book! Now unless you want to get all of your hair pulled out and your face scratched up, I suggest that you back the hell up off of me!" Angela took Charlene's threat seriously but handed her a business card before she moved away from her.

"If you change your mind, just give me a call," Angela said as she backed away from Charlene.

Charlene got in her car, tossed the business card on the floor, and pulled off.

It was now Valentine's Day evening and Charlene didn't want to be bothered by anyone for any reason. She'd drawn all of the curtains shut so that she could drown in her misery in peace. She was drinking gin and orange juice while aimlessly clicking her remote control, trying to lose herself in a mindless program. She tried not to cry about all of the negative press and character assassinations that she'd been going through. The combination of gin and juice convinced her emotions to purge the hurt that she was attempting to contain. Charlene began to think about her actions. She thought about the evil streak that she had within her and how it sometimes had a way of taking over when things didn't go the way she wanted them to or when she couldn't get her way. She could be downright sinister when she wanted or needed to be. That darker part of her nature surfaced whenever life or someone tried to mistreat her. That darker side of her also surfaced and guided her when she had to pull one of her schemes in order to get what she wanted. Like when she was in undergraduate school and needed clothes. Since she had only limited funds, she'd go to a small department store and play a game of tag. If she saw something she wanted but couldn't afford, she'd retag the item with a more reasonable price and then take it up to the register and pay for it. Or she'd grab a shopping cart and place one of those large outdoor plastic trash cans into it. She'd fill the inside of the trash can with all of her needs and then pay only for the trash can itself and not its contents.

Some lucky contestant screamed out in joy on the game show. His happiness added to the depth of her sorrow. *Lucky bastard,* she thought as she clicked the TV show off. Charlene took another gulp of her alcohol and wiped the tears from her eyes. She thought about why she had allowed herself to even get involved with Raymond when she knew that he wasn't exactly free. She was a repeat offender in the department of loving someone else's man. She wanted her relationship with him to work, as long as she was the dominant person in the relationship. *It could have worked,* she told herself in spite of the fact that he wasn't divorced yet. In retrospect, Charlene realized that she was forcing their relationship to be something that it wasn't. She thought about why she did that and the answer that the alcohol gave her was that she always had to be in control of everything in her life. She couldn't allow herself to be manipulated in anyway, shape, or form. She thought about how she wanted people to perceive her. She wanted to be approached like a real live queen. She wanted a privileged lifestyle that made people respect, fear, and envy her. She wanted a soft man who was wealthy and would take orders from her as well as provide her with a bit of passion, excitement, and adventure from time to time. Charlene didn't believe in all of that love-at-first-sight crap. To her, everything was about sex, money, and dominance.

"My Grandmother Hazel tried to find that true love shit and look what happened to her. She claimed that she found true love in the arms of someone else's man," the gin started talking to her. The alcoholic combination was starting to speak the truth. She took another swig and finished the glass.

Charlene got up from the sofa and mixed herself another drink. When she returned to the living room, she picked up the wooden picture frame sitting on the end table next to her sofa. The picture was of Hazel, her Uncle Stony, and herself. The photo was very old and the color had begun to fade. Charlene was about twelve years old in the photo. They were standing on her grandmother's front porch down in Glendora, Mississippi. It was hot that day and Charlene was squinting her eyes because the sun was so bright. Her grandmother had her hand in the saluting position to block the sun, and Stony, who was afflicted with epilepsy and mental retardation, was standing next to her wearing an old football helmet, in case a seizure decided to attack him suddenly. The man who was taking the picture was her grandmother's ex-husband, Bo. Charlene clutched the photo to her bosom, leaned back on the sofa, and rested her head on a sofa pillow. She thought about another summer night when she and Grandma Hazel were sitting on the front porch. Grandma was trying to calm her nerves after one of Stony's spells by sitting on the steps and looking up at all the stars in the sky. Charlene was bringing her a glass of freshly squeezed lemonade. As Charlene stepped out onto the porch, she allowed the screen door to slam shut.

"Why are you making such a ruckus, child?" Hazel scolded her. "The last thing I need right now is for you to wake Stony back up." Stony's real name was Paul, but everyone called him Stony, because he was as tough as a rock.

"I'm sorry, I didn't mean for it to shut so quickly," Charlene said as she handed her grandmother a glass jar filled with ice and lemonade. She sat down next to her grandmother and looked up at the night sky. The summer night air was warm, and a breeze carried the sound of crickets singing.

"Are you okay?" Charlene asked, noticing the concern on her grandmother's face.

"Yeah, I'm fine," she answered. "What's on your mind, Charlene? You're usually not up this late."

"I'm just thinking about stuff," she answered.

"Stuff like what?" asked Hazel.

"Somebody said something to me the other day at school that hurt my feelings. It made me cry."

"How many times have I told you about wearing your feelings on your sleeve, child?" Hazel's tone was stern. "You can't go around all of your life getting upset because somebody said something about you that hurt your feelings." Hazel took a sip of her lemonade. "You've got to be in control at all times, Charlene. You have to control every part of your life. The minute you start allowing other people to dictate your life to you, they will use and manipulate you until they get tired of toying with you."

"They weren't talking about me. They were talking about you," Charlene responded. "They said something about you and Bo."

"Is that a fact?" Hazel asked with indifference.

"They said that you were a jezebel because Bo has a wife, and that the Lord up above was going to punish you for being with him."

"Let me tell you something." Hazel turned and glared directly into Charlene's innocent eyes. "What goes on between Bo and I is between him and me. That's grown folks' business, you hear me?" Hazel's eyes suddenly had a fire in them that Charlene had never seen before. It was then that she knew she'd struck a sensitive nerve. "You'll be surprised at who you will find in heaven and hell. Those high-and-mighty hypocrites are always worried about somebody else's business instead of their own."

"Do you love him, Grandmomma?" Charlene asked, hoping that at least there was some type of untamed romance between them. Hazel smirked and Charlene could tell that she was thinking about him.

"Baby, love is funny. I do love Bo, but in a different way. Bo and I are in sort of a complicated situation."

"What do you mean, you love him in a different way?" Charlene was curious about love and how it worked.

"How old are you now?" Hazel asked, even though she already knew the answer.

"I'll be thirteen in two months," Charlene answered.

"Yeah, I guess you're reaching that age where you're getting curious about things like that." Hazel paused as she got her thoughts in order. "Baby, as you make your way through life, love is going to take you through some changes. Bo and I go way back. There was a time when I did have him all to myself, but at first, Bo couldn't deal with the fact that Stony came out the way he did. Most everyone around town whispered about our sick baby behind our backs. They said mean things about me having a baby with problems. Whenever they looked at Stony, they knew right away that something wasn't right with him. Then they'd glare at me like it was my fault. That hurt me to my heart. After a while, I got tired of getting my feelings hurt. So I made myself stronger. I took control over my emotions and I refused to let the things that people said upset me." Hazel paused again while she listened to the sounds of the night. "I love Bo because he doesn't treat me and our son like I've been punished by the angels with a baby that didn't come out normal. He treats me good, and doesn't allow all of the talk to keep him away from his son. I know that it must be hard on him. Stony is in his twenties but has the mind of a nine-year-old boy. Bo has a good heart, but that witch of a wife he has—" Hazel caught herself and bit down on her tongue because she'd said more than she wanted to.

"If you and Bo were together when you had Uncle Stony, why did he leave? And why doesn't he just leave his current wife and come back to you, me, and Stony?" Charlene asked. "I know that he loves you. I've heard him say it."

"It's like I said, baby, love takes you through some changes. It's not that simple. Things are kind of complicated between us," Hazel said as she took another gulp of her lemonade to cover the memory of their breakup while Charlene looked down at her toes, which had chipped red polish on them. Both she and Hazel were silent for a long moment, then Charlene spoke again.

"Grandmomma, how come you won't let me go stay with my momma?"

"Your momma has lost her way in the world, Charlene. You know that, we've talked about it before. Besides, your momma isn't going to do what's right for you."

"What about my father? Who is he? And where is he?"

"Don't concern yourself with him, child." Hazel's tone suddenly became edgy and irritated. "He's the reason your mother turned out the way she has. You don't need to know anything about him, do you hear me? Because he isn't worth the spit in my mouth." Hazel plunked her lemonade down, stood up, and marched back inside the house, allowing the screen door to slam loudly behind her. Charlene's feelings were hurt once again because she didn't understand why the subject of her parents caused her grandmother's mood to suddenly shift. The moment left a deep scar in her heart.

Charlene placed the picture frame down on the floor and then went into her bedroom. Thinking about the past while drinking was making her head spin. As soon as she rested her head on the pillow, she drifted off into a deep sleep.

An earsplitting pounding jolted Charlene awake. Someone was banging on her front door with a fist.

"Angela Rivers, if that is you at my goddamn door, you and I are about to go at it," Charlene shouted. "Damn, why don't you leave me the hell alone?" Charlene got out of bed and marched to her front door with a foul attitude and a massive headache. She was ready to snatch a patch of the reporter's hair clean off her head. *That would give her nosy ass something to write about,* she thought. *And it would teach her ass a lesson about getting in my business.*

"Wait one goddamn minute!" Charlene roared. She looked through the peephole in the door and saw a messenger standing there. *What the hell IS this about?* Charlene wondered as she tried to focus her thoughts.

"Yeah, what do you want?" she asked not opening the door.

"I have a letter here for Dr. Charlene Hayward," the messenger said.

"A letter?" Charlene was puzzled as she opened the door.

"Sign here," the messenger said as he handed her a clipboard. Charlene signed her name, took the envelope, and shut the door. She looked at the envelope, and noticed that it was from her malpractice insurance carrier. She opened the envelope, read the letter, and discovered that they'd been trying to contact her by phone but had been unsuccessful. She was being asked to come into their office to discuss the complaint that had been lodged against her.

"Damn!" She suddenly felt numb, as if all feeling had somehow magically left her body. "You've really screwed yourself this time, Charlene. The shameful thing about it is that Raymond is not even worth it."

8

NINA

On the evening that Nina picked Gracie up from the airport looking like she'd just escaped from a war, Nina had a multitude of questions that she wanted answered. As she drove her daughter home, she fixed her tongue to start firing them off one after another, but after seeing how broken she was, Nina decided that she would hold off her questions until later. She reassessed the situation and concluded that it would be wiser for her to ask her questions after Gracie had some rest. When they arrived back at Nina's apartment, Gracie noticed all of the packed boxes.

"Oh, Mom, I'm so sorry." Gracie burst open with tears. "You're moving out. I guess I hadn't thought about that part. I'll fly back in a day or so. I'll just face whatever is waiting for me."

"Nonsense, Gracie." Nina almost whispered the words because a boulder was forming in her throat. "Come with me," Nina said and took her hand. She pulled her daughter down a corridor and into her bedroom.

"I want you to get in this bed and get some rest. You're safe now, you're home with me. I don't want to hear any more of this nonsense about you going back."

"But—"

Nina cut her off by putting her index finger to her lips. "Just rest for now, Gracie. We'll talk tomorrow." With that said, Nina closed the bedroom door and went back into the front room where her sofa was. She sat down, put her face in her hands, and tried not to let her emotions run away with her. She exhaled loudly, tilted her head back, and gawked at the ceiling mindlessly. After a long moment of deep thought, she leaned over, coiled her legs up on the sofa, and drifted off to sleep.

The following morning Nina got up early, tossed on her navy blue cotton sweatpants and jersey, then left the house for the grocery store while Gracie was still asleep. She needed to pick up some food so that she could cook breakfast for her daughter. She knew that it was going to be a long and emotionally draining day and she wanted to be prepared for it. In that regard, she was like her mother, Cora. Whenever there was a major decision that needed to be made or some conflict that needed to be resolved, her mother always made sure that everyone sat at the kitchen table to talk about the issue on a full stomach. Nina massaged the back of her neck with her fingertips while she sat in her car at a stoplight as the thought of her mother entered her mind. There were so many days that had come to pass when she longed for her to still be living. Nina missed her scent, her voice, and the wisdom of her seventy years. Nina exhaled as she sped up the on-ramp of Route 53 and headed for the Jewel Food Store on Dundee Road. She dug into her purse, which was sitting on the passenger seat beside her, pulled out her cellular phone, and phoned Richard.

"Hey, baby," she said as he answered the phone.

"Well, good morning, sugar baby." Richard was always coming up with cute pet names for her. For so early in the morning, his voice was upbeat, warm, and cheerful. Nina suddenly had second thoughts about mentioning the situation with Gracie because she knew that it would cause him a considerable amount of concern not only for her well-being but for Gracie's as well. Throughout their courtship, she'd noticed that about Richard. He had somehow attached his emotions to hers, and whenever something affected her spirits, it affected his as well. She knew that the tone of his voice would change, and she didn't enjoy the thought that she was going to be the source of the shift.

"Are you on your way over here?" he asked. "Nathan and I are making you breakfast. There is so much that we need to do and talk about. I'm calling a few moving companies today to get some quotes on how much it's going to cost to move you over here. We have to plan the wedding, plan our honeymoon, and then discuss the particulars of buying our first practice."

"Richard," Nina tried to interrupt him. He wasn't making her feel any better.

"Hang on a second, Nathan has something to say to you." Nina could hear Richard hand the phone to Nathan.

"Hello," Nathan said in the sweetest voice.

"Hello, Nathan," Nina answered.

"Thank you for thinking about me when you went shopping. Daddy told me that you picked me up some overalls." Nina's heart suddenly received a jolt of positive emotions. Nathan was finally starting to loosen up to her a bit, and that made her glow on the inside.

"Well, I thought that you might be an overalls kind of man," she answered him.

"Are you going to bring them over?" Nathan asked.

"Yeah, sweetie, but it may not be today," Nina said.

"Why?" Nathan asked. Nina could hear the sound of uncertainty and mistrust in Nathan's voice. She felt as if her next words were going to determine whether or not this breakthrough in communication was going to completely collapse.

"Sweetie, let me speak to your dad again for a second," Nina said, not answering his question. She heard Nathan tell Richard that she wanted to talk to him again.

"I had nothing to do with that." Richard's voice was sounding even brighter. She could tell that he was truly overjoyed to have her in his life. "Nathan did that on his own. I think that things are finally falling into place for us." Richard was jovial. "We're not going to have to worry about a thing."

Why did he have to go and say that? Nina thought to herself. "Richard, honey, I'm not coming over today."

"You're not coming over? Why?" Richard asked. Nina could hear the sound of something frying in a pan. "I'm making my special veggie omelette. Egg whites only."

"There is no easy way to say this so I'm just going to come out with it. It's my daughter, Richard. She came home last night and she doesn't have a place to stay." Nina paused and heard only silence. She didn't even hear the sizzling of the frying pan anymore. At that moment Nina wanted to get inside of Richard's head to hear what he was thinking but she knew that was impossible.

"It's not what you're thinking," she said, wanting to ease any fears that may be resurfacing about family members moving in on him.

"I'm just slowing down and listening. What's going on?" Richard seemed to be questioning her instead of asking her. She didn't like the sound of the words "slowing down" either. At first, he was rushing into everything so the words "slowing down," in her mind, seemed to indicate that he was abruptly rethinking everything.

"What do you mean, 'slowing down'?" Nina got an attitude out of the blue with him.

"Nina, talk to me. Tell me what's going on? Why are you so edgy all of a sudden?" Nina finally reached Dundee Road and turned left to continue on her errand to the Jewel Food Store, which was three stoplights down the road.

"She called me up late last night from the airport asking me to come and pick her up." Nina paused again and heard pure silence.

"Hello! Are you there?" Nina asked, thinking that perhaps she'd lost the call.

"Yes, I'm here," Richard answered.

"So I went to pick her up and she looked pretty bad."

"What happened to her?" Richard asked and Nina felt a bit better that he was starting to show some concern.

"I'm not sure yet because we haven't had a chance to talk. But I do know this: That fool of a husband has been beating up on my baby," Nina voiced with a sudden flare of unbridled emotion.

"You're kidding me?" Richard's voice had a higher pitch to it.

"No, I'm not. Apparently it was so bad that she told me she had to escape. I'm not exactly sure of what that means, but I'm glad she found the courage to get out. I never did care for her husband, Mark."

"Is she okay? Does she need medical attention or anything?" Richard asked, voicing more of his concern. "Working at the group practice, I see domestic abuse cases from time to time. A male spouse can really do some damage. Loosen teeth, knock them out, or even worse, break a jawbone."

"My goodness, Richard, you never told me that."

"I'm not trying to frighten you, Nina, I'm just trying to help. I know of some counseling centers in the area if she needs support. But she has to be willing to take that step. She has to be willing to get help." Nina sighed with relief. She was glad that Richard had compassion and concern for her daughter, even though they hadn't met yet. She was equally happy that he didn't come out of an ugly bag on her, out of some fear that she might have been thinking about trying to move her daughter in with them.

"You are one of a kind, Richard. Did you know that?"

"No, but now I do."

"I love you, baby," Nina said pleased with the fact that she and Richard didn't end up having a nasty dispute.

"Let me know if there is anything I can do. And take your time, we can always discuss our plans at a later date."

"Okay baby, I'll call you back once Gracie and I decide what will be best," Nina said as she turned into the Jewel lot and found a parking space. They said their good-byes for the moment and Nina went to take care of some shopping.

When she returned to her apartment, it was quiet except for the low hum of the refrigerator. Nina set the bags down on the kitchen counter and then walked down the hall and peeked in on Gracie, who was curled up peacefully under the forest green comforter. She gently pulled the door closed again then headed back into the kitchen to make a pot of tea. Nina unpacked her groceries then pulled a pan out of one of her packed boxes. She set the pan on the stove but just stared at it because at that moment she told herself she needed to be strong. She had to somehow find the strength to keep it all together just like her mother would have. In a bizarre kind of way, she felt what her mother felt when she admitted that she'd gotten pregnant at such a young age. She could still see the hurt in her mother's eyes. It was like the breath had been knocked out of her, but she never admitted how much pain she was feeling.

Nina heard the sounds of feet swishing against the carpet and knew that Gracie was finally up and shuffling her way toward her. She took a deep breath in preparation for a conversation that was going to be a pivotal point in both of their lives.

"I'll have some tea ready in a minute," Nina called out as she began slicing a fresh lemon.

"Just like Grandma used to make, right?" Gracie said as she walked into the kitchen and flipped the power switch on Nina's small countertop radio. The soft mellow voice of the newscaster reporting the local weather came on.

"Yeah, just like she used to make," Nina said, taking a good look at her daughter under the light of day. When she'd hugged her the night before, she'd felt a bit frail, but now Nina could see that she wasn't frail at all. Gracie had picked up weight, and her face and hips were much fuller. Her hair looked as if she hadn't been taking very good care of it. She had it braided in two large French braids that ran away from her face and down the back of her head. Her skin was also in bad shape. It was riddled with splotches and a black ring ran from one side of her nose to the other. Nina was thinking about getting her some Neutrogena products to help clean and balance out her skin so that it looked healthier. After Nina took all that in, she concentrated on the bruise around Gracie's right eye. It was black and looked hideous against her skin. It was like looking at a patch of pepper in a bag of sugar.

"I was going to cover it up with a bit of makeup but sometimes that only makes it look worse." Nina could no longer hold back her questions so she just came right out and asked her what happened.

"How long has this been going on, Gracie?" Nina made sure that her tone was soothing and not confrontational.

"Does it really matter?" Gracie answered as she took a seat at the kitchen table. "I mean, to be honest, I can't remember the exact beginnings of it. It just sort of started happening."

"You know that love doesn't begin at the end of a fist, right?" Nina was looking directly into Gracie's eyes.

"Yes." Gracie broke her eye contact with Nina and stared out the kitchen window. Gracie studied two squirrels chasing each other around the base of a tree. Nina sensed that her comment had jabbed a delicate wound.

"Baby, I'm not here to make you feel bad. I just want to help you."

"You are helping me, Mom," Gracie paused as she still eyed the squirrels that were now rushing up the tree. The squirrels were a welcome distraction because the pain in Gracie's heart was ballooning and she was trying to deflate it before it burst and her emotions got the best of her. Once the squirrels disappeared, she began talking again.

"I guess it started after my accident. He was rather calculating with his criticism of me." Gracie turned her head back from the window and looked down at the flower pattern on the tablemat. "He somehow made me feel worthless because I couldn't have a baby for him. When we made love, he said that I didn't feel the same. He complained that I wasn't satisfying him. After a while he stopped asking for sex and turned me down when-ever I wanted it. Whenever we went out to places, we got into arguments over tiny things, silly things like slamming the car door too hard. Or I'd get mad at him for walking in front of me as if we weren't together. We began picking on each other like we were in second grade or something. I felt like he was an-noyed by me, but took pleasure in trying to break me down. I think he wanted me to worship the ground he walked on or something queer like that." As Nina listened to Gracie, she swiveled her head from side to side, not wanting to believe what she was hearing because what Gracie was telling her sounded all too familiar. "I felt so bad, I felt like my life had no value or meaning if I couldn't make a baby for him." Nina placed a steaming cup of tea on the table in front of Gracie, and then sat opposite her at the table. She palmed her cup of tea and contin-ued to listen to her. "I mentioned adoption a few times but that didn't go over very well. He got to bitching about why should he raise another man's child when he should be raising his own."

"What an insensitive—" Nina caught herself because she was about to call the man out of his name and she didn't want to do that, at least not while Gracie's wounds were still fresh.

"He's like that. He constantly searches for something to argue about. Anyway, he began staying out late. He said that he was out with his military buddies, which I wanted to believe was true, but in the back of my mind I had my suspicions. One night, he came to bed and I could smell the scent of another woman on him. The scent of her womanhood was all over his breath and body. The dirty bastard didn't even have the decency to wash the scent off his body. I sprung up, pissed as hell, and confronted him. We got into a vicious shouting match; we were bitter and cold with each other. I accused him of creeping around on me and he told me to grow the hell up. One word led to another, and before I realized it, I was venting about every-thing that wasn't going right with our marriage—his criticism of me both privately and publicly along with his lack of support for anything I wanted to do." Gracie paused again as she began reliving the moment. "I didn't even see his hand coming. I just remember my ear ringing loudly. He hit me so hard, it felt like he'd split my ear open. I backed up from him and my back hit the wall. I slide down to the floor next to the laundry hamper and cried because I didn't know what to do." Gracie's words went straight to Nina's heart. Under no circumstance does a parent ever want to see someone harm their child, no matter what their age.

"Baby, you could have called me. I would have sent an airline ticket for you."

"As bad as it sounds, I thought the entire thing was my fault. I kept asking myself if I'd missed something. I thought that perhaps he was under a great deal of pressure that he wasn't telling me about. I found myself making excuses for what he'd done. I didn't think that it would ever happen again so I let it go." Nina reached across the table and placed Gracie's hand in hers. "You can always call me, Gracie. I'm here for you no matter what. You didn't have to suffer like that, and don't ever have to again."

"I didn't want to bother you with all of my drama and I really didn't want to bother Dad with it."

"Speaking of him, I need to call him and tell him that you're back now," Nina said.

"No!" Gracie shouted out. "No, I don't want him to know. I don't want him to see me like this. I can see the pain in your eyes, Mom, and I don't want to see pain in his as well. I'll tell him when I'm ready."

"Okay," Nina agreed. "So how did you get here? Spare me the details about him hitting you. I can see that he's done that."

"He went out again for the night but forgot his cellular phone at the house. It started ringing so I answered it. It was a woman calling for him. She was a woman that I didn't know, so I asked who she was. She asked me the same question. I told her that I was his wife, and then she told me that she was the mother of his child." Gracie released a sigh from a deep chamber in her heart. "When he got home, we fought about it. After he did this to me, he rushed out to a bar and came back intoxicated. He hit on me some more, and then used me for sex." Gracie's hands and neck were twitching uncontrollably. "When he fell asleep, I packed my suitcase and took his car and his credit card. At first, I was going to just get a hotel room, but I suddenly realized that I didn't even want to be in the same city with him so I drove to the airport, bought a ticket, and here I am." Nina was silent for a moment as she processed what Gracie had just told her.

"Are you going back to him, Gracie?" Nina asked in an attempt to figure out if Gracie had left him for good or if she just wanted some time away to give him something to think about.

"No," Gracie answered. "I don't want a man who doesn't want me. I can't make him want me."

"So what are you going to do? Have you thought about that?" Nina asked.

"I haven't had much time to think about the future, Mom. I just needed to get away from him. I needed to escape from the reality I was living. I was unhappy, afraid, and miserable. I deserve a much better life than that one. I know that my timing is horrible, with you about to get married. Believe me when I say that I don't intend to screw up any of your plans." Nina noticed Gracie glancing around her apartment at all the packed boxes. "You're moving, aren't you?"

"Yes," Nina answered her.

"I'm already screwing things up for you." Gracie hung her head down shamefully. I'm sorry, I'll go back. I seem to mess up everything. I'm such a failure at everything. Mark was right, I'm stupid, I'm fat, and I'm worthless," Gracie said, beating herself up before anyone else could. Nina watched as tears rolled down from Gracie's cheeks and splashed against the edge of the table. Nina stood up, walked over to Gracie, put her arms around her, and kneeled beside her.

"Gracie." Nina paused for a moment to choose her words carefully, while at the same time managing the swell of emotion lodged in her throat. "Hold your head up, baby. Don't you ever let any man take away your dignity, pride, or self-esteem. You were not raised like that. You have a good head on your shoulders, honey, but somehow, some way, you started believing in what someone else said about you instead of believing in yourself."

"You're right," Gracie responded with her head still slumped down. Nina grabbed a napkin from the tabletop and handed it to her so that she could dry her tears.

"You know, while I was on the plane, a random memory jumped into my head. I began thinking about the day when you and I went downtown to the old State and Lake Movie Theater to see a rerun of *The Wiz*. I was so excited that day because I wanted to see Diana Ross and hear her sing. When she finally sang that song, 'Believe in Yourself,' I felt my heart soaring. I remember you saying that Diana Ross's version of that song didn't do it for you; I remember tears in your eyes when Lena Horne sang the song. You said that it had more meaning for you coming from Lena because of what she'd endured in her life. I remember you saying that she believed in herself no matter what everyone else thought or said and in the end she came out on top. Well, now that I've endured a bit of psychological hardship of my own, I like Lena Horn's version of the song better as well." Nina sighed as she thought about the day Gracie was recalling.

"Honey, I was just trying to teach you that life is more than vinegar and salt, life is also sweet like honey. I wanted you to understand that in the face of adversity and difficulty, you have to be stronger and better but, most importantly, you have to believe in yourself, when no one else does."

"I think that Mark was trying to reprogram me. I think that he wanted to break me down and make me more obedient, like I was his damn dog or something."

"Gracie, I need to ask you something." There was an awkward moment of silence between them, and unspoken tension hung in the air. "Do you want your marriage back? I mean, is it really over or are you just infuriated right now?"

"Mom, I told you already, it's over," Gracie answered without hesitation.

"Then here is what I propose we do. I have some money saved up. I want you to take this apartment. It's already furnished, and you'll have everything you need."

"Mom, I can't—" Nina cut her off by raising her right eyebrow and looking deeply into her eyes. Gracie was very familiar with the glare that Nina was giving her. It was the one that said, *don't bite the hand that feeds you.* "Okay," Gracie said, not challenging her mother.

"Good," Nina said as she stood back up. Nina was going to help Gracie out for the moment but she was also going to work on her. She was going to convince her to go back to school so that she could become a strong and independent woman. Her only concern was the amount of damage that Mark had done to her baby, both physically and mentally. It would not be easy getting Mark out of her system.

"Mom," Gracie called to her as Nina went back to her side of the table.

"Yes," Nina answered.

"I really wanted to have children for him," Gracie's voice trembled and she broke down sobbing once again. *Oh, lord,* Nina thought. *How am I going to convince her that he isn't worth all of the torture she's putting herself through? How am I going to tell her that she needs to press assault charges against him?*

9

RICHARD

Richard was sitting in his private office at the group practice making notes in a patient's chart. Just as he was finishing up, one of the dental assistants came into his office and gave him the chart of his next patient.

"I've put Mr. Orchard in Room 2, Dr. Vincent," said Andrea, his twenty-five-year-old dental assistant and the senior member of his dental team, which consisted of three hygienists, two assistants, and a secretary. She placed the chart next to him on the desk.

"Thank you," said Richard. "This is my last patient, right?" he asked, making sure that no one had called in with an emergency.

"Yes, it is," answered Andrea and then turned to walk out. "Oh, by the way, when am I going to get my invitation to the wedding?"

"Don't worry, we haven't sent them out yet. Nina wants to have a small wedding. You should be getting one fairly soon, though, now that we've agreed on a church."

"I just wanted to make sure that I'm on your 'small' wedding list." Andrea's Hispanic accent surfaced with a hint of playful attitude.

"Andrea, you're my right arm around here. Without you, I wouldn't know if I was going or coming. You know that I couldn't get married without inviting you."

"Good, I'm glad you feel that way, because if I don't get an invitation, my boyfriend and I are going to crash your wedding," Andrea said as more of a joke than a threat. "You know how much I love going to weddings."

"Don't worry," Richard put her at ease, "you will get an invitation."

"Good." Andrea tucked her hair behind her ear. "One of these days I'm going to get married. I'm working on my man right now."

"I'm sure he'll say yes soon," Richard chuckled.

"Well, if he doesn't propose to me, I will have to find myself a new Prince Charming." Richard laughed out loud. "Shoot, I'm telling you, Dr. Vincent, Nina is one lucky woman. It isn't pretty out there in the dating world these days. People are just plain old loco. Plus, I'm tired of going to everyone else's wedding, I want to go to my own," Andrea added.

"You know . . ." Richard stopped the business of his writing. "She may be a lucky woman, but I'm a blessed man to have found someone I'm compatible with, someone I can communicate with and who will not take me for granted." Richard reflected on what he'd just said. "I sound like a sap, don't I ?"

"No, you sound like a man that most women would die for," Andrea responded with pure honesty. "You're handsome, sincere, caring, and honest. Are you sure you don't have any brothers lurking around somewhere? My sister is looking for a good man like yourself."

"No, I don't have any brothers, Andrea." Richard chuckled.

Andrea groaned. "More men need to be like you and be in touch with their feelings. Anyway, enough of my pouting. Let me go tell Mr. Orchard that you'll be right in."

"All right," Richard answered as he went back to the business of writing his notes. When he was finished, he closed up the file and put it in his out basket so that it would be refiled. He looked at a photograph that he'd taken of Nina standing in the water wearing her yellow bathing suit when they were in the Bahamas. Her wanting eyes were looking directly at him. It was almost as if she were standing right in front of him. He mulled over what had happened over the past three weeks with Nina and her daughter, Gracie. Nina had let Gracie take her apartment and finally moved her belongings in with him and Nathan. When she got off work, she dropped by to check on Gracie to make sure that she was doing well both physically and emotionally and also to make sure that she didn't have a relapse and head back to her husband. Richard had given Nina information on some local centers that offered help to woman who were victims of domestic violence. Richard's heart ached a bit when he thought about what Gracie must have gone through and how all of this was affecting Nina. Although she was showing an amazing amount of strength and composure in front of Gracie, when she came back to him in the evening she was emotionally drained, and during the middle of the night on several occasions she'd had crying spells, because she felt as if she'd somehow failed as a mother. Richard would hold her tightly as he tried to be of comfort to her.

"When your heart hurts, mine does as well," he whispered to her as he rubbed her shoulder. "I wish I could make your pain go away."

"Just hold me," she said and Richard held her all night, rocking and comforting her and giving her reassurance that everything would be all right.

Richard stopped looking at the photo and was about to go in and see Mr. Orchard when his phone rang. He picked it up and heard Nina's voice on the other end.

"Hey, handsome, you're still getting off on time, right?" Richard could tell that she was on her cellular phone by all of the static.

"Yes, I'm about to see my last patient now. How are things going with you and Nathan?" Richard needed to know because it was the first time that Nathan and Nina had been out together alone. The adjustment for Nathan was a difficult one. He wasn't willing to accept Nina as his stepmother right away. He constantly brought up his mother, Estelle, especially when Nina was present. When she made his favorite food, he complained that it didn't taste good because his mother hadn't made it with her special touch. Whenever Nina and Richard showed each other any type of affection in front of him, Nathan would ask why Richard never did those things with Estelle. It was very clear that Nathan was choosing not to get along with Nina. However, Nina wasn't willing to give up on Nathan, and had been adamant about spending some time alone with him so that they could develop a more solid relationship. Nina was determined to win Nathan over, even though she knew that it was not going to be an easy task.

"Well, he wasn't very talkative at first, but when we hit the electronics section at Wal-Mart, then he wanted to communicate. He decided to share with me that he wanted some new video game," Nina said, "but, the little devil, he tried to trick me into buying some horror game called Resident Evil."

"You didn't buy that game for him, did you? That's one of those mature games."

"No, I didn't buy that," Nina answered, almost offended that Richard thought she'd fall for Nathan's antics. "I brought him a car racing game, though."

"Oh, okay, other than that, did he behave himself?"

"He is still uneasy about me trying to be a mother to him. I guess I want him to instantly like me but I know that's just not going to happen right away. He brought up his mother and grandmother several times today. He really misses his mother, more so than his grandmother. I told him that it was okay for him to talk to me about them, and that it would not hurt my feelings if he did, but I don't think he wants to fully open up to me yet. I can tell that he is a bit uncertain about things. I assured him by telling him that I was all ears when he was ready to talk. Once we made it over that hurdle, our day together was smoother. I can also see that he likes to do things for himself, though. When we left the house this morning, he wouldn't let me tie his shoes or tell him when his shoes were on the wrong foot. He walked out of the house with one shoe pointing east and one pointing west. It was so funny watching him walk like a duck. I said, 'Nathan, do you want me to help you with your shoes?' And he said, 'Nope, I have them on and I tied them up by myself.'"

"Oh, lord." Richard rolled his eyes. "Did you fix his shoes?"

"No. When he got in the car, he realized that something wasn't right and did it himself."

"So where are you at now?" Richard asked, trying to speed up the conversation.

"Well, we're on our way over to pick up Gracie. Then the three of us are going to head over to Roosevelt University and gather some information. After that, we'll meet you at Shaw's Crab House for dinner."

"Okay, baby, then I'll see you tonight. I have a patient waiting on me."

"Okay. Oh, Richard?"

"Yes?"

"Gracie is looking forward to meeting you tonight."

"So am I," Richard answered and then said his good-bye for the moment.

When Richard arrived at Shaw's Crab House in Schaumburg, he found Nina, Gracie, and Nathan sitting on a bench in the waiting area. Nathan saw him first and called out, "Daddy!" then rushed over to him. Nathan leaped into his arms and Richard hugged him.

"I got a new video game." Nathan was eager to start discussing his day. His young voice was bold and raspy. "I also met a new lady today."

"You did?" Richard asked with excited surprise in his voice.

"Yup," Nathan twisted around in Richard's arms so he could see behind him. "Come here, Gay-C." Nathan couldn't fully pronounce her name yet.

"Hello." Gracie walked over to Richard and extended her hand. Richard sat Nathan down and shook her hand.

"It's good to meet you," he said as Gracie's eyes held his for a brief second before she broke contact. Gracie twisted her neck around to look for Nina, who was talking to the hostess. Richard studied Gracie for a moment, trying to distinguish which features of Nina's she possessed. She had Nina's facial structure but not her skin tone. She had more of a cinnamon tone rather than a caramel one and she wasn't taking good care of her skin the way Nina did.

"Okay, the hostess is going to seat us now," Nina said as she greeted Richard with a quick kiss on the lips. The hostess seated them at a table at the rear of the restaurant. Nina and Richard sat across from each other, and Gracie and Nathan sat across the table from each other. Nathan had felt an instant fondness for Gracie in the same fashion that he had with Rose. Richard could tell that Nathan liked Gracie by the way he was asking her one question after another. Richard noticed that Gracie didn't seem to mind at all. She enjoyed talking to his little guy and gave him the attention he was demanding.

"Gracie, now that you're all settled in, do you like your new apartment?" Richard asked.

"It's nice," Gracie answered. "I'm thankful for it." Richard studied Gracie longer than necessary and noticed that she covered up the right side of her face with the palm of her hand. He could tell that he was making her self-conscious, but he didn't mean to.

"Gracie and I have made some new plans." Nina offered up a bit more information. "She's having her academic records transferred and is going to continue with her education."

"That's great," Richard said. "Where are you going to go to school?" he asked Gracie although he already knew the answer.

"Uhm, I'm probably going to go to Roosevelt University,

which is where my mom went. They have a campus out this way."

"How long will it take you to complete your degree?" Richard asked.

"That depends on how many of my credits transfer. I'm hoping that at least sixty of them transfer over. That would put me at about the halfway mark."

"I'm going to help her out with the apartment until she finds a job," Nina jumped back into the conversation. "And this time we're going to stick to our plan, right?" Nina looked at Gracie.

"Yes." Gracie spoke softly and for a moment Richard thought he detected a hint of depression in Gracie's tone.

"Can I go to school with you?" Nathan interrupted the flow of the conversation.

"No, I'm afraid not, sweetie," Gracie said. "My school is for big kids like me. When you grow up and become big like me, you'll be able to go to my school."

"Will you still be there?" Nathan asked.

"I hope not." Gracie smirked. "I still haven't called Dad yet," Gracie said, changing the subject. "I'm hoping he will help me out with getting a car so I can get around."

"Oh, I see," Richard said, nodding his head in the yes motion.

"I'm sorry, I didn't mean to make you feel awkward by mentioning my dad."

"No, you didn't upset me." Richard quickly defused the moment. "I was actually thinking of something else. I was thinking that when I open up my practice, I would need a staff person at the front desk of the office. I was thinking that if you couldn't locate a job that would offer you some flexibility with your class schedule, you could come and work for me."

"Gracie looked at Richard with wide-eyed surprise. Are you serious?" she asked.

"Yes, I am."

"Thank you so much." Gracie was filled with glee. "There

are so many things that are changing in my life right now and I can use all the help I can get."

"Well, as long as you're willing to work, I'll do what I can to help you."

"That is so generous of you, Richard." Nina reached across the table and clutched his hand. She knew that Richard was doing this to make things simple and less stressful.

"You guys are doing an awful lot," Gracie commented. "You're getting married, and opening up a new practice. Isn't all of that going to be rather expensive?"

"Can I get a job at your office too, Daddy?" Nathan once again interrupted the flow of the conversation.

"You can be the toy manager, how does that sound?" Richard answered Nathan.

"Okay," Nathan said and attempted to pick up the glass of water in front of him. Gracie quickly reached over to help him hold it.

"Richard is, well," Nina paused briefly, "financially able to handle the responsibilities that he is placing on himself."

"So how are the wedding plans going?"

"They're moving along, right baby?" Richard looked at Nina.

"Yes, they are. We're going to get married on May twenty-second at a church on Williams Street in Palatine."

"May twenty-second was Grandma's and Grandpa's wedding anniversary," Gracie said.

"I'm surprised you remembered that," Nina responded.

"Of course I remember. Every year you would send a large care package down to them for their anniversary."

"What about your wedding dress?" Gracie asked.

"Well, your nutty-ass Godmother Rose and I are still trying to find one that we both like. She wants me to get one with a long-ass train and I want something that is a bit more daring. But I think we're narrowing things down."

"Well, the next time you guys go out looking, let me know. I want to go."

"You're going to have to come because you're one of my bridesmaids."

"Oh, yeah, I forgot. It slipped my mind. I'm dumb like that. Mark was always saying that I couldn't remember anything."

"Gracie, honey, you're not dumb." Nina couldn't stand it when Gracie cut herself down like that. She hated the fact that, somehow, Mark had completely squashed all of Gracie's self-worth.

"I'm sorry," Gracie said, rotating her neck clockwise trying to reduce the tension in it. "It's going to take me a while to get him out of my system."

"What does 'dumb' mean?" Nathan asked.

"It just means that a person has some trouble learning new things," Richard answered his son.

"You're not dumb, Gay-C, you remembered my name."

Gracie laughed a bit.

"You're right, Mr. Nathan, I'm not dumb, but I may need you to remind me of that, okay."

"Ok, Gay-C, you're not dumb, you're smart."

10

CHARLENE

Charlene had to drive all the way to downtown Chicago to meet with her malpractice insurance carrier's attorney. His corporate office was on Dearborn Street, which was in the heart of Chicago's Loop area. When she arrived, she took the elevator up to the sixteenth floor and informed the receptionist that she had an appointment. After waiting in the lobby for a few moments, she was escorted to a conference room by the receptionist, where she was seated at a round table. After waiting for about ten minutes, a short, young Irishman with red freckles, a short haircut, and large ears rushed into the room with a brown accordion folder.

"Hi, I'm Brad McCann, and I'm sorry I had to keep you waiting," he said, rushing the words out of his mouth as Charlene stood up to shake his hand. "I got tied up on a phone call."

"It's okay." Charlene put him at ease as she sat back down and slid her purse from in front of her.

"Okay, here is what has been going on since you got the letter and contacted me. I've spoken with Kay from the emergency answering service, and I've also been gathering information on your case." Brad couldn't seem to slow down his words as he opened up the folder and pulled out some papers. "And I'm going to be honest with you, Dr. Hayward, this is the type of case that we don't want to go to trial with."

"Okay," Charlene said as she stared at him and tried to digest what he was telling her.

"A jury would be sympathetic to the patient and would award millions of dollars in a case like this, and quiet frankly, you don't have that type of coverage."

"So what are you saying?" Charlene felt an ugly attitude surfacing.

Brad began gesturing with his hands. "I'm just saying, according to the information that I gathered on this, what you did was a very malicious act." Charlene noticed that Brad's style of speech was very proper and he was grammatically correct with every word he spoke.

"Well, I know that already!" Charlene's tone was sharp. "Just tell me how I can get out of it."

"Well, that's the thing." Brad's voice was now filled with a hint of nervousness, and Charlene could tell that she'd intimidated him a bit. "You're only covered for one million dollars, and your level of exposure in this instance extends far beyond that amount." Brad was once again gesticulating with his hands to emphasize his point. Charlene released an aggravated sigh.

"Look, the expert witness that the plaintiff gets is going to take one look at the patient record and say that there is no clinical reason that six upper anterior teeth had to be removed from Raymond's mouth. Even our own expert witness says that. So now, it looks like this guy came into the clinic for emergency treatment, and for whatever reason, you disfigured the man and made him look like a jack-o-lantern. Now if there is a valid clinical reason that you had to remove all of those teeth, please tell me now."

"He pissed me off!" Charlene replied with aggression and venom in her voice.

"Okay"—Brad was talking with his hands again—" "what

did he do to piss you off? Did he try to attack you or something? Because if he did, we could perhaps take a different approach."

"It doesn't really matter why he pissed me off, he just did."
There was thick tension in the air and an awkward moment of
silence between the two of them. Charlene noticed Brad studying her as if she were from another planet. "It's a woman thing,"
Charlene said, wanting him to discontinue his prying into the
reasons why she did what she did.

Brad huffed before he spoke again. "There may be a way to
get you out of this. It's a long shot," Brad paused, "and I do
mean a very long shot, but I'm going to try it. I'm going to see if
they'll agree to an arbitrator. If they do, this case doesn't have
to go in front of a jury, which means that the settlement amount
will be more manageable."

"Do you think they'll agree to that?" Charlene asked.

"To be frank with you, no, I don't think they'll agree to it. If
I were the plaintiff in this case, I wouldn't, but perhaps we can
excite Raymond with the proposal of a quick settlement."

"Well, when do you think you'll have an answer?"

"I'll put in a call to the other attorney this week. I'll feel him
out and see if he nibbles. If he does, I'll let you know right
away."

"What if he doesn't go for it?" Charlene asked even though
she really didn't want to know the answer. Brad looked into
Charlene's eyes and paused for a brief moment.

"If they don't agree, they will be in a position to ruin you financially."

The words "ruin you financially" resonated in Charlene's
head like an echo that wouldn't fade away. Her mind was in a
bit of a haze as she mixed in with the pedestrians and headed
back to the parking garage on the corner of Lake and Randolph
Streets. All she wanted to do was pay Raymond back for trying
to play her for a fool, and now, with the way things were going,
she'd end up paying him. She needed to talk to him. She somehow needed to meet with him.

When Charlene got back to her apartment, she went into her bedroom and sat Indian-style on her bed. She grabbed a pillow and hugged it tightly as she rocked back and forth while thinking intensely about her uncertain future. The pit of her stomach was going sour and began grumbling. Charlene closed her eyes for a moment so that she could put her thoughts in order. The first thing she needed to do was call Raymond and get him to drop the charges against her. After all, he did bring all of this on himself and there was no one to blame except himself. Had he been man enough to meet with her face to face, and end their relationship, things would have perhaps turned out differently. That was one of the things she didn't understand about men. One minute they could be all over you, showering you with affection and attention, and the next minute, they flip out and decide they need their space, or decide that they're suddenly bored with you and want to see if there is another woman who can hold their interest a bit longer. It was frustrating dealing with men and their moods.

Charlene took a deep breath and decided that it was time to do something audacious. She was going to go directly to the root of her problem. She was going to confront Raymond, at his house, with his tiny twig of a wife. *What in the hell does he see in her anyway?* She wondered. She barely had breasts, no hips, and a flat ass. Charlene had full juicy lips, hips that could rock a mountain, a generous and plump amount of ass, and scrumptious breasts. *There was no way that wife of his could possibly do anything better than Charlene could.*

The following day Charlene found herself sitting in her car glaring at Raymond's car, which was sitting in his driveway. His new home was situated at the crest of a hilly street. It wasn't difficult to find since the local newspaper had covered his inauguration and had listed the area he'd be living in. All she had to do was drive down the streets and search for his car. The day was gray and the clouds were dropping light snow flurries. Charlene was tickled by the mood of the day because it mirrored how she felt—gray and bitterly cold. She was about to make a calculated move. If Raymond was so worried about his public image, she was about to really give him something to consider. She was about to use the only weapon she had left—humility with a twist. She opened up her purse and removed a small canister of pepper spray, which she'd use if things got out of hand. She trotted through the snow on the sidewalk, up his porch steps, and rang the doorbell. She folded her arms across her chest and shifted her weight from one foot to the other. She heard the locks on the door turn and then finally it opened up. Charlene was thankful that Raymond had opened the door and not his wife, because she knew that she'd more than likely slam it in her face and call the police.

"What are you doing here?" Raymond was less than cordial as he spoke through the screen door.

"Now is that any way to talk to the woman you were so in love with a few weeks ago?"

"You and I have nothing to talk about, now get off my property! I have a restraining order against you and I'm not afraid to use it."

"But we do have something to talk about, Raymond!" Charlene yelled, but before she could get her point across, Raymond slammed the door shut.

"Raymond!" Charlene howled at the top of her voice. "If you're so damn concerned about your public image, consider this. If you ruin me financially, I will be forced to go to the press. And trust me, baby, they want the story. I will tell them everything. I will disclose every detail of our affair including your fondness for wearing female underwear! I will even release the photos that I took of you wearing my damn panties! I will make the story national fucking news and have your ass on *Good Morning America* explaining yourself." Charlene stood there as the door opened back up. She smiled, because she knew that now she had his full attention.

"Listen, you psychotic b—"

"Watch what you say to me," Charlene warned him as she felt electricity building in her veins. "You brought this ugly side

of me out. All is fair in love and war, Raymond, and right now
you and I are at war. You thought that you had a leg up on me,
but just like most men, you don't realize that women have two
legs up opposed to your one dangling one. Don't take this case
into a courtroom, Raymond, or I'll put your ass on display like
Anita Hill did Clarence Thomas." Charlene had his attention
and focused her gaze on him through the screen door. Charlene
noticed his chest heaving with contempt and knew that she had
him by the balls.

"I've got you by the nuts, Raymond." Charlene's attitude
was cold, bitter, and malevolent. "Don't fuck up and make me
twist them, because I will crack them open." Raymond was
stunned into silence and she could tell that he was itching to
bring physical harm to her but she wasn't about to get cold feet
and shut up. "You brought this on yourself, Raymond,"
Charlene was now taking advantage of her new position. "I
know that you want to hurt me, but you can't, at least not without facing some pretty stiff consequences."

"What you did to me was uncalled for," Raymond hissed.

"Yes, it was, I'll admit that. But you had to pay for toying
with my emotions and taking my money."

"You knew that I was married when we got together. I was
up front with you. And if you want your money back, I'll write
you out a damn check."

"Fuck the damn money, Raymond!" The very sight of Raymond infuriated Charlene and she suddenly began to wonder
why she'd even wasted her time with him.

"You also told me that you were divorcing!" Charlene abruptly
reacted to what he'd said.

"Lower your voice before you wake my wife up."

"What! You think I fear that toothpick of a woman? Negro,
please!" Charlene rolled her eyes in defiance. "I'll kick your
scrawny ass and hers with one hand tied behind my back. And
that's another thing! Why in the hell did you choose her over
me?" Charlene asked, wanting to know the answer. If there was
anything she truly wanted to know, it was why she was not cho-

sen. "I have long beautiful black hair, thick lips, thick hips, and a more than ample behind. And I've seen more bumps on an ironing board than on her."

"She knows how to love a man! You only want to control him. You need help, the psychological kind of help." Charlene saw the fire and fury in Raymond's eyes, but she didn't give a damn because she wanted to have it out with him about their relationship.

"What! Excuse me! You're the one who needs the damn shrink! You were the one telling me how much you loved me and how you wanted me to have your baby. You were the one telling me how I was the smartest and most intelligent woman you've ever met. And now you want to turn around and tell me that I'm too controlling. How does that sound, Raymond? That shit doesn't even make sense."

"Look, if you want to know the fucking truth, our relationship was nothing more than—"

"Raymond, who is that you're yelling at?" Charlene heard Raymond's twig approaching.

"I think you'd better leave," Raymond said.

"What? You think I'm afraid of her? She can bring her tiny ass out here if she wants to, I've got something for her."

"Just leave, Charlene! It's over between us."

"You know what!" Charlene was reacting with scorn. "I'm glad I fucked up your mouth." She pointed her index finger at him. "You think about what I've said, Raymond, and you think about it long and hard. Angela Rivers has been contacting me for my side of this story. Don't let this case go in front of a judge and jury. Have your attorney agree to an arbitrator. If you don't, I will make you regret it for the rest of your miserable life." They glared at each other like two unyielding stone statues before Raymond finally slammed the door shut.

When Charlene arrived back at her apartment, she decided to check the mailbox, which was something she had neglected to do. When she opened up her silver box, she discovered that it was crammed tightly with mail. Most of the mail was late notices from her creditors. She hadn't paid a single bill in nearly forty days. A random memory of her grandmother popped into her head as she sifted through her mail. Whenever Hazel got mail from her creditors, she always said, "I'm not behind, I'm just late."

Charlene wished that she had her grandmother's indifference about such things but she had far more creditors than her grandmother. Her car note was behind; her Lerner's, Marshall Field's, Target, and Wal-Mart charge cards were all overdue. Her automatic deduction of her student loan payments had bounced, along with her rent payment. Not having a paycheck hit her account was beginning to take its toll quickly. As she walked up the stairs to her unit, she continued to go through her mail. Her cellular phone bill had arrived and the word URGENT was printed in bold red letters on the outside of the envelope. She knew that unless she paid it in full right away, it would be cut off. Her light bill had tripled, her gas bill had tripled, and her home phone was about to be disconnected. Charlene opened the door and walked inside her apartment. She tossed her mail on the table because she didn't want to think about how she'd screwed herself around. As the mail spread out on the table, a small personalized envelope caught her eye. She picked it up and noticed that it was from her mother. She took the letter, walked into her bedroom, and sat down in her reading chair. She clicked the switch on her reading lamp, opened up the letter, and began to read.

Dear Charlene,
I hope that my letter reaches you this time. Since you refuse to return my phone calls, I thought that writing you would be the best way to communicate with you. Even though you refuse to talk to me I still worry about you a great deal. I'm your mother, and that's what mothers do. I want more than anything for us to at least be cordial with each other. It hurts, to know that you have so much contempt and animosity towards me, although I can under-

stand why you do. I don't blame you for the way you feel, though.

I wanted to let you know that I am doing well. I think that I'm going to make it this time. I haven't had any relapses in a year. I've been praying a lot lately and that helps. Anyway, my phone number and address are below. You can call me anytime, day or night. I just want to hear from you so that I know you're ok.

Your loving mother,
Dean

Charlene folded the letter back up, sat it on her lap, and began to think about her damaged relationship with her mother. When Charlene was a little girl, she was always wishing that some way, somehow, she would be able to go and live with her mother and father. She daydreamed about how she'd be the perfect little girl. She wouldn't be sassy or disrespectful. She'd do all of her homework without being asked and even do chores around the house without complaining. All she'd ever wanted was to live in the same house with her mother and her father. She'd wanted to be close to them, but that just hadn't been her reality. Her Grandmother Hazel had refused to let her mother take her back to Chicago with her and never spoke of her father. Even her mother, when she called her on the phone each year for her birthday, didn't like to talk about her father. Charlene thought back on her fourteenth birthday.

"Don't worry your pretty little head with such things, child," Dean had told her.

"But I want to know who he is. What is he like? Does he know who I am? Why doesn't he write me or at the least call me on my birthday?"

"Charlene, I didn't call to talk about your daddy."

"But I want to meet him. Everyone else has a dad and I don't. It's not fair."

"Life isn't fair, baby, remember that, okay? Life is not fair at all. And this world we live in is bitter, cold, and cruel." Charlene remembered the tone in her mother's voice when she told her that. Dean's voice was filled with a type of sadness that she couldn't understand at that time. But her instincts told her that her mother's heart had been bruised and she was carrying her pain around because she didn't know what else to do with it.

In the summer of 1973 Charlene's mother had come down to Mississippi to visit her for her fifteenth birthday. Charlene was hanging out on the front porch with a few of her girlfriends—Monica, Tracy, and Tyronna—when she saw a brand-new tan-colored Ford Mustang coming down the road. Charlene could hear the humming of the motor from a far distance.

"I wonder who in the world that is?" Charlene said as the car came to a stop in front of the house. Dean got out of the car with her Afro blown out. She was dressed in a white tube top, a white belt, matching white hot pants, which were riding high on her ass, and a matching pair of white high heel shoes.

"Well, are you just going to sit there with your mouth open or are you going to come and give your sexy momma a hug?" She spoke loudly, making sure that everyone in the neighborhood heard and took notice of how foxy she thought she was.

"Mom!" Charlene rushed down the porch steps and hugged her mother. "Why didn't you call and let us know that you were coming?"

"Because I wanted to surprise you, sugar." She kissed Charlene on the forehead and continued to talk loudly. "Where is your grandmother and Uncle Stony at?" Charlene followed her mother to the trunk of the car.

"Grandma is in the house watching her soap operas. Bo took Uncle Stony out on a fishing trip." Her mother opened the trunk and Charlene saw a bunch of shopping bags filled with clothes from big department stores in Chicago.

"Wow! Who is all of this stuff for?"

"Most of it is yours," Dean said. "I got you some tube tops, hot pants, miniskirts, boots, some hip huggers, and a few leather jackets. There is even a small blue fur coat in there if you want it. Baby, you and I can dress up like girlfriends, get in my car, head into town, and turn it inside out." Her mother snapped her fingers and twitched her neck with drunken joy. "Here, take them." She began handing Charlene the bags of clothes.

"Oh, my god, this is out of sight, Mom. Grandma is so old-fashioned. She only buys me dresses that come down to my ankles. She even went to the thrift shop and brought me home a hideous pink dress with a poodle on it. I almost went to meet Jesus when she brought that home."

"Well, your grandmother is stiff like that, child. She wouldn't know good fashion if it came up and introduced itself to her."

"Charlene Hayward," a voice shrieked out from behind her. "Don't you bring a single stitch of those street walker clothes into this house!" Her Grandmother Hazel was coming down the front porch steps.

"Oh, lord, here we go," Charlene heard Dean mumble under her breath.

"Grandmomma, why are you shouting like that?" Charlene turned and looked at her grandmother at the same time noticing her girlfriends waving good-bye to her. Charlene realized that, to them, it seemed as if some serious drama was about to jump off and they didn't want to be in the eye of the storm.

"Didn't I tell you not to come back down here? Didn't I tell you to stay away?" Hazel was furious as she limped toward them. She had fallen at work and hurt her leg, which wasn't healing up right.

"Momma, I can come down here and see my baby if I want to." Dean stood in defiance of her own mother.

"You don't have any right to come down here and taint this child's upbringing with this garbage that you call gifts."

"Momma, I didn't come down here to fight with you, okay? I just came down here with some gifts for you, Charlene, and Stony."

"We don't want your gifts!" Hazel roared like an angry lion as she stood behind Charlene and rested her hands on her shoulders for balance.

"I don't know what you're talking about, I want my stuff!" Charlene disagreed with her grandmother and began to reach for the bags. Hazel grabbed Charlene's arm by the wrist and squeezed with all of her strength until Charlene stopped reaching for the items.

"Momma, Charlene is at that age. She needs some nice things." Dean was twitching with discomfort.

"I give her nice things already. She doesn't need your stolen merchandise."

Dean got insulted. "Momma, none of this stuff is stolen."

"Then let me see the receipts for it. If you can show me the receipts for every stitch of clothing you got here, then I'll let her keep it." There was thick anxiety in the air as a mournful moment of silence settled around them. Charlene waited for her mother to pull out the receipts for her gifts.

"Mom, just show her the receipts. I know that you have them," Charlene said with blind innocence.

"I don't have the receipts with me," Dean said. "I didn't bring them. I mean, there was no need to, it's not like she can return this stuff down here. Besides, I know what size she is. I'm good at judging those kinds of things."

"Where did you get the car from, Dean?" Hazel asked.

"It's mine. I got a job and I paid for it."

"You got a job doing what?" Hazel's words were filled with venom.

"I'm in sales now," Dean responded and for the first time Charlene noticed that her mother seemed to be twitching uncontrollably.

"Selling what?" Hazel asked.

"Stuff, okay, Momma. Now, I came here to give my baby the damn clothes that I got for her! What kind of problem do you have with that?" Dean began shouting as her anger ballooned.

"Grandmomma, why are you ruining this for me? It's my birthday. Why can't I have the clothes?" Charlene asked.

Hazel sighed. "Charlene, you're old enough now. It's about time you know the truth about your momma."

"Don't you dare," Dean barked at her mother.

"Let me see your arm, Dean," Hazel said.

"What for? There isn't anything wrong with it."

"Then prove it." Dean handed her forearm to her mother and Charlene looked into Dean's eyes and saw a storm forming in them.

"I don't have any tracks, Momma." Dean said. Hazel wet the tip of her index finger with her tongue and began wiping the makeup from Dean's arm and exposed the needle marks that she'd tried to cover up.

"Then what do you call this?" Hazel said as Dean snatched her arm back from her.

"I just wanted to give my baby something for her birthday, okay?" Dean was now shaky and Charlene could see the tears in her eyes. Charlene felt her heart break. She never knew that her mother was a drug user.

"The last time she was here, Charlene, she stole eight hundred dollars from me." Hazel looked at Dean and Dean didn't release her gaze from Charlene's crying eyes.

"She's had this problem for some time now. I ignored it for a while and hoped that she'd see the light and change. But she didn't, she only got worse. One time, we were almost put out on the street because of her. But Bo came through for me at the last minute." Charlene could see the hurt in her mother's eyes as Hazel was telling the awful truth.

"Stop," Dean said, "don't say any more."

"Why?" Hazel said. "She's old enough now. If you want to do something for her, then tell her the truth about yourself. Go on, tell her. Tell her what her father looks like. Tell her how you met him, and where you got him from! Go on, tell her the reason why she's been living here with me all of these years!" Hazel growled her words at Dean.

"I said stop!" Dean finally broke her gaze from her daughter and smeared away the tears on her cheeks. "Look, baby, I'm going to mail you these clothes back, okay" Dean tried to give Charlene a hug but Hazel stopped her with the palm of her hand.

"Leave!" Hazel demanded. Her voice and demeanor were as sharp as an ice pick.

"Happy birthday, baby. And I'm sorry you had to find out like this." Charlene was hurt and heartbroken. She wanted to ask why? But the question was lodged in a chamber of her heart.

"I'll see you later, baby," Dean said as she got back into the car. Charlene turned and ran inside the house, sobbing uncontrollably. A few moments later, after Dean had taken off back down the road, Hazel came into Charlene's room, where she was laying on her bed facedown.

"Charlene, sit up," Hazel said as more of a command rather than a request. Charlene sat up but refused to look into her grandmother's eyes.

"I'm sorry you had to find out like that, but you were going to find out sooner or later. I know that you want to know about your daddy's people. But I'm not the one who has that information. Your mother does; you'll have to get it from her."

"But you've met him, right?"

"Baby, your daddy isn't worth the spit in my mouth, and that's just the truth of the matter. I'm protecting you from him and your mother. I'm sorry that I'm so blunt, but that's just how it is." Hazel paused to allow what she'd just said to Charlene to sink in.

"Look, I don't want to talk about what happened out there anymore. I came in here because I want to let you know that I'm getting on up there in age. I don't plan on leaving anytime soon, but when I do go, I want you to know that the house is yours. I want you to promise, that if something happens to me, you'll keep the house and make sure that Stony is taken care of. Can you promise me that?"

"Yes," Charlene answered.

"Good, because your mother may never find her way. I don't know where I went wrong with her." Hazel's voice trembled slightly, which was a sign that the confrontation had affected her. "She has evil in her and she's as treacherous as the devil himself." It was then that Charlene realized that although her grandmother was acting tough on the surface, the fact that Dean wasn't a respectable woman was a constant source of pain in her heart.

Charlene placed her mother's letter back in its envelope, crumbled it up, and flung it to the other side of the bedroom. She placed her face in her hands to think and to keep herself from shedding tears of pain. Dean had caused her so much suffering, and she didn't think she had it in her heart to forgive her. Then again, she longed for someone to talk to about the turmoil and misery that she was going through. It was at times like this that she longed for an unbroken home that had a mother and a father who understood her and could lend a shoulder to cry on when the world decided to treat her badly.

11

NINA

The small wedding that Nina had envisioned somehow grew into a much larger and much more expensive event. She'd had every intention of keeping it simple until Rose convinced her to splurge a bit.

"Girl, what is wrong with you? Honey, you have been afforded a second chance at happiness with a wealthy man. Do you know how many sisters would love to be in your shoes?"

"Rose, I don't want a really big and expensive wedding," Nina restated her position as she searched for a parking spot. They had just arrived at the tailors' shop where the seamstress was awaiting their arrival. Nina had finally found the perfect wedding dress. The style of the dress was called a Shannon and it was a silhouette sheath, which hugged the curves of her body. The dress was white with a scoop neckline and an attached sweep. Nina had decided to get a sweep on the dress instead of a long train, as Rose had suggested all along. Nina was having the dress taken in just a bit more and Rose was there tagging along so that she could be fitted for her bridesmaid dress.

"Yes, you do," Rose said, ignoring what Nina was telling

her. Nina rolled her eyes a bit as she turned the ignition off. Just as the two of them were getting out of the car and walking across the parking lot, Gracie pulled up in a white Dodge Neon that her father had purchased for her when she told him about the physical abuse she'd been enduring throughout her marriage to Mark. Gracie blew her horn and waved her hand at the two of them as she parked her car right next to her mother's. Rose and Nina milled around the parking lot and waited for Gracie to join them.

"How is my baby doing?" Rose asked as she gave her god-daughter a hug.

"I have a headache, my back hurts, and my knee hurts, but other than that, I'm okay," Gracie answered as they walked toward the shop.

"Do you want some aspirin or something?" Rose asked, already searching her purse. "Honey, why are you hurting like that?" Rose asked.

"I think it's just one of those aging things. I slept in a bad position and now I've got a cramp in my neck, pain in my lower back, and throbbing pain in my right knee."

"Honey, it sounds as if you need to purchase a new mattress. One with much better support." Rose justified Gracie's claims of body pains. "Here, I found some aspirin for you. These are pretty strong and will numb any pain you have."

"No, thank you, Rose, I'll be fine. I just took something stronger than those. I haven't been sleeping on a mattress because I prefer to sleep on the sofa. But I think I will have to stop doing that," Gracie said, blinking her eyes rapidly as if she had a foreign object in them, while at the same time attempting to keep her body from twitching.

"Are you sure you're all right?" Nina asked, noticing Gracie's strange jittery behavior. The first thing that came to Nina's mind was that Gracie was coming down with some type of hideous nerve condition like multiple sclerosis.

"Mom, I'm okay. I'm just going to come in here, get fitted with you guys, and then head back home."

"All right," Nina responded, trying not to be worried about Gracie.

"Don't worry, Mom, I'm going to take care of it. So how have you been, Rose?" Gracie asked.

"Good," Rose answered, snapping her purse closed.

"And how's what's-his-name?"

"John?"

"Yeah, he's your guy, right?" Gracie asked.

"Yeah." A large grin formed on Rose's face. "He's my man."

As Nina pushed the door open to the shop, a bell chimed, signaling to the shop owner that someone had come in. The Korean seamstress who was wearing glasses and a yellow tape measure looped around her neck came from the back of the store.

"So good to see you again, Nina," the shop owner said as she shook her hand. "I have everything all set up, follow me," she said and escorted the three of them to the rear of the narrow shop.

After the three of them were fitted, Gracie went back home and Nina and Rose took care of running some errands for the wedding. Richard had given Nina the money to pay the baker, the DJ, the caterers, the photographers, and the modest banquet hall they'd rented for their reception.

"You just don't know how happy I am for you, Nina," Rose admitted. "I can see how happy you are, it's all in your eyes."

"Well, now that John has landed the job here in Chicago, I know you must be happy about that," Nina said.

"Oh, believe me, I am," Rose admitted. "Hanging out with you and watching you go through all of this preparation for your wedding has me feeling a bit envious."

"Just be a little more patient, Rose. I think that John is the one for you, I really do."

"Honey, you can bet your bottom dollar that I'm working on his ass, especially since he's living with me until he finds a place of his own."

"How is that going anyway? Him living with you?"

"It's not too bad," Rose said as she lost herself in thought. "He's so funny. When he first moved in he asked me all kinds of questions about my pet peeves."

"Oh, really?" Nina responded.

"We sat down and had an entire conversation about it. He said that he didn't want any of his habits to get on my nerves while he was there. He told me that he had a habit of clipping his toenails and didn't want the loud popping sound to annoy me. He also told me a multitude of other things about himself which he thought might be annoying." Rose laughed, expressing her amusement.

"That's good," Nina said. "At least he's letting you know these things."

"I know that John is a neat freak and I told him that, sometimes, I let the housecleaning slip a bit. I thought that would turn him off, but he said don't worry, he'll pick up the slack in that area, and do the cooking as long as I didn't slack up on the lovemaking. Honey, that man likes to do it a lot. Keeping up with him is becoming a job in itself."

"Well, shit, you shouldn't have any complaints then. The man is cleaning, cooking, and screwing your brains out."

"You're right," Rose confessed as a coughing attack began. Nina could hear the distress in her lungs.

"Are you okay?" Nina was concerned by what she was hearing. "Do you need me to pull over?"

"No, I'm fine. Keep driving," Rose insisted. "I'm only coughing because my throat is a bit dry. Turn the heat down some." Nina clicked the heat switch to the off position. Once Rose stopped coughing, she continued her conversation about John.

"He has to cook for the men in his rescue team," Rose said, clearing her throat. "The man makes a damn good pot of chili. He adds honey to it, which gives it a sweet flavor. His chili is the damn bomb."

"So what is he doing about his home in Atlanta? What about all of his furniture and stuff?"

"His daughter, who is pregnant with her first child, and her husband are in the market for a home and have made a bid on his. If everything goes through, his home down there will stay in the family. As far as his furniture goes, he's been talking about selling some of the stuff and putting other things in storage until he gets his own place."

"Do you like him living in the house with you, Rose?" Nina asked.

"Of course I do," Rose replied. "Having a man in my bed at night cuddling up next to me makes me feel so safe and cared for. And I really like the fact that he had the presence of mind to have a discussion about pet peeves."

"Rose, John seems to be looking for the type of committed relationship that you want. It sounds to me as if he really wants to know everything about you. I think he's studying you. He's trying to obtain a degree in Roseology. You two are perfect for each other. You're a nurse, you help save lives, and he's a member of a rescue squad, and they basically do the same thing. If I were you, I wouldn't let him move out on his own, especially without me."

"Nina, you don't have to tell me that. Now that I have him, he's not going any damn place without me. And if he does try to leave, a sister has a couple moves that she's going to put on him to make him stay. You can bet your bottom dollar on that one." Both Nina and Rose chuckled.

"What kind of moves are you talking about, girl?" Nina asked.

"What, you don't know? Shit, I'll turn inside out on his ass. I'll change my entire appearance in a heartbeat. He'll come home and discover a brand-new damn woman with an entirely different viewpoint."

"Hey now!" Nina chimed.

"Babygirl, I don't play when it comes to my dick! Do you know what I mean?" Rose glanced over at Nina. Nina laughed loudly. "Neither do I, Rose." Nina said.

*   *   *

It was Friday night, May twenty-first and Nina couldn't sleep at all because she was wrestling with herself with all of the plans. She wanted to make sure that everything would go well so she sat at the kitchen table and kept going over the list of things to make sure that she'd done them.

"Girl, if you don't take your ass to bed, you're going to look like a damn zombie on your wedding day," Rose had scolded her. "Whatever glitches come up, we'll just deal with them then." Nina and Rose were spending the night with Gracie at Nina's old apartment.

"All right already," Nina huffed impatiently. "I'm just a bit nervous, that's all."

"So am I," Rose said, "but if you don't take your nervous tail to bed, you're going to force me to put a sleeper hold on you." Nina smirked because although Rose was kidding, she knew that if it came to that, Rose would try to put the move on her.

"Mom, you're still up?" Gracie had come into the kitchen to run a glass of water so that she could pop a pill.

"I'm going to bed now," Nina said. "Are you okay? Why are you taking that pill?"

"Sleeping on the sofa will most certainly leave me with a neck cramp. I'm just taking a preventative measure so that I don't wake up all evil in the morning," Gracie answered.

"An ounce of prevention is worth a pound of cure," Rose commented. "At least that is one of the things my mother told me." Nina snickered a bit as she thought about her own parents. She thought about her mother and some of the things she'd told her.

"Don't ever fall in love with a man's potential," Nina blurted out.

"What?" Gracie asked.

"That's what your grandmother always said. Don't ever fall in love with a man's potential because he may never reach it."

Gracie had a puzzled look on her face.

"You never told me that one?"

"Oh, I'm positive that I have, Gracie. You may not have been listening to what I was trying to tell you."

"And what's that supposed to mean?" Gracie had suddenly gotten offended.

"Hold your horses, babygirl." Rose jumped right in the conversation. "There is no need to be on edge tonight."

"I'm not on edge," Gracie countered.

"Good, now can we go to bed? It's already midnight, and if we don't get some sleep, all three of us are going to look like the children of the Grim Reaper." Both Nina and Gracie laughed. Rose just had a way of turning rain into sunshine.

"You are so silly," Nina commented as Rose did a few dance moves and headed out of the kitchen.

"I can't wait for tomorrow afternoon to roll around. I'm going to get my party on!" Rose said.

At 6:00 A.M. Saturday morning the alarm clock buzzed, and Nina slapped it with the palm of her hand so that it would shut up. She turned her back to the clock knowing full well that she needed to get up but wanted to try and squeeze in a few more minutes of sleep since she didn't actually fall asleep until about 2:00 A.M.

"Oh, no, you don't." Rose hustled into the room and yanked the covers off the bed. "We're not even going to play like that."

"Rose, let me sleep for ten more minutes!" Nina whined like a child.

"Nope." Rose went to the window and opened up the blinds and a full force of yellow sunlight filled the room. Nina finally gave up and sat up in the bed. She was already tired and the day hadn't even started.

"I knew this was going to happen," Rose complained.

"What!" Nina had the same edgy tone that Gracie had the night before. She and her daughter were just alike when it came to catching a quick attitude.

"You look tired, Nina. Why didn't you go to sleep?"

"Because I couldn't." Nina stood up and lazily made her way to the bathroom.

"I've made some strong black coffee." Then Rose blurted out. "You're going to need it," huffing her dissatisfaction with Nina away.

Richard was up and ready to go bright and early on the morning of his wedding. He was steadfast about making sure that the day started off without a glitch. He entered Nathan's bedroom and stood watching him sleep. He hated to wake his son, but he wanted to get him dressed first. Richard raised the blanket up and exposed his feet. He took his fingers and tickled the soles of Nathan's feet to wake him up. Nathan quickly coiled his legs up to protect his feet from being touched. Richard tickled them again and Nathan finally came to life.

"Stop," he whined but Richard didn't stop. Nathan tried to act annoyed but he couldn't because he began laughing and kicking his legs.

"Come on, Mr. Lazy Bones, it's time to get up," Richard said as he turned to leave the room.

"Wait a minute, Daddy," Nathan requested.

"What is it, Nathan?"

"Pick me up." Nathan held his arms up. Richard rolled his eyes playfully at his son as he scooped him up. "You're a big boy now, Nathan," Richard said. "You're getting too heavy for Daddy to be picking you up all of the time."

"Carry me to the bathroom," Nathan said, ignoring what Richard had just said.

"No," Richard responded and put him down.

"Bend down for a second, Daddy, I got something that I want to ask you."

"Just ask it, Nathan."

"I want to whisper it, in your ear." Richard kneeled down so that Nathan could tell him what was on his mind.

"Is today that special day?"

"Yes, it is," Richard answered.

"Okay," Nathan said as he pressed his lips against his father's cheek and blew air from his mouth, making a loud flapping sound. "I got you," Nathan said as he rushed off to the bathroom before Richard could catch him. As Richard walked past the guest room, he heard John stirring around inside. Richard decided to knock on the door.

"Are you up, man?" he asked. John opened the door and Richard saw that he was already dressed.

"I've been up," John said. "How are you feeling?"

"Nervous, man," Richard answered with honesty.

"You'll be okay," John said with confidence. "Before you know it, you guys will be on your way to Maui."

"Yeah, I can't wait to get there either," Richard said as he leaned against the doorframe. John had turned and sat down on the edge of the bed to put on his shoes.

"Rose was telling me that you rented a condo instead of getting a hotel."

"Yeah, I did," Richard answered. " I rented out a two-bedroom condo in South Kihei. The property is right in the heart of shopping, dining, plus the beach is right across the street from the property."

"When you guys get back, you have to let me know what it was like. Once I get settled in up here, I plan to take Rose on a nice vacation."

"No problem," Richard said. "Say, I just want to let you know that I appreciate you being my best man."

"Brother, please, I would have been upset if you hadn't asked me. I know that Nina makes you happy, and that's what is important. You're both starting over in life, and finding that someone who is compatible with you makes all the difference in the world."

"I agree with you on that one," Richard said.

"It's getting to be eight o'clock. You'd better go ahead and get dressed. I can't have you arriving late. Rose would kick my ass if that happened." Richard burst out laughing.

"Hell, you think I'm joking. Rose doesn't play around when it comes to stuff like that."

"I believe you, man," Richard said as he left the room to get dressed.

*   *   *

Richard stood at the altar glancing around at the modest number of friends, colleagues, and family members who had been invited to the event. Each pew had a flower arrangement at the end of it and the flowers that were near him made the entire area smell like spring. His hands were sweaty as he waited for the organist to begin the wedding March. When the song began, Richard focused his attention down the aisle as he saw Gracie and Rose come in first, and then he was overcome when he saw how beautiful Nina looked in her dress. She carried a bouquet of flowers as she measured her steps carefully, locking her gaze directly on him just as they'd done at their wedding rehearsal. The ceremony began and Richard exhaled, relieved that the moment he'd been waiting for had finally arrived.

The banquet hall and the caterers had done an outstanding job with the decorations and the food. The photographer was also doing a fine job by Nina's estimates and she couldn't wait to see how the photos turned out. Nina and Richard sat at their table greeting guests and meeting each other's extended family members. Two of Richard's aunts had attended along with a few of Nina's cousins and their adult children. The hired DJ was playing the jams, and Rose was showing off her dancing ability. She had taught John how to step, and the two of them looked graceful together.

Richard had a hilariously embarrassing time when he was blindfolded and had to remove Nina's garter, which was very high on her thigh. When Richard tossed the garter over his shoulder to all the single men in the room, everyone side-stepped, with the exception of John, who caught it. On the other hand, when Nina tossed up her bouquet of flowers, there was a mad scramble for them. Rose tossed her weight around and knocked a few sisters aside so that she could snatch the flowers out of the air. If John wasn't afraid of being jinxed with marriage, neither would she.

As the afternoon changed over into evening, the festivities continued. Nina and Richard danced to their wedding song, which was, "You Bring Me Joy," by Anita Baker. Rose, who had gotten tipsy by that time, was moved to tears as she watched Nina and Richard slow-dance.

On Monday, Nina, Richard, and Nathan boarded their 8 A.M. flight for Maui. When they arrived at the airport, Hertz had their rental car waiting for them along with driving directions to their rented condo. Thirty minutes later the three of them arrived at the property where they'd be staying. It was a very beautifully landscaped property in South Kihei, Maui, with an assortment of brightly colored garden flowers. Richard parked the car and walked into the rental office and picked up the key to their unit. The unit she and Richard had rented was absolutely perfect. The second-floor two-bedroom, two-bathroom residence had a fully equipped kitchen, complete with pots, pans, and silverware. Their dining room had a bamboo dinner table with a tropical pattern on the seat cushions and the place mats on the table. All of the wall art and sculptures around the unit had tropical colors of pink, green, and blue. The master bedroom was fabulous; it included a whirlpool surrounded by mirrors and a gas fireplace to get cozy and cuddle once you left the whirlpool. There was also a private, bricked in balcony, which could be accessed from the master bedroom. Also in the master bedroom was a massive in-wall entertainment center, which Richard began fumbling with right away. After he figured out how to turn on some soothing Island music, he went back down to the car to gather the rest of their luggage. Later that afternoon, once they were settled in, the three of them put on their bathing suits, walked outside, and crossed the road to a small beach. They spread out a blanket on the sand and Nina immediately began putting suntan oil on both Richard and Nathan's backs so that they wouldn't get a sunburn. Once Nina was done with Nathan, he hurriedly snapped on his life vest and began jumping up and down in place because he was anxious to get in the water.

"Hold your horses, boy," Richard said. "The water isn't going anywhere."

"I'm ready to go swimming, Daddy." Nathan was ready to turn and sprint toward the water.

"Go easy on him, baby." Nina rubbed oil on Richard's slumping shoulders. "He's just excited." At that moment, the buzzing sound of a couple zooming by on a Jet Ski caught both Richard and Nina's attention. A woman was riding her man on the watercraft. Richard and Nina smiled at each other as they watched the couple buzz around the water. Richard nudged Nina to see if she was thinking about the adventure they'd had when they were in the Bahamas.

"Don't you say a word," Nina responded because she knew what he was thinking about.

"I want to ride one of those," Nathan said, pointing.

"All right," Richard answered, trying to sound as excited as his son. "I'll go see about renting two of them." Richard rented two Jet Skis but Nathan wanted to ride with Nina, not his father. Nina sat on the watercraft and Nathan sat in front of her to hold on to the handlebars. Nina was about to lightly pull the throttle back when Nathan stopped her.

"I can do it," he said.

"Aren't you afraid of falling into the water, sweetie?" Nina asked.

"Nope, I like the water," Nathan answered. Nina instructed him to push the throttle lightly so that the craft wouldn't get away from him. Nathan did as he was instructed and the craft buzzed around at a slow speed. Nina studied Nathan, who seemed to be in heaven. Richard slowly drifted up alongside the two of them.

"Hey there, man." Richard pretended to be a friend of Nathan's. "That's a mighty nice Jet Ski you have there."

"Yup," Nathan answered with a matter-of-fact tone.

"Do you mind if I talk to that lovely lady you're riding around with?"

"No, you can't talk to her, she's with me," Nathan said and turned the craft away from Richard. Nina was surprised by Nathan's protection of her.

"It seems as if he gets his jealousy streak and his love for Jet Skis from his father," Nina said joyfully as Nathan continued to drive her around in circles.

Later that evening after they'd returned from their water sport activity, they drove over to Wailea, Maui, where they attended a luau at sunset.

"I've got to get you a grass skirt," Richard said as he watched the Hawaiian dancer shake her skirt to the rhythm of the music. "Do you think that you can rock your hips like that?" Richard teased.

"Don't mess around and get cut now." Nina rolled her eyes at Richard. "I know you're looking at more than her grass skirt."

"Who me? No, I'm not."

"Stop while you're ahead, Richard." Nina was feeling bloated and cranky.

When they returned to the condo from the luau, Nina was tired and looking forward to resting comfortably on the bed in her silk pajamas. Nina had planned to make love to Richard that evening after Nathan fell asleep but ran into a major snag, because her cycle had begun. When Richard got into the bed, where she was resting, he began kissing all over her. Nina eagerly responded but then stopped him as he began rubbing on her thigh.

"Baby, we can't," Nina informed him.

"Oh, don't worry about Nathan. I'll lock the door," Richard said.

"No, it's not that," Nina said. "My monthly visitor came tonight."

"Oh, wow," Richard said. "It's okay, that's cool."

"I'm sorry about that, but I'm more than willing to please you in another way, if the lollypop store is still open." Richard kissed Nina on the lips as he clicked on the stereo.

"I think the lollypop store does keep late hours." Joe Cocker was singing his beautiful love ballad called, "You Are So Beautiful."

"Where are you going?" Nina asked, noticing Richard leaving the room.

"Nowhere," Richard said as he grabbed some lotion from the dresser. He sat at the edge of the bed, and began rubbing her feet while he spoke the words to Joe Cocker's love song. Richard wondered what woman had inspired the words to that song. Whoever she was, she had to have touched the man's soul to write such simple yet passionate lyrics.

"That feels so good," Nina was encouraging him to continue.

"Whatever I can do to make you feel good, I will do it," Nina said to him as she melted into the bed. Richard smiled a mannish smile. "Oh really?" He was about to say much more but at that moment Nathan rushed into their bedroom and turned on the television.

"*The Lion King* is on." Nathan pranced around in place as he growled like Simba.

"Can I watch it in here with you, please?"

"Yeah, have a seat," Richard said, patting the spot next to him.

"I want to sit up there with Nina," Nathan said and climbed into the bed with her. To Nina's surprise, Nathan snuggled up next to her and rested his head on her chest.

"I used to snuggle like this with my mom all the time. Is it okay if I snuggle up to you?" Nathan asked.

"Yes," Nina answered, "you can snuggle with me whenever you like."

She ran her fingers through his curly hair and kissed him on his forehead. Richard continued to rub her feet as the three of them watched *The Lion King* together as a family.

12

CHARLENE

Charlene could have been bought and sold for a dollar when she had a telephone conference with her malpractice insurance attorney Brad the following week after she'd had her confrontation with Raymond.

"You're not going to believe this," Brad said, hurrying his words, "but the plaintiff doesn't want to take this in front of a jury. The guy actually wants to settle the dispute with an arbitrator. I can't believe it." Brad was almost screaming with joy into the receiver. He was happier than Charlene was. "This is a big step for us in this case," Brad continued on.

"So what happens next?" Charlene asked because she'd grown annoyed with the fact that Brad actually thought he was the one who'd convinced the plaintiff to arbitrate. She was going to burst his bubble but then thought better of it. She needed to stay on his good side so that he could do what he needed to do in order to protect as much of her assets as he could.

"We go in front of the arbitrator on Friday, June 4th. We can settle this thing up then. One other thing you should know, which I forgot to tell you, is that your professional liability insurance doesn't cover punitive damages. He still has the right to seek those if he wants to. I'll try to discourage him from doing that to protect your financial assets. I know that I can make an effective argument to keep him from doing that but that is outside the scope of what I'm allowed to do for you."

"What do you mean, outside of the scope?" Charlene didn't like what Brad was saying to her and she demanded clarification. Brad instantly picked up on the aggressive tone in her voice and upstaged her tone with his own.

"It means that if you want me to keep him from taking your 401K Plan and liquidating all your assets, you will need to pay me for my services."

"How much are we talking here, Brad?" Charlene felt as if the little shit was trying to dupe her.

"A modest amount, somewhere between five and ten thousand dollars."

"Excuse me!" Charlene didn't want to pay him that amount of money.

"You have three choices here. Number one, pay me to keep him off your back. Number two, pay some other attorney who isn't familiar with the case. Or three, pay Raymond a ridiculous amount in punitive damages." Charlene was angry and clenched her jaws so tightly that she thought she'd crack her teeth. She didn't like or appreciate Brad springing this on her this way.

"Hello, are you there?" Brad asked because of the long pause.

"Yes, I'm here." Charlene would be forced to max out her credit card in order to pay the little runt off. "Are you sure you can keep him from filing for punitive damages?" she asked.

"I'm ninety-nine percent sure," Brad answered with a cockiness that annoyed Charlene.

"All right," Charlene reluctantly agreed to his terms.

"Great." Brand's voice rose about six octaves, which made

him sound like a child squealing at a playground. "I'm going to get to work on this right away. I'll have my assistant call you before June 4th so you can be deposed."

"Fine," Charlene answered, trying to think about how she was going to make some money.

"Just relax, okay?" Brad said. "I know this is a stressful time, but I think that we'll be able to pull out of this one."

"It's your ass if you don't get me out of this, Brad." Charlene tried to sound nonthreatening, yet very stern at the same time.

"I'll be in touch." Brad shrugged her comment off as he hung up the phone.

Charlene's untamed thoughts demanded that she pace the floor between her sofa and cocktail table. She was concentrating and thinking of what she should do next. She was already in financial trouble and the unexpected expense of an attorney's fee was the last thing she needed to add to her dreadful situation. She had a twenty-five-thousand dollar credit limit on her Visa card but only about eleven thousand dollars of credit were left for additional charges. She'd already used her charge card to cover her bills so that she wouldn't fall too far behind. The only smart option available to her was to find herself a job and quickly. "But how?" she whispered out loud. No private dentist in the county would hire her as an associate with a scandal dangling above her head. Charlene was positive that she'd been blacklisted among her colleagues. She'd seen it happen before with another dentist, who used his prescription drug license to support his addiction to painkillers.

"What am I supposed to do?" She spoke out to the empty room. "Take a mindless office job somewhere? An employer would take one look at my resume and say that I'm overqualified without hesitation. Then I'd have to come up with some logic as to why I wouldn't leave at the first chance a better offer came along." The heel of Charlene's foot began to ache so she plopped down on her sofa and stared out the window. At a time like this, she wished she had a girlfriend she could confide in, but she didn't because she'd ruined one with her long-standing

friendship when she started sleeping with her best friend's husband down in Springfield, Illinois.

"Oh, what a mess that was. I had to put my girlfriend in a
headlock and tell her husband to come get her before I hurt
her," Charlene said out loud as she began to revisit how she'd
ended up in Kankakee in the first place.

Her girlfriend wasn't supposed to have found out about
Charlene's relationship with her husband until he and Charlene
had moved out of town." He was a heart surgeon with dashing
good looks, power, status, and money. He was also a charming
flirt who admitted to her that he had a desire for her. Charlene
ignored him initially, but then she started wanting him all to
herself. He had all the qualities that Charlene wanted with the
exception of being married to her girlfriend. Charlene couldn't
recall what exactly made her cross the line, but when she did, it
felt good. She felt special, as if he'd magically realized that she
was really the woman for him and that he'd leave his wife for
her. *It happens all the time.* She convinced herself that her secret
affair would be where she'd find what she was looking for. If
she could nab him, she would have the kind of love that her
grandmother and Bo shared. Looking for love in inappropriate
places was one of Charlene's largest flaws.

"I'm a repeat offender." Charlene guffawed once again to the
empty room and to her twisted and bruised heart. She couldn't
explain to herself why she did the things she did. She only knew
that she'd find herself at a crossroads with two signs. One saying DO THE RIGHT THING and the other one saying DO WHAT
YOU WANT TO DO. Whenever she did what she wanted to
do, she always felt justified, self-righteous, and reasonable. Once
she got her mind fixed on what she wanted, there was no right
or wrong, and anything in her path preventing her from getting
what she wanted would be dealt with accordingly.

Charlene began cleaning up her home even though there was
really nothing out of place. The mindless acts of repositioning
her sofa cushions and picking the dead leaves out of the flower-

pots offered her a temporary escape from her thoughts. She went down the corridor to her bedroom to see if there was anything that needed to be picked up. As she searched the room, she ran across the letter that her mother had written. The sight of the letter once again opened up a wound between the two of them that had never healed properly.

The sad news of Hazel's death came in the spring of 1978 on Charlene's twentieth birthday. Charlene was away at Clark Atlanta University at the time when word arrived about her grandmother. Charlene borrowed and scraped up money to rush home so that she could take care of the service arrangements and honor her Grandmother Hazel's request to keep the house and take care of her Uncle Stony.

When the taxi dropped her off at the front door of her grandmother's home, Charlene was surprised to see Dean, her mother, standing on the front porch saying her good-byes to a few elderly ladies who had dropped by to offer their condolences. Charlene and Dean still hadn't patched up the sore that was lingering from her fifteenth birthday. When it had come out that Dean was a drug user and a thief. Charlene's heart froze into a block of ice on the limited occasions she saw her mother. Over the past five years, her heart had grown bitter and cold toward her, and animosity had replaced the love in her heart for her mother.

"When did you get here? And how did you get here so quickly?" Charlene asked as the taxi driver set her luggage beside her on the front porch and held his hand out to be paid. Charlene gave him his money and he thanked her as he walked back to his white cab and pulled off.

"Does it really matter?" Dean answered with the same mind-set that Charlene had given her.

Charlene sucked wind through her teeth, grabbed her tattered suitcase, then walked past her mother and into the house. She plopped her suitcase down on the floor beside the sofa and glanced around the house with disgust and repulsion. There were bowls, plates, and trash sitting on the cocktail table and the floor. Two white laundry hampers were in the living room with clothes spilling over onto the floor. The once tan carpet had so many stains on it that it needed to be pulled up and tossed out. This was not how her grandmother kept her house—Hazel was a stickler when it came to keeping it clean. She didn't even like to leave dishes in the sink once she was done cooking. Charlene turned her attention back to her mother, who was stepping inside the living room with one side of her lip and cheek drawn back like drapes. Charlene had a major problem with her mother's sly and defiant grin.

"So, how long have you been here hovering around like a vulture waiting for her to die?"

"You'd better watch who you're calling a vulture, tweedy-bird." Dean marched by her, and kicked a pair of her dirty black underwear which were on the floor. "I've been here for a few weeks. By the way, it's good to see you too, Charlene." Charlene noticed the poison in her tone of voice and knew right then and there that she and her mother were not going to see things eye to eye.

"Where is Uncle Stony?" Charlene added a bit of snake bite to her voice, just to let her mother know that she was not about to bow down to her. Charlene had lost respect for her mother a long time ago, and the animosity that she had for her was about to rear its ugly head.

"He's someplace safe right now," Dean answered as she walked back into the living room with a bowl of singed popcorn. She plopped her wide sloppy ass down on Hazel's favorite sitting chair, which still had Hazel's brown throw draping down the back of it.

"What do you mean, he's someplace safe?" Charlene watched as Dean struck a match to light herself a cigarette while she nibbled on her snack.

"Just what I said." It was clear to Charlene that Dean wasn't willing to offer any additional information. Charlene's anger was raging by the second, and her blood was roaring like a river. In an effort to control her uncultivated emotions, she took a few deep breaths to calm herself. She had half a mind to go and remove the brown throw from the back of the chair so that it wouldn't smell like an ashtray, but then again, now that she thought about it, the entire house smelled like an ashtray. None of the familiar scents of her deceased grandmother lingered in the air. The last bit of Hazel's spirit's scent was gone and she blamed her mother for that.

"What do you mean he's someplace safe?" Charlene repeated, deciding to push the issue, because she was worried about Stony's well-being and knew that her mother could have cared less about him even though Stony, was her younger half-brother. Charlene studied her as she awaited her answer, noticing that Dean was bouncing her leg up and down on the ball of her foot uncontrollably. It was as if her leg was having a major nervous spasm.

"Why did you walk through the door bitching? Damn! We're supposed to pull together at a time like this."

"Because I don't trust you, that's why. You're a cantankerous person who doesn't care or think about anyone but yourself. And the fact that you've turned my grandmother's house into your personal ashtray is irritating the hell out of me." Dean sniffed the air then shot daggers with her eyes over at Charlene.

"Cantankerous, what's that? Some fancy college girl word for 'bitch'? What? You think that, because you're in college, you're better than me? Is that what you think?" Dean was glaring into Charlene's eyes for her answer. "Yeah, I know that's what you think. It doesn't matter, because I've been called worse by better people. You sound just like those two big heifers that just left here. They came over here to snoop around, asking me some crazy shit, like, do I need any help getting the house together for guests? I told them hell no, because I was selling the house." Dean thumped the ashes from her cigarette on the mahogany coffee table and Charlene's eyes lowered to slits, mother or not, she was itching to jump on Dean and kick her out of the house her grandmother had left her.

"Look at what you're doing!" Charlene roared like an out-of-control freight train. "You're putting burns in the damn table!"

"What does it matter, I'm getting rid of the shit anyway! And don't be yelling at me. I'm still your mother—show me some fucking respect."

"The only mother that I knew just died." Charlene's chest had ballooned with angry tension.

"Oh, that's real rich, Charlene," Dean said as her leg bounced and twitched more rapidly. "You can say what you want to, but no matter how you feel, the fact remains that you crawled out from between my legs, not hers."

"You know what?" Charlene was completely repulsed now, and began expressing herself with her hands. "I came back here to do what Grandmomma wanted me to do. She left the house to me, not you, so I don't know where in the world you got the idea that you were going to sell it, because that is not happening. I made her a promise five years ago to take care of Uncle Stony if something happened to her. So no matter what you say, that fact remains that this is my house, and as soon as the arrangements are made, you have got to go. You cannot stay here." Charlene was taken by surprise when Dean sprung to her feet and moved swiftly into her social space. The smoke billowing up from Dean's cigarette was stinging her nostrils.

"Let me tell you something, you nappy-headed black child of God! This house is mine! The law says so! And I've already got a buyer that I'm going to sell it to."

"You can't do that! Grandmomma signed papers that said she was leaving the house to Uncle Stony and me. They're in her room under her mattress!" Charlene hurried into her grandmother's room and lifted up the mattress but none of her grandmother's important papers were there. Charlene flipped the mattress all the way off the bed and removed the sheets, but still she didn't find the papers. *Where in the world could she have put them?* Charlene's heart began to race. She searched the entire room. She looked in the closet, in the dresser drawers, and in her Grandmomma's Bible, but she couldn't find the papers.

Charlene's mind began clicking and thinking as fast as a tornado.

"Mother!" she shouted at the top of her voice as she marched with heavy steps back into the room where Dean was.

"What did you do with the papers?" Dean relaxed in the chair and inhaled deeply from her cigarette. She closed her eyes, and allowed the nicotine to calm her nerves.

"What papers? I have no idea of what you're talking about." Charlene's chest was heaving with contempt; she was ready to get into a catfight with Dean. She was about to leap toward her mother when the phone rang. It was the funeral home calling about burial clothes for Hazel. Charlene took the call and decided that she'd have to deal with her mother later because, at that moment, she needed to focus on Hazel's arrangements.

On the morning of Hazel's funeral, Charlene and Dean had a colossal argument because Charlene discovered that Dean had sent Stony to live with Bo, Hazel's married lover.

"What in the hell is wrong with you?" Charlene bawled at the top of her voice. "Why did you do that to your brother?"

"Half-brother," Dean answered back with a vindictiveness in her voice, "besides, Bo is his daddy. On top of that, Bo was more than willing to take him in." Charlene watched as Dean jerked and pulled at the clothes in Hazel's closet.

"Why doesn't she have anything decent to wear?" Dean's voice was beginning to grow hoarse and soft.

"Oh, no, you're not doing what I think you're doing, are you?"

"Yes, I am. Do you have a problem with that?" Charlene was stunned into silence. She didn't know what to say or do. She'd never had to deal with her mother on a level such as this before. She'd never had to face the dark, bitter, and deeply bruised side of her mother's heart.

"What is the matter with you? What you're about to do is unthinkable. Why are you doing this?"

"Because I'm weird and strange like that! Didn't your precious grandmother tell you that about me? Huh? Didn't she tell you that?" Charlene focused her attention on the glaze in Dean's eyes, and to her, it appeared as if her mother had flipped completely out.

"Momma, look, I know that you're not in your right mind now, okay. I know that all of this has caused you some pain. I know that I caused you some pain, too." Charlene began to blame herself for not being able to see how deeply troubled her mother was.

"Wearing your mother's clothes to her funeral is morbid. You shouldn't do that; people will talk."

"They're already talking, or haven't you noticed." Dean pulled down one of her mother's yellow dresses and held it up to herself in the mirror.

"I think this will fit perfectly, don't you? I'm much heavier than she was but I can squeeze into this dress." Dean had an unreasonable glaze in her eyes that Charlene had never seen before. Charlene could only gawk at her mother as she tried to process what was going on. Since Charlene couldn't answer, Dean answered her own question. "Yes, Dean, I think that this will look just fine on you." Charlene noticed an unzipped pouch sitting on her grandmother's bed. She causally took a peek inside and noticed that it contained paraphernalia for her mother's drug habit.

"Momma, have you been using this morning?" Charlene's voice trembled because her heart was broken all over again and she could feel her tears rising up to spill over. Dean didn't answer and wouldn't even look her daughter in the eye. She just took the dress and her bag and locked herself in the bathroom.

"Momma, you need to get some help," Charlene squealed as her tears spilled over and dripped down her cheeks. "Please, I don't want you to do this." Charlene banged on the bathroom door with the palm of her hand. "Let me help you. I'm sorry if I pushed you into using again." Charlene, like a child, willingly placed the burden of her mother's addiction on her shoulders. "I don't know what happened between you and Grandmomma, but I got a feeling that I'm the source of your pain." Charlene slapped on the door harder. "Please open the door, Momma, please!" Dean refused to open the door and Charlene knew that her efforts were ineffective.

By the time the funeral car had arrived to pick the two of them up, Dean decided to come out of the bathroom. Just as Charlene had feared, she was wearing her grandmother's bright yellow dress. Dean didn't say a word as she roamed like a doped-up robot toward the front door and out to the funeral car. Charlene felt sympathy for her mother at that moment and wanted to understand her, but that was difficult given her present state of mind. When it was time for the final viewing of the body before it was laid to rest, Dean didn't get up to view it.

"Do you need me to stay with you, momma?" Charlene asked, attempting to accommodate her mother, but Dean refused to speak. "I'm here for you," Charlene whispered.

"Get away from me," Dean hollered at the top of her voice. "Leave me alone!" She sprang to her feet as if something had possessed her.

"Oh, God!" Charlene said as a wave of uncertainty filled the room. Charlene grabbed Dean's arm to help her through the sudden emotion that had consumed her.

"I'm in pain, Momma!" Dean hollered out. "You hurt me and I hurt you back!" Charlene was no match for the strength that Dean had summoned and could not hold her back. Dean stomped up to the casket and stared at Hazel. Shock and awe hung in the air as all of the mourners gawked at what was taking place.

"Why?" she screamed. "I want to know why you wouldn't tell me who he was. Why did you make me hurt you like that! Why? Why? Why?" Momma!"

Charlene was a publicly embarrassed nervous ball of emotions. Bo and Stony walked up behind Dean to pull her away from the coffin but Dean fought the two of them until she no longer had the strength or will to wrestle with them. Charlene had no idea of what her mother was talking about and she had no idea of how to help her. The only thing that she could gather was that something between Hazel and Dean had gone terribly wrong, and whatever it was, it never got resolved.

After the funeral, when Dean had calmed down, Charlene attempted to reason with her mother about selling the house. However, reasoning with Dean proved to be pointless because she was going to have it her way. The two of them engaged in bitter disputes about the sale of the house, which caused pain, resentment, limited communication, and eventually distance from each other. Dean sold the house and went back to Chicago to live with the unsavory man she'd been shacking up with. Charlene went back to school to finish up her education. Charlene had left a very thin line of communication open between them over the years, because in spite of everything, Dean was still her mother and at least she knew where she was and how she was faring in the world.

Charlene was poised and confident on the morning of the arbitration. The hearing went pretty much how Brad had said it would. He spoke and negotiated on her behalf while she sat and listened. She had to grudgingly hand it to the little maggot; he really knew his stuff and held true to his word, and protected her assets. The insurance company awarded monetary damages to Raymond for loss of income, present and future health care expenses, and pain and suffering. That pleased Charlene because it meant that she could move on with her life, leaving the misery and disappointment of her relationship with Raymond behind her.

Afterward she and Brad met outside the hearing room in the hallway near a stairwell.

"I'm going to be getting some papers into my office in the next few days that I will need you to come in and sign." Brad was rushing his words as usual.

"Once we have everyone's signature on the damage amount, then that will be it as far as the plaintiff is concerned."

"Well, I'm just glad that all of this crap is over with." Charlene was feeling a bit of relief.

"So am I. You did great in there. You just sat back and let me handle it. Most doctors when they go through something like this are on the verge of having a breakdown. But not you. I've never seen anyone with the steel nerves that you have."

"Yeah, that's the story of my life. A woman with a hell of a lot of nerve." Charlene mused at what she'd just said.

"What does that mean?" Brad wanted in on the gag because he didn't understand.

"Never mind, Brad, it's not important."

"Well, look, I'm going to head back to the office and draw up the paperwork so that the plaintiff can be paid and be out of your life. I'll give you a call once I need you to come on in."

Charlene said good-bye to Brad and headed home feeling good. Now she could just go and work at another clinic or group practice in another town where they didn't know all of her business. She walked out of the courthouse and across the parking lot to her car. *Charlene, girl, it's time for you to pack your bags and move on,* she told herself. She'd start by putting everything in her apartment up for sale. When she returned home, she ran into the mailman.

"Dr. Hayward, I have a registered letter here for you," said the postman. Charlene signed for the letter and walked up the stairs to her unit. Once she got inside and kicked off her shoes, she glanced down at the letter, which was from the Illinois Department of Professional Regulations. *What in the hell do they want?* Charlene's chipper mood was turning to anger and confusion rather quickly. She ripped open the letter and began reading it.

Dear Dr. Hayward,
You are hereby ordered to appear before the State Dental Board for a hearing regarding a complaint from Dr. Seth Wood.

Charlene stopped reading the letter because a fit of angry dizziness had swiftly consumed her body. She thought she'd gotten away with what she'd done. She thought once she settled up with Raymond, no one else could touch her. She hadn't considered Dr. Seth Wood lodging a compliant with the damn Dental Board. She wasn't in a position to threaten the Dental Board as she had done Raymond. She was in over her head now. The Dental Board was like the Internal Revenue Service— once they sank their teeth into you, it was going to cost a pretty penny to get them to release their grip.

13

RICHARD

The sun was setting and painting the sky with brilliant and vibrant shades of orange and yellow. It was the Fourth of July holiday, and Nina and Richard were having a pool party and barbecue at their Spanish-style home. They'd invited Rose and John along with two of Nathan's neighborhood friends. Richard had gone into the house to flip on the patio and pool lights along with the insect zapper. While on the inside, he changed the radio station.

"Let that song play, Richard!" Rose blurted out from the steps inside of the pool, where she was submerged up to her waist in the warm water. Richard turned the music up slightly so that Rose could hear better.

Nina was wearing a green two-piece bathing suit with a matching green sarong tied around the waist. She'd just come from the garage, where she'd grabbed a small bag of nonexploding fireworks to entertain the kids with once the sun went completely down. She sat in her chair at one of the patio tables and picked up her glass, which contained the fruit smoothie she blended together earlier that day. She took a sip, and as soon as her glass hit the table again, Nathan ran up to her. He stood at her side, fidgeting and dripping wet wearing his orange water wings.

"Can I have some more?" Nathan asked, making a move to clutch Nina's glass before she could answer him.

"Are you and your friends ready to get out of the pool yet?" Nina asked as Nathan put the glass to his lips and gulped down the remainder of her drink.

"Nope," Nathan answered with his face buried in her glass.

"Well, let me know when you boys are ready to play with the sparklers."

"Okay," Nathan said. He set the empty glass back down on the table, ran to the other side of the pool, making a flapping sound with his feet, and then leaped off the edge of the pool and back into the water with his friends.

"Girl, Nathan must be part fish or something," Rose commented to Nina.

"I am a fish, ladybug," Nathan responded back to her from across the pool.

"Well, thank you for the clarification, Mr. Nathan Fish."

"Who is Nathan Fish?" Richard asked because he'd heard only the tail end of what Rose had said as he walked back out onto the pool deck.

"Your son," Rose answered. "That boy has taken to water like he has gills or something."

"Nathan isn't all fish," Richard remarked. "He loves to get into the pool, but I have to hear a song-and-dance act when I tell him to take a bath at night."

"Man, that's just the way kids are," John interjected as he coated the grilling chicken breasts with the barbecue sauce that Rose had mixed up.

"My daughter was the same way when she was little. She didn't like taking a bath at night, but the minute she saw a puddle of water outside on the street, she just had to go and splash around in it."

"Why are kids like that?" Richard asked, perplexed.

"Well, if you listen to Bill Cosby, he'll tell you they're brain damaged." Richard split open with laughter because he recalled what the famous comedian had said about his own kids.

"Don't you mess up and burn my chicken, John," Rose shouted out across the pool deck.

"Baby, please." John glanced over at Rose. "You know that I'm a trained professional."

"Well, you just make sure that you score the chicken and don't scorch it, Mr. 'Trained Professional.'" Rose rolled her eyes playfully at John.

"Don't worry, baby, I've got this under control." John was playing along with Rose.

"You know what, Nina . . ." Rose was shifting her eyes back and forth between Nina and John. Nina could tell that Rose was about to make a wisecrack. "Why is it that a man acts like he can't cook dinner, but the minute the coals get hot in the tub of a grill, he's suddenly an expert chef?"

"Oh lord, here we go," John announced with amusement as he once again flipped the chicken over.

"Girl, I don't know, men are funny like that," Nina answered.

"Now wait a minute. Don't go around generalizing men," Richard said. "Not all men are like the one Rose just described."

"That's right," John turned his attention away from the food and backed Richard up. "I'm certainly not like that."

"Guys, you're taking this way too seriously." Nina felt that she needed to defuse the swelling tension before their playfulness got out of hand. "Rose was just being sarcastic, right, Rose?" Nina asked, glancing over at Rose, who was sniffing the air.

"John! Are you burning up my damn chicken?" Rose hollered out as she stood up quickly in the water. Richard glanced at the grill and noticed that the flame had begun shooting up around the meat. He watched as John hurriedly removed the meat from the grill.

"Naw, baby, I'm just scoring it." John inspected the meat and sighed with relief when he discovered that he hadn't overcooked their meal.

Richard joked with John. "You lucked out that time, playa."
Richard slapped John on his shoulder. "I think that Rose would
have placed your neck in a noose if you had burned up the
chicken."

"Hey, my neck has been in a noose before and I haven't been
hung yet," John joked.

Rose sat back down and splashed some water on her arms.
"So where is Gracie at today, Nina?" asked Rose.

"Honey, she didn't want to come. She claimed that she just
wasn't feeling good. She claims that she's having body aches
again."

"Body aches?" Rose questioned. "She's starting to sound
like an elderly woman."

"I know, but that's what she said," Nina answered.

"Well, did you call her? How is she doing?"

"I just called her a moment ago but she wasn't home. I personally think she just said it so that she wouldn't have to come
over here. Now that she is divorced, I don't think she wants to
be around couples right now."

"Well, maybe you're wrong. Perhaps she's on her way over
here right now."

"I doubt it, but if she is out, she is more than likely somewhere with her father."

"Oh, okay," Rose mumbled and let that conversation rest.

Nathan and his friends tired themselves out playing in the
pool and playing with the sparklers that Nina had gotten for
them. When Nathan's last friend was picked up by his parents,
Nathan fell asleep on the sofa. It was eleven o'clock in the evening
when the adults finally had the evening completely to themselves.
They all sat at the patio table sipping their drinks while they listened to one of Nina's smooth jazz CDs.

"Nina, I love this music. The Spanish guitar is one of my favorite instruments. Smooth jazz music is for serious lovers,"
John stated as he allowed the melody of the music to lull him.

"Serious lovers?" Richard chuckled.

"Aw, don't sit there and act as if you don't know what I'm

talking about, Richard." John glanced at him with good-natured suspicion. "I'd be willing to bet that you consider yourself to be a serious lover as well." Richard mused at the way John phrased his words.

"I'm serious, man," John said as he swayed his head to the groove.

"I know you are, John," Richard agreed. "I'm not poking fun at you."

"Can you guys believe that at the end of this year we will be looking at an entirely new century," Rose said.

"A new century with each other, baby. Don't forget that," John reminded Rose.

"Well, John, sounds as if you're making sure of that," Nina said, noticing the way John corrected Rose.

"You know, when you find someone you're compatible with, it makes all the difference in the world," he said. "It has taken me a long time to find someone that I'm compatible with and whom I can trust. When I divorced my wife I thought that I would never find anyone else. To be honest, I really didn't want to be bothered with women anymore." John paused to reflect on his thoughts.

"John's daughter purchased the round trip tickets to the Bahamas for him," Rose said. "If it wasn't for her worrying about her father enjoying life, we never would have met."

"That is so nice," Nina chimed in.

"I had a real problem trusting women after my ex-wife walked out on me," John mentioned.

"That's the problem with some sisters," Rose said, loading up to go on a tangent. "They have a good man, who is faithful, with a job, and suddenly he's too boring. Or they have a male friend who they've known for years. They know that he is a decent man, with good character and strong values, but for some reason they can't see themselves with him because he has bad skin or he's a large man or something like that. I say, who cares? If the man is good to you," Rose began, using her fingers to count off her points, "and you can communicate with him, he's willing to work, and takes care of the home front, I say that's the man you need to be with. And another thing, these sisters out here think that just because they have a trophy case of college degrees that they know everything about relationships. What they don't realize is that a piece of paper doesn't have a damn thing to do with loving a man."

"Amen to that," John said. "One of the reasons my marriage failed was because my ex-wife wasn't a good listener. She had the best education that money could buy but didn't know how to listen to me. In my line of work, I see a lot of sad things happen to people. Sometimes I would need to talk about it but she didn't care to listen to what was on my mind. That was the start of our problems because I began to feel as if she didn't care about the things that had affected me. But with Rose, things are so different. We're like the best of friends and lovers at the same time. I don't think that I've ever felt this strongly about anyone."

Richard smiled at his friend. "I know how you feel." "Nina and I are also the best of friends. We love each other with passion and we're also a team."

"And don't forget business partners," Nina added.

"Yes, and now we are business partners," Richard added.

"Wait a minute, business partners? What are you two talking about?" Rose was confused and needed clarification.

"Well, Richard and I have an announcement to make." Nina and Richard stood up, and each slid an arm around the other's waist.

"We closed the deal on the dental practice this week," Richard said proudly.

"Well, congratulations!" Both Rose and John clapped their hands.

"That's a very big step," Rose added.

"I know, and I'm excited, nervous, and afraid all at the same time," Nina said. "I've already put in my two week's notice. It is going to be such a wonderful feeling to be working for myself and not someone else. I'm going to run the office while Richard handles the patients."

"Well, come on now, don't be shy about sharing the details, Richard," Rose said. "Where is your practice at? And when are you going to open it up?"

"Actually it's an existing practice that I purchased from a retiring dentist. The practice has about one thousand patients. I'm keeping the dental support staff that is already there, so that I don't have to worry about hiring new dental assistants or hygienists."

"Wow, that must be costing you an arm and a leg," John commented.

"Well, it's not cheap, that's for sure, but I've been blessed with a wife who happens to be one of the smartest accountants the world has ever seen." Richard kissed Nina on the cheek and then sat back down in his seat. Nina sat on his lap.

"Get this, we're going to market the practice as a dental spa," Nina added.

"Dental spa? What in the world is a dental spa?" Rose was now all ears.

"I want my patients to be as comfortable as possible when they sit down in my chair. Patients oftentimes fear or dread coming to see their dentist, and as a result, they're all tense. I mean, let's face it, no one enjoys getting a root canal. So to ease the anxiety, what we're going to do is pamper the patient. We are going to offer at no extra charge paraffin hand wax treatments, foot treatments, and headphones so that the patient can listen to the soothing sounds of the ocean or some other pleasant sound rather than the dental drill."

"Aw damn!" Rose blurted out. "Just like the smooth music we're listening to right now?"

"You got it, Rose," Nina confirmed for her.

"It sounds like it's going to be a nice-ass practice. Hell, I'd see my dentist every other week if I was getting that kind of treatment."

"That is what I'm counting on, Rose. Patients like yourself, who keep coming back, not only for their oral health but also because of the service that we'll be providing."

"We even go a step further," Nina interjected. "We are re-molding the waiting area and equipping it with a flat-screen television that will hang on the wall and show comedy movies so that while patient's are in the waiting area, they aren't experiencing dental anxiety while they wait."

"I'm even having the contractor create another small play area for people who have children. That room will be equipped with plastic toys and a Sony PlayStation. That way, while their parents are being treated, their children can play a video game."

"It sounds as if you're building one hell of a dental office, Richard," John said as he listened carefully.

"We're investing a lot of money in it," Richard said, "but this is what I've always wanted, to be my own boss while I practice my profession."

"There is so much we have to do. We have to set up accounts with dental product providers and join HMO's and managed care networks. I have to contact the yellow pages and place ads there and in the local newspaper. I need to set up payroll and vendor accounts, Richard and I need to order new furniture and computers for our offices. There is just so much that needs to be done."

"It sounds as if you're going to need some help," Rose said.

"Gracie is going to be my assistant," Nina said. "She's going to be a salaried employee during the day and go to school at night."

"Well damn, isn't the world just sunny for you all," Rose said with good-natured sarcasm and a little envy. "Can I get a job too?" she joked.

"No, I don't think it would be a good idea for me to be your boss," Nina joked back as she stood up from Richard's lap and sat down in her own seat.

"Well, I'd like to propose a toast." John held up his glass and everyone followed his lead. "To success, health, friendship, and most of all, love."

"Cheers," everyone said and clinked glasses.

*   *   *

On the last Sunday in July, Nina and Richard were spending the afternoon at their new dental office organizing the new office furniture that had been delivered the day before. Nina loved the fact that Richard's office was next door to hers because she was discovering that she was so in love with him that the thought of spending too much time away from him was enough to drive her crazy. She took a break from setting up files and work schedules for the staff to peep in on her honey bun.

"How are you coming along in here?" asked Nina as she hovered around the doorway of his office.

"Pretty good," Richard answered, leaning back in his burgundy leather chair as he organized his desk drawer. "I shouldn't be too much longer." Nina glanced over at the sofa, which had a fall leaf pattern with vibrant colors of brown and orange.

"The sofa looks really good in here," Nina commented. "It matches the desk and the wallpaper pattern perfectly."

"Of course it does, babes. You picked it out for me." Nina slipped her tongue between her teeth as she smiled.

"I'm glad you like my taste. The next thing I'm going to get is some nice art for these walls. One of my former coworkers from the accounting firm sells black art on the weekend. In fact, I've been meaning to call her to find out when and where her next art show is going to be, because I also want to get some art for the house. Rose and Gracie have been waiting on me to do that."

"Where does she have her shows?" Richard was curious.

"She usually hosts them at either her house or someone else's. She brings samples of the artwork with her."

"Well, when you do go, I'd like to come along as well if that's okay with you. I may see a piece or two that I want to get for myself personally."

"Okay, I'll give her a buzz," Nina said. "I don't mean to rush you, but when you have a minute, you need to come down to Patient Room 4. It looks like the drain is clogged up. We may need to call a plumber before we can use that room for patients."

"You're kidding me." Richard stopped fumbling around in his desk drawer and glanced at Nina with an annoyed look about the drain.

"You may be able to unclog it yourself, but take a look at it so that you can see what I'm talking about."

"All right." Richard grumbled at the thought of having to spend money for a plumber if he couldn't unstop the drain. "Give me about twenty minutes, then I'll go and take a look at it." Nina said okay and walked down the hall, leaving Richard to his organizing.

When she got a good distance away from his office door, she chuckled to herself. She went into Patient Room 4 and closed the door softly behind her. *Richard, Richard, Richard, wait until you see what I've got in store for you.* Today, Nina planned to catch Richard off guard. Today she had a sizzling sexual fantasy that she was dying for him to fulfill. Enacting each other's sexual fantasies was something that both Nina and Richard agreed to do for each other. They'd had a lengthy discussion about the passion, fire, and desire of their intimate life one night after making love.

"I want our lovemaking to always be fresh, passionate, and exciting," she told him. "I don't want it to grow stale or routine. If there is something that I'm not doing, or something that you want me to do, I want you to tell me, Richard. For you, I will do anything."

"I will," Richard said. "In fact, I've been thinking about that and I have an idea, but I'm not sure how you will feel about it."

"Talk to me, baby, I'm all ears." Richard sat up in bed and crossed his legs Indian-style, then asked Nina to do the same.

"I would like to propose that we agree to fill each other's deepest and wildest sexual desires without question."

"Without question?" Nina wasn't totally comfortable with that one.

"Yes, without question. I trust you fully and completely and I hope you trust me the same way."

"I do." Nina cleared away any doubt that Richard may have had.

"Good. As long as we have that trust, we will not have to fear each other's fantasies. I would like for us to make a commitment to each other, that every so often, we break from the routing of predictable lovemaking and do something adventurous, wild, and spontaneous."

"Like making love in the middle of the Atlantic Ocean on a Jet Ski?" Nina studied Richard's expression.

"Now see, that's what I'm talking about! And just like we were spontaneous on the Jet Ski, I want us to fill each other's desires in the same fashion, without question, or fear of having our request denied."

"Okay, I think I can handle that." Nina was keyed up about all the adventures she could and would have with her husband.

Richard initiated the first fantasy when he came home with a game called Twister. Nina had no idea of what he wanted to do with it until he spun the arrow on the game, told her to get naked, bend over, and put her right hand on green. He had her in the strangest positions while he sucked on her breasts and licked her coochie. He told her not to collapse when she had an orgasm, or she'd lose the game. When it was her turn to do him, she made him get into similarly awkward positions and gave him a blow job that broke him down and had him speaking out of his head.

"What did I tell you about speaking in tongues when you're not between my legs," Nina playfully scolded Richard for babbling as he removed his manhood from deep in her mouth.

"You can talk shit all you want to," Richard said, "because in a moment I'm going to have your ass howling like a wolf at the moon."

"Oh, really?" Nina said feeling exuberant. She loved and enjoyed giving Richard oral sex just as much as he enjoyed giving it to her. She loved the taste and feel of him. She got so turned on by the way he responded to her, which made her eager to please him all the more.

After the Twister game, it was Nina's turn to come up with something wild. She'd always wanted to get freaky in a dark movie theater and stop an elevator and make love in it. So one night they caught a late movie—she couldn't even remember what movie it was because she was enjoying Richard's long middle finger probing her and toying with her clit. He brought her to a climax three times and she had to mask her sighs of pleasure with coughing sounds. After the movie, they walked back to the public parking garage to get their car. When they got in an elevator, Nina stopped it, pulled her skirt above her hips, and told him to get it up quickly because she was aroused and needed to feel him inside her right away. She turned around, bent over at the waist, spread her ass cheeks, and Richard took great pleasure in fucking her from behind.

The next fantasy that she filled for Richard, she had to admit, was a wild and imaginative one. Richard had Nathan spend the night with Rose so that they could get up in the middle of the night for his fantasy. Richard had his car fitted with new cloth seat covers and black light lamps. They were mounted in the cab of the car under the dashboard just above her feet. Nina had seen black light lamps on license plate frames, motorcycle frames, and even mounted on the undercarriages of cars, which colored the ground beneath them blue as the car sped by. At midnight they got into his car and drove south toward Grant Park, Illinois. The only things out that way were open prairie and highway. Richard turned on a dark and deserted two-lane farm highway and he plugged in the black lights, which lit up the entire cab of the car in a magnificent hue of blue.

"Wow." Nina was amazed as she surveyed herself and her glowing blue skin. She suddenly felt like she was in some really kinky and erotic film. Richard put in a CD from a group called Enigma and selected a song called "The Sound of Sadness." It was a sultry and erotic instrumental with a heavy bass beat mixed with the sounds of a woman and a man whispering love coos in French while breathing heavily as if they were making love to each other. Nina looked over at Richard and his eyes were glowing under the black light along with his white teeth. Richard told her to take off her clothes and play with herself. Without hesitation or question, Nina honored his request. She stripped off all her clothes and tossed them in the backseat. She began touching her breasts and raised her caramel nipples to an erect state. She rubbed her stomach just below her belly button, and then allowed her fingers to begin massaging and teasing her womanhood.

Richard inhaled deeply. "The scent of your arousal turns me on," he admitted and his words ignited Nina's passions. She placed the soles of her feet on the windshield, opened her legs like butterfly wings, and began massaging her clit while at the same time cupping one breast. Soon she began to feel the butterflies dancing around in her stomach.

"Keep your eyes on me while you work yourself up," Richard said as he sped down the highway, "and moan loudly for me. I want to hear every whimper and cry that you release. Don't hold back your screams. You have a tendency to try to control your gasps of pleasure. I want you to let loose; no one can hear us way out here." Nina couldn't believe that he'd noticed that about her. Controlling her sexual moans was something that she did to keep from losing complete control over herself. The way Richard made love to her made her feel as if she were losing her mind. Now Richard was asking her to do just that, lose all control and express herself fully and openly. Nina kept her eyes on him and worked her passion up until she was shouting out his name during the rapture of her orgasm.

"Scoop some of your love juice out with your finger and put it on me like lipstick." It was the way that Richard was in control and knew exactly what he wanted her to do that made her hot and sticky with desire. She placed her middle finger inside herself, covered it with her love juice, and brushed it on his lips. The white juice began glowing on his lips. Suddenly, it seemed like some type of erotic potion. She watched in total erotic ecstasy as his tongue traveled across his lips, licking up every drop of her.

"Ooooo." Nina shuddered at the sight of his tongue sweeping his chocolate lips. Nina closed her eyes and exhaled as another wave of passion consumed her.

"Did you just make some more pussy elixir for me?"

"Yes." Nina's voice was twitching with untamed passion and lust.

"Feed me some more of it." Richard ordered up another meal and Nina gladly filled his order. After Richard slurped up her sticky liquid for the second time, he pulled off the pitch-black deserted two-lane farm road and drove toward an old abandoned farmer's barn, which was fifty yards from the road. He pulled the car completely inside the abandoned barn, turned off the headlights, shut the car off, but left the music and black lights on.

"There's a bag on the floor behind me. Get it." Nina reached behind the seat.

"Okay, I have it," Nina said, gazing directly into his glowing eyes, waiting for his next instruction. Richard removed his shorts, T-shirt, and underwear. His erect cock was standing tall, and Nina felt her mouth watering for it.

"Open the bag, and pull out the small jars." Nina pulled out the small jars of body paint. Richard took one and unscrewed its cap. He stuck his index finger inside the jar, scooped up the paint, and began fingerpainting on her body, just above her breasts. She could feel his finger spelling out the words, "My Woman."

"Now, you write something on me." Nina was charged up by the game they were playing. She scooped up some paint with her finger and wrote the words "I want it" on his stomach. The letters were glowing on his brown skin.

"How badly do you want me?" Richard asked. "Write how badly you want me on my body." Nina eagerly obliged her man and wrote the words, "Very badly" on his chest. Richard dipped his finger in the paint and drew a circle around her belly button that tickled her. Nina started writing on his thigh, "I want my dick, now." Richard wrote on her thigh, "Come and get it." When they ran out of space to write on each other, they were both glowing like children who had gotten into a bag of white flour.

"This is so kinky, baby, I'm on fire," Nina admitted. "I want to taste you." Nina was anxious to get Richard inside her mouth.

"Then go and get what you want," Richard said and reclined his seat all the way back. Nina leaned over and wrapped her lips and mouth around his silky cock. While she leaned over his lap, Richard was probing her womanhood with his fingers, keeping her love tunnel flowing with cunny juice. Hearing Richard's moans heightened her lust as she sucked and moistened Richard's delicious cock . Nina reclined her seat all the way back, and pulled Richard over to her side of the car. She was ready for him and needed him in her well of desire. Nina smeared a healthy amount of the body paint on the palms of her hands, and as Richard positioned himself above her and entered her she slapped her palm prints all over his back and ass as he pumped her into a screaming frenzy. For Nina, the entire moment was surreal, erotic, intense, and wickedly fun.

"Look at me," Nina was now the aggressor. "Don't close your eyes when you shoot your hot juice. I want to watch it build up in your eyes. I want us to climax together." Nina slapped his muscular ass again and clutched his dick with her pussy muscles.

"You like that, don't you?" Nina slapped and squeezed his ass as she asked him again.

"Damn, I love it when you clutch my shit like that," Richard growled with pleasure. He was pushing off against the floor of the car to thrust himself deeper inside of her. "I feel your walls squeezing it again, baby," he said.

"Climax with me, Richard," Nina shouted as she felt herself reaching the point of no return. "Cum with me!" She began howling out as the bliss of the moment overpowered her and her skin became blanketed with goose bumps . . .

Nina walked over to the window in Patient Room 4 and yanked the curtains closed. Making love the way they had that night, in a damn abandoned farmer's barn, was something that Nina often replayed in her mind. Whenever she thought about "Barn Love," which is what she called it, she became totally and completely caught up in the rapture of the memory. Now it was Nina's turn again and she was about to bring something new into their love life. She set the room up so that her fantasy would look and feel a certain way. She changed her clothes and appearance for Richard, which was an idea she'd gotten from Rose the day they were getting fitted for the wedding. She just couldn't wait for him to wander into the room so that he could see what she'd been cooking up for him. Richard was about to meet another side of Nina that had been silent for far too long.

When Richard opened the door to Patient Room 4 thirty minutes later, he didn't see Nina but he noticed that all the curtains were drawn and all the lights were out with the exception of the one on the dental chair. The white light glowing over the dental chair gave it a surreal look, as if it were from some weird science fiction movie where some type of strange and unnatural experiment was about to take place.

"What in the world?" Richard took in a gasp of air as he stepped all the way in the patient room. Nina swung the door, slamming it shut behind him. Richard turned around and watched as she hit play on a boom box that she'd brought from home and a sensual melody began playing. Nina sashayed toward him from the shadows of the room, and when Richard saw her, a look of wonder covered his face. Nina had somehow changed her entire appearance. She had on a long black wig with hair that came down to her shoulders. Her makeup was done differently, and she'd placed contacts in her eyes that were a lighter shade of brown. She had on a peach headband and one of his white lab coats, which was dangling open to show off her new peach-colored lace bra, thong, and garter belt set. Nina had on heels that made her just as tall as Richard.

"Damn, you look so different," Richard commented with wide-eyed excitement. "I've never seen you like this before."

"There are a lot of things about me that you've yet to discover, mister." Nina found the sensual pitch of voice that she was searching for. She decided that she'd give that voice, that other woman within her, a name. "My name is Cinnamon," she said, "and I believe that you have a few cavities that are in need of filling." Richard was grinning so hard that his cheeks began to ache. He knew that it was time for one of their wicked sexual adventures.

"Are you a doctor?" Richard asked, instantly playing along with her.

"Why, yes I am, but that doesn't matter." Dr. Cinnamon raised her freshly trimmed and recently arched eyebrow in defiance.

"Well, Dr. Cinnamon, I'm a happily married man, and if my wife ever found out that I was in here with you, she'd have my head."

"I give much better head than your wife does," Dr. Cinnamon taunted him with the double meaning of her words. "I swallow," she said as she walked past Richard, rocking and bouncing her hips and caramel heart-shaped ass toward the light of the dental chair. She extended one arm around the chair as if she were displaying it like Vanna White from *Wheel of Fortune*. She drew back one side of the white lab coat and placed her hand on her hip so that Richard could see her body illuminated under the white light.

"I need you to get completely undressed and have a seat," said Dr. Cinnamon as she swung the silver dental instrument tray, which was covered by a white cloth, over to the side. Richard followed her command and began undressing.

"What kind of cavities do you plan on filling?" Richard teased.

"Careful," Dr. Cinnamon warned. "Don't mess this up by asking meaningless questions."

"Oh," Richard answered, picking up on the fact that she wanted him to speak only when spoken to. He got undressed and sat down in the black leather dental chair. From the pocket of her lab coat Dr. Cinnamon removed a brown leather collar with silver letters that said PATIENT. She put the collar around Richard's neck and snapped it tight. The simple act of the collar being placed around his neck made him feel owned. Nina put a similar collar around her neck that read DR. CINNAMON. Both collars had a silver loop ring in the center for a small leash strap. Dr. Cinnamon sat on the dental stool, took the dental chair remote, and rolled around to the side where her patient could see her. She looked at her patient as she pressed the button to let the back of the chair lie all the way down like a bed.

"Are you comfortable?" Dr. Cinnamon asked as she clicked another button and raised the dental chair upward toward the ceiling.

"Yes, Dr. Cinnamon," Richard answered, understanding that his role had become that of Mr. Patient. Dr. Cinnamon swung the dental tray back over to her and removed the white cloth that was covering her equipment. She had body oil, the leash straps for the collars, peacock feathers, a blindfold, and a gold vibrator. She held up a small bottle of oil and let him watch her unscrew it. She dabbed a bit of the oil on her index finger and rotated it around one of his nipples. Once the oil was on, she puckered up her lips and blew a wisp of air on it. Mr. Patient suddenly felt a warm sensation on the area where she'd applied the oil.

"Do you like the feel of the warm oil on your skin?"

"It feels strange," answered Mr. Patient as Dr. Cinnamon dabbed more oil on his other nipple.

"I like the way it makes your nipples get real erect," Dr. Cinnamon said with a mischievous glint in her eyes. She grabbed the blindfold and covered up Mr. Patient's eyes.

"I can't see a thing," he said.

"Good," she answered him back. "I see that the mystery of what I'm about to do is turning you on. I love the sight of your chocolate sword extending."

"What you're doing is turning me on," replied Mr. Patient. "Will you squeeze my chocolate sword for me?"

"Perhaps, but only if you're a good patient who takes his medicine. Do you like to take your medicine?"

"Yes, I will take whatever medicine you prescribe," answered Mr. Patient.

"Are you willing to prove it to me? If I give you your medicine now, will you take it?"

"Yes," answered Mr. Patient.

Dr. Cinnamon took the peacock feathers and brushed them up and down her patient's body. She saw goose bumps pop up on his skin and he began to quiver. Her patient reached out to grab her but she quickly slapped his arm with her hand.

"Stop that! You do not touch," she said and continued to rub the feathers over the head of his manhood and along his long shaft and around his chocolate jewels. He began panting as she continued to tickle, tease, and excite him with the feathers. She removed her thong and rubbed it around his lips and nose so that he could inhale the scent of her readiness. She knew how much her scent turned him on.

"Your scent is driving me wild," he said through a quivering voice that was on the edge of lust.

"Why do you love it so much?" She dangled her thong above his nose.

"I don't know, it just drives me wild. It makes me thirsty for you." She rubbed the feathers around the sticky head of his manhood and the sight of his juices dripping off his long silky chocolate cock made the walls of her sugar basin contract. She had to taste him, so she began rubbing her tongue along the length of his sugar stick.

"Oh damn! Don't stop, you're making me so hard." She let

the tip of her tongue swirl around his helmet and mop up his river of sugar nectar. She put him in her warm, moist mouth, drank up his nectar, and swallowed it.

"You have sparks of electricity rushing all through me," confessed Mr. Patient as he felt her sucking hard on his love muscle. "Squeeze it, right there at the base," he pleaded with her. She squeezed that magic spot with her pinky finger, the way he'd taught her to, and his cock twitched and jumped with excitement. Nina loved it when that happened. The spot was like a magic button that she could control.

"Are you ready for your medicine now?" asked Dr. Cinnamon as she slurped up the rest of him.

"Yes, goddamn it, yes."

"Good." She grabbed the leash strap from the tray and fastened it to the ring attached to her patient's neck collar. She held the remote in her hand and lowered the dental chair all the way down. She straddled the dental chair just above her patient's head, noticing that his toes were curled up into fists of excitement. She coiled the strap around her hand twice so that she had a strong grip. She clicked another button on the remote and watched as the dental chair elevated his head and lips upward to meet her pussy. A quick gasp of air escaped her lips when he gently kissed the lips of her sugar basin. She jerked on the leash to hold his head and neck at the spot she wanted him to concentrate on, while she straddled above him.

"It's so good to see you again." Mr. Patient was now speaking directly to her womanhood as if she were a real person. It turned her on whenever he behaved as if he and her pussy were having a personal conversation. "Do you come here often?" Richard asked her pussy as he removed his blindfold. "By the way, your Mohawk hair style looks fabulous on you. I mean a lot of ladies can't wear an exotic hairstyle such as yours." Dr. Cinnamon laughed because she got tickled by the fact that Richard was talking about how she'd shaved the hair around her pussy.

"Stop talking!" She tried to sound stern but she didn't, so she jerked on the leash.

"Eat!" she ordered him. "Drink all of your medicine."

"What kind of medicine is this?" Mr. Patient asked.

"PPD," Dr. Cinnamon answered.

"PPD?" Mr. Patient repeated. "Is it good for me?"

"Pussy Pie Delight from me is always good for you. It freshens your breath and keeps your teeth nice and white." Without asking further questions, Mr. Patient began French-kissing and sucking on her womanhood.

"Yes"—her words were coming quickly and spontaneously—"you're making me melt," Dr. Cinnamon admitted as she worked her hips in a tight controlled circle.

"Oh, right there." She jerked on the leash and pressed her clit hard against his tongue. "Damn, you eat some good pussy!" She squirmed and shivered uncontrollably then melted all over his lips and tongue.

"I need to be inside you," said Mr. Patient with absolute resolve. Dr. Cinnamon straddled his sugar stick. Her back was toward his face. As she lowered herself down on him, she had to make an adjustment by stretching herself a bit wider in order to control every long delicious inch of him as she submerged him into the moist warmth of her love tunnel. He placed his hands on her hips and took great pleasure in watching the agility of her movements, which were quick and light at first before turning into more passionate thrusts of pleasure. Nina grabbed the gold vibrator and twisted it to the on position. The power of the vibrator in her hand felt good. She rubbed the vibrating toy up and down her stomach, which caused all of the butterflies in her stomach to prance with excitement. Touching and pleasing herself in this new fashion was taking her to a new level of sexual awareness. She was controlling how deeply Mr. Patient entered her and controlling when she wanted to orgasm. She'd locate a spot that was sexually sensitive inside her love tunnel and stimulate the spot by bouncing up and down on Mr. Patient hard until her release burst open and made her shout with plea-sure. Dr. Cinnamon placed the buzzing vibrator on her patient's skin and noticed immediately how he responded. His toes curled into tight fists of delight.

"You like me touching you with the vibrator, don't you? I can feel you," she said. "I can feel that you're about to un-leash."

"Yes," he answered, "I like the strong buzzing pressure of it." Hearing Mr. Patient say that detonated Dr. Cinnamon's pas-sions like a nuclear bomb. She wanted to reciprocate by provid-ing him with just as much pleasure as he was providing her with. She placed the gold vibrator on his balls and felt Mr. Patient's cock twitch and dance inside her. The sudden flinch was like a battery spark that caused her to orgasm unexpect-edly.

"Oooo!" Dr. Cinnamon shouted out at the top of her voice. The sound of Dr. Cinnamon's wail excited Mr. Patient. He took control over her movements now. He grabbed her by the hips and began lifting her up and down on his manhood. The sight of her caramel ass bouncing up and down against his brown skin made him want to devour her.

Mr. Patient's sudden spark of energy caught Dr. Cinnamon by surprise and he caused her to orgasm yet again.

"Damn!" she cried out, suddenly feeling light-headed.

"Right there, baby!" Mr. Patient said as Dr. Cinnamon began screwing her hips around in a tight circle, causing his dick to sweep against every wall of her pussy.

"Goddamn!" The undulations of her back, ass, and hips forced Mr. Patient to smack her fanny approvingly.

"Smack my ass again," Dr. Cinnamon cried out. Mr. Patient complied and smacked it over and over again.

"Yes!" Dr. Cinnamon felt a colossal orgasm swelling up from every part of her body. Mr. Patient noticed Dr. Cinnamon's movements becoming quicker and much more powerful. Dr. Cinnamon placed the gold buzzing vibrator directly on the muscle behind his chocolate Jewels and felt Mr. Patient's cock expand, then twitch spastically and hit her magic spot. Dr. Cinnamon's orgasm flowed downward and melted on Mr. Patient's cock like an ice cream cone melting in the hot summer sun. In order to make the feeling last, she needed Mr. Patient to shoot his juice inside her. She then pounded down on Mr. Patient's joystick as hard as she could, forcing him to explode deep in the depths of her love cave. When she felt his nectar mixing with her own, Dr. Cinnamon's eyes rolled up into her head. At the moment of his release, Mr. Patient howled out with pleasure as he became entwined in the rapture of the moment.

Once the intensity of the moment subsided, Nina and Richard began reaffirming their feelings for each other.

"I love you so much," Nina said as she leaned backward resting her body on Richard's. "That was a big one. You screamed so loudly," Nina said, amused.

"I did not!" Richard playfully disagreed.

"Okay, if you say so." Nina was feeling too good to disagree with her honey.

"I love you, too," Richard said.

"Do you like my new toy?" Nina asked.

"Hell yeah," Richard answered with a quickness. "Now I've got to find a toy that makes you lose your damn mind," Richard said as he toyed with her breasts.

"We should go shopping for our toys together," Nina suggested.

"You are such a wild woman, and I love you deeply."

"You're the one who made me this way." She laughed. "You're the one who brought all of this out in me. You're my pussy's prince." Richard laughed because he was so tickled by her comment.

"I'm the Pussy Prince, eh?"

"Damn right, baby," Nina said, rising up off him. "I'm going to be tender for a few days."

"So I gather that the sink isn't clogged up." Richard grabbed the remote and brought the dental chair back into an upright position.

"Baby, I am completely unclogged. You just put down one hell of a pipeline."

"You are such a mess." He swung his head from side to side as they both laughed.

14

CHARLENE

Charlene went to see Brad as soon as she got the complaint, which was right after he'd settled the malpractice lawsuit with Raymond. She wanted him to represent her in the new case with the State Dental Board but he declined to do it.

"Why won't you take it?" Charlene was pissed that he was telling her no.

"Because everything listed in the complaint is true. There is no strong argument that I could make on your behalf." Brad was stuttering and racing his words at a frantic pace. He was so damn excitable when it came to explaining things to her. In one way, it annoyed her, but in another way, she got a charge out of being confrontational with him because she knew that she made him nervous. She felt a sense of superiority over him because of it.

"Well, what about someone else? Can you recommend someone?" Charlene was aggravated with him, and it came across clearly in her tone of voice.

"Look, I'm going to be honest with you." Brad was trying to get firm with the inflection in his voice. "It's going to cost you a significant amount of money to defend a case like this. The fact that you haven't been working and have limited resources to pay attorney's fees is going to make lawyers shy away from you and this case. You cannot file a counter suit against the Dental Board for money; it just doesn't work like that."

"I just paid you in full, didn't I." Charlene's temper flared and she got snappy with him.

"Hey, I did my job. Raymond agreed to settle the lawsuit and not take you to civil court. This new complaint is something you're going to have to deal with." Charlene didn't appreciate the way he was talking to her, like she was stupid or something. At that moment, she wanted to unleash all of her frustration with men, love, and life on him even though her situation wasn't his fault. She just wanted and needed someone to kick in the ass other than herself.

"Okay." Charlene stood up to leave his office. "I'll handle this on my own."

"I wish there was more that I could do for you, but I'm afraid I can't."

"Yeah, and I bet," Charlene remained short with him, "if I had a shitload of money I bet that you'd be more than willing to give the case a shot." When Brad didn't answer her, that confirmed for her that the little prick was thinking just that. Aggravated, annoyed, and irritated, Charlene left his office and slammed the door on their business relationship. She didn't need him in her life, she reasoned.

Charlene was up very early on Monday, July 26th, because she had trouble sleeping. She had been reflecting on how she'd put her career in jeopardy. She had to appear before the State Dental Board and was sitting at her kitchen table reading the complaint lodged against her. Everything the complaint said was true. She did act maliciously and unethically and she did bring harm to her patient, which was a serious violation of the State's Dental Practice Act. As tough and unyielding as she wanted to be, she knew that the members of the Board could not be bullied and would not take what she'd done lightly. She figured that the only shot she had was to see if she could somehow cloud the thinking of the men with a hint of sexual charm. She'd wear the right type of skirt with a hemline that would be well above the knees and the right kind of high heels that would make the men perhaps consider going easy on her since, after all, she was a woman.

When Charlene stepped into the Board Room, she saw that twelve members were women and only one was a man.

"Damn," she hissed under her breath, knowing that women would show her no mercy. The members were all sitting around an elongated conference table glaring at her. The chairperson was a cocoa brown black woman in her mid-sixties with a skin tone that matched Charlene's. The chairperson stood up and directed her to have a seat at the opposite end of the table where everyone could see her. Charlene stood suspended in time attempting to read the body language of the women on the review panel.

"Dr. Hayward, please, have a seat," said the chairperson. Charlene clicked out of her daze, held her head up, walked to the other end of the table, and took her seat. Her heart began pounding so hard that she thought it was going to burst through her chest. Her hands were all sweaty and she felt perspiration trickle down her torso from under her arms. She glanced around the room at the members of the board once again and knew that her career and her very livelihood rested in their hands. Their vote and decision would alter the course of her life.

Charlene snapped open her briefcase and pulled out the file, which contained the complaint along with copies of Raymond's charts and her medical notes. She took in a deep breath as she prepared herself to fight and argue whatever they tossed her way.

"Before us comes a complaint filed by Dr. Seth Wood against Dr. Charlene Denise Hayward, Dental License Number 035-0455575. The complaint states that Dr. Hayward practiced the profession of dentistry with negligence, malice, and unprofessional conduct when she treated Mr. Raymond Dolton on the evening of January 1st, 1999." Charlene was about to speak up and deny the fact that she behaved unprofessionally but was stunned into silence when the chairperson called for a witness to validate the charges. The door to the board room swung open and Dr. Seth Wood, her former employer, walked in. He sat down in one of the chairs next to a board member and began testifying against her. Charlene tried not to show the discomfort she was feeling as Seth explained everything that happened that evening. The x-rays and notes in the patient's charts validated everything that he said.

"Clearly," Seth said, "Dr. Hayward knew that Mr. Dolton did not need to have six upper anterior teeth removed." After Seth's damaging testimony, Charlene was asked to share her side of the story.

"I cannot give you a reasonable explanation for what I've done." Charlene swallowed hard. She hated having to eat crow by apologizing, but she was trying to save her career and showing some faint form of remorse may help.

"I can only say that my actions were regrettable and I am deeply sorry." After her brief apology, the chairperson excused both Seth and Charlene while it met in executive session to determine the fate of Dr. Hayward. In a few weeks she'd receive another letter which would contain the opinion and recommendation of the Board.

Both Charlene and Seth waited on an elevator in the hallway without speaking to each other. When it arrived, they got on together, and as the elevator descended to the ground floor, Seth finally spoke.

"There is a coffee machine in the basement if you want to grab a cup."

Charlene nodded her head in the yes motion because at that moment, there was an emotional block lodged in her throat. Once they reached the small lounge area, she got a cup of black coffee from a machine and sat down with Seth.

"I know this has to be hard on you." Seth was attempting to be a comfort to her. Charlene knew that Seth had a bit of desire in his heart for her, but he just wasn't her type. In the past, she'd turned down his request for a casual date countless times. But Seth was the type of guy who lingered around, waiting for her to get either weak or desperate.

"I'm okay," Charlene answered as she took a sip of the coffee. "This will blow over." She said feeling a bit better now that she was away from the hot seat.

"You do realize that this is very serious, don't you?" Seth said, surprised that she wasn't a sobbing emotional wreck. "I didn't want to file a complaint against you, but I had no choice. The media and the city officials would have ruined my reputation, if I didn't file a complaint."

"I understand Seth. None of this is your fault. There is no use in crying over spilled milk," Charlene articulated, finding personal strength from somewhere deep inside of her. She would need that strength while she waited for the decision and opinion of the Board.

"You could have at least apologized with more feeling. That may have helped."

"I'm not sorry for what I did, Seth. I was pissed off at Raymond and all I did was pay him back for pissing me off."

"Damn, you're a real piece of work, Charlene," Seth said with a disapproving glare and tone. Charlene took another sip of her coffee and stared Seth directly in the eye.

"I'm more like," Charlene paused, "a work in progress."

"Woman, those board members have the power to ruin your career." Seth raised his voice to a loud whisper.

"What do you care?" Charlene questioned the motive behind his interest in her case.

"Because I'm trying to help you!" Seth was clearly irritated with her.

"Huh! That's a laugh. If you wanted to help me, you would not have shown up. You put the dagger in my back with your testimony, and if that's your idea of help, shit, you can keep it."

"I had to give the testimony. I told the truth."

"Yeah, well, sometimes the truth should not be told," Charlene uttered and acknowledged to herself that she sounded like both her mother and her grandmother when she said it.

Seth leaned in closer to Charlene and whispered, "I'm trying to save your career in a roundabout way."

"Stop beating around the damn bush and get to the point. I don't have time for your riddles or your bullshit, Seth."

"You're just too impossible to deal with." Seth stood up. "You won't even fucking apologize to me for the shit you put me and the office staff through. Raymond isn't the only victim in all of this. I'm sorry that the men in your life have made you so bitter, cold and empty. I thought that there was hope for you. I thought that I could save you. I thought that during this time of distress you and I could get closer to each other."

"I don't see how." Charlene pinched her eyebrows and rolled her eyes at him. He had some damn nerve thinking that she was going to get weak and want to be with his skinny ass for some sex. Or perhaps he thought she'd view him as her knight in glimmering armor, but that thought made her stomach churn.

"My mother is the chairperson, that's how I'm helping to save your ass, Charlene. I told her that your career was worth saving, but now I see I may have been wrong. I went out on a limb for you."

"I didn't ask you to go out on a limb for me, Seth!" Charlene didn't mean to sound ungrateful, but she wasn't about to be talked into some type of guilt complex because he'd tried to help her. There was just no way she was going to allow him to trick, manipulate, or con her like that in order to get what he wanted from her, which she assumed was an unlimited supply of her wet and juicy pussy, which she had to admit was in need of servicing.

"I don't know what else to say to you so I'm not going to say anything else."

"No, you shouldn't say anything else. You should leave." Charlene made sure that her words stung him. Seth swiveled his head disapprovingly as he walked away from her. Charlene remained seated at the table with her cup of black coffee. She took another sip and begin to think about what she would do if the worst case scenario happened.

On Monday, August 9th, Charlene received a letter in the mail containing the decision and recommendation of the Dental Board. Once she signed for the letter, she just gawked at it, too terrified to open it up. Finally, she mustered up the courage to pull out the decision, which was about six pages long. She began to read the "Findings of Fact," which recapitulated the charges against her. She then moved on to the "Determination of Guilt" section, which read:

> *After carefully reviewing the evidence available at the hearing, the Board unanimously concludes that the Respondent is guilty of the specification of charges.*

Charlene gasped a bit as her heart pounded inside her chest like the thunder of a drum. Charlene moved forward to the section called, "Determination as to Penalty," which read:

> *Upon the specification of the charges of which Respondent has been determined to be guilty, the Board imposes the penalty of Dental License Suspension for a period of six months. During such time Respondent is ordered to take remedial training in ethics and chair-side manners. After the six months have come to pass, Respondent's Dental License will be placed on probation for a period of 36 months. Respondent is ordered to pay Dr. Seth Wood, $15,000 in damages for said actions. Respondent is also ordered to pay a fine of $25,000 to the State of Illinois. All fines must be paid within thirty-six months. If all fines are not paid within said time, Respondent's Dental License will be revoked. Respondent is also ordered to seek psychiatric counseling to determine if anger management therapy is warranted.*

Charlene felt numb, as if she'd been hit on the head with a club. She allowed the document to fall to the floor beside her chair. *I must be tough and strong,* she told herself, so that she wouldn't overreact to the decision. She took in a few deep breaths and exhaled them out. She closed her eyes for a long while and then opened them back up when she heard something being slid under her door. Someone had slid an envelope under her door.

"Now what!" She damned the letter as she got up to see what it was. She ripped it open and saw that it was an eviction notice. Charlene crumbled the letter up and flung it to the other side of the room because she didn't want to deal with reality at that point. She sat down in one of her chairs and placed her feet up on the footstool.

"Son of a bitch!" she hissed. She picked up the television remote and turned on the TV. A rerun of the comedy program *Living Single* was on.

"That's what I need," she said out loud, "something to make me laugh, instead of losing my mind." She watched the program and got mad at the character Sinclair.

"If that goofy heifer can get a simple sucker like Overton to be crazy about her, why can't I?" Again, she spoke her feelings out loud. At that moment, Regine walked into the room carrying a shopping bag, wearing sunglass, and a stylish wig.

"Smooches, everyone," Regine said and Charlene found humor in it. "That heifer knows that she has some smoking ass wigs," Charlene said out loud. Then Maxine, the extremely confident, arrogant, and sarcastic attorney, walked into the room and Charlene perked up a bit. Out of all the characters on the show, Maxine was more a reflection of her, except that Charlene had a sharper edge than Maxine would ever have and Charlene was much more treacherous. Charlene's mind began to drift a bit as she wondered how Maxine Shaw, Attorney at Law, would handle the desperate situation that she found herself in.

"Maxine," Charlene said to the television. "You would probably blame someone else for your situation. You'd make someone sympathize with you and your circumstances all the while using them until you figured out which direction you needed to go." When the show went off the air, the local news came on and Charlene once again began to think. The heavy fines were the straws that broke the camel's back for her. There was no way she could gather up the type of money that the Board demanded she pay without working. Not only that, but not being able to work for six months was going to place her in financial ruin. She exhaled deeply and locked her fingers behind her head.

"Oooooh, Charlene, Raymond was not worth all of this." There was no one that she could talk to and no one who would understand her, except for her mother, Dean. Charlene had difficulty admitting to herself that after all this time she needed her mother. There were unresolved issues between them, which kept them apart and left Charlene bitter with her, but now she'd have to somehow resolve the issues between them so that she could move in with her and have a place to stay for six months until she got back on her feet. She located the letter that Dean had sent her over the holidays, and for the first time in a long while, she gave her mother a call.

By the time September arrived, Charlene had a moving sale and sold all of her furniture in order to have some money. She paid up her car note, which was several months behind so that she wouldn't have to worry about it being repossessed, at least not for the time being. She hated having to sell her belongings but since she would be starting over, she thought it was best. Dean seemed to be happy that Charlene wanted to stay with her for a while until she was able to find work. Charlene didn't tell her mother the complete truth about her situation, only that she and her boyfriend had broken up and the town that they lived in was too small for the both of them.

*   *   *

When Charlene finally arrived at her mother's apartment complex off Route 53 in Rolling Meadows, Illinois, reality hit her hard. She parked her car a few spaces down from a blue dumpster, which was overflowing with trash. The two-story row buildings reminded her of low-income housing and that made her lips and stomach curl up into fists. At the other end of the parking lot she saw several young men hanging out with the trunk of their car open, listening to loud rap music, the kind where every other word was "bitch" or "whore." Charlene sighed disapprovingly as she pressed the trunk release button, which caused it to leap open. She got out of her car and went to pull some of her things out. Two young boys, around the age of ten, came riding their dirt bikes up to her trunk.

"Do you need any help carrying your bags inside?" one of them asked.

"No, I've got it," Charlene said and watched as they continued on about their business. Charlene had to yank and pull on her suitcase before it finally broke free of the confines of the tight trunk.

"Charlene!" she heard a voice squeal her name. She let down the trunk and saw her mother sticking her head out of the second-floor window. "I'll be right down," she said with wild excitement in her voice. Charlene slammed the trunk shut. *Oh, lord,* she thought to herself as she rolled her eyes. As soon as she reached the walkway with her bag, Dean came rushing out of the building with her arms extended for a hug. She embraced Charlene tightly and wouldn't let go for a long moment. Charlene was taken aback by her mother's open display of affection. Dean was wearing blue jeans and an oversized button-down blue jean shirt with her cigarettes and door keys stuffed in the shirt pocket.

"It's so good to see you," Dean said, squeezing her very hard. "I'm so happy that you're here." Charlene felt odd returning the embrace because she'd locked up that emotional part of herself long ago, vowing never to let her mother get close to her again, or at least not in a way that would bruise her heart.

"Let me take a look at you." Dean clamped her hand on Charlene's shoulders and took a good look at her.

"You look fabulous," Dean declared, beaming with joy. Charlene could see the toll that Dean's drug use had taken on her. Her facial skin was black in places, most noticeably under her eyes, which didn't seem to open up fully. Dean seemed to be perpetually squinting. When she smiled, the deepness of her smile wrinkles told the tale of a woman who'd traveled the road of hard knocks.

"Do you have any more stuff in the trunk?" Dean asked, grabbing the suitcase that Charlene had.

"I have one more suitcase in the backseat of the car." Charlene answered.

"Well, go and grab that one, and I'll take this one," Dean said, lugging the suitcase toward the door of her apartment building and talking loudly to herself, "I've cleaned out a closet for you and I bought one of those cardboard dressers for you from my job at Wal-Mart." Dean continued rambling on as if she were trying to remember to tell Charlene that she'd done the best that she could to make her stay a pleasant one. "I went to the grocery store and picked up some pork chops, pork roast, and some sliced ham. We have to make up for lost time, and we can't do that on an empty stomach, no sir, we've got to have food in our stomachs because so much time has passed." Charlene looked up at the clear blue sky and said to herself. *This is not going to work.*

When Charlene stepped inside Dean's small one-bed apartment, everything about the place felt tight. The dining room was in front of her, and when she turned to the left, there was a small nook where a cheap-looking neon yellow dinette set was. She set her remaining bag down at the door and took a critical look around.

"Don't be shy now, my home is your home." Dean took her by the hand to show her around. "Right here is the kitchen," Dean said, flipping on the light switch. Charlene noticed that all the kitchen appliances were pea green, and the kitchen could have easily been mistaken for a pantry. There was only one way in and one way out.

"And this door here behind us is the bathroom." Dean opened the door and Charlene noticed that the sink and toilet were practically on top of each other. "And down here is the bedroom." Dean opened the door and they walked in. The bedroom was arguably the largest room in the apartment. Here is the dresser I got for you." Dean proudly displayed a short three-drawer flower-print cardboard dresser, which wasn't big enough to hold three pair of shoes.

"Don't you worry none. I got what I could for right now. If you need me to get another one, I'll take care of it."

"Dean," Charlene said in a soft voice.

"Can you call me Mom?" Dean had a sad look in her eyes and Charlene knew that it was because she felt guilty. *She's probably felt guilty about a ton of things,* Charlene reasoned to herself.

"Dean." Charlene ignored her request because she didn't care about the guilt her mother was dealing with. "I just want to rest for a while, okay. It was a long drive up here and I'm just very tired."

"Okay, sure, no problem," Dean said, wanting to be very accommodating. "Just go ahead and lay your head down. Get some rest, and we'll talk later." Dean walked out of the bedroom and shut the door behind her. Charlene sat down on the side of her mother's bed, which squeaked like a bed in a sleazy motel. She began thinking hard. *This was a bad move,* she thought to herself, *I can't stay here. Visit yes, but living here would drive me crazy.* Charlene lay down on the bed, shut her eyes, and fell asleep before she realized it.

The following morning she awoke to the smell of bacon and the sound of it sizzling in the skillet. Dean had come into the room overnight and placed a blanket over her. For a brief moment, the warmth of the blanket and the scent of the food reminded her of her Grandmother Hazel.

"I miss you so much, Hazel," Charlene whispered. She

tossed the blanket back and wandered down the short narrow corridor to the bathroom.

"Good morning," Dean chimed cheerfully.

"Good morning," Charlene returned the greeting.

"I left a fresh face towel and a fresh toothbrush on the sink in there for you."

"Okay," Charlene answered. After she freshened up, she sat down at the small neon yellow dinette table.

"You must not be getting much sleep at night," Dean commented. "You've been asleep for a good twelve hours."

"That's strange because I still feel tired," Charlene said, running her fingers through her hair.

"Well, that happens when you have a lot of things on your mind. Trust me, I know about that kind of stuff. Things get in your head and you can't get them out. They just stay there bugging you all the time." Charlene yawned and then began scratching her head. She had a ridiculous amount of new growth under her perm and she needed a touch-up quick, fast, and in a hurry.

"I hope that you like what I'm cooking," Dean said. "I'm making some bacon, grits, eggs, and biscuits."

"That sounds good, Dean," Charlene said as she rubbed her eyelids with the tips of her fingers.

"I'm not sure if my cooking is as good as your grandmother's, but I try to remember the things that she taught me when I was a little girl."

"I'm sure that however you make it, it will be just fine." Charlene took another survey of her mother's apartment, and although it was very small and tight, it was clean and orderly. Nothing like the way she had seen her grandmother's house when she'd come home for the funeral. Dean brought out her plate and set it in front of her.

"Hang on, I'll bring you some butter and jelly for your grits and biscuits. I only have fruit juice, is that okay?"

"Yes." Once Dean got everything they both needed, she sat down at the table with Charlene.

"You said something a few moments ago that made me think," Charlene said as she buttered her biscuit.

"What, the thing about how your grandmother taught me how to cook?"

"Well, yeah, sort of." There was no easy way to phrase Charlene's question because it has always been a tender issue. But she decided that she would ask anyway, since Dean appeared to want to be so accommodating.

"My father," Charlene said. "Why wouldn't Grandmomma or you tell me who he is?" Charlene glared directly into her mother's eyes and saw pain in them. Dean's eyes turned sad, and a shameful glint appeared in them.

"Baby." Dean reached across the table and put her hand on top of Charlene's. "Let's just be a mother and daughter having breakfast this morning. Let's leave the past where it is." Charlene noticed that Dean's eyes were turning glassy with tears.

"It's important to me." Charlene tried not to bark at her but she did. "I want to know."

"Baby." Dean had a nervous laugh in her voice. She changed the subject. "There is so much I want to know about you and your life as a doctor. There is so much I've missed. Your father doesn't matter at this point; he really doesn't. But I will tell you this; Hazel did the right thing by taking you away from me. As much as it hurts my heart to admit that, she did do the right thing. In spite of everything that happened between us, she made sure you didn't go down the same tragic road that I did."

15

NINA

Nina was lounging around in her pajamas in front of the fireplace listening to the soothing sound of clarinet player Kenny G play the holiday tune "Winter Wonderland." Nina was amazed that another year had come and gone so quickly. Tomorrow would be New Year's Eve, and according to the news reports, by January 1, 2000, everyone needed to prepare for the end of the world. However, neither she nor Richard was buying into the Y2K madness. Since it was snowing outside, Richard and Nathan decided to go out and play in it.

"Now I don't want to hear it when you two get sick as I don't know what," Nina scolded them as she got up and helped Nathan put on his snowsuit.

"We're only going out to make some snow angels," Richard said. "We will not be that long."

"Yeah, well, just make sure that you take the flashlight so you don't make any angels in yellow snow."

"We will not be long, baby," Richard said, kissing the top of her forehead.

"We'll be back, Mom," Nathan said, arching his back at an

odd angle to look up at her because his snowsuit made move-
ment difficult. Nathan decided to start calling Nina "Mom" all
on his own one day when they were sitting at the kitchen table
coloring pictures in one of his coloring books. She was showing
him how to color inside the lines when he said:

"How does this look, Mom?"

"It looks beautiful," she answered him. Nina's heart warmed
when he reached that milestone.

Nathan had grown so much over the past year, she thought
to herself as she held the front door open for them to go outside. He'd just started first grade and was a ball of energy, eager
to help out with everything and talk about everything he'd done
in school all day. He still had his sad moments when he thought
about his mother, and he and Nina still had their squabbles, but
overall, Nina was satisfied that things were progressing well.

Nina shut the door and headed back over to the sofa. She
picked up her book and reading glasses from the end table next
to the sofa. She was reading "Knowing" by Rosalyn McMil-
lian, a book that Rose had passed along to her before she and
John left for Atlanta to spend the holidays with his daughter
and his new grandson. Nina was well into the book when she
heard the front door open.

"Richard, when you get a moment, would you bring me a
glass of orange juice," Nina hollered out, not wanting to leave
the comfort of the sofa or interrupt the flow of her reading.

"It's me, Mom. Richard just let me in," said Gracie, who
walked over to her.

"Hey." Nina shut the book and stood up to give Gracie a
hug. Gracie then took a seat in one of the straightback chairs.

"What brings you over?" Nina asked.

"Nothing. I'm just tired of sitting in the house by myself
aching. You got any ibuprofen?"

"I have some extra-strength Tylenol," Nina said, walking
out of the room. "What's the matter with you? Are you cramp-
ing up?"

"Yeah," Gracie answered her. "You know how that goes."
Nina returned with a white bottle of extra-strength Tylenol for her.

"You don't have anything stronger?"

"Stronger?" Nina glanced at Gracie strangely.

"Never mind, these will work just fine."

"Baby, you've had this aching problem for some time now.
What did the doctor say when you went back to see her?"

"She ran some tests, ran up a bill and said I was healthy."

"What?" Nina was surprised at what Gracie was telling her.

"Well, let me rephrase that." Gracie huffed and rolled her
eyes a bit. "She said that I should try an over-the-counter medication for my muscles when they feel real tense. I told her that
a machine can't feel the pain that I'm in, and that I wanted
something stronger. She then told me that I was probably just
stressed and needed a break."

"What are you stressed out about, honey? I thought that you
said school was going well."

"It is. I just feel old as hell when I'm in the class."

"Child, please! Try going back when you're in your thirties,
honey. The students looked like babies to me," Nina stated.

"I talked to Dad today," Gracie said cautiously.

"Oh really? How is Jay doing?" Nina was only slightly interested in hearing how her ex-husband was faring.

"Okay. He's lost a little weight but that's because he got sick
with a nasty flu germ. I made some hot soup and took it over to
him then spent some time there."

"Is that right," Nina said, half wondering where all of his
extra girlfriends were now that he was totally available.

"Yeah, his last girlfriend didn't work out, but I know that
you don't want to hear about that." Gracie stopped herself before she said too much.

"Is he still staying at the house?" Nina asked.

"Yeah, he's still there. He hasn't even changed the phone
number. It's still the same."

"Do you want something to drink?" Nina asked, "I've got
juice, pop, or wine coolers . . ."

"I would say let me have a wine cooler, but since I'm driving, I'll just take pop." Nina left and then returned and handed Gracie her drink.

"Can I ask you something, Mom?"

"Sure, anything." Nina sat back down and covered her legs and feet with the blanket on the sofa.

"I've been thinking about taking in a foster child. What do you think about me doing that?" Nina paused so that she could choose her words carefully. She knew that Gracie has been struggling with the fact that she couldn't have children of her own. Nina knew that it bothered her a great deal.

"I mean, there are some really great kids out there who need a home," Gracie continued.

"That's true," Nina agreed with her, "but children need stability as well. They need love and someone who will not betray their trust."

"I know that, but I wanted to know what you thought."

"You want to know what I think." Nina paused. "Okay, that's a huge step, Gracie. I know that you want children and it is a noble thing to want to be a foster parent. However, at least, at a minimum, finish what you started, dear. Finish up your bachelor's degree. You don't have to worry about going to law school if you don't want to. But if you finish that degree, then I will know that you'll be able to provide for not only yourself but for your future foster child as well."

"Oh, don't worry, I plan to finish. I was just wondering how you felt about it."

"Baby, just finish what you started, because you can't work for Richard and me forever. I like the fact that you're in the office with me but I would be doing you a grave injustice if I told you that you could stay employed by us indefinitely. There is a whole world out there for you to see and explore, Gracie. Don't give yourself the short end of the stick, okay?"

"Yeah, you're right," Gracie said as she took the Tylenol. "Is there anything good on TV?"

"I don't know," Nina said as she picked up the remote.

"Let's see." Nina clicked on the television and flipped through the channels.

"Wait, go back," Gracie said and Nina flipped back a few channels. "Right there."

"That's Scrooge," Nina said. "Remember how we use to watch it every year?" Nina smiled, recalling the number of times she and Gracie had watched *A Christmas Carol*.

"Yes, I remember and I miss that tradition," Gracie said. "I miss being around family during the holidays."

"You'll always have family, Gracie. You're welcome to come here anytime you like."

"I know, I guess that's why I came by." At that moment, Richard and Nathan walked back in the house.

"Don't leave those wet clothes in the middle of the floor, guys. Take them and put them in the laundry room so they can get washed," Nina yelled out at them.

"Hey, Gay-C." Nathan waved to her. Once he was out of his snowsuit and boots, Richard let him run over to her. Nathan climbed up on Gracie's lap and proceeded to tell her all about making snow angels.

"Nathan, come on so that you can get a bath," Richard called for him once he'd taken their clothes to the laundry room.

"I'll be back, okay, so don't go," Nathan said to Gracie.

"Okay I'll be here," Gracie said as Nathan sped out of the room, making a sound like a race car.

"I'm going to make a great foster mom," Gracie said.

"Don't forget about finding love again, Gracie."

"I'm not interested in men right now," she answered. "I just want to have a child around me. Someone who will love me un-conditionally." The way that Gracie said that concerned Nina. For the first time she began to wonder if Gracie was dealing with a full deck; her thinking seemed to be a bit twisted to Nina. Something wasn't right with Gracie, and Nina made a mental note to herself to keep a close eye on her daughter.

16

CHARLENE

Charlene fulfilled her obligation to take additional training in ethics and chair-side manner along with sitting down with a shrink, who determined that there was no need for anger management therapy. In February 2000, Charlene received a letter from the Dental Board stating that her dental license had been reinstated but warned that she was still on probation and that any additional complaint against her could result in the complete suspension of her privileges. Charlene was ecstatic when she got the letter because that meant that she could find a better job than the one she'd been forced to take as an English teacher at Harper Community College. She was glad she'd landed that job fairly quickly because as soon as she got her first paycheck, she moved out of her mother's tight little apartment and found a place of her own not too far from Dean's. She had to admit that staying with her mother for a short time was helpful in repairing their bruised relationship. Although her mother still hadn't told Charlene what she wanted to know, having an open line of communication helped.

Charlene was heading toward the college to teach a ten o'clock class when she heard an ad on the radio.

The first thing that people notice about you is your smile. If you're struggling with bad breath, or teeth that are badly stained or uneven, then you don't have a confident smile. If you want that healthy glowing smile that everyone will rave about, then come see Dr. Richard Vincent at the Great Smiles Dental Clinic and Spa to see what he can do for you. The Great Smiles Dental Clinic and Spa not only provides you with outstanding oral health care, and a healthy sparkling smile, but also offers paraffin wax treatments to make your visit to the dentist a joy and comfort. See just how comfortable your next dental visit can be. Call us today at 1-800—.

"Son of a gun!" Charlene said as she scrambled for a pen and quickly wrote down the number while she waited at a stoplight. Then she rushed to the school campus. Once she got to her office, she tossed her purse on her desk, picked up her phone, and called the Great Smiles Dental Clinic and Spa.

"Good morning, Great Smiles Dental Clinic and Spa, this is Gracie. How may I assist you?"

"Hello, I have sort of a strange question. I want to know if Dr. Richard Vincent is an African-American man who went to Northwestern Dental School."

"Yes, he is," Gracie answered.

"Thank you." Charlene smiled.

"Would you like to make an appointment?" Gracie asked.

"No," Charlene said, feeling as if a great burden had been lifted off her shoulders. "I'll be in touch with Dr. Vincent in the near future. Perhaps you can tell me what time he arrives at the office."

"He's here all the time. Are you sure you don't want to make an appointment?"

"No, dear, but thank you for your help." Charlene hung up the phone and leaned back in her chair.

"Richard, Richard, Richard," she babbled, "I wonder if you're still that handsome sapsucker I fell in love with back in undergraduate school. It has been such a long time. Oh, it's going to be so good to see you, baby, and talk about the good times we shared together."

17

RICHARD

Richard was in Patient Room 3 finishing up with his last patient, Mr. DeSadier, who'd just undergone a wisdom tooth extraction.

"I need you to bite down on this," Richard stated while he raised the dental chair back to the upright position. Mr. DeSadier bit down on the sterile gauze as Richard's hygienist, who had been assisting him, removed the bib from around the patient's neck.

"I'm going to write you a prescription for a painkiller," Richard continued. "You should have this filled as soon as you can because the anesthetic will wear off in about an hour." Mr. DeSadier nodded, indicating that he understood. "If you have any problems or questions, just give me call. My hygienist will give you a sheet, which has some information about how to take care of your mouth. One of the most important things is to not drink with a straw. I want a good blood clot to form where the tooth was. I want you to come back in a week so that I can take a look at the extraction site to see how you're healing up." Mr. DeSadier nodded his head again. "Gracie at the front desk will schedule your next appointment with me, okay? How do you feel?"

"Man, right now I feel great. I don't feel a damn thing." Mr. DeSadier had a funny sound to his voice because of the gauze in his mouth. "My hands feel all soft, and the music that I was listening to through the headphones really relaxed me."

"Great, I'm glad you enjoyed that part. My wife, Nina, suggested the New Age music and the sounds of nature."

"I've never had an experience like this with a dentist. To be honest, I don't want to get out of the chair." Both Richard and Mr. DeSadier laughed.

"I know how you feel, but I'm afraid that you must get up, because I've got to get home." Mr. DeSadier nodded his head, shook Richard's hand, then followed the hygienist out of the room and to the front desk. Richard made some notes in the patient's chart then went into his office, where he put the file in his out basket for Gracie to pick up and give to Nina so she could file an insurance claim. Richard picked up the phone to check his voice mail to see if Nina had called him from home since she'd already left for the day. Sometimes she'd leave a message for him to stop at the store before he came home.

"Dr. Vincent."

"Yes," Richard answered Tracy, his hygienist, without looking up.

"There's a person in the lobby waiting to see you."

"Is it a patient who needs emergency care?" Richard listened to the prompts of his voice mail while he looked at Tracy.

"No, but she says you'll want to see her." After determining that Nina hadn't phoned, Richard hung up the receiver. "What's her name?" Richard asked, a bit perplexed.

"She said her name was Charlene. Dr. Charlene Hayward, and if you ask me, she's a bit arrogant. Do you want me to tell her that you've already left?" Richard pinched his eyebrows as he began to think very hard.

"Are you sure she said her name was Dr. Charlene Hayward?"

"Yes, I'm sure. She said you'd know who she is." Richard leaned back in his chair and sat in silence for a moment because he was at a complete loss for words.

"Dr. Vincent, are you okay? You look as if you've just seen a ghost or something."

"Yeah, I'm sorry," Richard paused again. "Send her in." Richard tried not to appear uncomfortable. A few moments later, Charlene strolled into Richard's office with power, confidence, and purpose. She was wearing a blue blouse, a white belt, blue jeans, and blue heels.

"Charlene," Richard said, "it's been a long time." Richard extended his hand for a handshake.

"Richard, come on now, let me have a hug. It's not like we're strangers," she said. Richard reluctantly gave her a brief hug and Charlene embraced him tighter than Richard thought she should have. Charlene was hoping that Richard would glance down at her full hips and consider the option of trying to rekindle the romance they once had.

"Have a seat." Richard pointed to the chair in front of his desk. He shut his office door then took his seat behind the desk. "What can I do for you?" Richard was direct with her.

"It looks as if you've done very well for yourself, Richard," Charlene commented as she glanced around his office. "I'm sure that Mom and Dad would have been proud of their son." Charlene didn't mean for her comment to sound sarcastic, but by the expression on Richard's face, she could see that she did come off that way.

"Do you want to get to the point, Charlene? Why are you here?"

"My goodness, Richard, you're not happy to see me? Not even a little bit? Is that any way to speak to your ex-fiancée?" Richard leaned back in his chair and put the tips of his fingers together like a church steeple. He wanted to make sure there was no mistake about his body language; he didn't appreciate her dropping in unannounced.

"Okay, I guess not," Charlene said, standing up. She could

feel the unspoken tension in the air. She strolled around his office so that she could take a look around. She was still holding out hope that Richard would be fascinated by the way she swung her hips and hot ass around the room. Richard had matured since the last time they were together; she could tell that right away. She'd been hoping that he was still the same quiet, passive sapsucker of a man that she'd once been intimate with. After reading Richard's standoffish body language, she knew right then and there that getting him to do what she wanted wouldn't be as easy as she'd hoped. However, Charlene was glad that she didn't call him before she came, because now he had to figure her out instead of her trying to read his mind. This awkwardness would give her the edge she needed. Charlene stood on the opposite side of the room and noticed a silver-framed photograph on his desk, which was facing toward Richard.

"May I take a look?" she asked as she walked back over to it.

"Be my guest," Richard answered, nodding toward the frame as he leaned back in his chair once again, studying her every move like a cat studying a moving object. Charlene picked up the frame and looked at a wedding photo of Richard and Nina. "So, this is your lovely bride." Charlene scrutinized the photo. "She was your second choice for a wife." Charlene said it more as a statement than a question. Then, realizing that her tone was a bit edgy, she decided to follow up with a nicer comment. "She's very pretty." Richard continued to glare at Charlene but didn't respond to her comment.

"So, she's the one you met while you were in dental school? I heard that she got pregnant on you?"

"Charlene, our relationship was over when I met Estelle, who was my first wife. The woman in the photo is my second wife." Richard could tell that Charlene was the same woman she was when they broke up back in the early eighties. She was a snake—very calculating, very swift, and razor sharp.

"Yes, I suppose our relationship was over after that incident at my apartment. But there was the one time we bumped into each other after our separation. I could still feel the passion that you had for me."

"The last time that I saw you, Charlene, was what—thirteen or fourteen years ago? I wasn't trying to get back with you then. To be frank I just wanted to understand why you bit the hand that was feeding you."

"Don't be so self-righteous, Richard!" Charlene got irritated when she thought about the moment in time Richard was referring to. She hadn't wanted to lash out at him—it was just a reaction she couldn't control. "I'm sorry," she quickly offered. "Sometimes you have to do unconventional things in order to survive in this crazy world. What did our sociology professor at Clark Atlanta University call it?" Charlene acted as if she had to search her memory although she was simply pausing for effect. "A necessary evil," she finished her thought, "sometimes you just have to perform necessary evils in life. If the U.S. hadn't dropped the Atomic Bomb on Japan, we may very well have been speaking Japanese today. That's just the way it is. That's what happened to our relationship back then Richard—a necessary evil."

"I don't agree with that, Charlene. What you did was very low-down."

"Oh really." Charlene was tickled by Richard's conviction. "You should have joined in; that would have been fun." Charlene paused in thought for a moment. "I suppose you're going to sit there and tell me you've never done anything out of the ordinary in order to survive in this world, right?"

"That's right," Richard answered.

"Okay," Charlene nodded her head and accepted his answer for the time being. "So, how long have you and Estelle been together? What, fifteen years or something like that?"

"That is not Estelle in the photo," Richard barked a bit. He was about to end their conversation and escort her out of his office.

"Oh, that's right, my bad," Charlene said. "Things didn't work out with the first one." Charlene was being a bit cynical.

"You should have stayed on my side of the fence, Richard; it would have saved you a lot of headache and heartache." Charlene smiled at him wickedly as she flounced over to the sofa and noticed Richard's degree framed on the wall.

"You finished dental school two years after I did," she said. "I didn't realize that."

"So, you became a dentist, too." Richard was surprised by that fact and now was getting very suspicious of Charlene. He watched her from the corner of his eye.

"Yes," Charlene answered. "After working in the dental office with you and your mother, I kind of liked the idea of becoming a doctor. So after you ran out on me, I decided that I wanted to go to dental school. I went to Southern Illinois School of Dental Medicine. I'm an oral surgeon now, just like your mother was." Charlene walked over and stood in front of Richard's desk. She paused for a moment and then got to the reason she'd come. "I need a favor from you, Richard."

"I'm afraid that I'm not in the business of granting favors," Richard answered.

"Okay, I'll put it another way. I'm looking for a job. Let me come work for you. I do good work," Charlene added.

"Why me, why my dental office? There are plenty of other places you can go." Richard was leery of Charlene's motives; he knew she couldn't be trusted.

"Because I know you and you know me. I figured we'd make a great team. If you had an oral surgeon in here, you could expand your practice and make more money." Richard leaned forward in his seat. He knew that Charlene was up to no good, and there was no way in hell he'd allow her to come work for him.

"I don't need any help, Charlene. I've been blessed with a growing practice and right now I'm not looking to take on an associate."

"Richard, how could you possibly pass this opportunity up? Right now you're just doing general dentistry. If I came abroad as an oral surgeon, your practice would grow at an even faster pace. You could perhaps open up a second office and hire another dentist so you wouldn't have to spend so much time in your office."

"Charlene!" Richard cut her off. "My answer is no! What part are you having trouble comprehending, the N or the O?"

"Why?" Charlene's temper flared up because she was losing her argument.

"Because I said so," Richard answered, unafraid of Charlene's mean personality.

"Okay, Richard," Charlene conceded for the moment. "If that's the way you feel, then there is nothing I can do about it." Charlene turned to leave his office in defeat. "Don't worry, I'll escort myself out."

Richard got up and followed her to the front door anyway. As Charlene was about to leave, she turned to Richard and invaded his social space. Her face was now very close to his and she could smell the sweet scent of his cologne.

"Damn, you smell good," she said. "Are you sure you don't want to reconsider my offer?" Charlene was attempting to charm him by batting her eyelids at him and appearing to be helpless and harmless.

"You're not offering anything I want," Richard rejected her.

Richard's words and unwillingness to give her employment enraged Charlene to the point that she wanted to scratch up his face, but she didn't allow him to see the malice in her heart. Instead, she played nicely because she was going to move to Plan B. Richard was going to hire her because she was going to leave him with no other option.

"It seems as if I have no choice in the matter. Unless, of course, I do another necessary evil in order to survive." Charlene smiled at Richard then walked out the door and across the parking lot.

"What's that supposed to mean?" Richard hollered out.

"Have a good day, Dr. Vincent, and don't forget to kiss that lovely bride of yours tonight."

Richard glared at Charlene like a hawk. He didn't appreciate how she'd attempted to force her way back into his life after all these years. *That woman must be a damn nut!* Richard thought to himself as he stepped back inside the clinic. He returned to his private office and checked his patient schedule for the following day. He tried to organize his day in his mind but he couldn't. Charlene was consuming his thoughts. Seeing her again after all this time was like having surgery on the same wound twice. Richard got up from his chair, stretched out on his sofa, locked his fingers behind his head, stared at the twirling ceiling fan, and reflected on the events that had broken his heart and terminated their wedding engagement.

Richard was twenty-one and a senior when he met Charlene at Clark Atlanta University in Atlanta, Georgia. He had gone to the library one evening to do research for a paper for his critical thinking class. The library was rather full that particular evening and the only seat available was the one that Charlene had her book bag on. He approached the wooden seat with an armful of books and set them down on the wooden table.

"Can I have this seat?" Richard asked and noticed that Charlene seemed irritated by the fact that he had broken her concentration. "The library is rather full tonight and this seems to be the only open seat," Richard explained.

"Just give me my book bag," Charlene said, and she reached out her hand toward Richard. Richard gave her the book bag and she went back to the business of studying. Richard sat down at the table, opened up one of his books, and began reading. A few minutes later Charlene spoke to him again.

"Don't I know you?" she asked.

Richard looked up at her and studied her face. He knew who she was but decided to play dumb. "I'm not sure if we know each other."

"You have sociology on Tuesdays don't you?" Charlene asked.

"Yeah, I do," Richard answered.

"You're that smart guy who sits up front, the one that the professor always call on."

"He doesn't call on me all the time." Richard chuckled, noticing her even-toned brown sugar skin for the first time. He admired her braided hair, bedroom eyes, pouting lips, and perky breasts.

"You're the one who sits up top and argues with him from time to time."

"We don't argue," Charlene said. "We just don't see eye to eye on some things."

"Well, you offer some pretty convincing arguments. I've watched you make him pause and rethink his position on more than one occasion. Perhaps you should consider going to law school," Richard suggested. "You'd make a good lawyer."

"Nah, I don't think I could defend some criminal that I didn't like."

"Well, there is always business law."

Charlene laughed. "Hell, they're the biggest criminals of them all."

Richard shifted his thinking and began to ponder the possibilities of a romantic relationship with her, based only on the fact that his physical attraction to her was very high. That evening they sat and studied with each other, and at the end of the night Richard walked Charlene back to her dorm room.

Over the next several months, they developed an intimate relationship, just as Richard had hoped.

During a warm spring afternoon the two of them had gone to a local park, spread out a blanket, lain on their backs, and watched the clouds float by. Charlene opened up to Richard that day and told him how she'd been raised by her Grandmother Hazel, who had died two years before. She talked about how she missed her grandmother and about how Hazel and her mother, Dean, didn't get along very well, and that she didn't know why. Charlene offered him only small slivers of information about Dean, saying that they weren't getting along very well either.

"Why?" asked Richard. "Why aren't you getting along?"

"It's a long complicated story, Richard," Charlene said. "I

guess my biggest issue with her is that she will not tell me who my father is. I mean, I have no idea who he is, who his people are, or what he was like. For all I know, I could pass him on the street and not even know it."

"Why won't she tell you? That just sounds crazy for her not to," Richard said as Charlene snuggled up close to him. She liked how sensitive he was to her feelings.

"I don't know," she answered, "but I do know that when my grandmother passed on, there was a deep unsolved issue between the two of them. My mother will not tell me what that was either."

"Charlene, baby, what are you going to do when we graduate in June? You are planning to go back to Chicago, right?" Richard asked, wondering if she'd thought about what she was going to do and where she was going to go.

"Yes, I'm going back to Chicago. It's not like I really have a choice," she said.

"Then you have to get this thing with your mother cleared up so that you'll have a place to stay."

"I know. She and I have talked, although very briefly. She told me that I could stay with her as long as I didn't cause any trouble."

"What kind of trouble could you possibly cause?" Richard asked, confused by what she said.

"The kind that aggravates her, I guess. She told me that I could stay with her as long as I stayed out of grown folks' business."

"Wow." Richard was trying to comprehend what Charlene was telling him.

"My family isn't like yours, Richard. We're pretty screwed up, if you ask me. Although my grandmother kept things stable, from what I understand, she was sneaking around with a married man."

"Really?" Richard said with wide-eyed amazement.

"Why did you say it like that?"

"Say it like what?" Richard asked.

"Do you think my grandmother was dirty or something?"

"No, I didn't say that, Charlene, I'm just trying to understand."

"There isn't anything to understand, okay? What she was doing was between her and him, all right?"

"All right, there's no need to snap at me." Richard backed down from Charlene.

"I'm sorry, Richard, I'm just very protective of my grandmother."

"Hey, I understand."

"No, you don't, but thank you for trying to. That means a lot to me."

When Richard and Charlene graduated, they both returned to Chicago. Since Richard was undecided about whether or not to attend graduate school, he decided that he'd work for his mother, who needed an office manager at her practice during that time.

Richard and Charlene continued to date each other, but Charlene's reality was much different from the one Richard was enjoying.

"I can't take it anymore, Richard," Charlene confided in him one evening while sitting in Richard's car in front of her mother's apartment building. "I want a job so damn bad so I can get the hell out of that woman's house."

"What happened?" Richard asked.

"Her married drug-dealing man is what happened!" Charlene hissed as tears streaked down her face.

"What did he do? Did he touch you or hurt you?"

"No, not exactly. It's my damn addicted mother. He's got her hooked on that shit and she isn't thinking right. God, sometimes I wish I was a man so that I could beat the hell out him for what he's doing."

"Charlene, what did he do?" Richard had to know.

"My mother came into my room last night all high and shit. She told me that her man Sledge wanted to have sex with me, and that if I didn't, he was going to put me out."

"What!" Richard was at a loss for words.

"It's okay." Charlene turned and glanced out the car window. She had a distant look in her eyes. "I'm tough, just like my grandmother was. I'm as tough as nails."

"Look, I've got to get you out of there," Richard insisted. "We need to find you an apartment of some kind."

"I need to start a new life, Richard. Your life is perfect; you don't have to worry about a thing. Me, on the other hand, I've got to fight and claw for everything."

"Just hold on, okay," Richard said. He wanted to be her savior. "What if I can get you a job with me working at the office? You could be my mother's receptionist. The current receptionist is about to go on maternity leave and chances are she will not be coming back. If you take the job, you and I could get a place to stay. Something small."

"Richard, I have a college degree, I can get a better job."

"Yeah, but until that better job comes along, you can take this one."

"You're strange, Richard." Charlene wiped her tears away. "You want to be my Prince Charming, don't you? You're willing to accept me with my shitty attitude and everything, aren't you?"

"Yes," Richard answered.

"You'd be so perfect if you were a millionaire," Charlene said and kissed Richard before he had a chance to process what she'd just said.

Richard convinced his mother to hire Charlene, which provided her with the money she needed to get a small apartment. Charlene and Richard worked well together and their relationship was able to continue and flourish and reached the point where Richard proposed to her. Charlene accepted Richard's proposal, which filled him with joy. They decided they'd get married in the fall but as the fall months approached, Charlene decided that she wanted a spring wedding instead. Shortly after she dropped that bomb on Richard, Charlene quit working for him and his mother because she found a higher-paying job. She never told Richard that she was even looking for a new job; she just came in one day and said that she quit. Being blindsided by Charlene left a sour taste in Richard's mouth, but he was willing to live with it if it meant that it would make their life together more fruitful. Richard soon noticed that Charlene didn't want him dropping by her apartment unannounced and requested he return the extra key that she'd given him. Richard refused to do that so Charlene began making her self unavailable to him. Richard became suspicious of Charlene's behavior and decided that he'd drop by her apartment one evening unannounced. He stood in the hallway of the brown three-story building that she lived in and knocked on the door.

"Just a minute." He heard Charlene rushing around the apartment. When she opened the door, she had on silk pajamas and the smile that she had on her face fell off when she saw him.

"Oh, what are you doing here? I thought I told you not to come by unless you called first." Richard walked inside the apartment without being invited.

"Why have you suddenly changed on me, Charlene? What has happened to us?"

"Richard, I just need my space, okay? Sometimes you can be overbearing and smothering."

"What! Just because I try to treat you nice and let you know how I feel about you I'm smothering you? I'm a good guy, Charlene, I'm a nice guy." Richard was more hurt than he was pissed off by her comment.

"Okay, perhaps smothering is the wrong word, but absence makes the heart grow fonder." Charlene shut the door and approached him. She rested her arms on his shoulders and looked him in the eye. She knew that she had to defuse him and do it quickly so that he would leave. Richard wasn't paying attention to Charlene as much as he was her apartment. Fresh flowers on her small cocktail table, sticks of jasmine incense burning around the room, and her silk pajamas, which he'd never seen her wear before.

"Looks like you're planning a cozy little evening," Richard commented sarcastically.

"No, not really. Just trying to relax after a long week at the office."

"How come you don't return my phone calls?"

"Richard, we're not in college anymore, okay? It's not like I have a ton of free time. I'm always busy."

"It only takes a few seconds to call just to say hello and that you're thinking about me," Richard snapped at her. Charlene ignored his snappiness and sat down on the sofa.

"Come here, baby, and sit down next to me." She patted the space beside her. Richard obeyed her and sat down next to her. She turned her body toward him and played with his hair.

"Look at you, coming over here all tense and angry like you're a big tough guy about to hurt somebody." Charlene rubbed the back of her hand along the side of his face. "Do you think I've been neglecting you?" she asked in a soft docile voice.

"Yes." Richard still had an edge in his voice, but to Charlene he sounded like a boy who was mad that someone had stolen his bike. That was Charlene's problem with Richard at the time—although he was twenty-three, he lived a very spoiled life and sometimes his punk ass just got on her nerves. He just didn't have enough bad boy in his blood for her. She enjoyed having Richard around for the time being only because she loved the way he went down on her and licked her kitty cat. She had to admit that Richard was a pussy connoisseur.

"You want me to make it better?" she asked, rubbing his thigh.

"What about our wedding, Charlene? There is still a lot of planning and stuff that needs to get done."

"Shhh." Charlene placed her index finger to his lips. "We'll talk about that later, but right now . . ." Charlene straddled him and felt his stiff manhood. "I want you to relax. Actually, I want both of you to relax. Miss Kitty will deal with both of you later on. Do you want something to drink?" Charlene asked.

"Yeah, I'll get up and get it," Richard said.

"No, I want you to sit tight, I'll get it." Charlene got up and walked toward the bathroom. She opened up the medicine cabinet and pulled down a bottle of sleeping pills that she kept inside. *This should do the trick,* she thought to herself. She went into the kitchen, pulled down a glass from the cabinet, opened up the refrigerator, then removed a can of pop from the door and an ice tray from the freezer. She popped the top of the sleeping pills and put two of them in her hand. She crushed up the pills, poured the powder into Richard's glass, plopped in a few cubes, and filled it with pop.

I can't allow you to ruin my evening with my new man, Richard, Charlene thought to herself.

She watched as Richard drank his pop and then decided she'd wait for the pills to take effect.

"Let me turn on the TV," she said as she got up and turned on her new television set.

"When did you get a new television?" Richard asked because he hadn't noticed it before. Richard looked around her apartment again and noticed a new stereo as well. "And the stereo, when did you get a new stereo?"

"Oh, I picked that stuff out at Montgomery Ward's a while back. They just delivered it two days ago. I can do that now that I'm making more money," Charlene lied.

"Oh, okay you should have told me. I would have helped you shop for it."

"Don't worry about it," Charlene said as she sat back down on the sofa.

"Be my baby and lay your head in my lap," she said because that would change the entire mood of the evening and get his mind off having sex. "*Barney Miller* is about to come on."

Richard didn't know when he'd drifted off to sleep on Charlene's sofa. He only knew that when he woke up, he was completely covered up from head to toe in Charlene's green blanket. Richard also noticed that he felt very drained and very tired and his mouth was incredibly dry. He sat up and tried to focus his eyes in the dark room. Still half sleeping, he wandered into the kitchen and opened the refrigerator. The white light from the frig split the darkness in the kitchen. Richard pulled out a can of pop and set it on the counter, but knocked over a bottle of pills when he did.

"Damn," he hissed as he stooped down to pick up the pills and put them back in their bottle. He read the label on the bottle and wondered what Charlene was doing with sleeping pills. He popped the top of the soda. He guzzled down the liquid but stopped when he heard the hissing sound of water coming from the bathroom. Richard assumed that for some reason Charlene was taking a shower and decided that he'd join her. When he walked out of the kitchen and past the living room toward the bathroom, he noticed that the bathroom light wasn't on because there were no slivers of light creeping up from under the door. *Why is she taking a shower in the dark?* he wondered. When he got to the door, he could hear the muffled sound of Charlene's voice. He slowly turned the knob and stepped into the bathroom, which was clouded with steam from the shower. Even though the small bathroom window was open and provided him with a little light from the streetlamps, the room was still thick with steam and he could hear Charlene and someone else much more clearly. Richard didn't want to peek behind the shower curtain, but he made himself do it. He slowly moved the pink curtain back, took a look inside, and saw Charlene getting it on with a huge, strong, muscular, enormous John Henry of a man. His shoulders and arms were massive and rippling with muscles. Water was cascading down on the two of them like a waterfall, and made their skin glisten. The man, who appeared to be in his mid-thirties, was clearly a bodybuilder. The man had Charlene pinned against the shower wall. Her legs were wrapped around his back and locked at the ankles. This huge man had his hands clamped on her waist and was using his powerful back and thunderous thighs to thrust himself in one solid motion deep inside Charlene's love tunnel. Charlene was moaning and breathing hard and heavy through her nose because she had stuffed a small face towel in her mouth to muffle her screams. She was clawing at the man's back, encouraging him to plunge himself deeper inside her. Richard was so stunned, he was frozen in place, like a statue. Charlene opened her eyes and caught Richard's gaze. Her hair was wet and dangling on her shoulders. He could tell by the lustful glint in her eyes that this man was taking her to a place that he had never taken her. Charlene removed the towel from her mouth and began biting on the man's neck. She released her moans freely now and continued to claw at his back while she glared at Richard. It was clear at that point that there was no way she was going to tell her lover to stop. There was also no way that Richard could win a battle against such a giant man. Richard found the strength to rush out of the room. He stumbled on a pair of pants in the living room, where he'd been sleeping. He picked them up and pulled the wallet out of the back pocket. He went to the front door and opened it. The light from the hallway crept inside her dark apartment, and Richard opened up the wallet and pulled out the man's identification. He looked at the man's photo and recognized him right away. It was Mr. Howell, one of the patients from his mother's practice. Richard tossed his wallet and slacks back inside and slammed the door shut. He rushed down the stairs and outside to his car. Richard felt as if he'd been stabbed in the heart and left in the gutter to bleed to death. He drove off in a fit of anger, humiliation, and disappointment. Not only was Charlene cheating on him, but Mr. Howell was cheating on his wife, Jessica, who was also a patient in his mother's practice.

The ear-splitting sound of the phone ringing in his office startled Richard out of his memories and made him sit up abruptly and stop thinking about the past. He snatched up his phone.

"Hello?"

"Baby, what are you still doing at the office? Did you have an emergency patient come in?"

"Yeah, something like that." Richard was being vague with Nina.

"What do you mean, something like that?" Nina asked.

"I was just working late, baby, I'm on my way home to you now."

18

CHARLENE

Three weeks later Charlene was driving back to Great Smiles Dental Clinic and Spa to have another chitchat with Richard. Charlene laughed to herself as she glanced over at the manila file folder of damaging information resting comfortably on the passenger seat. She pulled into the parking lot, got out, and damn near skipped over to the front door with the file. She was about to hand Richard a rotten egg he couldn't refuse to take, but in her mind, this was the only way to get out of debt and make a reasonable income. Charlene didn't care about the awkward position she was about to place Richard in—she cared only about herself. Charlene walked in and saw Gracie, the receptionist that she'd spoken to a few weeks ago.

"Gracie, how are you doing?" Charlene asked, feeling as bold and as strong as bad breath in the morning.

"Good, and you?" Charlene noticed that Gracie paused because she didn't remember her.

"Dr. Charlene Hayward." She extended her hand and Gracie shook it. "Would you please tell Dr. Vincent that Dr. Hayward is here to see him."

"Is he expecting you? Because he is with a patient right now."

"He'll want to see me," Charlene said with confidence. "Just let him know that I'm here."

She sat down in the waiting room and looked at the large television screen that was mounted on the wall. The movie *Boomerang,* starring Eddie Murphy, was playing. Charlene got a real kick out of the character that Eartha Kitt was playing.

"Marcus!" Eartha Kitt came up to Marcus, who was portrayed by Eddie Murphy. She was cynical, old, wrinkled, and manipulative. She was Charlene's kind of woman because she always got exactly what she wanted. "I'm not wearing any panties," she purred as only Eartha Kitt can. Charlene split open with laughter as she slapped the palm of her hand on her thigh. Laughter helped her to relax, and when she sashayed back into Richard's office, she didn't want to feel any shame or guilt about what she was about to do.

"Uhm, Dr. Hayward," Gracie called her, "Dr. Vincent will see you now."

"That's a funny movie," Charlene said, pointing to the screen as she stood up.

"Yes, it is," Gracie answered. "The patients also really enjoy it when I play *Vacation* with Chevy Chase as well. The scene where he's eating the sandwich after the dog has peed on it makes me crack up every time I see it."

"Well, it's a good idea to have funny movies like that playing."

"It was Dr. Vincent's idea," Gracie said as she escorted her back to Richard's office.

Richard was sitting behind his desk glaring at Charlene as if she'd lost her damn mind.

"Don't look at me like that," she said as Gracie closed the door behind her.

"What do you want, Charlene?" Richard asked and then even got more direct with her. "You're not wanted here."

"Richard! You are so edgy. Is the wife not taking care of her wifely duties?" Charlene was sharpening her daggers and gave him a surface cut with her comment. Richard wasn't about to take her bullshit and picked up the phone.

"What are you doing?" Charlene said, calm and cool.

"I'm calling the police, Charlene. You're trespassing." Charlene swiftly pressed the receiver button down with her index finger.

"I'd think twice if I were you before I did that," Charlene said as she held her finger down on the receiver. "Do you recall a patient of yours by the name of Jessica Howell?"

"I don't have a patient by that name," Richard growled at her.

"Oh, silly me," Charlene said. "You're having trouble remembering. Let me help you recall who she is." Charlene released the receiver. "Hang up the phone, Richard. There is no need for two professional people to get ghetto-fabulous." Charlene knew that she was getting her way when he hung up the phone.

"You're right," she said, waltzing over to the wall with the file folder in her hand and glancing at his degree again. "Jessica Howell was not a patient of yours; she was a patient of your mother's, Dr. Katherine Vincent. However, according to this, there seems to be some discrepancy as to whether or not Dr. Vincent treated Mrs. Howell back in 1983, or if Mr. Vincent treated her."

"What the fuck are you talking about?" Richard's blood pressure was rising. Charlene slapped the file folder on his desk, which contained the dental records of Jessica Howell from 1983. She opened up the file and pointed to the treating physician's signature, which read Dr. Richard Vincent. Richard gasped for air and his eyes grew wide when he saw his signature. In 1983, Richard's mother had developed arthritis in the joints of both of her hands, which limited her ability to perform complicated dental procedures. When situations like that occurred, he helped his mother out while the patient was sedated. It was during this time that his family was putting pressure on him to go to dental school and become a doctor. After the dental procedure with Jessica Howell, Richard's mother was beaming with pride because he'd done an outstanding job.

"You sign the patient's chart, Richard. So you can see how the letters 'D-R.' look in front of your name," said his mother.

Charlene was giving him a cynical glare as he gaped at her, speechless. "Hello, Earth to Richard, you look as if you've seen a ghost, that is your signature isn't it?"

Richard found his voice and raised it in fury. "Where did you get that!"

"Oh, no." Charlene pointed her finger at him. "You will not raise your voice at me."

"Where did you get that file?" Richard asked through clenched teeth, trying to control his rage.

"It doesn't matter how I got it, Richard," Charlene said, brushing off the question. She wasn't about to tell him Jessica Howell moved to Hopkin's Park, Illinois, and was a patient in Dr. Seth Wood's practice in Kankakee where she once worked. When Jessica came to the practice, she had copies of her dental records. Charlene had an extra set of keys to Dr. Wood's practice. Dr. Wood never changed the alarm code, which made it easy for Charlene to sneak back into the practice late at night and steal Jessica Howell's original file. Charlene remembered Jessica Howell clearly, not only because Richard told her he'd done the procedure at his mother's instruction, but also because Charlene had had an improper relationship with Mrs. Howell's husband—a stud of a man who knew how to use his tool, and didn't mind spending handsome amounts of money on her.

"I have the original record, and this is a copy of it. You see, Richard darling"—Charlene was cocky now—"you said you've never had to perform a necessary evil before." She cackled like a happy phantom casting a malicious spell. "Medical fraud mean anything to you, Richard?"

Richard's jaws were locked so tightly that he thought he was going to crack his own jaw.

"According to this dental record, you were performing dentistry in 1983 without a license. In fact, you hadn't even enrolled in an accredited dental program until two years later in 1985, and according to your lovely degree displayed here on the wall, you didn't actually get a license until 1989. Did you know that this state carries a minimum sentence of ten year's imprisonment for medical fraud?"

"That happened damn near twenty years ago, Charlene."

"True, but there is no statute of limitations on medical fraud in this state. It's all right there in black and white. I took the liberty of doing the research for you, so you know that I'm not bluffing." Charlene sat down on his sofa and crossed her legs at the knees, enjoying the art and thrill of controlling and manipulating Richard. "It didn't have to come to this, you know. All I wanted was a job. I only planned to work for you for about a year. Then I was going to move on. But no, you wanted to be difficult, and now I have to play dirty."

"You can't prove that this is my signature," Richard shot back at her.

"True, Richard, very true. In order to prove anything, I would need to produce a credible witness who can verify that you at least worked at that office during that time." Charlene looked at her manicured fingernails and blew air on them. "Funny how people stay in the same area for years. The phone number in the chart is current."

Richard was so enraged he was feeling dizzy, and lightheaded. He felt his shoulders tensing up, which was causing his neck to grow stiff.

"I have no doubt, Jessica Howell would leap at the chance to make money off of your necessary evil. Hopkins Park, Illinois, is a poor community. Many of the residents are the type who welcome a big payday." Charlene grinned once again, thoroughly enjoying how she'd done her homework and was making a solid case. "I can just see that pretty little bride of yours right now packing her shit and leaving your ass once you're convicted." Charlene began rocking her leg as twitches of excitement rushed through her. She found herself getting a bit turned on by the dark cloud she was dangling above Richard's head.

"What do you want? Money?" Richard wanted Charlene to go away and now he was going to attempt to buy his way out of his situation.

"Richard, darling, your pockets are not that deep. Besides, I'm not that evil. Right now, I need you. I'm going to make you an offer you can't refuse."

Richard was silent.

"I'm willing to earn my pay. I want to come in, work for you, and reestablish my good credit rating so that I can get my own practice. It will only take about a year. I'll even sign an agreement that says that I will not steal your patients when I leave. However, I do expect you to do whatever you need to do to pay me well." Charlene stood up. "It's a small price to pay to keep yourself out of prison, Richard."

"And what if I refuse your offer? What if I choose to fight this?" Richard's eyes were flowing with the red wine of anger. Charlene laughed.

"Richard, let me put it to you this way." Charlene was about to break it all down. "I'm like a zit on prom night. I'm the last thing you want to see, but I've shown up and I'm right in the middle of your damn forehead. Everyone will see me and notice me. You can ignore me, and I'll eventually go away, or you can take a chance and squeeze me, but I can assure you that I will leave a sticky mess and a hideous stain. Do yourself a favor, Richard—don't refuse my offer, or I will send that information to the state board, and trust me, they will not be as kind as I am."

"I can beat this," Richard hissed.

"True, you may be able to beat the case but at what cost? Can you imagine the bad press you'll get from this? Can you imagine your patients finding out that at one point you were a fraud? Think about it, Richard. It would cost you a considerable amount of money to fight this."

Richard's jaws were locked tight as he processed everything that was happening to him. *Ain't this a bitch!* he thought to himself. He just couldn't believe that Charlene had come into his life again after all these years with the power to destroy everything that he had built for himself and his family.

"I will come back to start in exactly two weeks. Oh, and I will want my own office." Charlene scooted over to his doorway. "Richard, honestly, this can be as painless or as painful as you make it. You have exactly two weeks to get things together for my arrival. I'll see you then." Charlene winked at Richard and then left him as a wounded prisoner of his own thoughts.

19

NINA

Nina didn't know what was wrong with Richard when he came home. He was all wound up and wouldn't speak to either her or Nathan. He didn't eat the meal that she'd cooked, and when she tried to rub the tension out of his shoulders, he jerked away from her as if her touch annoyed him.

After she put Nathan to bed, she expected to have a conversation with him about what was going on. Instead, Richard surprised the hell out of her when he went into the guest room to sleep. That was where she had to draw the damn line. Something was wrong and she was going to find out what was on Richard's mind. She didn't want to live in a house where the communication got interrupted. *Been there, done that,* she mumbled to herself. *If something is bothering him, he needs to tell me about it.*

When Nina opened the door of the guest bedroom, she found Richard pacing the floor like a caged tiger. He was mumbling to himself and was so deep in thought that he didn't even notice her standing in the doorway. He had an impaling glare in his eyes as if he were about to torture or kill something or someone. Richard's behavior distressed Nina because she'd never seen him behave like this before. This was a dark and dangerous side of him that he had not shown her. Nina didn't say anything to him because he looked as if he were about to pop a blood vessel or something by the way his veins were pulsating in his temples. Finally, after mustering up some nerve, she cautiously made her way to the edge of the bed and sat down. Her heart rate picked up because whatever it was that had her man like this, it was massive. Nina sat there for a full ten minutes with her hands folded in her lap waiting for Richard to acknowledge her but he didn't. She could see that he was in an entirely different place; he was someplace inside of his mind where he didn't want to be reached. She waited for a few more moments and decided to be brave and strong. She spoke and broke his concentration.

"Richard, baby, what is it?" Nina's voice seemed to startle Richard and he glared at her like a deer caught in headlights. He looked at her as if he had no idea of who she was. Richard was as stone as a sculpture and wouldn't speak.

"Richard?" Nina spoke his name again. "Come on now, baby, you're scaring me." Richard wanted to speak but he couldn't. He tried to say "Help" but the word wouldn't come out. He felt terrified, panicky, nervous, distressed, and confused. His voice was refusing to obey his order to speak. Suddenly, he felt his whole body betray him, and systemically it began shutting down on him, and there was nothing he could do to stop it.

"Richard!" Nina now yelled out his name as she noticed the glare in his eyes going rather blank.

"Richard!" Nina howled out his name again. Richard's body went limp and fell to the floor as if someone had unplugged him.

"Girl, we got here as quick as we could." Rose came running up to Nina and Nathan, who were sitting in the emergency room at the hospital.

"Come on with me Nathan," John said. "Let's go see if we can find a vending machine." Nina thanked John for having the presence of mind to remove Nathan from the adult conversation she and Rose were about to have.

"It's okay, sweetie," Nina told Nathan. "You can go with John." Nathan took John's hand and the two of them walked down the corridor.

"What happened?" Rose put her arms around Nina, who was finally getting a chance to allow her tears to flow. She had been holding them back because she didn't want to upset Nathan.

"Oh, girl, take your time," Rose said and she reached into her purse for some Kleenex. Nina put her face in her hands and then ran her fingers through her hair. Her eyes were red with fatigue and worry. Her words were caught in her throat, and it would take a few moments for her to get them out.

"He came home with something gnawing away at his thoughts." Nina's words were choppy, which made Rose hang on her every detail.

"He was in the guest room, pacing, like he'd lost his mind or something." The emotion of the moment was choking Nina, so she paused until the emotion passed.

"I called to him and he just glared at me, like I was a poltergeist or something. Then his eyes started losing the life in them. He was just fading away, like a vapor of air." Nina looked at Rose, who was studying her. Nina noticed the lines of burden and worry etched under Rose's eyes.

"Nina." Rose was speaking soft and clear. "Where is Richard now?"

"I don't know if he was awake or unconscious when they brought him in. I guess they're still back there working on him. You're a nurse, Rose, tell me the truth: Is he going to make it?"

"Baby, in a situation like this, no news is good news. It means that he's still with us, okay?"

Nina inhaled a jerky breath of air and said, "Okay."

An hour later, a black female physician called out Nina's name.

"Right here," Rose answered for Nina. She approached Nina.

"Mrs. Vincent?"

"That would be me," Nina answered as she held on to Nathan, who had fallen asleep in her arms.

"Hi, my name is Dr. Mary Douglas, I'm the cardiologist who's been looking after your husband. If you want, there is a private room over here." The doctor pointed. "We can talk in there"

"Hold him for me, John." John scooped Nathan up and out of Nina's arms and held on to him for her.

"Come with me, Rose." Nina clutched her girlfriend's arm for support as they followed the doctor to a private room. They all sat down at a small table, and the doctor began to speak.

"The good news, Mrs. Vincent, is that your husband did not have a heart attack as we originally thought when he came in." Nina exhaled a sigh of relief. "We've run some tests and his heart is in good shape."

"So what happened to him?" Nina asked.

"Your husband has been living with hypertension, which is a common trait among black men. Your husband's hypertension caused him to have a severe anxiety attack. It's not a heart attack, but it was close. Has he been under any heavy burden or stress?"

"No," Nina answered, "just the normal stress of running the dental practice but that's it."

"Well, running a practice is a monster all its own, especially if he is the only dentist treating patients. If the burden of the practice results in anxiety attacks like this one, he should consider hiring an associate to balance out his workload."

Nina nodded her head in agreement with what the Dr. Douglas was telling her. "As soon as he recovers, that will be one of the first things we do," Nina said. The doctor placed her hand on top of Nina's.

"He's going to recover from this attack just fine. However, I am concerned that he may not be so lucky the next time. Stress is a strange animal and can do harm in a variety of ways. When

Richard came in, his blood pressure was extremely high—it was 197 over 105."

"Oh, my god." Both Nina and Rose gasped.

"Normal blood pressure is around 125 over 80. Right now I have him on medication that has his pressure under control and he is resting comfortably. His blood pressure is back down to normal levels right now, but I'm going to monitor him for a day or two to see how he does."

"When can I see him?" asked Nina.

"They're taking him out of the emergency room and up to a private room right now. You should be able to see him in about twenty minutes or so. Once they have him in his room, I'll have the nurse let you go up to see him."

"Thank you," Nina said. Dr. Douglas gave her a comforting smile and then escorted both her and Rose back to the waiting room.

When Richard woke up the following morning, he was aware of the fact that he was in a hospital. The needles that were jabbed in the joint of his right arm and in his fingertip were annoying to him. He glanced around the room and saw Nina slumped down and asleep under a blanket in a chair next to the bed. He didn't want to wake her from her peaceful sleep; he knew that she more than likely needed to get as much rest as possible. He knew that Nina could drive herself crazy worrying about him.

Richard would not have been so concerned with what Charlene had on him if he'd at least been a dental student at the time—then he could have argued that his mother was instructing him—but the fact he wasn't in dental school left him without justification. Even if he fought and won the case against him, the legal expenses and public exposure would more than likely ruin him and his reputation. Richard was livid with himself for allowing Charlene to get to him the way she had. He couldn't bring himself to stop playing the tape that was running in his head. It was a tape that kept saying that he'd go to prison and lose everything, his freedom, his family, and his practice. He couldn't bring himself to think clearly and devise a plan for dealing with Charlene, who he knew was as scandalous and as treacherous as his ex-mother-in-law, Rubylee. Charlene just didn't care or give a damn about anyone except for herself, and Richard was wondering why she chose a health profession if she was so self-centered, *but then again,* Charlene more than likely became a dentist because of the high social status that health professionals carry in modern society, and for the financial wealth that dentists can achieve with a healthy and thriving practice. Now that Richard had calmed down, he could think with a clear head. He was glad he'd only told Charlene about one patient he'd worked on, or she'd blackmail him for the rest of his life. He wasn't about to lie down and allow Charlene to ruin him. *There is just no damn way in hell,* he said to himself. He'd come up with a plan to handle this. He'd bring Charlene on board for the time being as an associate. He'd have his attorney write up the contract and have a clause in the agreement that said he could terminate her at will with or without a reason. He'd also make sure that there was a noncompete clause in it so that when he released her, she would not be able to practice within fifty miles of him, and she would not be allowed to contact any of his patients of record. However, before he could fire her, he'd have to somehow get her to tell him where she kept that original file, so that she would no longer be able to use it against him. He would have to play dirty just like her, but it didn't matter—he was willing to do whatever it took to get that original file from her so that he could rescue and protect the privileged life that he'd built with Nina and his son.

Nina awoke from her sleep and caught Richard in deep thought. "Hey, baby, I didn't realize you were awake," Nina said to Richard as she got up and stood beside his bed. She put her hand in his and gave it a squeeze.

"Stop worrying," Richard said, attempting to ease her fears. "I'm not going anywhere."

"You better not," Nina said, kissing the back of his hand. "How do you feel?"

"Very mellow," Richard answered, trying to chuckle. "I see that they spared no expense when it came to providing me with the good stuff." Richard was referring to the medication he'd been given. "Where is Nathan?"

"I gave Rose the keys to the house and sent him home with her," Nina said.

"Good," replied Richard. "I don't want him to see me all wired up like this. I don't want him to get afraid. Does he know what happened?"

"No, I didn't tell him."

"Good." Richard nodded his head.

"The doctor says you're going to be just fine. They are going to keep you here for a day or so, she said."

"I need you to call Dr. Weaver for me, and ask him to cover my patients for me for two days. I'll pay him for his services. Give the staff two days off at full pay, but tell them to expect a full schedule when I return," Richard said as he began organizing his thoughts as to what he needed with regard to his practice.

"Baby, you need to get your rest." Richard noticed that Nina had that look of worry engraved on her face. "I'll be fine," Richard reassured her again.

"Dr. Douglas thinks that you should take on an associate, so you don't get stressed out again and have another setback. My nerves can't take you going through something like this again." At that moment, Richard recognized that he was at a crossroads in his marriage. He could either be forthcoming about taking on Charlene and their past, or just agree with her and hide the truth from her until he dealt with Charlene and got her out of his practice and their life.

"Yeah, you're right," Richard said. "I know someone who would be willing to start right away." Richard didn't offer any more information about the person he had in mind. *It is neces-*

sary, he thought. *Keeping the full truth hidden from Nina at this point is necessary. It's a necessary evil.* Richard felt bad about doing that because in his heart he knew that if Nina were faced with a similar situation, she'd tell him, but he wanted to handle this one on his own. For now, he didn't want to worry Nina with this problem. When Nina didn't probe more by asking whom he had in mind, Richard knew that Nina trusted his judgment fully and completely.

20

CHARLENE

Charlene knew that what she'd done was ugly and foul, but in her mind, she could see no other way out of her situation, or at least that was what she told herself so that she wouldn't feel any remorse. She had to work as a dentist but knew that, given her recent disciplinary action, no practitioner in his or her right mind would touch her. To make things as smooth and as easy as possible, if there was such a thing in an instance like this, Charlene agreed to every one of Richard's terms. She signed the associate agreement, she agreed that she wouldn't practice within fifty miles of his current practice when she left, and she agreed not to steal his patients when she finally moved on. Richard offered her an attractive salary, but made it very clear that he expected her to earn every penny of it.

"I don't have a problem with working for the pay, Richard," Charlene proclaimed when she was in his office on the day she was going to start. "In fact, I want to prove to you that I do good work."

"Yeah, I'll bet you do," Richard said with a bitterly cold winter chill in his tone. "I looked you up on the State Dental Board's website and saw the disciplinary action taken against you. Once I saw that, it became clear to me why you decided to come back into my life." Charlene was impressed that Richard had done his homework, but then again, she'd expected him to check out her background and she was prepared to deal with that aspect of their prickly business relationship.

"If I even think that you've mistreated or harmed one of my patients, I'm going to lodge a formal complaint against you, and that, my dear, would mean the end of your career as a dentist."

"You don't have to remind me of that, Richard, but I will say this: If I go down in flames, I'm not going alone. Remember, I still have that original file, tucked safely away at home, and I will not hesitate to use it."

"How long do you plan on remaining here, Charlene? How long do you think it will take for you to get your shit together and split?" Richard's heart was ice cold, and it was reflected in his body language.

"I'll only be here a few months, to a year Richard, and that's it." Richard huffed a breath of disdain, "Let me lay down a few ground rules, then."

"I don't follow rules very well, Richard. Clearly you know that by now."

"You will follow my rules in this practice," Richard answered her sternly. For some reason, which Charlene couldn't quite figure out, she found Richard's hard-nose approach toward her to be a bit of a turn-on. Even though she had him by the balls, she liked the fact that he was still letting her know that he was in control. She liked that in him.

"This business relationship is between you and me and no one else. You will not discuss our arrangement with anyone else on the staff."

"Including that lovely bride of yours?" Charlene was egging him on and she knew it, but it didn't matter to her; she was getting a twisted thrill out of it.

"Especially my wife. I'm paying you out of my personal account."

"Keeping secrets from her, are we?" Charlene smirked a bit. "That sounds like a strong and healthy marriage to me." Richard gave her a glare of disdain.

"You will be professional in this office at all times."

"I think I can handle that. So, where is my office, and when are you going to introduce me to the staff? I'm ready to work for you, Richard."

"Yeah, I'll bet you are."

"Don't be like that now." Charlene used a lighter, more understanding tone of voice. "You just never know, you may find it in your heart to forgive me for what I've done and keep me on board."

"Oh, that will never happen, so don't even get that notion in your head."

"Never say never, Richard, because life is full of surprises. You just never know what will happen further on down the road."

Charlene proved true to her word and took pride in the work and treatment that she was giving. She worked well with the hygienists and dental assistants and for the most part came into the office, did what she had to do, then went home. During the first eight weeks, Richard kept a keen eye on her every move. Charlene knew that he would but she didn't mind—he could watch her all he wanted to, but she wasn't about to do a thing that would place her back in front of the dental board.

By June of 2000, Charlene had been working for Richard for sixteen weeks and noticed that his business was booming. Richard had been blessed with a thriving practice and he even had a few well-known professional athletes as patients. During those sixteen weeks, Charlene and Nina had frequent contact and trivial conversations whenever they ran into each other in the break room. This usually happened in the morning when Charlene was getting her cup of coffee, and Nina was placing her bottled water and protein shakes in the office refrigerator. Charlene couldn't help sizing Nina up to her own standards whenever she saw her. Nina was a bit taller than she was, had shorter hair, which

Charlene noticed was professionally styled every four or five days. Nina was fit—in fact, fitter than she was—although Charlene didn't consider herself to be out of shape; she just needed to firm up some areas that she'd let get out of hand. It was obvious that Nina was going to great lengths to keep herself together. With a successful practice like the one Richard had, Charlene couldn't control her thoughts. Being around Richard and Nina gave her a clear view of the life that she would have had with him. Somehow, some way, deep in the back of her mind, envy and jealously were lurking about, pacing back and forth like two animals stalking their prey, trying to decide when and where to strike. It was annoying to Charlene that Nina had taken her damaged goods and turned Richard into a man she wanted back.

Instead of striking directly, Charlene decided she'd try to compete with Nina. After all, Richard wasn't being truthful with his lovely bride about their past relationship, and in Charlene's twisted thinking, that was a weak spot she had to exploit. So during one of her causal encounters with Nina in the break room, she struck up a more meaningful conversation. She was curious about how she and Richard met and if he'd ever mentioned a former girlfriend named Charlene during the days that they were courting, but she knew that she had to be tactful, because Nina didn't appear to be the type of sister who'd like it if she just came out and started asking about her man.

"How do you keep yourself in such fantastic shape?" Charlene was giving Nina a compliment while she poured her morning cup of coffee.

"Girl, it is not easy. I get up every morning at 5 A.M. religiously and go out to the coach house to hit my treadmill and the weight room." Charlene couldn't stop her eyes from blinking rapidly as she tried to process what Nina had just said.

"Excuse me, did you say 'coach house'?" Charlene needed clarification.

"Yes, the house that Richard and I live in has a coach house for servants, which I converted to a gym." Charlene couldn't help her thoughts as she began to add up in her mind how much a home with a detached coach house would run in this area. Charlene tried not to draw suspicion to herself.

"So what does a semi-in-shape woman like myself need to do to drop a few pounds?"

"Just the usual things," Nina said, opening up the refrigerator and putting a few cans of her protein shake inside. "Stuff that you probably already know."

Nina was being vague and Charlene wanted her to open up a bit more. "Stuff like what? I mean, can you be more specific? Like what do you do before you come to work?"

"Well, I hit the treadmill for about forty-five minutes to get my heart rate pumping. After that I usually pop in my sit-ups video and do that for thirty minutes and then I lift some light weights so that I keep my arms and thighs toned up."

"Oh, so you're really into the fitness thing, I see."

"Yeah, I am. I use to be an aerobics instructor, but I had to stop teaching class because I moved out here with Richard."

"Oh, I see," Charlene said. "I used to run but that was years ago when I was an undergraduate at Clark Atlanta University."

"You went to Clark Atlanta University?" Nina chirped with surprise. "What a small world, Richard went there as well." Charlene could see that Nina had not made the connection.

"Yes, it is a small world," Charlene answered, realizing that Richard had not mentioned her at all when he discussed what his life was like prior to meeting Nina, and for some reason, which Charlene couldn't fully understand, she took offense to that. She took offense to the fact that Richard didn't think she was significant enough in his life to mention.

Charlene tried hard not to ogle Nina as she began making comparisons and assumptions about her without any solid evidence. Soon Charlene's thoughts began to take on a life of their own. *Nina is probably a total bore in the sack. She's probably really stiff in the lovemaking department.* Charlene willed her assumptions to become the truth. She decided that her full succulent lips, larger breasts, juicy and plump rear end, and full and inviting hips were far superior to Nina's tall, slender but rigid frame. *Hell, a woman is supposed to feel soft to the touch, not hard like a damn rock. Richard must have forgotten how much he adored my luscious, soft, and succulent body.*

"How in the world do you work out and keep your hair so together?" Charlene asked to divert Nina's attention from her longer-than-necessary glare. She really didn't give a damn about Nina's hair, but felt that another compliment was due. "I mean, if it were me, I'd sweat out every curl in my head, until it was just a nappy ball of tangled-up hair," Charlene added.

"Honey, every five days I'm in the beauty shop. I've finally found a hair stylist who really knows what she's doing," Nina said ignoring the fact that Charlene was glaring at her so strangely. When she first saw Charlene come into the office, she got a bad vibe from her, but now Nina believed that she understood why she felt that oddly. Based on the way Charlene was studying her, Nina concluded that Charlene was a lesbian.

"Is she out this way?" Charlene asked, "I like a sister who really knows how to style hair."

"Yeah, she is. In fact, I have one of her cards back in my office. I'll grab it for you," Nina offered.

"Grab what?" Richard's voice boomed when he entered the break room.

"Putting a little bit of bass in your voice, Richard?" Charlene asked in a playful manner that Richard didn't find humorous.

"That's Dr. Vincent," Richard corrected her.

"We were only discussing girl stuff, Dr. Vincent," Charlene answered as she maneuvered past him while sipping on her cup of hot coffee. Richard cut his eyes at her as she left the room.

"Richard, why are you looking at her like that? I was only letting her know where I got my hair done."

Richard regained his composure. "Looking at her like what?" Richard asked playing dumb.

"You were looking at her like you wanted to beat her up or something."

"Was I really?" Richard was trying to deny the contemptuous way he was glaring at Charlene.

"Yes, really. Man, if looks could kill, that poor child would be lying in her grave right now."

Richard played down the seriousness of what Nina had seen by laughing it off.

"That's exactly why looks can't kill," Richard responded, trying not to show how much he distrusted Charlene. She had that cynical look in her eyes when she left the room, and Richard could tell that she was up to no good.

Richard switched the focus of their conversation by asking what the status of their trip to New Orleans was. Richard and Nina were flying down for a dental convention and planned to stay there a few extra days to unwind and enjoy the city's nightlife, Southern culture, and each other.

"I'm glad you asked," Nina said, resting her behind against the gray marble countertop. "I've booked the airfare, and I've also taken care of our hotel reservation and your convention registration."

"Great." Richard relaxed a bit because the thought of getting away appealed to him.

"Rose said that she'd watch Nathan for us and I figured that Charlene could handle the patient load for the few days we'll be out of town." Nina instantly noticed that Richard's body language changed. He rotated his neck as if he suddenly had a cramp in it.

"Are you letting that stress level build up again?" Nina asked. "Turn around and let me rub your shoulders." Richard turned and Nina placed her hands on his shoulders and began rubbing them.

"Richard, sweetie, you are way too tense."

"I know," he answered as he shut his eyes for a moment. "I don't want Charlene in charge of the practice while we're gone," Richard said, rotating his neck. "I've already spoken to Dr. Weaver about covering any emergency patients for me and I'll have Gracie reschedule everyone else."

"Baby, wouldn't it be easier for Charlene to handle it?"

Richard suddenly found Nina's questioning of his decision to be threatening, and before he could stop himself, he jerked away, spun around to face her, and snapped at her. "That's the way it's going to be, all right!"

Nina could see the electricity in Richard's eyes, but she couldn't figure out why he had suddenly barked at her.

"Don't use that tone of voice with me, okay?" Nina didn't approve of Richard raising his voice at her.

Richard caught himself and lowered his voice. "Look, I'm sorry I yelled at you." He caressed the side of her face with his hand. "We will give Dr. Hayward a few days off while we are gone, okay?" Richard placed his hands on Nina's shoulders, but she could still see fire and rage in his eyes. It was as if his eyes were screaming out in pain or for help, but she couldn't determine which it was.

"Baby, what is going on? Talk to me, I'm worried about you." Nina locked her fingers around Richard's wrists. Richard was once again at the crossroads of deceit. He wanted to disclose the situation to Nina, but he just couldn't bring himself to do it, at least not yet. He needed to get that damn file but he didn't know how to do it. That was something he was still working on. During the weeks that Charlene had been working for him, he'd been more concerned about her harming one of his patients than he was with the file, but now getting that file would have to become a priority because it was causing him to behave erratically and Nina was noticing it.

"Nothing is wrong, baby," Richard answered her. "I'm just a bit wound up. My last patient was a bit difficult to deal with, that's all." Richard felt like a jackass for lying to his baby.

When Charlene left Richard and Nina in the break room, she walked up to the front of the dental office to pick up the next patient's chart. She glanced out into the waiting room and noticed how full it was. And how Richard had gone to great lengths to make sure that all his patients were entertained while they waited. The wall-mounted flat-screen television was play-ing *The Best of Saturday Night Live* and Eddie Murphy was doing his impression of James Brown trying to get inside the hot tub. Everyone in the waiting room was smiling and laughing as if they were sitting at home in their living room instead of in a dental office waiting to get their mouth drilled in. At that mo-ment, Charlene instantaneously caught an ugly attitude fueled by her envy. She was once again staring right in the face the life that she could have had with Richard. She and Richard could have had a healthy growing dental practice, wealth, respect, and social status. Charlene twisted things around in her mind and began analyzing Nina and Richard's relationship. She al-ready knew that Richard was deceiving his wife, and if there was deception within their relationship, she could use it to her advantage to get Nina to question his loyalty and commitment to her. If she played her cards just right, she'd get Nina to leave him and conveniently take her place. If she had Richard's nose open once before, she didn't see why she couldn't open it up again. Besides, it had been so long since anyone had stroked her kitty cat and she needed to be broke off. All she had to do was compete with Nina and offer Richard something that Nina wouldn't or couldn't. Charlene was poised to use the power of temptation to get what she wanted.

She walked back to Patient Room 4 with the file she needed. As she approached the room, she glanced in the break room and noticed that Nina was massaging Richard's shoulders. By her estimations, Nina didn't know what the hell she was doing because Richard's face had a sour look on it. When Charlene saw that, ideas began coming to her. She'd have to be critical of Nina and somehow get Richard to confide in her. She'd have to change her attitude and make Richard recall just how good they were together and make him desire and lust after her once again. If she could do that, she'd be able to work his lovely bride out of the picture. Beside, *I had him first,* Charlene thought to herself. Charlene walked into the room to see her patient, who was getting her blood pressure taken by the dental assistant, because the patient had a heart condition, and the patient's physician recommended getting a blood pressure reading prior to each procedure.

"Good afternoon," she said to her patient, who returned the greeting. Charlene searched her lab coat for a pen but couldn't find one. She excused herself and wandered into Nina's office for another one. She looked around on Nina's desk and noticed the airline confirmation page for a trip to New Orleans the following month. She hurriedly opened up Nina's desk drawer in search of something to write with when she ran across the red PAID ink stamp and the black ink stamp with the name GREAT SMILES DENTAL CLINIC. Charlene's mind began clicking rapidly as she came up with a plan that would work to her benefit.

"Yes," she said, holding the red ink stamps and speaking softly as a menacing grin etched itself on her face. "If I approach my scheme that way, I'll come out on top no matter what."

Nina left the break room irritated by the fact that Richard wouldn't open up to her and tell her what was wrong. Although he said that everything was just fine, her intuition told her something altogether different. As she walked down the corridor, she saw that Richard's office door was open. That was strange because he always locked his office door when he wasn't in there and she knew that she'd just left Richard in the break room. She approached Richard's office, looked inside, and found Gracie in there taking something out of Richard's lab coat pocket, which was draped on the back of his office chair, and placing it in her own.

"What are you doing in here, Gracie?"

"Oh!" Gracie gasped for air as she placed her hand over her heart. "Mom, you scared me half to death." Gracie walked from behind Richard's desk and over to her. "I was searching for a key to the supply room. I thought that Richard might have had it in his lab coat. I just saw him go in with a patient and didn't want to bother him."

"I thought you kept the keys up in front by you." Nina was suspicious of Gracie.

"Uhm, yeah." Gracie was hesitating and repeating her words. Right then and there, Nina knew that Gracie was about to lie to her about something. "Uhm, yeah, I gave the keys to him for something and I think he just forgot to give them back." Gracie walked past Nina and rushed back up front. Nina walked over to the chair with the lab coat and reached into Richard's pocket but the only thing she found was a stack of blank prescription pads. Nina stood there with her eyebrows pinched together trying to figure out why Gracie had just lied to her. She knew that Gracie had to have the door keys to get into Richard's office.

"Gracie, what are you up to?" Nina mumbled to herself.

During the middle of the night, Richard woke Nina up from her sleep by playing with her womanhood. She really wasn't in the mood to make love to Richard but she consented to his advances because she knew that he had a way of taking his time to get her in the right frame of mind. But for the first time, Richard didn't take his time with her. He rushed their lovemaking and did it to her hard and rough. She didn't mind hard and rough but she had to be in the mood for that. Richard quickly got his release without letting her get hers and rolled off her. Nina couldn't believe that Richard had made selfish love to her like that but decided to let it go because she knew that he was wound up about something. She decided that she'd cuddle up next to him to see if she could at least get him to talk about it, because the last thing she wanted him to do was have another one of those anxiety attacks. Before she could even snuggle up to him, Richard got out of bed and headed toward the bathroom.

"Where are you going and what in the hell was that you just did to me?" Nina was now even more irritated as she sat up in the bed.

"I'm sorry," Richard responded as he continued on to the bathroom. "Give me a few minutes. I'll be back." Nina flopped back down on the bed exhaling her frustration away. Nina now felt both mistreated and used as she tried to understand why and how her perfect world was beginning to crumble apart.

21

RICHARD

Richard sat in his office considering what his problems might look like from Nina's point of view. He feared that if she discovered what was really going on, not only would she question the trust and communication of their relationship, but she'd also probably think that to some degree he was a weak man, and he just couldn't allow that misperception.

"You need to really handle this, Richard!" he scolded himself and reinforced the need to take care of his business.

Richard also wanted to let Nina know that what happened the prior evening would not happen when they traveled to New Orleans for the dental convention. He needed to tell her that right away.

Richard stood up from his office chair and was about to walk next door into Nina's office to talk about it, but his dental assistant peeked her head into his office and told him that his first patient of the day was ready and waiting for him.

"Okay, I'll be right there," Richard answered as he walked out of his office and over to Nina's but she wasn't there.

"*Damn!*" Richard hissed. Now he'd have to wait until he

was done with his patient. He was kicking himself in the ass for not even coming back into the bedroom last night. He'd gone into the family room and slept on the sofa because he was wound up.

Nina was irritated, frustrated, and aggravated because Gracie left her a voice mail message claiming that she was feeling achy and had a bad headache. When Nina called her back at home, Gracie didn't answer the phone. Nina had half a mind to take a trip over there but she didn't want to leave the front area unattended since she would have to take up the slack for Gracie. She concentrated her thoughts on Gracie and the health problems she was having. Nina couldn't determine if her daughter's claims were real or imagined, although in the back of her mind, she believed that they were more imagined than real.

After forwarding the phone in the reception area to voice mail for a moment, Nina went down the hall to the employee break room to get one of her protein shakes from the refrigerator. As she approached the lounge, she heard loud laughter coming from the break room. When she entered, she found Charlene gossiping with Samantha, who was the dental assistant that worked with her. As soon as the two women acknowledged her presence in the room, they stopped laughing.

"What's so funny?" Nina asked. "I could really use a good laugh right now."

Charlene felt catty and feisty when she saw Nina. Charlene's envy oftentimes guided her actions with the precision of a military missile. She found Nina's unexpected intrusion to be annoying and decided to make her pay for it. Besides, in her mind, it was high time she started firing artillery at Nina. She wanted to exploit the deception that Nina didn't realize was going on in her marriage so that she could benefit from it. In fact, now that Charlene thought about it, she was glad that Nina had interrupted her and Samantha because their conversation, which was causing all of the laughter, was a sexual one. It was a sexual conversation that Charlene knew would slice at the fabric of Nina's perfect world.

"You really don't want to know what we were talking about," Charlene chimed.

"Yes I do, please tell me," Nina said. "I could really use a good distraction right about now." Charlene grinned like a cartoon character about to pull a foul prank. Nina fell directly into her trap. Charlene was going to take great pleasure in surveying the damage she was about to do.

"Are you sure?" Charlene asked once again just for effect.

"Yes, I'm sure." Nina smiled, not knowing that Charlene had just launched a missile at her.

"Well, we were sitting here talking about men who eat pussy really well." Charlene got a charge out of watching Nina's jolly smile fall and shatter on the floor before her. Charlene had already pegged Nina for the stiff type of woman who would never refer to her pleasure pot in public by its slang name. Before Nina had a chance to back out of the conversation, Charlene continued on.

"I was telling her that I had trained my college boyfriend and ex-fiancé on the fine art of eating pussy. He was so eager to learn about all of the secrets and mysteries of my pussy. Once I trained him, he took to pussy eating like a fish to water. In fact, he enjoyed tasting my pussy so much, that he talked to it like it was a real person. He would ask my pussy if she came around often, and then he'd tell my pussy that he liked her haircut and he'd also ask my pussy if he could French Kiss her."

Charlene noticed that Nina's eyes suddenly began darting from right to left and she began to blink so rapidly, that Charlene swore that she saw dust flying up from the floor. Charlene knew right then that Richard hadn't changed in that department and Nina was processing what she'd just heard.

"What was your man's name?" Nina felt her blood starting to boil now that she realized that Charlene wasn't a lesbian.

"I think his name was either Ralph, Ray, Richard, or Roy. I

can't remember exactly. We had a very bad breakup and when I left, I tried to ease all of the bad memories out of my mind."

"Well, it's a damn shame you didn't marry him." Nina took a verbal swing at Charlene.

"Yeah, it is a shame, but perhaps I'll find him again and snatch him up, if he isn't already taken, of course." Nina felt a sudden urge to give Charlene a smack-down for toying with her.

"Ooooh," said Samantha, who sensed that the conversation had taken a turn for the worse. "On that note, I think I'll get back to work."

Nina found out what patient room Richard was in and interrupted him in the middle of a procedure.

"When you're finished, I need to see you in my office right away, okay," Nina was curt and to the point. Richard noticed the strange look on her face and the anger in her voice.

"Yeah, okay," Richard answered Nina and went back to his patient. As soon as he was done, he went into Nina's office and shut the door. He wanted to talk with her as well.

"Hey, babes, what's going on," Richard said with a pleasant tone as the door clicked shut. Nina was about to completely unload on Richard about exactly who Charlene was when the heifer had the nerve to knock twice on the door and enter before she was even invited in.

"Excuse me, Dr. Vincent, may I see you down in the radiology lab. I would like to get your opinion on a patient's x-ray."

"Can it wait a moment?" Richard wanted to speak with Nina first before he got busy again.

"Well, I'd really appreciate it if you came down now. I don't want to harm a patient." Charlene smiled innocently like a schoolgirl using her charm in order to get her way. The word "harm" caught Richard's attention.

"Go on, Richard." Nina huffed. "Take care of the patient. We can discuss what's on my mind once we get home." Nina cut her eyes at Charlene. Richard left the room to head down to the radiology lab, and Charlene was about to follow behind him. But before she left, she caught Nina's gaze.

"Tony was his name, Nina," Charlene said.

"Excuse me?" Nina was clearly irritated and Charlene knew that she was the reason for it. It was all too easy for her to ruffle Nina's feathers.

"Tony was my ex-fiancé's name, I just remembered. I hope that I didn't give you the impression that Richard was the man I was speaking of," Charlene lied without even flinching.

"There is no need for us to carry on this conversation Dr. Hayward." Nina wasn't about to fall into this wench's trap again, and at the moment she was on the edge of beating her ass for attempting to fuck up her good relationship with her husband. Nina had worked too damn hard to find a man who loved her like Richard did.

"I don't mean any harm," Charlene said, still playing the innocent role. "I hope I didn't cause any conflict."

"Isn't there a patient waiting for you, Dr. Hayward?" Nina was fuming and wanted Charlene to get out of her face with the bag of bullshit she was trying to sell her.

"Of course," Charlene said and shut the door behind her with a sinister grin plastered on her face.

Richard stood in the dark radiology room looking at the x-rays that were on the illuminated screen. When Charlene walked into the room, she shut the door behind her for privacy.

"You know, Richard," Charlene exhaled softly, "we don't have to be such enemies." Charlene wanted to work her way onto Richard's good side.

"What are we supposed to be, Charlene?" Richard didn't take his eyes off the x-rays.

"I would like us to be really close friends again," Charlene said, "if that is possible."

Richard turned to look at her. "Good friends don't do what you've done to me."

Charlene wasn't the least bit ashamed of how she'd forced her way into Richard's life or the odd position her presence put him in. "You're right, Richard, and as soon as I get on my feet, I will bring the original dental records from my apartment and give them to you, I promise." Charlene stepped closer to Richard and purposely entered his social space. Richard decided that he would try to use the moment to his advantage. If Charlene wanted to be friendly, he'd play along with her long enough to get the damn dental records from her, then he'd get rid of her quick, fast, and in a hurry.

"It would be so nice if you'd pull yourself away from that lovely bride of yours, and have a drink for old time's sake with me sometime."

"That would be nice," Richard answered, which delighted the hell out of Charlene because it was a sure indication to her that Richard wasn't all that happy with that rigid muscle woman he called a wife. "When I come back from New Orleans, we should spend some time together. I think I could sneak out for a few hours and talk about the old times." Charlene raised her eyes and gazed at Richard with longing. A twinge of excitement was making her kitty cat purr; the thrill of being caught was a bit of a turn-on. She wanted to make sure that Richard didn't misread her body language. She placed her hand on Richard's chest, found his nipple, and twirled her finger around it. She was glad to see that he didn't remove it or stop her.

"I'd like that a lot," Charlene said and let her fingers walk up his chest to the base of his neck. "I really want to be your friend, Richard. You can talk to me about anything that is on your mind." Charlene needed Richard to open up to her about his relationship with Nina so that she could cut her down every chance she got. She needed to find a tender spot in their relationship and exploit it.

Richard knew that he was walking a very thin line, and if Nina saw what was going on in the radiology room, that would be it. There would be no explaining what she saw going on between him and Charlene. The site of Charlene rubbing his chest would have broken her heart and enraged her at the same time. Nina would have felt deceived and betrayed, and that was not what he wanted. All he wanted was to get the file back in his hands, fire Charlene, and bring his life back into some type of order. Richard finally turned his full attention to the x-ray and Charlene stood beside him.

"We work so well together, Richard," she said, feeling as if things were going just the way she wanted them to. "You and I make an awesome team. We could be just like your mother and father were. Two doctors with a successful practice and a handsome son." Charlene had just said more than she'd wanted to but she couldn't help feeling the way she did at that moment. Richard was a successful black doctor and she wanted to be in his life, she wanted to be at his side, and she was willing to do what it took to make that happen.

"Yes," Richard agreed. "You and I would be like my mother and father were." Richard's words went straight to Charlene's head. She was so happy he didn't damn her for rubbing his chest, or for feeling the way she did. In her mind, Nina's days were numbered, because she had every intention of making Richard her man once again.

22

NINA

"Excuse me, Charlene." Nina caught Charlene as she was exiting the bathroom. "Do you have minute? I need to see you in my office." Nina's tone was direct and hard like granite.

"Does it have to be right now?" Charlene didn't appreciate the fact that Nina was trying to exert some type of authority over her.

"Yes, it does." Nina didn't care for her insubordinate behavior. Charlene followed Nina into her office and Nina gently shut the door behind her.

"Have a seat," Nina instructed and Charlene went to a chair at the conference table on the other side of the room.

"No, here, in front of my desk, where I can see you." Nina pointed to the seat. Charlene huffed a bit as she got up from her chair and sat in front of Nina's desk.

"At the end of the day, today, you need to give me the keys to the office."

Charlene instantly got defensive. "What for?" She pinched her eyebrows and got sharp with Nina.

Nina wasn't the least bit intimidated by the pudgy woman's

predilection. "You will not be seeing any patients while Dr. Vincent and I are away on vacation." Nina rolled her neck at her like she was itching for Charlene to do something that would justify an all-out confrontation with her. Now, she was happy that Richard had instructed her to get the keys from this jezebel. "Arrangements for emergency care have been made with another dentist."

"Does Richard know about this?" Charlene questioned Nina's authority and Nina was quick to notice it.

"Excuse me!" Nina's eyes were full of fire and Charlene decided to back down for the time being.

"What I'm trying to ask is, did Dr. Vincent approve this?"

"It doesn't matter who approved it, Dr. Hayward, the fact is, at the end of the day I expect you to hand me your keys until we return." Charlene took offense at being chastised by this he-woman.

"You know what?" Charlene now had an edge to her voice. "I'll make sure they are on your desk at the end of the day. How's that?" Charlene wanted to get into an argument with Nina so that she could tell her all about her past relationship with Richard. But she didn't, because she had a much bigger plan in the works.

"Thank you, that will be all, you may leave my presence," Nina said, abruptly ending their conversation and dismissing Charlene from her office. Charlene was insulted by the fact that Nina gave her permission to leave her presence like she was a damn queen or something.

Charlene left Nina's office and went into the break room. She was fuming over what Nina had just told her.

"Richard probably didn't approve of my not having access to the office while they're out of town," she mumbled to herself as she poured herself a fresh cup of coffee. "I'll bet she's carrying a grudge about the break room conversation we had a while back. Yeah, I'll bet that's what this is all about." Charlene plopped down at the break table and began thinking. The more she thought about how Nina had stepped to her, the more Charlene wanted to show Nina that she was not the one to threaten.

"Miss Nina," Charlene mumbled as she took a sip of her hot coffee. "You're not good enough for Richard and he is not happy with you. Why else would he offer to sneak away from you in order to be with me?" Charlene was about to play foul, because she didn't want Nina to go down to New Orleans with Richard; she just couldn't allow that. She needed to move quickly and swiftly in order to do what she needed to do since the two of them would be leaving for New Orleans in the morning.

Charlene kept an eye on Nina, and when Nina stepped out of her office, Charlene quickly darted inside with her coffee. She flipped the power strip, which was on the floor, to the off position. She tilted Nina's computer tower forward so that she could see the back of it. She then poured her coffee into the vent holes in the back of the computer.

"That should do it." She grinned and quickly fled the office. As Charlene walked out, she ran into Gracie, who was coming out of Richard's office. The papers that she was carrying fell out on to the floor.

"Excuse me, I am so sorry," Charlene said and quickly bent down to pick up the papers that she'd knocked out of Gracie's hands.

"No, I'll pick them up." Gracie quickly got down on her knees to pick up the papers but it was too late. Charlene had already noticed that Gracie had one of Richard's prescription pads hidden in her stack of papers. She studied Gracie, who refused to look her in the eyes. Gracie quickly stood up with her papers and walked away without saying anything more.

Nina was sitting at Gracie's desk checking the appointment book to see how many more patients Richard had to see. She wanted to talk with him about Charlene. She wanted to know what kind of bitch Richard had allowed to come into their life and why. She wanted to know why Charlene tried to treat her like she was insignificant.

"What are you doing at my desk?" asked Gracie, who seemed to be edgy and aggravated.

"What's wrong with you?" Nina didn't like the tone of voice that Gracie was addressing her with. Gracie huffed and plopped the papers she was carrying on her desk. The papers tipped over and once again fell to the floor. Nina reached down to pick them up and noticed the prescription blanks.

"Gracie, what are you doing with these?" Nina was extremely suspicious of her daughter now.

"Oh, uhm, yeah, I picked up some papers on Richard's desk and those must have been inside the stack." Gracie's paused and then repeated herself, and Nina knew that she was lying to her again.

"Gracie, when I get back from New Orleans, you and I are going to have a talk."

"Uhm, okay, yeah, that's cool. No problem." Gracie seemed wired and wound up to Nina as she got up to leave and head back to her office. Nina's thoughts were now focused on Gracie and what she was up to as she sat down at her computer to do the monthly payouts and payroll. She noticed that her computer screen was blank so she hit the on button. When nothing happened, she became puzzled.

"Now what's wrong?" Nina said out loud. She looked down at the computer tower and noticed that it wasn't on either. She hit the power button but nothing happened.

"What in the world?" Nina became nervous because she feared that her computer had crashed. She glanced over at the power strip and saw that it was off. She flipped the switch to the on position and then pressed the power button on the computer tower. The system started to come alive and Nina felt a bit of relief. As she typed in her password, a burning smell filled the air around her. She quickly began looking around and then noticed smoke billowing up from under her desk where her computer tower was.

"Oh my god!" she hollered out as she saw red sparks leaping in the air. She quickly ran out of the office and into the hallway, where the fire extinguisher was mounted on the wall. She broke the thin glass, pulled it out, and ran back to her office. The computer now had flames leaping out of it. Nina pulled the pin, hosed down her computer, and extinguished the fire. Once she was sure that it was safe, she hit the power strip and cut off the electricity to the computer. At that very moment Richard rushed into the room.

"Baby, what happened?" Richard quickly checked to see if she was okay, "You're not hurt, are you?"

"No, I'm fine," Nina said with a look of bewilderment on her face. "Why did my computer suddenly catch fire like that?"

"I don't know," Richard replied. A few moments later Gracie came into the room. "I smell something burning," she said and then noticed the melted computer.

"What happened to your computer?"

"It looks like some kind of electrical fire." Richard said, "Maybe the computer got too hot."

"But the computer was off, Richard. I had just turned it on."

"Yeah, that is odd. Let's send it out to the repair shop and see what they say the problem was."

"Richard, baby, right now that is the least of my concerns."

"What do you mean?"

"Everything was on the hard drive of that computer. Payroll, purchase orders, billing, everything! And I don't have it all backed up!" Nina felt a colossal migraine building up in her head. She put her hand on her forehead as stress began to blanket her face.

"Shit!" she hissed, then began pacing the floor and running her fingers through her hair. Stress was now making its deep etches.

"Damn near everything is due to be paid today." Nina

quickly began thinking of a way to resolve the predicament she was in. She could delay some of the vendors but not all of them.

"Richard, let me use the computer in your office," Nina said, and before he could respond, she left the room and marched over to his office.

"Well, I'm going back up front," said Gracie. Richard nodded his head and acknowledged that she was leaving. He then went into his office to join Nina.

"Baby, we can take care of this when we get back from New Orleans," Richard said.

"New Orleans?" Nina had momentarily forgotten about her vacation with Richard. "Baby, I can't go to New Orleans and leave all of the billing like this. My mind would be stuck here at the office."

"Well, then I won't go. I'll stay here with you."

"No," Nina said as she logged on to his system, "you should go. Just come right back after the convention."

"Baby, I don't want to go if you're not with me."

"That's sweet, baby, and I appreciate your willingness to stay. But go; you should go. Hopefully by the time you return, I'll have this all fixed," Nina said and went back to the business of logging on to his PC. "I can't believe I didn't have my files backed up." Nina glared at the computer screen like a zombie. "I knew I should have backed up the files, damn!"

Richard walked out into the hall and bumped into Charlene.

"Is everything okay?" she asked.

"Yeah, Nina's computer just went haywire," Richard explained.

"Well, I hope she had everything backed up," Charlene said. "A good office manager should always have her files and systems backed up. It's stupid not to have some type of backup."

"Yeah, she didn't though," Richard answered.

"Ouch, bad move on her part." Charlene was being openly judgmental. "I'm sure that after this, she'll take steps to ensure it doesn't happen again. Hopefully, she's not causing you and your practice to lose money." Charlene was driving a pitchfork through Nina's credibility.

"I'm not even worried about that," Richard said.

"What are you worried about then, Richard?" she asked. "Remember how I told you that I wanted us to be friends."

"Yeah." Richard looked at her funny.

"Well, I'm all ears. Tell me what's on your mind. I know that you're angry with her for screwing up like this."

"No, I'm not," Richard answered.

"Are you sure? I mean, if this were my practice and my office manager didn't have things backed up, I'd fire her." Charlene was taking a hard line.

"Nina is good at what she does. If I know her, by the time I return from New Orleans, she'll have things up and running again."

"So, you're going to New Orleans alone?" asked Charlene, trying hard not to smile.

"Yeah, it looks that way."

Charlene damn near wanted to jump up and down when Richard told her that. Crashing Nina's computer had had the desired effect.

"Well, I hope you're still going to give me a few days off." Charlene smiled because she was going to fly to New Orleans so that she could be with Richard, alone. She was going to have him, and temptation was going to be the weapon she would use to have her way with him. She planned to bring a digital camera with her so that she could take pictures of Richard enjoying the taste of her pussy. Once she had the photos, it wouldn't be hard to get that lovely bride of his to leave him.

"Yes, take the days off, Charlene," Richard said.

"Well, I plan to take off more than that," she mumbled under her breath.

Later that evening when Charlene was in her bedroom packing for her trip to New Orleans, she checked her phone messages and listened to one she got from her mother, Dean.

"Hey, Charlene, this is your mother calling. Uhm, I did

something, something that I wish I hadn't, but I did it for you. When you have a moment, give me a call. Okay, bye."

"Whatever, Mom." Charlene didn't give a damn about Dean at that moment because she had bigger things to deal with. She was about to set a scandalous trap for Richard.

23

RICHARD

When Richard arrived in New Orleans, he took a taxi over to the Le Pavilion Hotel, which was on Causeway Boulevard. He checked into his hotel room, plopped down on the bed, picked up the phone, and called Nina to let her know that he'd arrived safely.

"How are things going there?" Richard inquired.

"They're moving along," Nina said. "I was able to get the payroll done, and tomorrow I'm going to the bank to get hard copies of our deposit slips so I can check their records against my own hard copies. Everything will be back to normal once you return, I promise." Richard smiled.

"I know it will baby," he said.

"Richard, honey, I'm sorry that I messed up our vacation, but I just couldn't leave knowing that this wasn't taken care of."

"Don't stress yourself over this," Richard said. "There will be another time."

"How is your hotel room?" Nina asked.

"The hotel is really nice," Richard said. " I'm just down the street from the mall and the football stadium."

"Well, don't forget to bring Nathan and me something back."

"I won't. How is Nathan doing anyway?"

"He's fine. He's in his room playing with his toys. Do you want to talk to him?"

"No, that's okay, I'll call him back before bedtime. Right now I just want to get something to eat and relax."

"Well, you just hurry up and get back here, okay? There's something I need to talk to you about."

"What is it?"

"It can wait, baby. Just hurry up and get back to me."

"All right, " Richard replied and was about to say good-bye when Nina said, "Richard?" She paused then continued, "I know that on this trip you were planning to have me fill one of your sexual fantasies. I'm sorry I'm not there."

"It's okay, baby. Like I said, there will be other times."

"Well, just so that you're not lonely out there, I'm going to call you at 10 P.M. every night so that we can have phone sex."

Richard burst open laughing. "Phone sex?" Then he thought for a moment. "Okay, that sounds like it might be fun."

"Don't worry, I plan to make it fun. Just make sure that you have your ass in that room when I call. Also, check your suitcase. I placed a special care package in there for you when you weren't looking."

"Care package?" Richard walked over to the closet and pulled out his suitcase. He laid it flat and opened it up.

"Do you see what I've packed for you?"

"What's in this plastic bag?" Richard asked as he tried to untie the knot.

"Just a few little reminders to help keep your mind focused on me."

"Listen to you, sounding all bad and stuff." Richard was tickled by Nina's display of jealousy.

"Just make sure that you're there when I call, do you hear me?"

"Yes, baby, I hear you. I'll be here," Richard said and then hung up the phone as he struggled to release the knot she'd tied in the plastic bag.

That evening at 10:00 P.M. Richard was lying on the hotel bed watching Old School Videos on BET when the phone rang.

"What are you in there doing?" Nina asked without saying hello because she could hear noise in the background.

"Nothing, baby, I just got out of the shower and I'm lying here on the bed with a white towel wrapped around my waist."

"What is that noise I hear?"

"Oh, that's just BET. I'm watching videos," Richard answered, then picked up the remote, aimed it at the television, and pressed the red off button.

"Did you open my care package?" Nina asked, adding a hint of sexiness to her voice.

"Yes," Richard answered, "you are a mess. I can't believe you did that."

"I have to make sure that my man has me on his mind at all times." Nina's tone was direct.

"Well, this will certainly help. I've already changed the pillowcase and put the pillow in the case that you sent. I like the way you sprayed the pillowcase with your perfume. But why did you send me one of your thongs?" Richard said, holding it in his hand. He thought that Nina had perhaps placed it in his suitcase by accident.

"So that you can sniff the scent of my sweet paradise while we are having phone sex." Richard couldn't help but smile at the extra effort Nina had taken to make sure that he missed her.

"Now, put my thong up to your nose and inhale deeply," Nina said more as an order than a request. "My thong is going to be your oxygen mask. I want you to get high off the scent of my pussy."

"Damn, baby," Richard breathed. "I feel myself getting a buzz already."

"Now, I want you to close your eyes, and imagine that you have me soaking wet. Imagine me lining your lips with my love juice. It's time for 'Barn Love' baby."

"Aw shit! " Richard said as he allowed his fingers to creep under the towel toward his manhood. "You have me hard already."

"Damn right I do," Nina responded. "In a moment I'm going to be sucking your ass bone dry."

"Well, suck on, sister. Suck on."

Richard didn't have a chance to look around New Orleans until the last night he was there, because after spending a full day at the convention center, he'd just come back to his hotel room and get some rest. But now it was early Tuesday evening and he decided that he'd hit Bourbon Street to see what it was like. Richard was surprised to find that Bourbon Street was jam-packed with partygoers on a Tuesday night. He was also surprised to discover an untamed, wicked pulse of sexual energy flowing through the street like a river to the sea. It was easy to get washed away by it. As he walked down the popular street, he came across clusters of men gazing up at balconies urging women to flash their breasts at them in exchange for colored beads. Richard found that to be rather fascinating. What was even more bizarre was that women had men expose their manhood for beads as well. When a woman from a balcony pointed to him, Richard laughed.

"Show me your beef, baby," a young white girl pleaded with him. Richard laughed and shook his head no, then continued on up the crowded street.

Charlene's hotel was in the heart of the French Quarter and on Bourbon Street. She was standing on the balcony of her hotel room, urging men to show her some beef, when she saw Richard wandering down the street.

"It's about damn time that I ran into you, Richard," she said as she headed down to the street to surprise him.

Richard saw a sex toy shop and decided to take a peek inside to see if he could find something interesting for him and Nina to play with. There seemed to be a pleasure toy to fit every taste but what he found humorous were the outrageous costumes. A large, floppy orange tiger-stripped hat with matching pants, shirt, and boots intrigued Richard. If he got the outfit, he'd look like a pimp who'd escaped from a paint factory. He laughed to himself as he thought about the kinky kind of fun that he and Nina could have with the costume. He wondered what Nina would do if he called her into the bedroom and he was wearing a pimp daddy outfit such as this one. They'd probably laugh the entire time they made love.

"I never thought you were the type of man who liked the color orange."

"I'm just looking," Richard replied as he continued his inspection and moved on to the leather clothes.

"Yes, I'm more of a leather woman myself." Richard caught the voice this time. He quickly spun around and looked at Charlene.

"What are you doing down here?" he asked.

"I received an invitation to the convention as well," Charlene smiled. "And since you and your lovely bride said that I wouldn't be responsible for seeing patients in the practice, I figured I'd use the extra time and come on down here."

Charlene strolled to the other side of the room, where the sex toys were displayed on the wall. Richard noticed her erect chocolate nipples through her sheer white blouse. He could tell that she wasn't wearing a bra. He noticed how her skin-tight blue jean shorts looked as if they had been sprayed on her body. He also paid attention to how she slung her round, plump, and mouth-watering ass around the room like a magic wand. Richard tried hard not to stare at her, but he couldn't get himself to stop looking. Something about the sight of a black woman's behind mesmerized him. The power of the booty was as potent as a narcotic. Charlene was also wearing a pair of cutout thong strap boots, with a generous heel that made her appear like a much taller woman, like an exotic Amazon Woman. The boots most certainly said, *Come get this choochie.*

"I like this one." Charlene sashayed over to Richard with a

chocolate vibrating dildo in her possession. "If I remember correctly, it looks just like yours. It curves a bit to the right." Charlene stuck her tongue between her teeth, bit down on it, and looked at Richard with a wicked innocence. Richard read the lust and passion in her eyes and didn't want to get hypnotized by it. He looked at his watch, which said seven-thirty. It would be another two and a half hours before Nina phoned his room.

Charlene studied Richard, whose reckless staring at her was adding more fuel to the heat between her legs. She felt her thong panties getting wet with unbridled lust and desire. Getting away from it all had a way of making her come alive sexually, and right now, she was hot enough to make hell feel like the Antarctic.

"You know, Richard, what happens here in New Orleans can stay here in New Orleans." Charlene tossed her offer out to Richard to see if she could lure him into the web of sin that she was weaving.

Richard tried not to listen to the lust that had surfaced within him. But lust was a powerful emotion, and if he couldn't contain it, he knew that he'd regret it.

"Well, I hope that you find something to keep down here," Richard said. "Have a good night, Charlene." Richard turned and walked back out onto the crowded street.

"Wait a minute," Charlene called after him, "Richard!" He stopped on the sidewalk and turned to face her.

"Look, can we just sit down and have a drink?" Richard rolled his eyes at Charlene, turned, and walked away again. Charlene had to think quickly because she couldn't allow Richard to get away from her.

"Richard," she said as she caught up to him, "if you have a drink with me tonight, I promise that I will give you the dental file as soon as we get back," Charlene was lying, but it had the effect that she wanted it to. "We can go right in here." Charlene pointed to the door of one of the many clubs on the strip. "We'll just sit and talk, okay?"

"All right." Richard was willing to take the chance if it meant getting the dental file back and removing her from his life. They entered the dark nightclub, which had black lights that illuminated everything that was white, including the sheer white blouse that Charlene was wearing. Richard could see her generous, inviting breasts, which were perfectly shaped. A waitress wearing nothing but a green thong and high heels walked over to the table.

"Welcome to Bourbon Burlesque," she said. "Can I get you something to drink?" Richard took another quick glance around the room and suddenly realized that they had wandered into a gentlemen's club.

"I'll have a rum and Coke," answered Charlene.

"And for you, cutie?" The waitress smiled at Richard.

"Come on now, Richard, I know that you're not that damn stiff. Surely you've been in a gentlemen's club before."

"Yeah, uhm, I'll have the same thing she's having."

"Okay, baby," said the waitress, who spun on her heels and made sure that Richard got a good view of her big brown ass as she walked away. Before they could even begin a conversation, a woman dressed in a black trench coat, black satin gloves, high heels, and a black fedora with the brim curled just enough to hide her eyes came out and sat in a chair on the stage with her head tilted down. A tune began playing that Richard instantly recognized. It was a song called, "Get Off" by Prince. A fog machine began blowing white smoke onto the stage, adding mystery to the dancer's performance.

"Do you like her, Richard?" Charlene asked. She could see that Richard didn't frequent clubs like this, and she was going to use it for all it was worth. If watching women perform got him in the mood, it would be much easier to get him over the line that she wanted him to cross. Her hotel was within walking distance of where they were; and she had everything all set up for him.

"She's interesting," Richard answered, not taking his eyes off her. "She's very well built, that's for damn sure."

"Here, Richard." Charlene gave him a twenty-dollar bill. "Go give it to her." Richard glanced at Charlene and then at the money.

"No, that's okay" Richard answered "We need to talk."

"Come on, Richard, don't be such a damn pussy. Go give the woman the damn money. That's why she's up there dancing." Richard turned his attention back to the woman.

"Go on, it's okay," Charlene said. "What happens in New Orleans, stays in New Orleans, remember?" Charlene laughed. "We can talk once she's done dancing."

"I have my own money, Charlene."

"Suit yourself, but if you like what you see, by all means, pay the woman."

Richard walked over to the stage and sat down in one of the seats in front of the stage. By the time Richard sat down, the woman was completely naked, with the exception of her high-heeled shoes and the black fedora. The stripper walked the length of the stage toward him, swinging her mesmerizing hips at him. Richard leaned forward, completely intrigued by this woman. When she got to him, she got down on all fours and put her face up close to his. She had a look of complete desire for him in her eyes and that turned Richard on. She stood back up, turned her back to him, spread her legs apart, and bent down to glare at him from between her legs. She winked at Richard, and he placed a twenty-dollar bill between her teeth.

"Thank you, baby," she said, then went to work the other side of the stage.

Richard got up from the stage seat and sat back down with Charlene. The song went off and another, less appealing girl came out onto the stage. At that moment, the waitress brought back their drinks. Richard paid for them and gave her a generous tip. The waitress was about to walk away, but Charlene called to her.

"Excuse me." Charlene waved her over and stood up to whisper in the woman's ear.

"Okay." Richard heard the waitress say, "I'll let her know."

"So, you're going to give me the file as soon as we get back, right?" Richard tried to focus on business as he took a sip of his drink.

"Do you ever let yourself unwind, Richard?" Charlene smiled at him.

"Sometimes," Richard answered, not knowing what to make of the peculiar grin plastered on her face.

"Richard, I want you to unwind with me tonight." Charlene stood up, moved over to him, and began rubbing Richard's shoulders. "You're so tense," she said.

"Yeah, I know," Richard said, closing his eyes and rotating his neck. "Aw, man, that feels good." Charlene was weaving a web of lust and temptation and Richard was getting caught up in it, just like she wanted him to.

"I can't believe how good that feels," Richard complimented Charlene once again.

"I'm not rubbing your shoulders anymore, Richard," Charlene said, and Richard quickly popped his eyes open and glanced at Charlene, who was sitting back in her seat. Charlene nodded her head in the direction of the woman who was rubbing his shoulders. Richard looked up and met the gaze of the stripper he'd just tipped.

"Thank you for the generous tip, baby," she said. "Your girl-friend wants to give you something special. Come with me."

The stripper began to lead Richard away from the table and toward the back of the club and into a private lap dance room. Richard stopped at the door of the dark room.

"I'll bet that lovely bride of yours doesn't play kinky sex games like this, now does she?" Charlene pressed her erect nipples against Richard's back as she whispered in his ear, and placed her hand on his stiff manhood. Richard felt lust run down the length of his spine, as he became entangled in Charlene's web of sexual bliss.

"You're so hard, Richard." Charlene began stroking his manhood as she continued to whisper in his ear. "You know that you want this, baby, two women all over you at the same time. Every man has the sexual fantasy of being with more than one woman. The stripper is willing to be discreet as long as she's paid well for her time." Richard closed his eyes as he got caught up in the idea of the fantasy.

"And for a little extra money," the stripper was now whispering in his other ear, "I can work in something special for you. No one will come into the room, I can guarantee that."

"Come on, Richard, let's play pussy so that you can get fucked the right way. If you don't like this place, all of us can go back to my hotel room and—"

"Hotel room!" Richard's eyes leaped open. "He looked at his watch, which said ten-fifteen. "Damn you, Charlene!" Richard had missed Nina's nightly call. He caught himself, snapped out of his daze, and extricated himself from his dangerous situation. He rushed back to his hotel room, angry and upset with himself for allowing Charlene to manipulate him once again. It was at that point that he realized that Charlene was like his ex mother-in-law, Rubylee; she was too much for him to handle on his own. As soon as he got back home, he'd tell Nina the heartbreaking truth—he needed her help, and that was no joke.

Charlene rushed out onto the street to catch Richard but he was gone.

"Dammit!" she hissed as she began making her way back to her hotel room. Maybe Richard was truly in love with Nina, she thought but then dismissed the idea because she just didn't believe in true love—she'd never seen it or experienced it. Since she couldn't tempt Richard with sex, she'd have to hit him where it hurt, and she knew just how to do it. She'd make Nina look bad enough to get Richard to want to leave her, instead of trying to get her to leave him. But right now, she was going to pack and rush to the airport to catch the first flight back to Chicago.

24

NINA

Nina didn't call Richard for their nightly phone conversation because she rushed over to Rose's house after staying at the office late trying to figure out where she went wrong with her accounting. When she couldn't figure things out, she decided to head over to Rose's house. Nina sat in one of Rose's dining room chairs and began running her fingers through her hair. Nathan, whom she'd brought with her that night, was happy to see Rose.

"Hey, ladybug," Nathan said as he handed Rose his jacket.

"Hey there, Mr. Nathan," Rose answered, taking his coat. Rose hung Nathan's jacket up and then came back into the dining room, where they were.

"Child, what is wrong with you?" Rose said as Nina began raking her fingers through her hair as if trying to sort out her thoughts.

"Girl, I just don't know what to do," Nina answered. "Everything is messed up."

"What are you talking about? Is Richard okay?"

"He won't be after he hears this."

"Hears what, Nina?" Rose glanced at her friend.

"Can you turn on the cartoon network for Nathan?" Nina asked.

"Yeah, sure," Rose said. "Nathan, follow me. You can watch TV in the bedroom." Rose and Nathan got up and went into the bedroom to set up the TV for him to watch while she and Nina talked.

"Why can't I stay in there with you guys?" Nathan asked, sitting down on the edge of the bed.

"Because Nina and I have to discuss some grown folks' business," Rose said.

"Grown folks' business?" Nathan looked puzzled.

"In other words, you don't need to hear what we're talking about, honey. When you get older, you'll understand."

"Are you guys keeping secrets?" Nathan asked as *Bugs Bunny* came on.

"It's sort of like a secret," Rose said. "When grown-ups have these types of conversations, it's so that wonderful children like yourself don't have to deal with our burdens and worries."

"What does 'burden' mean?" Nathan had a million questions, but Rose didn't have the time or the inclination to explain it to him.

"Honey, just sit here and watch TV okay? Can you do that for me?"

"Okay" Nathan answered with an unhappy sigh. Rose went back to the dining room table and sat down.

"Whatever is going on, it has to be pretty deep to bring you all the way out here this evening. Do you want something to drink?"

"Do you have any Scotch?" asked Nina.

"Scotch, girl. I'm not about to give you some damn alcohol. You have to drive all the way back home. I've got some freshly squeezed lemonade."

"That will do," Nina said. A few moments later Rose returned with her drink and sat back down beside her.

"Okay, let it out. What's going on?"

"Rose, there is so much shit going on that I don't know what to do. Nine thousand dollars are missing from the practice, the new doctor that Richard has hired is going to get her ass drop-kicked if she keeps on playing her little games with me, and the worst and most troubling thing is . . . "Nina paused.

"What is it?" Rose put her hand on Nina's shoulder.

"You're a nurse, Rose, so I want you to be straight up with me. Give me the real answer."

"Now you know that I've always been honest with you. What is it?"

"It's Gracie. I ran into her at the office and knocked a bunch of papers out of her hand. One of the things that she had was a few of Richard's prescription blanks. Why would she have them, Rose?"

Rose exhaled and leaned back in her seat. "Do you think she's stealing them?" asked Rose.

"Yes, I think so," Nina answered.

"Oh Jesus," Rose said, and Nina noticed the look of concern and worry covering her friend's face. "I'll go get you that glass of Scotch, but you stay here with me tonight. John will be on duty all night." Rose got up, walked into her kitchen, and poured both herself and Nina a stiff drink.

"So what does it mean, Rose?"

"Nina." Rose paused, trying to find the right words but there was no simple way to answer the question, so she just did. "Do you feel that Gracie is stealing the pads in order to get pre-scription drugs?"

Nina hung her head down in shame. "I don't want to think that, Rose, but it would explain a lot. Ever since she came back, she's been complaining about being in pain. When she went to her Doctor, they said that she was fine, but she still insists that she's hurting."

"In the emergency room, we often get people who come in claiming to be sick but are really not. The only thing that they want is for the doctor to write them a prescription for some-thing, usually a painkiller that they've gotten addicted to. If Gracie has an addiction, she needs to get help for it. If she's

been stealing prescription pads to get drugs of some sort . . ."
Rose paused again and stared up at the chandelier on the ceiling. She exhaled the breath that had got caught in her voice. "If
she's been doing that, and Richard doesn't report it, he could
lose his license. If he does report it, Gracie may go to jail for
prescription drug fraud."

"I can't do that, Rose." Nina felt her emotions welling up. "I
can't turn in my own child and send her to jail."

"I know, but if you think that she has a problem, you have to
tell Richard."

"I can't do that either, Rose." Nina's voice was trembling
and she felt like crying. "If Richard has to choose between his
livelihood and my daughter's . . ." Nina didn't want to say what
she was thinking.

"I know, but you shouldn't keep this from him." Rose
sighed, feeling the sting of Nina's situation. "Have you talked
with Gracie?"

"No, because my computer caught fire at work and I lost all
of my electronic accounting records, which were stored on the
hard drive."

"How in the world did your computer catch fire?" Rose had
a perplexed looked on her face.

"Girl, I don't know. The repair people said that there was
some type of liquid in it. They said it looked like coffee to them,
but I don't even drink coffee so I don't see how that happened.
I told Richard about it over the phone the other night, and he
couldn't figure out how coffee got inside of the computer either."

"That doesn't sound right, Nina." Rose was trying to understand what was going on.

"Yeah, I know, but that's the least of my worries right now.
I've been putting in a lot of hours trying to make sure that all of
the bills get paid on time and making sure that my records
match the deposit slips that I requested from the bank, but I've
discovered that there is a nine-thousand-dollar discrepancy between my printed records and the bank's deposit slips."

"Damn!" Rose almost shouted the word. "How in the world are your records and the bank's records that far off?"

"Girl, I don't know. I've been going over all of the records, and they just aren't matching up. Richard is not going to be happy about that type of money missing from the practice, and if I tell him that I think Gracie has a damn drug habit, who do you think he is going to point his finger at?"

"Gracie," Rose whispered.

"Exactly." Nina gulped down her Scotch.

"So what are you going to do, Nina?" Rose asked.

"I know don't yet, but I do know one damn thing: I'm not about to spring all of this on Richard. No" —Nina shook her head—"especially not after all of the drama he just went through with his crazy-ass ex-mother-in-law, Rubylee."

"Nina, let me tell you something that you may not want to hear. Keeping stuff like this from your husband is not good. I understand why you don't want to tell him, but baby, if you can't discuss difficult issues that will have an impact on your relationship and your marriage, then you will leave the door open for misunderstanding, deceit, resentment, and all of the other things that can destroy a healthy marriage."

"I know, Rose, but by the same token, I wouldn't be able to live with myself if I didn't do all I could to help my baby."

"Gracie hasn't been a baby for some time now, Nina. She's a fully grown woman."

"If you had children, Rose, you'd understand me better." Nina didn't mean to say that; she just felt that she needed to defend her emotions.

"Excuse me? Don't you say that to me, Nina. Don't you dare say that to me." Nina could see that her words had hurt Rose. She could see that her eyes were turning glassy with tears.

"I'm sorry." Nina got up from her seat and hugged Rose. "I didn't mean that. I'm so sorry."

"Perhaps if you talk to Richard, you guys can agree not to report her, and get her some help. I think that would be the best solution."

"Yeah, I think you're right, Rose, and somehow Gracie is going to have to pay back the nine thousand dollars she's taken. I just can't figure out what in the hell she did with that type of money."

"If she truly has a problem, nine thousand dollars is peanuts for a person with a habit."

"Where did I go wrong, Rose? Why is my baby taking me for granted?"

"I don't know. I don't know why our baby is doing this to us," Rose said, taking on some of the responsibility as Gracie's godmother.

"I just want to cry, Rose. I just want to cry."

"So do I, Nina. So do I."

25

RICHARD

Richard got home from New Orleans at 12:00 P.M. the following day. When he walked inside his home, the house was empty. Neither Nina nor Nathan was there. He was anxious and wanted to speak with Nina right away. He was tired of carrying the burden of his secret; it was taking too much of a toll on him and his relationship with his wife. He phoned Nina at the office and hoped that she was there.

"Hello," Nina answered her office phone.

"Hey, baby," Richard said.

"Hey," Nina said, already feeling on edge about how she was going to bring up the subject of Gracie, who hadn't shown up for work yet.

"We need to talk," Richard said. "I'll be there in about twenty minutes."

"Okay." Nina's voice was filled with nervousness.

"Are you all right? What's wrong?" Richard asked.

"I really need to speak with you about a few things as well," Nina confessed.

"A few things like what?" Richard wanted to know now.

"We can talk once you get here. Oh, by the way, Charlene came in today. I thought she had the day off."

"She does," Richard said, stunned that she'd come into the office. "I'm the only one with patients today. My first one doesn't come in until 2:00 P.M."

"Well, she's here, but for what, I don't know."

Richard's nerves were tingling and he suddenly felt jumpy because he knew that conniving heifer was up to something no good. She must have taken a red-eye flight back to beat him to the office. The last thing he needed was for her to tell Nina that she'd been in New Orleans and that she had spent an evening with him at a damn gentlemen's club.

"You know what, baby," Richard said, rushing his words, "I'm on my way right now."

Charlene was sitting at the front desk answering a collect phone call from Gracie when Richard walked in the front door. She wanted to ask if she should accept the call but Richard refused to even look at her. He just marched right past her. Charlene decided to accept Gracie's phone call.

"Hello?" Gracie's voice was full of whimpering sighs, and Charlene had to contain her malevolence and delight.

"Yes," Charlene answered casually, trying not to bring attention to herself.

"Charlene, can you transfer me to my Mom, please."

Charlene could hear Gracie's sniffling, which was an indication that she'd been crying.

"Are you okay?" Charlene asked.

"No," Gracie answered. "Now can you please get my mom for me?"

"Well, sweetie, I think that she is in a closed-door meeting with Dr. Vincent. Is there a number where she can call you back?"

"Listen, Charlene, I don't care. Put me through to her right now, okay!" Gracie shouted at her.

"Okay, hang on." Charlene put her on hold and started snickering at how pathetic Gracie whined. This was what Charlene had been waiting around the office for; this was the straw that would break the camel's back. Charlene had her suspicions about Gracie's drug habit. She flew back from New Orleans so she could hang around the office and find out exactly how Gracie was supporting her habit. Charlene overheard Gracie calling in a prescription for herself earlier. Gracie mislead the pharmacist into believing she was a patient of Richard's. When Gracie left to pick up her medicine, Charlene picked up her phone and redialed the local pharmacist. She tipped him off about an employee with prescription blanks stolen from Dr. Richard Vincent. She gave the pharmacist Gracie's name so that when she came in to supply herself with her drug of choice, the pharmacist would have no choice but to call the police and have her arrested. Charlene transferred the phone call.

"Hello?" Nina answered the phone.

"I'm so sorry to bother you and Richard, but you have a very important phone call." Nina didn't like the catty tone of Charlene's voice.

"Take a message, I'll call them back," Nina said, irritated.

"No, sweetheart," Charlene scolded, "you need to take this." Without giving Nina a chance to respond to her, Charlene transferred the call. She then leaned back in Gracie's seat and waited for the shit to hit the fan.

"Mom, I'm in trouble," Nina heard Gracie say.

"Gracie? Where are you? Why haven't you come to work?"

"I'm in trouble, Mom, I need your help." Gracie was clearly crying.

"Trouble, what kind of trouble? What are you talking about?" Richard noticed a look of horror cover Nina's face.

"I'm in jail, Mom. They arrested me for prescription fraud."

"Oh, Jesus!" Nina dropped the phone and covered her face with her hands.

"Nina, what's going on?" Richard stood up from his chair

THROUGH THICK AND THIN 259

and was about to pick up the phone, but Nina picked it back up before he did.

"Where are you?" Nina asked.

"I'm at the Barrington Police Station."

"I'll be right there," Nina said. She exhaled and hung up the phone. She hadn't even had a chance to tell Richard about her suspicions of what Gracie was doing.

"You're going to find out about this anyway but I want you to hear it from me." Nina began sniffling, "I was trying to tell you about Gracie." A large boulder lodged itself in Nina's throat and made it difficult for her to speak. "Gracie has been stealing your prescription blanks and now she's just been caught and is in jail."

Richard didn't think that he'd heard Nina correctly.

"What did you just say?" Nina saw the electricity in his eyes and didn't want to repeat herself, but she forced herself to do so.

"She's just been arrested for prescription fraud with your prescription blanks." Nina's neck was stiff and twitchy. "I have to go see her." Tears were forming in her eyes. Richard stood there clenching his fists, ready to explode like a cork from a champagne bottle.

"What the fuck do you mean, she's been stealing blanks!" Richard howled at Nina like an animal gone mad.

"Richard, don't holler at me, okay, please. It's not my fault."

"Do you know what this means, Nina? Do you! We could fucking lose everything!" Richard felt an anxiety attack mounting.

"Richard, I'll be back, okay? I just need to go to the Barrington Police Station. I'll be back." Nina left Richard's sight before he said or did something he wouldn't be able to take back.

Charlene saw Nina rush out of the office in a hurry. Now was her chance to get Richard—he was vulnerable, and angry at his wife. She'd heard him yelling at her all the way in the front of the office. She scribbled down her home address on a scrap piece of paper and walked back to where Richard was.

"Is everything okay?" she asked as she noticed Richard sitting in his chair trying to process what he'd just been told.

"No, Charlene, it isn't. You should go. I've got a lot on my mind right now."

"Here." Charlene gave him the piece of paper.

"Believe it or not, I'm your friend, Richard. If you want to talk about it, I'm available for you. Anytime day or night, I'm there for you." Richard didn't answer Charlene.

"Baby, I know what you're going through. I've been through a disciplinary hearing and it's no fun at all. I can at least give you a sense of what to expect." Charlene turned to leave him alone with his thoughts. When she got to the doorway, she turned to him and looked at him once more. She wanted to put damaging information about Nina in his head.

"Just so that you know, I think that Nina has known about Gracie for some time now, but she just never told you. You thought that I was the bad guy, Richard. I hope you can see clearly now that I'm not. I'll help you if you allow me to." Richard turned his gaze from the wall and met Charlene's.

"What do you mean, Nina knew?"

"I overheard her talking to Gracie about sneaking into your office one day. She asked Gracie what she was doing with your prescription blanks." Richard didn't want to believe what Charlene was telling him, but given the circumstances, he believed that she was telling him the truth.

"In spite of everything that I've done, you can trust me, Richard. I was at least honest and up front about what I was going to do and what I wanted. I've never hid any of my intentions from you. I want you to think about that." Charlene could see that she was getting through to Richard but didn't want to overdo it.

"I'm here for you, Richard. Just call me or drop by."

26

RICHARD

Richard was bewildered, anxious, confused, and had difficulty organizing his thoughts. He didn't know how to react to what was going on; he didn't know if he was angry, shocked, or just wounded. Either way, all he felt was numb and lost like a zombie who didn't have a clue that he was already dead. Richard had Rose do him a huge favor and pick Nathan up for him while he tried to sort things out. He told her that he'd pick him up later.

Richard couldn't exactly figure out his rationale for driving over to Charlene's apartment later that evening, but for some reason, he thought that speaking with her about his situation would give him some type of insight on what to expect from an investigation. He rang Charlene's doorbell and she opened the door right away as if she'd been standing there waiting for him.

"Come on in," she said, taking his hand, shutting the door, and leading him over to a sofa she'd purchased for the small apartment that she was renting. "I've been waiting for you."

"Waiting for me?" Richard's thoughts were as clouded and as thick as night fog on an open highway. He couldn't see the road in front of him and didn't know which way it twisted.

"Yes, I knew you'd come, Richard, and I'm glad you did," Charlene said. "Have a seat." Richard sat down on the sofa and suddenly felt strange and out of place.

"I may lose everything," he mumbled.

"Relax, Richard," Charlene said, "it's not the end of the world, you know. You'll survive this, and I'm going to help you get through it." Charlene went behind the sofa and began rubbing her hands across Richard's chest to help him relax.

"You're so tense, baby, I can tell," she said as she attempted to work the tension out of his neck muscles.

"I can't believe this is happening to me." Richard was still trying to process what was going on. He didn't want to believe that it was the truth.

"Hey, shit happens, Richard," Charlene muttered. "What you need to do is get rid of that low-down bride of yours." Charlene was all set to work up Richard's anger toward Nina so that she could have her way with him.

"Nina wouldn't do something like that," Richard said. Charlene didn't appreciate the fact that he was in denial.

"Richard, she just did! Wake up, baby, and smell the damn coffee. She placed her daughter, who has a chemical dependency problem, in your office, where she had access to drugs. I'll bet you she's known that Gracie has had problems for years."

"She never said that Gracie had a problem." Richard was still speaking as if he were in a fog, trying to find his way out of his nightmare.

"Of course she wouldn't say anything Richard. It's her daughter."

"Maybe you're right, Charlene," Richard said and Charlene liked the fact that she was twisting things around.

"Wait right here, baby." She leaned down and kissed him on the neck and purposely spoke in his ear. "I'm going to make some coffee and get a bit more comfortable." Charlene had every intention of slipping his ass some more sleeping pills; that way he'd stay all night, and when he woke up the next morning

THROUGH THICK AND THIN   263

with her wrapped in his arms, she could say anything that she wanted to about the night before and he wouldn't remember. If she couldn't get him to leave Nina so that she could be at his side, she would say that she was pregnant so that she could get paid to disappear from his life.

"Okay," Richard answered. Charlene left the room and Richard sat there glancing around. He noticed that the closet door next to the front entrance was open. He took off his jacket and got up to hang it inside the closet. When he went to the closet, he saw a small beige metal file cabinet sitting on the floor of the closet. Instantly his mind began racing with new thoughts, and something told him to take a peek inside to see if that was where she had the dental record that he'd been trying to get. Richard stooped down, quietly opened up the top drawer, and searched through the files. There wasn't much in the top drawer so he opened up the second drawer and there it was, sitting on the bottom of the drawer. It was the only thing in that drawer. Richard quickly snatched up the file, closed the file drawer, and stood erect. Some of the fog was lifting from his mind now.

"I'm in the wrong damn place talking with the wrong damn woman about my problems," Richard mumbled under his breath. "What in the hell am I thinking? Didn't this crazy-ass woman try to seduce me?" He began to think rationally. Then he heard it, a voice deep within himself that told him to leave and leave now! Without questioning his inner voice, Richard made himself disappear from Charlene's apartment like an echo in the wind.

When Charlene returned to the living room holding Richard's cup of drug-laced coffee, the only thing she was wearing was the skin that she'd been born in. She had decided to be very direct with Richard and show him just how well she could relieve all the tension he was feeling. Besides, after rethinking things, she decided that it couldn't hurt to try and get a little action before she slipped him his drink.

"Richard?" she called out. "Where are you?" Charlene set

the cup down on the cocktail table. When she got no answer, she thought that he might have gone to the bathroom so she walked around the corner but saw that the bathroom door was wide open and Richard wasn't there.

"Richard?" She called out his name again as she walked back into the living room. She stood in the center of the floor with her face winkled into an ugly expression.

"Oh, no you didn't!" Charlene shouted as she rushed over to the closet where the file cabinet was. She opened the bottom drawer and saw that the original copy of the file was gone.

"Son of a bitch!" she hissed. Charlene stood there with her hands on her hips angry with herself for not putting the file in a safety-deposit box as she'd intended to do. "Damn," she growled. Then she forced herself to calm down and formulate a new plan. She knew that she had to get out of town now and she had to do it quickly. Now that she no longer had Richard by the balls, she knew that there was no reason for her to go back to the practice because Richard was surely going to tell her that she was fired.

"That's okay, Richard. "She nodded her head. "You've served your purpose as far as I'm concerned. I didn't get all of the money that I wanted to get from you, but the extra nine thousand that I stole from you will be enough for me to start over with." Charlene walked back to her bedroom and began pulling her clothes from the closet, because she wasn't going to stay there any longer than she needed to. By the following evening, she would be out of her apartment and out of town. She smirked and then chuckled a bit as an old Kenny Rogers tune from a movie called *The Gambler* surfaced from somewhere deep in her mind. She'd gambled on being able to control Richard and make him obey her, and in the process of all of the conniving and deceit, she lost the bet that she'd placed. She lost to Richard's love for Nina. Now Charlene knew that it was time to fold things up and run away.

* * *

Richard rushed to the Barrington Police Station so that he could catch Nina and finally tell her everything. When he got to the station, he didn't see her. He went up to the desk sergeant and asked if Gracie Howard was still being held.

"Yes, she's still here," said the sergeant.

"May I see her?" asked Richard.

"Yeah, give me a minute, I'll have someone come out and take you back there to her." A few moments later, a uniformed officer escorted Richard to the visiting area where Gracie was sitting with her shoulders and head slumped down. Richard walked up to her table and sat down.

"Gracie?" Richard tilted his head to meet her gaze. When she looked up at him, he could tell that she'd been crying consistently for some time. The whites of her eyes were red and they were very swollen.

"You're the last person that I expected to see." Gracie's chest was swelling up with emotion. "I didn't mean to do that. I'm sorry for what I've done," Gracie apologized as she burst open with tears. "I'm so sorry."

"Hey," Richard said, "it's going to be okay."

"No, it's not," Gracie said. "I've ruined everything. I'm such a screw up, and if you want the judge to throw the book at me, Richard, it's okay I deserve whatever I've got coming to me."

"Do you want to change your life, Gracie? Are you willing to get some help?"

"Yes, it's not like I wanted to get hooked on those Vicodin pills. They just made me feel better."

"Vicodin is a very addictive drug. Where is your mother? We'll get an attorney and find out what your options are."

"Well, she sort of agreed to meet with my dad."

"Oh, really?" Richard was surprised that Nina would agree to see her ex-husband, Jay, without letting him know about it. Jealousy was suddenly rearing its ugly head.

"They are meeting at a bar in Palatine called Dirty Nelly's. It's near the train station."

"I think I know where it is," Richard said and was suddenly eager to get there. "Look, just sit tight, and we'll figure out something, okay?"

"Okay." Gracie said, "and Richard, be careful. I overheard the police talking to the pharmacist. Dr. Hayward is the person who turned me in."

"What?" Richard was suddenly thunderstruck.

"Dr. Hayward tipped the pharmacy off. I just found out a few minutes before you came in."

"Okay." Richard said as he walked out.

When Richard arrived at Dirty Nelly's, he saw Nina's car. He sat silently for a minute to prepare himself just in case he saw something that would upset him; after all, she did spend twenty years of her life with the man. Richard walked into the bar, and saw Nina and Jay sitting in a booth talking. There didn't seem to be any type of intimacy going on between them, and for Richard, that was a huge relief. At that moment in time, Richard understood that Gracie was their daughter, and as a parent, you don't want to see your child imprisoned at any age. Richard thought that it would be best for the time being to let them talk, especially since the last time he and Jay were together, they almost got into a physical confrontation. Although he didn't like the idea of leaving Nina there with her ex-husband, he felt that he had to trust her enough to believe that she wouldn't try to rekindle any old feelings for him. Richard picked up Nathan, went home, put him to bed, and sat in a chair on the pool deck. He'd planned to wait there most of the night for Nina, but to his surprise and delight, she arrived home just fifteen minutes after he had.

Nina walked out onto the pool deck, where she found Richard sitting in a lawn chair and staring at the pool. She went over to him and sat down beside him.

"Hey," she said.

"Hey," Richard answered back, "where were you tonight?" He wanted to see if she'd tell him the truth. This was a crossroad in the stability of their relationship. If she lied to him, it would break his heart, but if she told him the truth, he'd feel like an ass for not telling her the complete truth about Charlene from jump street.

Nina exhaled before she spoke. She was going to take Rose's advice and be truthful about everything. "After I went to see Gracie, I called my ex-husband, Jay. We met up at a bar in Palatine called Dirty Nelly's. I told him what happened with Gracie and he said that he had a friend down at the District Attorney's Office. He said that he'd call him and see what could be done."

Richard closed his eyes. Nina had put honesty and the truth above deception and fraudulence. "There is something else too, Richard," Nina was confessing. "We're missing nine thousand dollars from the practice and I don't know what happened to it. I think that Gracie may have stolen it, but she says that she didn't." At that moment Richard wasn't concerned about the missing money; he was more concerned about being truthful with Nina about Charlene.

"I have something to tell you that I've been hiding from you. I should have told you this from jump street but I made a foolish choice." Richard took his gaze from the pool and faced Nina. "I hope that you'll forgive me for this, but I did it because I didn't want you to worry. I thought by not telling you the truth, that I'd be protecting you."

"Richard, what are you talking about?" Nina asked, although deep in her heart, she knew that Richard was about to tell her something about Charlene. She was praying that he wasn't going to say that they'd been having a damn affair, or that she was pregnant with his child. She'd have to kick his ass if he said something like that to her.

"Charlene is my ex-girlfriend."

"What! Why you low-down dirty mother—" Nina caught herself.

"I'm sorry, I'm sorry, I'm sorry," Richard kept apologizing. "We dated when I was in undergraduate school."

"Yeah, I figured that one out, but why did you allow that bitch to come into our life? And why didn't you tell me, Richard!" Nina felt her blood beginning to boil.

"Hold on, don't get angry."

"Too late, Richard, I'm already pissed off!"

"Baby, let me explain. She showed up in my office with this," Richard slid the file across the table to Nina.

"What? A patient's chart? I'm not following you."

"My mother had gotten to a point where she couldn't perform complex procedures because of her inability to keep her hands steady. So, while certain patients were sedated, I came in and she instructed me on what to do." Richard noticed how a look of surprise suddenly came over Nina's face. "I was working on patients without a license. My mother wanted me to go to dental school after performing a procedure on this patient."—Richard pointed to the chart—"and she told me to sign it because, in her eyes, I was already a doctor. I signed this chart two years before I entered dental school."

"What does that have to do with Charlene?" Nina was confused.

"I was dating Charlene at the time and she knew what I was doing. When we broke up, she went on to dental school herself. And I hadn't seen her for a good sixteen years until she showed up at my office one day with this damn chart. She threatened me with it. She threatened to report me for fraud if I didn't give her a job."

"Why did she need a damn job from you?"

"Because the Dental Board had recently disciplined her for misconduct, and no practitioner in his right mind would hire her willingly."

"Richard, I can't believe you didn't tell me this."

"I know. I wanted to, but I thought that I could handle it on my own. I thought that I could convince her to give me the chart back and leave us alone."

"So how did you get the chart, Richard?" Nina had a nasty tone in her voice.

"I was at her apartment tonight. I was so bewildered about what had happened with Gracie, so I went to her to talk about it. While she was getting me something to drink, I searched her file cabinet and found the original file. Once I got it, I left and went to see Gracie."

"You didn't . . ." Nina couldn't bring herself to ask.

"Of course not. I don't have any feelings like that toward her. You are the only woman for me. You're the woman that I breathe for."

"What happened, Richard? Why didn't you tell me? If you had told me, we could have avoided all of this madness."

"I was trying to protect you from the truth. And I see now, that was a big mistake. Because a lot of the shit that we've been going through was unnecessary."

"So that bitch is the reason that you damn near had a heart attack on me? That bitch, was the reason for that selfish sex the other night?"

"Yes," Richard answered with shame in his voice. "That bitch, also turned Gracie in."

"I need to drop-kick that bitch and you." Fury and anger were flowing through her blood. Nina paused for a moment and redirected all of her anger at Charlene. "Ain't no way in hell I'm going to let that bitch come into my life and try to fuck up my good thing! I'm going to be pissed with you for a while Richard. But right now, I can't wait for Charlene to come to work in the morning. I've got something for her ass!"

27

CHARLENE

After withdrawing all of her money from the bank the following day, Charlene got into her car, which was loaded up with her possessions, and headed over to her mother's house before she left town. The least she could do was say goodbye to her and let her know that she'd contact her once she got settled in someplace else.

"What do you mean, you're leaving town?" Dean asked.

"I have to go, Dean. Sometimes you've just got to make quick moves when things get hot." Charlene noticed a sad look fall into her mother's eyes.

"I'll call you, okay?" Charlene attempted to comfort her.

"You're on the run, aren't you?" Dean asked.

"Let's just say that I want to be long gone by the time some people discover what I've been doing."

"Just like your father," Dean mumbled. "Lord, she's just like him!" Dean raised her eyes and hands up to the heavens.

"What about my father?" Charlene's emotions were suddenly heightened because her mother was actually saying something useful about him.

"Sit down for a moment, Charlene."

Charlene pulled out a seat at the small neon yellow dinette table and sat down.

"Wait here a minute," Dean said and disappeared into her bedroom. A few moments later she came back with a small flower-print box and set it on the table.

"I called you a couple of days ago and asked you to call me back, but you never did."

"I know, I was just tied up and didn't have time to get back to you."

"If you want to know about your father, you'll have to hear it all. I'll have to tell you the painful truth about what happened between your Grandmother Hazel and me. You'll have to hear about grown folks' business," Charlene watched as her mother paused. She wanted to know what happened but didn't dare say something and cause her mother to lose her train of thought.

"We shared a man, your grandmother and me."

"What?" Charlene's eyes were wide with surprise.

"If you must know the truth, you must hear the whole truth about your grandmother, about me, about your father Stan-back, Rubylee, and Justine, the child that they had together. You have a half-sister named Justine."

"Rubylee? Who in the hell is Rubylee? And why hasn't anyone told me about my half-sister Justine?"

28

RICHARD

The following morning, Richard dropped Nathan off at school and met up with Nina, who was in the office still trying to figure out what happened to the money that was missing. When Richard arrived, he found Nina sitting in her office frustrated.

"Are you okay?" he asked as he sat down in a chair in front of her desk.

"No, I can't figure out why I stamped these invoices as paid, and no money was deposited from them."

"Are they from patients or insurance companies?" asked Richard.

"They're all from patients, who paid by check. I even called one of them to see if the money had cleared from their account and the person said that it had."

"That is strange. Why would you stamp it paid if you didn't deposit the check?"

"It's obvious that the money was stolen from us, baby, but I'm trying to figure out how Gracie did it."

"Are you sure that Gracie stole the money?" Richard didn't

want to get aggravated by the situation; he just wanted to resolve it and make sure that it didn't happen again.

"She said that she didn't, but I'm not holding my breath on
that one."

"Let me see the invoices." Nina handed them to him.

"All of these patients belong to Charlene," Richard noticed.
"Hang on a minute." Richard sprang to his feet, "Let's go take
a look inside her office. Did she show up today?"

"No, but I'm still waiting on her ass." Nina and Richard
walked down to her office and searched around to see if
Charlene was hiding any money in the office. Nina opened up
one of the supply drawers and was stunned when she found a
red ink stamp, which was identical to hers, that said PAID.

"Why, that no-good swindling bitch!" Nina was irate because now she knew that Charlene had taken advantage of her.
She began putting things together in her mind as to how Charlene
had clipped her. She began thinking like a shady, desperate woman
who needed cash. "She probably told her patients to leave the
payable line blank, saying that we would stamp the clinic's name
for them," she said out loud as Richard came over to where she
was standing. "That way, she could just write in her own name
and deposit the money into her account. Then, she'd just stamp
the file paid, and backdate it so that when I got it, the only thing
that I would have done was give it back to Gracie for filing. We
can nail that jezebel on insurance fraud," Nina said as Richard
put his arm around her.

"No, we can't," he said.

"What are you talking about! I want her ass to be put under
the damn jail. She can't come in here and fuck with me like this
and get away with it." Nina was pissed that Charlene had
hoodwinked her.

"She only took the money from self paying patients—this is
more like embezzlement."

"Either way, we need to call the damn police and report her
ass so that a warrant can be issued for her arrest," Nina said,

then stormed away back to her office. Richard followed her and listened as she called the police department. When the uniformed deputy arrived, he filled out a complaint form but was heartbreakingly honest with Nina and Richard.

"Look, I'll file the complaint, but to be honest with you, the courts are overburdened with more serious offenses. I can pretty much tell you for a fact that the judge doesn't even consider cases such as this a priority. This could drag out for some time, and the chance of you getting your money back is, well, very slim."

"You've got to be kidding me," Nina and Richard both said at the same time because they couldn't believe what they were hearing.

"I wish I was. I'll also tell you right now, I'm the officer in charge of investigating complaints like this one, and I have so many other things that are priority that it will be some time before I get to this one."

"Can't you send a squad car over there to arrest her for this?" Nina asked.

"Mrs. Vincent, the only thing that you have is a red ink stamp found in her office. I can't arrest her for that."

"What about her bank records? Can't you subpoena her bank records and check them against what we have?"

"Like I said, the judge isn't going to consider this a priority. Especially for an amount this small." Nina growled with aggravation. "Okay," the officer corrected himself, "it's not a big amount to the judge. Besides that, you'll probably want to get permission from each one of those patients to release their dental records, which some of them may not want to do because of privacy issues. Then you have to consider how they'd feel if they knew that someone at your office cashed their check illegally.

"Damn!" Richard shouted as he began to see the bigger picture.

"We just can't let her get away with this shit!" Nina didn't want to give up on this.

"I'll submit the complaint. If the judge thinks that this is worth pursuing, you'll be hearing from me." With that said, the officer gave them a copy of the complaint and left. As he was leaving, Rose was walking in.

"Okay, I'm ready," said Rose, who was wearing sweatpants, a sweat jersey, and a baseball cap. "Has she come to work yet? We can put this bitch in a headlock and whip her ass while we bounce her trifling ass out of here." Richard tried not to laugh but he couldn't help it because Rose was dead serious.

"I'm not playing. I'm a big woman, but I'm light as hell on my feet and I'll throw her ass!"

"Girl," Nina said. "You have a way of making the most upsetting situations bearable. I don't think the bitch is coming back. But people like her always get it, one way or another."

29

CHARLENE

Dean opened up the box and pulled out a few items that were in it. She pulled out Hazel's faded obituary, a brush that contained strands of Hazel's hair, the will that stated that she wanted Charlene to have the house, and a few old photos that were tucked away in a clear plastic sleeve. Charlene wanted to get upset about Dean having the will all this time but decided to just let it go.

"Your Grandmother Hazel never told me who my father was," Dean said as she carefully handled the photos. "She took his identity with her to her grave. I don't know why she never told me who he was. She only said that he wasn't important and that I shouldn't concern myself with it."

"Didn't you want to know who your people were and where they came from?" Charlene asked softly.

"Of course I did." Dean sighed. "I know that you want to know about your father's side of the family as well. I'm sorry that I never told you about him in all of these years, but there was just so much heartache and pain associated with my life with Stanback."

"How did you guys meet?" Charlene asked.

"He was your grandmother's boyfriend." Dean paused and Charlene noticed that a shameful look masked her mother's face. Charlene could see that even after all these years, that scar was still fresh. Charlene held her hand.

"It's okay," Charlene said, "tell me. I want to know the truth." Dean exhaled loudly and glared up at the ceiling as if it were a movie screen projecting her life story.

"Like I said, I never knew who my daddy was. When I was a little girl, your grandmother had married Bo and they had your Uncle Stony. Hazel blamed herself for the way Stony came out because she was given direct orders from her doctor to rest if she wanted a healthy pregnancy. Hazel didn't listen because she needed the money I suppose and worked at the factory until she went into labor on the job. When Stony was born messed up, she and Bo had problems and misunderstandings. Your grandmother was deeply in love with Bo, and it broke her heart when he left. She did everything that she could to get him to come back, but he married another woman and Hazel had to face reality. It was just the three of us for a while—Hazel, Stony and myself. Then she met this young fella named Stanback, who was twenty-four at the time. Hazel was a good ten years his senior. She began courting him and eventually he moved into the house after he and his older brother, Packard, got into an ugly fight over some money, I think, I can't quite remember. I was seventeen at the time he moved in. At first, things were okay. Stanback was funny and made Hazel happy. Somewhere along the line, Stanback and I both started," Dean paused again and swallowed hard, "we started liking each other, okay."

"I understand, Mom," Charlene comforted her.

"I knew that it was wrong to have feelings for him like that, and I tried to fight it, but I found myself competing with my own mother for the same man. I didn't want anyone my own age, because I wanted an older man. Stanback had a smooth way about him. I knew that he was a manipulator but that didn't matter to me, because I was turned on by the fact that he could sing. You see, Stanback had dreams of hitting it big as a singer

in the music business. One day, when Hazel wasn't home because she was with Stony at the doctor's office, Stanback called
me into their bedroom. When I went in there, he told me to sit
down on the bed and listen to him as he sang. He serenaded me,
by singing a song that he wrote. I was so turned on by him, his
smooth voice, and his beautiful dark brown skin. I guess that he
could tell what he was doing to me because he asked me to
stand up and dance with him. I stepped into his embrace and he
sang the words in my ear, and I melted. Right there, I melted
like butter on a hot stove. One thing led to another, and the
next thing I knew, he took me. I didn't resist him because I
wanted him just as much. We both fell asleep afterwards and
the next thing that I knew Hazel was yanking me out of her bed
by my hair, screaming at me and calling me all types of sluts and
bitches. And well," Dean paused again, "you get the picture."

"What happened after that?" Charlene was on the edge of
her seat with intrigue.

"She put both of us out, baby. Stanback had a little money
tucked away so we came to Chicago." Dean placed the plastic
sleeve with the photo down on the table. "This is him right here,
that's Stanback." She pointed to the photo, which was taken
with a Polaroid camera. Charlene looked at the photo, which
was taken in a bowling alley sometime in the early 1960s, judging by the hairstyles and the clothing they were wearing. Her father was a brown-skinned man with his hair slicked up into a
pompadour hairstyle like the singer Jackie Wilson used to wear.
Her mother's hair was twisted up high and resembled a beehive.

"When we got to Chicago," Dean continued, "I realized that
I was pregnant with you. I forced Stanback to marry me because I wanted our relationship to work. After the way I hurt
Hazel, I couldn't go back to her. I wanted to prove to her that
Stanback and I were in love and that nothing else in the uni-
verse mattered, because love conquered all." Charlene looked
at the photo again and noticed a large scar on her father's face.

"How did he get the scar?" Charlene asked.

"I gave it to him," Dean answered. "Stanback was a woman

beater and he beat me up pretty badly one night. When he drifted off to sleep, I cut him."

"What!" Charlene was astonished by what she was hearing. "And he stayed with you after that?"

"Well, it was more like I stayed with him. Passion will make you do things like that. You were about two years old when I cut him in his sleep. The police put me in jail and the only person that I trusted to keep you was your grandmother, because by that time, Stanback and I were doing illegal things. So I called Hazel and she and your Uncle Stony came up to Chicago on a Greyhound Bus. I signed custody of you over to her and she brought you back home with her."

"That doesn't make any sense. Why did you sign me over so quickly?" Charlene asked.

"Baby, that wasn't the first time that I had been in jail. Like I said, Stanback and I had gotten involved with drugs and other things. The family services people said that I was an unfit mother, and rather than turn you over to the state to be mistreated, I had to call your grandmother. And bless her heart, she came right up and took you home knowing that you were a result of the passion that Stanback and I had."

"Were you in love with him?" Charlene asked.

"Yes," Dean answered, "I was madly in love with him. I couldn't live my life without him."

"Well, what happened?" Charlene was trying to figure out where their relationship went sour.

"A snake-in-the-grass woman named Rubylee Wiley is what happened, baby."

"Now, who is she?"

"She was some young, fresh neighborhood girl with a young baby named Estelle, who lived in the neighborhood that Stanback started dealing with."

"Why did he go with another woman if he was in love with you?"

"I think that I was more in love with him than he was with me. I turned a blind eye to his fling with her, thinking that all men do it and that it would just be a passing thing. I thought for sure that he'd come back to me. But it didn't happen that way. You see, baby, Stanback and I were a team. We did damn near everything from selling and using drugs, to shoplifting and credit card fraud. Stanback was a creative mastermind with finding loopholes in the justice system."

"Loopholes?" Charlene questioned.

"You know what I mean, Charlene. He knew how to do his dirt and still stay one step ahead of the law." Charlene thought about that unique trait, which was something that she'd inherited from him. She smiled because her mother was helping her to understand why she was the way she was.

"He came up with this idea of running a church raffle ticket scam, and decided that he didn't want me to be part of it, because he said I wasn't tough, fearless and hard like Rubylee was."

"Wait a minute, he admitted to you that he was seeing her?"

"Yes, but I already knew that. I wasn't about to lose my man to the likes of her so I confronted her. I met her on the corner of Madison and Laramie Streets one day and we got into it."

"Well, what happened?" Charlene was egging her mother on.

"Stanback was right, Rubylee was ruthless, fearless, and wasn't about to take an ass-whipping from me. She wasn't willing to fight me for Stanback. She was willing to kill me to get me out of the picture. Before I knew it, she wrestled me down to the pavement and put the barrel of her gun right in the center of my forehead. I didn't think that she'd pull the trigger, but the evil glare in her eyes told a different truth. Rubylee pulled the trigger, but the damn gun jammed and saved my life. She was arrested but got off on a self-defense plea because witnesses said that I started the fight, which was true. After that, Stanback left me to be with her."

"Damn!" Charlene said as she took all of this new information in. The two of them sat in silence for a moment before Dean continued.

"I went off the deep end after that. I had dark days and hurt the ones dearest to me because of my drug habit. I do know that Stanback and Rubylee had one daughter together. Her name is Justine; she's your half-sister. Over the past several weeks I've been in touch with a few people that I really didn't want to contact to get information about where she is. No one knew except for Rubylee." Dean pulled out a notepad from the box. "I took some time off of work and went to see Rubylee for you to try to find out some more information about your sister. It was very hard for me to go see that woman, but I did it for you. I figured that if it was that important to you, I'd do it."

"How did you find Rubylee and what did she say?" Charlene asked.

"Rubylee had a street reputation, so discovering that she was locked up wasn't a surprise. I went to the prison where she was, Charlene. When I saw her, she got to rambling on about hooking up when she got out. Apparently she made some type of deal with the state and got her sentence reduced significantly. She'll be out in a couple of years. Anyway, I wanted no part of her criminal life; I just wanted to get some information about your sister for you."

"Well, where is my sister?"

"She is at a state correctional facility. She's doing some time for auto theft. Here is her contact information if you want it." Charlene took the notepad. "She will not be there that long. She'll be getting out soon, from what I understand."

"But whatever happened to Stanback? Whatever happened to my father?" Dean hung her head down and huffed.

"He was killed over a drug deal that went sour. The word on the street was that Rubylee had set him up. I think that the rumor was true since she didn't even show up for his funeral. Legally we were still married and I had to bury him."

"Damn!" Charlene said once again.

"So, there you have it. Your father at one point was the love of my life but things didn't work out." Dean sighed.

"What about his brother, Packard?"

"I don't know much about him. I only know that he and Stanback never got along."

"What about the rest of his family?"

"I don't know anything about them either. Stanback never spoke about his mother and father."

"Mom." Charlene paused to phrase her question delicately. "Do you think that there is such a thing as true love?" Charlene wanted to know her thoughts on it because she realized that she had a problem with dating men that didn't belong to her, just like her mother and her grandmother had. Dean pondered the question for a moment.

"I think that your grandmother and Bo truly loved each other, but Bo wasn't willing to leave his second marriage to come back to your grandmother. I don't know why, but then again I really don't want to. When I was using drugs, I had a habit of seeing married men, because they promised to love me, but in the end, they didn't. If there is such a thing as true love, I haven't found it yet, but I've been looking for it in the wrong places. Nine times out of ten you won't find true love in the arms of someone else's man."

Charlene spent a few more hours with her mother absorbing all that she could about her father. She'd finally found a bit of peace knowing what the truth was. Dean asked Charlene to consider forgiving her for not being in her life the way a real mother should. A bit of Charlene's heart melted, and she forgave Dean.

She told her mother that she had to go because she'd stolen money from her employer.

"It's money that I need to start over, the right way," Charlene explained.

"Do you know where you're going?"

"I think that I'm going to head down to East Saint Louis, Illinois," Charlene answered. "I heard that they're starting up a public health clinic and are in need of a dentist to oversee the dental clinic operations."

"Baby, what if you don't get the job? Then what?"

"Trust me, I'll get it." Charlene smiled with confidence. She couldn't go without a job for any length of time, especially since she still owed the Dental Board and Dr. Seth Wood large sums of money. She had to pay the fines or that would be the end of her privileged career as a dentist. In her mind, Charlene knew that some new scheme would pop into her head during the drive down to East Saint Louis. She would find a way to get the money. She just had to be more like her father—do her dirt but stay one step ahead of the law. *Perhaps she'd contact her half-sister Justine at some point. She'd find out when she was going to be released and maybe between the two of them, they could come up with a way to get a large sum of money*, she thought to herself but then laughed at the idea.

"Charlene, girl, you're not a criminal," she said to herself. "You're just a survivor, doing what you have to do in order to make it." Charlene said her final good-bye to her mother, and then hit the highway.

30

FOUR YEARS LATER, JUNE 2004

The day had been perfect for Rose and John's wedding. Nina couldn't stop shedding tears of joy for both John and Rose, who had finally decided it was time to tie the knot. The wedding reception was outdoors and filled with friends and guests.

Gracie got help for her addiction and avoided jail time because her father, Jay, had enough clout to get the matter tossed out. Richard was given a light slap on the hand and fined a small amount of money for not securing his prescription pads, and Charlene was never charged with the crime of embezzlement.

Gracie finally finished her BA degree, got a teaching certificate, and took a job at the local school as a kindergarten teacher. She also became a foster parent of a six-month-old baby girl named Symeria, whom she decided to adopt. Gracie had also begun dating again and was willing to give romance another shot.

Nathan, who was now eleven years old, was standing next to Gracie and Nina under the shade of a tall tree. Nathan had shot up in height and was constantly measuring himself against Nina.

"Look, Mom, I've grown another inch taller than you," Nathan said, trying to look down at her.

"That doesn't mean I can't knock you down," Nina said playfully. "Remember, the bigger you are, the harder you fall."

"So Nathan, I hear that you're quite the swimmer," Gracie said.

"Yeah, I'm like Tiger Woods in the water. I'll be in sixth grade this fall and the swim coach has already contacted me about being on the swimming team."

"So, what events will you be doing?" asked Gracie.

"The hundred-meter freestyle, the hundred-meter butterfly, and sprint relays," Nathan answered, trying to add some bass in his voice.

"Oh, lord." Nina laughed at Nathan trying to deepen his voice as she cooed and spoke baby talk to Gracie's daughter, Symeria. "Look at that precious baby." Nina rubbed noses with Symeria, who had a pink headband around her head and was dressed in a matching pink dress. Symeria was smiling at Nina and drooling at the same time.

"Nathan, what is that on your lip?" Gracie squinted her eyes and leaned in closer to him. "What is that?" She pointed to his upper lip, "Are you trying to grow a mustache?"

"Yeah, you know." Nathan pranced a bit as he rubbed his thumb and forefinger across his upper lip. "Mom said she saw some hair forming up there," Nathan proudly boasted.

"Honey, I saw two black strands, and now he checks his lip every day and asks me if I see any more." Gracie and Nina busted up laughing.

"Naw, see, it ain't even like that." Nathan was gesturing with his hands. "I don't check every day like that." Nathan tried to deny the fact that he looked constantly in the bathroom mirror, but he couldn't and started laughing along with them.

"I finally stole these two lovebirds so that the photographer can get a photo of all of us together," Richard said, walking over with Rose and John on either side of him.

"Hell, I wasn't sure if they were truly lovebirds; it took them long enough to tie the knot."

"Hey, better late than never," John blurted out.

"Come on now, let's all get in here together," Richard said.

"Don't step on my dress, baby," Rose said to John as she gathered up her white dress in her hand.

"Don't worry, baby, I won't," answered John.

"Look at all of us," Nina said beaming with pride. "We look so good. We're family, and we're going to stay together through thick and thin." The seven of them huddled up close as the photographer aimed the camera.

"Say cheese," requested the photographer, and in unison they all repeated the word, "Cheese!" The camera clicked and captured their joyful moment forever.

ABOUT THE AUTHOR

Earl Sewell is the author of *The Good Got To Suffer With The Bad* and *Taken For Granted.* He is also a contributing author to *After Hours: A Collection Of Erotic Writing By Black Men* and *Sistergirls.Com.* He is also an athlete who is training to complete an Ironman Triathlon.

Earl resides in Palatine, Illinois, where he is training and working on his next novel. He would love to hear comments about this book. Readers can e-mail him at *earlsewell@earlsewell. com*; be sure to put the title of the book in the subject line. To learn more about him, readers can visit his website at *www. earlsewell.com.*

THROUGH THICK AND THIN

EARL SEWELL

ABOUT THIS GUIDE

The questions and discussion topics that follow are intended to enhance your group's reading of THROUGH THICK AND THIN by Earl Sewell. We hope the novel provided an enjoyable read for all your members.

1. Nina is insecure about her relationship with Richard and his son Nathan. She has concerns about the stability and direction of her relationship with Richard, as well as Nathan's refusal to accept her into his life. These concerns wrestle with Nina's emotions. What are the reasons fueling her insecurities? Consider Nathan's point of view; why is he refusing to open up to Nina?

2. Dr. Charlene Hayward finds herself dating a married man who has decided to return to his wife rather than begin a new life with her. Charlene is painfully aware of the inappropriateness of her behavior, yet she continually pursues unhealthy relationships. Do you think Charlene is easily seduced by what she can't have? Consider the history of the women in her family; how much influence has this had on Charlene's personality and behavior?

3. Gracie has fled her mentally and physically abusive marriage and returned home to Nina for emotional support and recovery. Gracie has traveled down a path similar to her mother's. Similarly, Charlene has followed a path similar to her mother and grandmother's. What message do you think the author is trying to deliver about how one's upbringing influences the choices that one makes?

4. Richard is moving at a blistering pace with his relationship with Nina. He's moved Nina into his home; he's married her and purchased a practice. All of this was done shortly after the death of Estelle, his wife. Should Richard have slowed down before making such large commitments? Do you feel that Richard only moved at this pace to keep Nina happy? Consider the relationship between Nathan and Richard. Should Richard have allowed Nathan more grieving time before introducing Nina into their life?

5. Nina and Richard openly admit that they feel as if their relationship is rock solid. However, when Nina has her sus-

picions about Gracie's addiction, she doesn't share her fears with Richard. When Richard allows Charlene to work at his practice, he isn't forthcoming with Nina about his prior relationship with her. Consider these major secrets that both Nina and Richard kept from each other. Why might two people who claim to be so in love be so secretive? What does keeping secrets say about the trust in their relationship?

6. When Charlene returns home to Mississippi for Hazel's funeral, she discovers that her mother Dean has been staying in the house. By this point Charlene is harboring deep animosity toward her mother, and Dean has unresolved conflicts with Hazel. Consider both women at this particular juncture in their lives. How has bitterness and anger shaped them? Openly discuss Hazel and what might have been her justification in keeping the identity of Dean's father a secret.

7. Charlene boldly parades into Richard's practice with damaging information that could ruin the life he has built with Nina. Richard becomes so distressed by Charlene's intrusion that he has to be hospitalized. During his recovery, he realizes that he has reached the crossroads of deceit and honesty in his marriage. Why do you think Richard opted to handle Charlene on his own?

8. Nina finds herself involved in a sexual conversation between Charlene and a staff member. Up to this point, Nina held the belief that Charlene's romantic interests were directed toward women. When Charlene indicates otherwise, for the first time, Nina's intuition suggests that Charlene may be a threat. Why wasn't Nina able to identify Charlene and her treachery sooner?

9. After failing to seduce Richard in New Orleans, Charlene gets wicked and tips off the local pharmacist about Gracie and her prescription pad thievery. Why do you think Charlene didn't just give up after she couldn't seduce Richard?

10. Dean finally discloses the identity of Charlene's father and the two women reach a milestone in their mother–daughter relationship. Now that Charlene has what she's been searching for, do you think she'll change her wicked ways? Why or why not?

11. Consider Nina and Richard. Did Charlene's intrusion into their lives strengthen their relationship? Or did it weaken it?